T...   ...ding

Ex...
sensu... ..., or romantic Moorish
pal... ...ises and harem...
...s such temptation,
it was —

DESERT
Seduction

Three fabulous novels by three
favourite writers: Alexandra Sellers,
Barbara McMahon and Susan Mallery

DESERT
Seduction

Alexandra Sellers
Barbara McMahon   Susan Mallery

M&B™ and M&B™ with the Rose Device
are trademarks of the publisher.
Harlequin Mills & Boon Limited, Eton House,
18-24 Paradise Road, Richmond, Surrey TW9 1SR

DESERT SEDUCTION
© by Harlequin Enterprises II B.V./S.à.r.l 2009

Sheikh's Woman © Alexandra Sellers 2001
Her Desert Family © Barbara McMahon 2004
The Sheikh and the Bride Who Said No
© Susan Macias Redmond 2005

ISBN: 978 0 263 86757 2

009-0409

Printed and bound in Spain
by Litografia Rosés S.A., Barcelona

SHEIKH'S WOMAN

Alexandra Sellers

Alexandra Sellers is the author of over twenty-five novels and a feline language text published in 1997 and still selling.

Born and raised in Canada, Alexandra first came to London as a drama student. Now she lives near Hampstead Heath with her husband, Nick. They share housekeeping with Monsieur, who jumped through the window one day and announced, as cats do, that he was moving in.

What she would miss most on a desert island is shared laughter.

Readers can write to Alexandra at PO Box 9449, London NW3 2WH, England.

For my sister Joy,
who held it all together in the bad times and
makes things even better in the good

Prologue

She crouched in the darkness, whimpering as the pain gripped her. He had made her wait too long. She had warned him, but he'd pretended not to believe her "lies." And now, in an empty, dirty alley, nowhere to go, no time to get there, her time was upon her.

Pain stabbed her again, and she cried out involuntarily. She pressed a hand over her mouth and looked behind her down the alley. Of course by now he had discovered her flight. He was already after her. If he had heard that cry…

She staggered to her feet again, picked up the bag, began a shuffling run. Her heart was beating so hard! The drumming in her head seemed to drown out thought. She ran a few paces and then doubled over again as the pain came. Oh, Lord, not here! Please, please, not in an alley, like an animal, to be found when she was most helpless, when the baby would be at his mercy.

He would have no mercy. The pain ebbed and she ran on, weeping, praying. *"Ya Allah!"* Forgive me, protect me.

Suddenly, as if in answer, she sensed a deeper darkness in the shadows. She turned towards it without questioning, and found herself in a narrower passage. The darkness was more intense here, and she stared blindly until her eyes grew accustomed.

There was a row of garages on either side of a short strip of paving. Then she saw what had drawn her, what her subconscious mind—or her guardian angel—had already seen: one door was ajar. She bit her lip. Was there someone inside, a fugitive like herself? But another clutch of pain almost knocked her to her knees. As she bent double, stifling her cry, she heard a shout. A long way distant, but she feared what was behind her more than what might be ahead.

Sobbing with mingled pain and terror, she stumbled towards the open door and pushed her way inside.

One

"**C**an you hear me? Anna, can you hear my voice?"

It was like being dragged through long, empty rooms. Anna groaned protestingly. What did they want from her? Why didn't they let her sleep?

"Move your hand if you can hear my voice, Anna. Can you move your hand?"

It took huge effort, as if she had to fight through thick syrup.

"That's excellent! Now, can you open your eyes?"

Abruptly something heavy seemed to smash down inside her skull, driving pain through every cell. She moaned.

"I'm afraid you're going to have a pretty bad headache," said the voice, remorselessly cheerful, determinedly invasive. "Come now, Anna! Open your eyes!"

She opened her eyes. The light was too bright. It hurt. A woman in a navy shirt with white piping was gazing

at her. "Good, there you are!" she said, in a brisk Scots
accent. "What's your name?"

"Anna," said Anna. "Anna Lamb."

The woman nodded. "Good, Anna."

"What happened? Where am I?" Anna whispered.
She was lying in a grey cubicle on a narrow hospital
trolley, fully dressed except for shoes. "Why am I in
hospital?" The hammer slammed down again. "My
head!"

"You've been in an accident, but you're going to be
fine. Just a wee bit concussed. Your baby's fine."

Your baby. A different kind of pain smote her then,
and she lay motionless as cold enveloped her heart.

"My baby died," she said, her voice flat as the old,
familiar lifelessness seeped through her.

The nurse was taking Anna's blood pressure, but at
this she looked up. "She's absolutely fine! The doctor's
just checking her over now," she said firmly. "I don't
know why you wanted to give birth in a taxicab, but it
seems you made a very neat job of it."

She leaned forward and pulled back one of Anna's
eyelids, shone light from a tiny flashlight into her eye.

"In a taxicab?" Anna repeated. "But—"

Confused memories seemed to pulsate in her head,
just out of reach.

"You're a very lucky girl!" said the cheerful nurse,
moving down to press her abdomen with searching fingers. She paused, frowning, and pressed again.

Anna was silent, her eyes squeezed tight, trying to
think through the pain and confusion in her head. Meanwhile the nurse poked and prodded, frowned a little,
made notes, poked again. "Lift up, please?" she murmured, and with competent hands carried on the exam-
ination.

When it was over, she stood looking down at Anna, sliding her pen into the pocket of her uniform trousers. A little frown had gathered between her eyebrows.

"Do you remember giving birth, Anna?"

Pain rushed in at her. The room suddenly filling with people, all huddled around her precious newborn baby, while she cried, "Let me see him, why can't I hold him?" and then...*Anna, I'm sorry, I'm so very sorry. We couldn't save your baby.*

"Yes," she said lifelessly, gazing at the nurse with dry, stretched eyes, her heart a lump of stone. "I remember."

A male head came around the cubicle's curtain. "Staff, can you come, please?"

The Staff Nurse gathered up her instruments. "Maternity Sister will be down as soon as she can get away, but it may be a while, Anna. They've got staff shortages there, too, tonight, and a Caes—"

A light tap against the partition wall preceded the entrance of a young nurse, looking desperately tired but smiling as she rolled a wheeled bassinet into the room.

"Oh, nurse, there you are! How's the bairn?" said the Staff Nurse, sounding not altogether pleased.

The bairn was crying with frustrated fury, and neither of the nurses heard the gasp that choked Anna. A storm of emotion seemed to seize her as she lifted herself on her elbows and, ignoring the punishment this provoked from the person in her head who was beating her nerve endings, struggled to sit up.

"Baby?" Anna cried. "Is that *my baby?*"

Meanwhile, the young nurse wheeled the baby up beside the trolley, assuring Anna, "Yes, she is. A lovely little girl." Anna looked into the bassinet, closed her eyes, looked again.

The baby stopped crying suddenly. She was well wrapped up in hospital linen, huge eyes open, silent now but frowning questioningly at the world.

"Oh, dear God!" Anna exclaimed, choking on the emotion that surged up inside. "Oh, my baby! Was it just a nightmare, then? Oh, my darling!"

"It's not unusual for things to get mixed up after a bang on the head like yours, but everything will sort itself out," said the Staff Nurse. "We'll keep you in for observation for a day or two, but there's nothing to worry about."

Anna hardly heard. "I want to hold her!" she whispered, convulsively reaching towards the bassinet. The young nurse obligingly picked the baby up and bent over Anna. Her hungry arms wrapping the infant, Anna sank back against the pillows.

Her heart trembled with a joy so fierce it hurt, obliterating for a few moments even the pain in her head. She drew the little bundle tight against her breast, and gazed hungrily into the flower face.

She was beautiful. Huge questioning eyes, dark hair that lay on her forehead in feathery curls, wide, full mouth which was suddenly, adorably, stretched by a yawn.

All around one eye there was a mocha-hued shadow that added an inexplicably piquant charm to her face. She gazed at Anna, serenely curious.

"She looks like a bud that's just opened," Anna marvelled. "She's so fresh, so new!"

"She's lovely," agreed the junior nurse, while the Staff Nurse hooked the clipboard of Anna's medical notes onto the foot of the bed.

"Good, then," she said, nodding. "Now you'll be all

right here till Maternity Sister comes. Nurse, I'll see you for a moment, please."

The sense of unreality returned when she was left alone with the baby. Anna gazed down into the sweet face from behind a cloud of pain and confusion. She couldn't seem to think.

The baby fell asleep, just like that. Anna bent to examine her. The birthmark on her eye was very clear now that the baby's eyes were closed. Delicate, dark, a soft smudging all around the eye. Anna was moved by it. She supposed such a mark could be considered a blemish, but somehow it managed to be just the opposite.

"You'll set the fashion, my darling," Anna whispered with a smile, cuddling the baby closer. "All the girls will be painting their eyes with makeup like that in the hopes of making themselves as beautiful as you."

It made the little face even more vulnerable, drew her, touched her heart. She couldn't remember ever having seen such a mark before. Was this kind of thing inherited? No one in her family had anything like it.

Was it a dream, that memory of another child? Tiny, perfect, a beautiful, beautiful son...but so white. They had allowed her to hold him, just for a few moments, to say goodbye. Her heart had died then. She had felt it go cold, turn to ice and then stone. They had encouraged her to weep, but she did not weep. Grief required a heart.

Was that a dream?

She was terribly tired. She bent to lay the sleeping infant back in the bassinet. Then she leaned down over the tiny, fragile body, searching her face for clues.

"Who is your father?" she whispered. "Where am I? What's happening to me?"

Her head ached violently. She lay back against the pillows and wished the lights weren't so bright.

* * *

"My daughter, you must prepare yourself for some excellent news."

She smiled trustingly at her mother. "Is it the embassy from the prince?" she asked, for the exciting information had of course seeped into the harem.

"The prince's emissaries and I have discussed the matter of your marriage with the prince. Now I have spoken with your father, whose care is all for you. Such a union will please him very much, my daughter, for he desires peace with the prince and his people."

She bowed. "I am happy to be the means of pleasing my father.... And the prince? What manner of man do they say he is?"

"Ah, my daughter, he is a young man to please any woman. Handsome, strong, capable in all the manly arts. He has distinguished himself in battle, too, and stories are told of his bravery."

She sighed her happiness. "Oh, mother, I feel I love him already!" she said.

Anna awoke, not knowing what had disturbed her. A tall, dark man was standing at the foot of her trolley, reading her chart. There was something about him... She frowned, trying to concentrate. But sleep dragged her eyes shut.

"They're both fine," she heard when she opened them next, not sure whether it was seconds or minutes later. The man was talking to a young woman who looked familiar. After a second Anna's jumbled brain recognized the junior nurse.

The man drew her eyes. He was strongly charismatic. Handsome as a pirate captain, exotically dark and obviously foreign. Masculine, strong, handsome—and impossibly clean for London, as if he had come straight from a massage and shave at his club without moving through the dust and dirt of city traffic.

He was wearing a grey silk lounge suit which looked impeccably Savile Row. A round diamond glowed with dark fire from a heavy, square gold setting on his ring finger. Heavy cuff links on the French cuffs of his cream silk shirt matched it. On his other hand she saw the flash of an emerald.

He didn't look at all overdressed or showy. It sat on him naturally. He was like an aristocrat in a period film. Dreamily she imagined him in heavy brocade, with a fall of lace at wrist and throat.

She blinked, coming drowsily more awake. The junior nurse was glowing, as if the man's male energy had stirred and ignited something in her, in spite of her exhaustion. She was mesmerized.

"Because he's mesmerizing," Anna muttered.

Suddenly recalled to her duties, the nurse glanced at her patient. "You're awake!" she murmured.

The man turned and looked at her, too, his eyes dark and his gaze piercing. Anna blinked. There was a mark on his eye just like her baby's. A dark irregular smudge that enhanced both his resemblance to a pirate and his exotic maleness.

"Anna!" he exclaimed. A slight accent furred his words attractively. "Thank God you and the baby were not hurt! What on earth happened?"

She felt very, very stupid. "Are you the doctor?" she stammered.

His dark eyes snapped into an expression of even greater concern, and he made a sound that was half laughter, half worry. He bent down and clasped her hand. She felt his fingers tighten on her, in unmistakable silent warning.

"Darling!" he exclaimed. "The nurse says you don't remember the accident, but I hope you have not forgotten your own husband!"

Two

Husband? Anna stared. Her mouth opened. "I'm not—" she began. He pressed her hand again, and she broke off. Was he really her husband? How could she be married and not remember? Her heart kicked. Had a man like him fallen in love with her, chosen her?

"Are we married?" she asked.

He laughed again, with a thread of warning in his tone that she was at a loss to figure. "Look at our baby! Does she not tell you the truth?"

The birthmark was unmistakable. But how could such a thing be? "I can't remember things," she told him in a voice which trembled, trying to hold down the panic that suddenly swept her. "I can't remember anything."

A husband—how could she have forgotten? Why? She squeezed her eyes shut, and stared into the inner blackness. She knew who she was, but everything else eluded her.

She opened her eyes. He was smiling down at her in deep concern. He was so *attractive!* The air around him seemed to crackle with vitality. Suddenly she *wanted* it to be true. She wanted him to be her husband, wanted the right to lean on him. She felt so weak, and he looked so strong. He looked like a man used to handling things.

Someone was screaming somewhere. *"Nurse, nurse!"* It was a hoarse, harsh cry. She put her hand to her pounding head. "It's so noisy," she whispered.

"We'll soon have her somewhere quieter," said the junior nurse, hastily reassuring. "I'll just go and check with Maternity again." She slipped away, leaving Anna alone with the baby and the man who was her husband.

"Come, I want to get you out of here," he said.

There was something odd about his tone. She tried to focus, but her head ached desperately, and she seemed to be behind a thick curtain separating her from the world.

"But where?" she asked weakly. "This is a hospital."

"You are booked into a private hospital. They are waiting to admit you. It is far more pleasant there—they are not short-staffed and overworked. I want a specialist to see and reassure you."

He had already drawn Anna's shoes from under the bed. Anna, her head pounding, obediently sat up on the edge of the trolley bed and slipped her feet into them. Meanwhile, he neatly removed the pages from the clipboard at the foot of her bed, folded and slipped them into his jacket pocket.

"Why are you taking those?" she asked stupidly.

He flicked her an inscrutable look, then picked up the baby with atypical male confidence. "Where is your bag, Anna? Did you have a bag?"

"Oh—!" She put her hand to her forehead, remembering the case she had packed so carefully…and then had carried out of the hospital when it was all over. That long, slow walk with empty arms. Her death march.

"My bag," she muttered, but her brain would not engage with the problem, with the contradiction.

"Never mind, we can get it later." He pulled aside the curtain of the cubicle, glanced out, and then turned to her. "Come!"

Her head ached with ten times the ferocity as she obediently stood. He wrapped his free arm around her back and drew her out of the cubicle, and she instinctively obeyed his masculine authority.

The casualty ward was like an overcrowded bad dream. They passed a young man lying on a trolley, his face smashed and bloody. Another trolley held an old woman, white as her hair, her veins showing blue, eyes wild with fear. She was muttering something incomprehensible and stared at Anna with helpless fixity as they passed. Somewhere someone was half moaning, half screaming. That other voice still called for a nurse. A child's cry, high and broken, betrayed mingled pain and panic.

"My God, do you think it's like this all the time?" Anna murmured.

"It is Friday night."

They walked through the waiting room, where every seat was filled, and a moment later stepped out into the autumn night. Rain was falling, but softly, and she found the cold air a relief.

"Oh, that's better!" Anna exclaimed, shivering a little in her thin shirt.

A long black limousine parked a few yards away

purred into life and eased up beside them. Her husband opened the back door for her.

Anna drew back suddenly, without knowing why. "What about my coat? Don't I have a coat?"

"The car is warm. Come, get in. You are tired."

His voice soothed her fears, and the combination of obvious wealth and his commanding air calmed her. If he was her husband, she must be safe.

In addition to everything else, being upright was making her queasy. Anna gave in and slipped inside the luxurious passenger compartment, sinking gratefully down onto deep, superbly comfortable upholstery. He locked and shut the door.

She leaned back and her eyes closed. He spoke to the driver in a foreign language through the window, and a moment later the other passenger door opened, and her husband got inside with the baby. The limo began rolling forward immediately. Absently she clocked the driver picking up a mobile phone.

"Are we leaving, just like that? Don't I have to be signed out by a doctor or something?"

He shrugged. "Believe me, the medical staff are terminally overworked here. When they discover the empty cubicle, the Casualty staff will assume you have been moved to a ward."

Her head ached too much.

The darkness of the car was relieved at intervals by the filtered glow of passing lights. She watched him for a moment in light and shadow, light and shadow, as he settled the baby more comfortably.

"What's your name?" she asked abruptly.

"I am Ishaq Ahmadi."

"That doesn't even ring a faint bell!" Anna exclaimed. "Oh, my head! Do you—how long have we been married?"

There was a disturbing flick of his black gaze in darkness. It was as if he touched her, and a little electric shock was the result.

"There is no need to go on with this now, Anna," he said.

She jumped. "What? What do you mean?"

His gaze remained compellingly on her.

"I remember my—who I *am,*" she babbled, oddly made to feel guilty by his silent judgement, "but I can't really remember my *life.* I *certainly* don't remember you. Or—or the baby, or anything. How long have we been married?"

He smiled and shrugged. "Shall we say, two years?"

"Two years!" She recoiled in horror.

"What of your life do you remember? Your mind is obviously not a complete blank. You must have something in there…you remember giving birth?"

"Yes, but…but what I remember is that my baby died."

"Ah," he breathed, so softly she wasn't even sure she had heard it.

"They told me just now that wasn't true, but…" She reached out to touch the baby in his arms. "Oh, she's so sweet! Isn't she perfect? But I remember…" Her eyes clenched against the spasm of pain. "I *remember* holding my baby after he died."

Her eyes searched his desperately in the darkness. "Maybe that was a long time ago?" she whispered.

"How long ago does it seem to you?"

The question seemed to trigger activity in her head. "Six weeks, I think…."

You're going to have six wonderful weeks, Anna.

"Oh!" she exclaimed, as a large piece of her life suddenly fell into place. "I just remembered— I was on my way to a job in France. And Lisbet and Cecile were going to take me out for a really lovely dinner. It seems to me I'm..." She squeezed her eyes shut. "Aren't I supposed to be leaving on the Paris train tomorrow...Saturday? Alan Mitching's house in France." She opened her eyes. "Are you saying that was more than two years in the past?"

"What sort of a job?"

"He has a seventeenth-century place in the Dordogne area...they want murals in the dining room. They want—wanted a Greek temple effect. I've designed—" She broke off and gazed at him in the darkness while the limousine purred through the wet, empty streets. Traffic was light; it must be two or three in the morning.

"I can remember making the designs, but I can't remember doing the actual work." Panic rose up in her. "Why can't I remember?"

"This state is not permanent. You will remember everything in time."

The baby stirred and murmured and she watched as he shifted her a little.

"Let me hold her," she said hungrily.

For a second he looked as if he was going to refuse, but she held out her arms, and he slipped the tiny bundle into her embrace. A smile seemed to start deep within her and flow outwards all through her body and spirit to reach her lips. Her arms tightened. Oh, how lovely to have a living baby to hold against her heart in place of that horrible, hurting memory!

"Oh, you're so beautiful!" she whispered. She shifted her gaze to Ishaq Ahmadi. He was watching her. "Isn't she beautiful?"

A muscle seemed to tense in his jaw. "Yes," he said.

The chauffeur spoke through an intercom, and as her husband replied, Anna silently watched fleeting expressions wander over the baby's face, felt the perfection of the little body against her breast. Time seemed to disappear in the now. She lost the urgency of wanting to know how she had got to this moment, and was happy just to be in it.

When he spoke to her again, she came to with a little start and realized she had been almost asleep. "Can you remember how you came to be in the taxi with the baby?"

Nothing. Not even vague shadows. She shook her head. "No."

Then there was no sound except for rain and the flick of tires on the wet road. Anna was lost in contemplation again. She stroked the tiny fist. "Have we chosen a name for her?"

A passing headlight highlighted one side of his face, the side with the pirate patch over his eye.

"Her name is Safiyah."

"Sophia?"

"Yes, it is a name that will not seem strange to English ears. Safi is not so far from Sophy."

"Did we know it was going to be a girl?" she whispered, coughing as feeling closed her throat.

He glanced at her, the sleeping baby nestled so trustingly against her. "You are almost asleep," he said. "Let me take her."

He leaned over to lift the child from her arms. He was gentle and tender with her, but at the same time firm and confident, making Anna feel how safe the baby was with him.

Jonathan. "Oh!" she whispered.

"What is it?" Ishaq Ahmadi said, in a voice of quiet command. "What have you remembered?"

"Oh, just when you took the baby from me...I..." She pressed her hands to her eyes. Not when he took the baby, but the sight of him holding the infant as if he loved her and was prepared to protect and defend the innocent.

"Tell me!"

She lifted her head to see him watching her with a look of such intensity she gasped. Suddenly she wondered how much of her past she had confided to her husband. Was he a tolerant man? Or had he wanted her to lie about her life before him?

She stammered, "Did—did—?" She swallowed, her mouth suddenly dry. "Did I tell you about...Jonathan? Jonathan Ryder?"

But even before the words were out she knew the answer was no.

Three

"Tell me now," Ishaq Ahmadi commanded softly.

She wanted to lean against him, wanted to feel his arm around him, protecting her, holding her. She must have that right, she told herself, but somehow she lacked the courage to ask him to hold her.

She had always wanted to pat the tigers at the zoo, too. Now it seemed as if she had finally found her very own personal tiger…but she had forgotten how she'd tamed him. And until she remembered that, something told her it would be wise to treat him with caution.

"Tell me about Jonathan Ryder."

Nervously she clasped her hands together, and suddenly a detail that had been nagging at her in the distance leapt into awareness.

"Why aren't I wearing a wedding ring?" she demanded, holding both hands spread out before her and staring at them. On her fingers were several silver rings of varied design. But none was a wedding band.

There was a long, pregnant pause. Through the glass panel separating them from the driver, she heard a phone ring. The driver answered and spoke into it, giving instructions, it seemed.

Still he only looked at her.

"Did I...have we split up?"

"No."

Just the bare syllable. His jaw seemed to tense, and she thought he threw her a look almost of contempt.

"About Jonathan," he prompted again.

If they were having trouble in the marriage, was it because he was jealous? Or because she had not told him things, shared her troubles?

She thought, *If I never told him about Jonathan, I should have.*

"Jonathan—Jonathan and I were going together for about a year. We were talking about moving in together, but it wasn't going to be simple, because we both owned a flat, and...well, it was taking us time to decide whether to sell his, or mine, or sell both and find somewhere new."

Her heart began to beat with anxiety. "It is really more than two years ago?"

"How long does it seem to you?"

"It feels as if we split up about six months ago. And then..."

"Why did you split up?"

"Because...did I not tell you any of this?"

"Tell me again," he repeated softly. "Perhaps the recital will help your memory recover."

She wanted to tell him. She wanted to share it with him, to make him her soul mate. Surely she must have told him, and he had understood? She couldn't have married a man who didn't understand, whom she couldn't share her deepest feelings with?

"I got pregnant unexpectedly." She looked at him and remembered that, sophisticated as he looked, he was from a different culture. "Does that shock you?"

"I am sure that birth control methods fail every day," he said.

That was not what she meant, but she lacked the courage to be more explicit.

"Having kids wasn't part of deciding to live together or anything, but once it happened I just—knew it was what I wanted. It was crazy, but it made me so happy! Jonathan didn't see it that way. He didn't want..."

Her head drooped, and the sound of suddenly increasing rain against the windows filled the gap.

"Didn't want the child?"

"He wanted me to have an abortion. He said we weren't ready yet. His career hadn't got off the ground, neither had mine. He—oh, he had a hundred reasons why it would be right one day but wasn't now. In a lot of ways he was right. But..." Anna shrugged. "I couldn't do it. We argued and argued. I understood him, but he never understood me. Never tried to. I kept saying, there's more to it than you want to believe. He wouldn't listen."

"And did he convince you?"

"He booked an appointment for me, drove me down to the women's clinic.... On the way, he stopped the car at a red light, and—I got out," she murmured, staring at nothing. "And just kept walking. I didn't look back, and Jonathan didn't come after me. He never called again. Well, once," she amended. "A couple of months later he phoned to ask if I planned to name him as the father on the birth certificate.''

She paused, but Ishaq Ahmadi simply waited for her to continue. ''He said…he said he had no intention of being saddled with child support for the next twenty years. He had a job offer from Australia, and he was trying to decide whether to accept or not. And that was one of the criteria. If I was going to put his name down, he'd go to Australia.''

His hair glinted in the beam of a streetlight. They were on a highway. ''And what did you say?''

She shook her head. ''I hung up. We've never spoken since.''

''Did he go to Australia?''

''I never found out. I didn't want to know.'' She amended that. ''Didn't care.'' She glanced out the window.

''Where are we going?'' she asked. ''Where is the hospital?''

''North of London, in the country. Tell me what happened then.''

Her eyes burned. ''My friends were really, really great about it—do you know Cecile and Lisbet?''

''How could your husband not know your friends?''

''Are Cecile and Philip married?''

He gazed at her. ''Tell me about the baby, Anna.''

There was something in his attitude that made her uncomfortable. She murmured, ''I'm sorry if you didn't know before this. But maybe if you didn't, you should have. ''

''Undoubtedly.''

''*Did* you know?''

He paused. ''No.''

Anna bit her lip. She wondered if it was perhaps because she hadn't told him that she had reverted to this memory tonight. Had it weighed on her throughout the new pregnancy? Had fears for her new baby surfaced and found no outlet?

"Everything was fine. I was pretty stressed in some ways, but I didn't really have doubts about what I was doing. At the very end something went wrong. I was in labour for hours and hours, and then it was too late for a Caesarean...they used the Ventouse cap."

She swallowed, and her voice was suddenly expressionless. "It caused a brain haemorrhage. My baby died. They let me hold him, and he was...but there was a terrible bruise on his head...as if he was wearing a purple cap."

No tears came to moisten the heat of her eyes or ease the pain in her heart. Her perfect baby, paper white and too still, but looking as if he was thinking very hard and would open his eyes any moment...

She wondered if that was how she had ended up giving birth in the back of a cab. Perhaps it was fear of a repetition that had made her leave it too late to get to the hospital.

"Why weren't you there?" she asked, surfacing from her thoughts to look at him. "Why didn't you take me to the hospital?"

"I flew in from abroad this evening. And this was six weeks ago?"

"That's how it feels to me. I feel as though it's the weekend I'm supposed to be going on that job to France, and that was about six weeks after the baby died. How long ago is that, really?"

"Did you ever feel, Anna, that you would like to—adopt a child? A baby to fill the void created by the death of your own baby?"

"It wouldn't have done me any good if I had. Why are you asking me these questions now? Didn't we—"

"Did you think of it—applying for adoption? Trying to find a baby?"

"No." She shook her head. "Sometimes in the street, you know, you pass a woman with a baby, or even a woman who's pregnant, and you just want to scream *It's not fair,* but—no, I just…I got pretty depressed, I wasn't doing much of anything till Lisbet conjured up this actor friend who wanted a mural in his place in France."

She leaned over to caress the baby with a tender hand, then bent to kiss the perfectly formed little head. "Oh, you are so beautiful!" she whispered. She looked up, smiling. "I hope I remember soon. I can't bear not knowing everything about her!"

He started to speak, and just then the car drew to a stop. Heavy rain was now thundering down on the roof, and all she could see were streaks of light from tall spotlights in the distance, as if they had entered some compound.

"Are we here?"

"Yes," he said, as the door beside her opened. The dark-skinned chauffeur stood in the rain with a large black umbrella, and Anna quickly slipped out onto a pavement that was leaping with water. She heard the swooping crack of another umbrella behind her. Then she was being ushered up a curiously narrow flight of steps and through a doorway.

She glanced around her as Ishaq, with the baby, came in the door behind her.

It was very curious for a hospital reception. A low-ceilinged room, softly lighted, lushly decorated in natural wood and rich tapestries. A row of matching little curtains seemed to be covering several small windows at intervals along the wall. There was a bar at one end, by a small dining table with chairs. In front of her she saw a cluster of plush armchairs around a coffee table. Anna frowned, trying to piece together a coherent interpretation of the scene, but her mind was very slow to function. She could almost hear her own wheels grinding.

A woman in an Eastern outfit that didn't look at all like a medical uniform appeared in the doorway behind the bar and came towards them. She spoke something in a foreign language, smiling and gesturing towards the sofa cluster. She moved to the entrance door behind them, dragged it fully shut and turned a handle. Still the pieces refused to fall into place.

Anna obediently sank down into an armchair. A second woman appeared. Dressed in another softly flowing outfit, with warm brown eyes and a very demure smile, she nodded and then descended upon the baby in Ishaq Ahmadi's arms. She laughed and admired and then exchanged a few sentences of question and answer with Ishaq before taking the infant in her own arms and, with another smile all around, disappeared whence she had come.

"What's going on?" Anna demanded, as alarm began to shrill behind the drowsy numbness in her head.

"Your bed is ready," Ishaq murmured, bending over her and slipping his hands against her hips. At the touch of his strong hands she involuntarily smiled. "In a few minutes you can lie down and get some sleep."

His hands lifted and she blinked stupidly while he drew two straps up and snapped them together over her hips. Under her feet she felt the throb of engines, and at last the pieces fell together.

"This isn't a hospital, this is a plane!" Anna cried wildly.

Four

"Let me out," Anna said, her hands snapping to the seat belt.

Ishaq Ahmadi fastened his own seat belt and moved one casual hand to still hers as she struggled with the mechanism. "We have been cleared for immediate take-off," he said.

"Stop the plane and let me off. Tell them to turn back," she cried, pushing at his hand, which was no longer casual. "Where are you taking us? I want my baby!"

"The woman you saw is a children's nurse. She is taking care of the baby, and no harm will come to her. Try and relax. You are ill, you have been in an accident."

Her stomach churned sickly, her head pounded with pain, but she had to ignore that. She stared at him and showed her teeth. "Why are you doing this?" A sudden wrench released her seat belt, and Anna thrust herself to her feet.

Ishaq Ahmadi's eyes flashed with irritation. "You know very well you have no right to such a display. You know you are in the wrong, deeply in the wrong." He stabbed a forefinger at the chair she had just vacated. "Sit down before you fall down!"

With a little jerk, the plane started taxiing. "No!" Anna cried. She staggered and clutched the chair back, and with an oath Ishaq Ahmadi snapped a hand up and clasped her wrist in an unbreakable hold.

"Help me!" she screamed. "Help, help!"

A babble of concerned female voices arose from behind a bulkhead, and in another moment the hostess appeared in the doorway behind the bar.

"Sit down, Anna!"

The hostess cried a question in Arabic, and Ishaq Ahmadi answered in the same language. *"Laa, laa, madame,"* the woman said, gently urgent, and approached Anna with a soothing smile, then tried what her little English would do.

"Seat, madame, very dingerous. Pliz, seat."

"I want to get off!" Anna shouted at the uncomprehending woman. "Stop the plane! Tell the captain it's a mistake!"

The woman turned to Ishaq Ahmadi with a question, and he shook his head on a calm reply. Of course he had the upper hand if the cabin crew spoke only Arabic. Anna had a dim idea that all pilots had to speak English, but what were her chances of making it to the cockpit?

And if it was a private jet, the captain would be on Ishaq Ahmadi's payroll. No doubt they all knew he was kidnapping his own wife.

Ahmadi got to his feet, holding Anna's wrist in a grip

that felt like steel cables, and forced her to move towards him.

The plane slowed, and they all stiffened as the captain's voice came over the intercom—but it was only with the obvious Arabic equivalent of "Cabin staff, prepare for takeoff." Ishaq Ahmadi barked something at the hostess and, with a consoling smile at Anna, she returned to her seat behind the bulkhead.

Ishaq Ahmadi sank into his seat again, dragging Anna inexorably down onto his lap. "You are being a fool," he said. "No one is going to hurt you if you do not hurt yourself."

She was sitting on him now as if he were the chair, and his arms were firmly locked around her waist, a human seat belt. The heat of his body seeped into hers, all down her spine and the backs of her thighs, his arms resting across her upper thighs, hands clasped against her abdomen.

Wherever her body met his, there was nothing but muscle. There was no give, no ounce of fat. It was like sitting on hot poured metal fresh from the forge, hardened, but the surface still slightly malleable. The stage when a sculptor removes the last, tiny blemishes, puts on the finishing touches. She had taken a course in metal sculpture at art college, and she had always loved the metal at this stage, Anna remembered dreamily. The heat, the slight surface give in something so innately strong, had a powerful sensual pull.

She realized she was half tranced. She felt very slow and stupid, and as the adrenaline in her body ebbed, her headache caught up with her again. She twisted to try to look over her shoulder into his face.

"Why are you doing this?" she pleaded.

His voice, close to her ear, said, "So that you and the baby will be safe."

She was deeply, desperately tired, she was sick and hurt, and she wanted to believe she was safe with him. The alternative was too confusing and too terrible.

The engines roared up and the jet leapt forward down the runway. In a very short time, compared to the lumbering commercial aircraft she was used to, they had left the ground.

As his hold slackened but still kept her on his lap, she turned to Ishaq Ahmadi. Her face was only inches from his, her mouth just above his own wide, well-shaped lips. She swallowed, feeling the pull.

"Where are you taking me?"

"Home." His gaze was steady. "You are tired. You will want to lie down," he murmured, and when the jet levelled out, he helped her to her feet and stood up. He took her arm and led her through a doorway.

They entered a large, beautifully appointed stateroom, with a king-size bed luxuriously made with snowy-white and deep blue linens that were turned down invitingly. There were huge, fluffy white pillows.

It was like a fantasy. Except for the little windows and the ever-present hum you would never know you were on a plane. A top hotel, maybe. Beautiful natural woods, luscious fabrics, mirrors, soft lighting, and, through an open door, a marble bathroom.

"I guess I married a millionaire," Anna murmured. "Or is this just some bauble a friend has loaned you?"

"Here are night things for you," he said, indicating pyjamas and a bathrobe, white with blue trim, that were lying across the foot of the sapphire-blue coverlet. "Do you need help to undress?"

Anna looked at the bed longingly and realized she was

dead on her feet. And that was no surprise, after what she had apparently been through in the past few hours.

"No," she said.

She began fumbling with a button, but her fingers didn't seem to work. Even the effort of holding her elbow bent seemed too much, so she dropped her arm and stood there a moment, gazing at nothing.

"I will call the hostess," Ishaq Ahmadi said. And that, perversely, made her frown.

"Why?" she demanded. "You're my husband, aren't you?"

His eyes probed her, and she shrugged uncomfortably. "Why are you looking at me like that? Why don't you want to touch me?"

She wanted him to touch her. Wanted his heat on her body again, because when he touched her, even in anger, she felt safe.

He made no reply, merely lifted his hands, brushed aside her own feeble fingers which were again fumbling with the top button, and began to undo her shirt.

"Have you stopped wanting me?" she wondered aloud.

His head bent over his task, only his eyes shifted to connect with hers. "You are overplaying your hand," he advised softly, and she felt another little thrill of danger whisper down her spine. Her brain evaded the discomfort.

"Did you commission work from me or something? Is that how we met?" she asked. She specialized in Mediterranean and Middle Eastern designs, painting entire rooms to give the impression that you were standing on a balcony overlooking the Gulf of Corinth, or in the Alhambra palace. But what were the chances that a wealthy Arab would want a Western woman to paint trompe l'oeil fifteenth-century mosaic arches on his palace walls when he probably had the real thing?

"We met by accident."

"Oh." She wanted him to clarify, but couldn't concentrate. Not when his hands were grazing the skin of her breasts, revealed as he unbuttoned her shirt. She looked into his face, bent close over hers, but his eyes remained on his task. His aftershave was spicy and exotic.

"It seems strange that you have the right to do this when you feel like a total stranger," she observed.

"You insisted on it," he reminded her dryly. He seemed cynically amused by her. He still didn't believe that she had forgotten, and she had no idea why. What reason could she have for pretending amnesia? It seemed very crazy, unless…unless she had been running away from him.

Perhaps it was fear that had caused her to lose her memory. Psychologists did say you sometimes forgot when remembering was too painful.

"Was I running away from you, Ishaq?"

"You tell me the answer."

She shook her head. "They say the unconscious remembers everything, but…"

"I am very sure that yours does," Ishaq Ahmadi replied, pulling the front of her shirt open to reveal her small breasts in a lacy black bra.

She knew by the involuntary intake of his breath that he was not unaffected. His jaw clenched and he stripped the shirt from her, his breathing irregular.

She wasn't one for casual sex, and she had never been undressed by a stranger, which was what this felt like. The sudden blush of desire that suffused her was disconcerting. So her body remembered, even if her conscious mind did not. Anna bit her lip. What would it be like, love with a man who seemed like a total stranger? Would her body instinctively recognize his touch?

She realized that she wanted him to make the demand on her. The thought was sending spirals of heat all through her. But instead of drawing her into his arms, he turned his back to toss her shirt onto a chair.

"What will I remember about loving you, Ishaq?" she whispered.

He didn't answer, and she turned away, dejected, overcome with fatigue and reluctant to think, and lifted her arms behind her to the clasp of her bra. She winced as a bruised elbow prevented her.

Her breath hissed with the pain. "You'll have to undo this."

She felt his hands at work on the hook of her bra, that strange, half electrifying, half comforting heat that made her yearn for something she could not remember. She wondered if they *had* been sexually estranged. She said, "Is there a problem between us, Ishaq?"

"You well know what the problem between us is. But it is not worth discussing now," he said, his voice tight.

She thought, *It's serious.* Her heart pinched painfully with regret. To think that she had had the luck to marry a man like this and then had not been able to make it work made her desperately sad. He was like a dream come to life, but...she had obviously got her dream and then not been able to live in it.

If they made up now, when she could not remember any of the grievances she might have, would that make it easier when she regained her full memory?

As the bra slipped away from her breasts, Anna let it fall onto the bed, then turned to face him, lifting her arms to his shoulders.

"Do you still love me?" she whispered.

His arms closed around her, his hands warm on her bare skin. Her breasts pressed against his silk shirt as her arms cupped his head. He looked down into her upturned face with a completely unreadable expression in his eyes.

"Do you want me, Ishaq?" she begged, wishing he would kiss her. Why was he so remote? She felt the warmth of his body curl into hers and it was so right.

A corner of that hard, full mouth went up and his eyes became sardonic. "Believe me, I want you, or you would not be here."

"What have I done?" she begged. "I don't remember anything. Tell me what I've done to make you so angry with me."

His mouth turned up with angry contempt. "What do you hope to gain with this?" he demanded with subdued ferocity, and then, as if it were completely against his will, his grip tightened painfully on her, and with a stifled curse he crushed his mouth against her own.

He was neither gentle nor tender. His kiss and his hands were punishing, and a part of her revelled in the knowing that, whatever his intentions, he could not resist her. She opened her mouth under his, accepting the violent thrust of his hungry, angry tongue, and felt the rasp of its stroking run through her with unutterable thrill, as if it were elsewhere on her body that he kissed her.

Just for a moment she was frightened, for if one kiss could do this to her, how would she sustain his full, passionate lovemaking? She would explode off the face of the earth. His hand dropped to force her against him, while his hardened body leapt against her. She tore her mouth away from his, gasping for the oxygen to feed the fire that wrapped her in its hot, licking fingers.

"Ishaq!" she cried, wild with a passion that seemed to her totally new, as the heat of his hands burned her back, her hips, clenched against the back of her neck with a firm possessiveness that thrilled her. "Oh, my love!"

Then suddenly he was standing away from her, his hands on her wrists pulling her arms down, his eyes burning into hers with a cold, hard, suspicious fury that froze the hot rivers of need coursing through her.

"What is it?" she pleaded. "Ishaq, what have I done?"

He smiled and shook his head, a curl of admiring contempt lifting his lip. "You are unbelievable," he said. "Where have you learned such arts, I wonder?"

Anna gasped. He suspected her of having a lover? Could it be true? She shook her head. It wasn't possible. Whatever he might suspect, whatever he might have done, whatever disagreement was between them, she knew that she was simply not capable of taking a lover while pregnant with her husband's child.

"From you, I suppose," she tried, but he brushed that aside with a snort of such contemptuous disbelief she could go no further.

"Tell me why you won't love me," she challenged softly, but nothing was going to crack his angry scorn now.

"But you have just given birth, Anna. We must resign ourselves to no lovemaking for several weeks, isn't it so?"

She drew back with a little shock. "Oh! Yes, I—" She shook her head. He could still kiss her, she thought. He could hold her. Maybe that was the problem, she thought. A man who would only touch his wife if he wanted sex. She would certainly hate that.

"I wish I could *remember!*"

He reached down and lifted up the silky white pyjama top, holding it while she obediently slipped her arms inside. He had himself well under control now, he was as impersonal as a nurse, and she tasted tears in her throat for the waste of such wild passion.

Funny how small her breasts were. Last time, they had been so swollen with the pregnancy...hadn't they? She remembered the ache of heavy breasts with a pang of misery, and then reminded herself, *But that's all in the past. I have a baby now.*

"Do you think I'll remember?" she whispered, gazing into his face as he buttoned the large pyjama shirt. It seemed almost unbearable that she should feel such pain for a baby who had died two years ago and not remember the birth of the beautiful creature who was so alive, and whose cry she could suddenly hear over the subdued roar of the engines.

"I am convinced of it."

"She has inherited your birthmark," she murmured with a smile, touching his eye with a feather caress and feeling her heart contract with tenderness. "Is that usual?"

He finished the last button and lifted his eyes to hers. "What is it you hope to discover?" he asked, his hands pulling at her belt with cool impersonality. "The... Ahmadi mark," he said. "It proves beyond a doubt that Safiyah and I come of the same blood. Does that make you wary?"

"Did you think I had a lover?" she asked. "Did you think it was someone else's child?"

His eyes darkened with the deepest suspicion she had yet seen in them, and she knew she had struck a deep chord. "You know that much, do you?"

Somewhere inside her an answering anger was born. "You're making it pretty obvious! Does the fact that you've now been proven wrong make you think twice about things, Ishaq?"

"Wrong?" he began, then broke off, stripped the suede pants down her legs and off, and knelt to hold the pyjama bottoms for her. His hair was cut over the top in a thick cluster of black curls whose vibrant health reflected the lampglow. Anna steadied herself with a hand on his shoulder and stifled the whispering desire that melted through her thighs at the nearness of him.

They were too big. In fact, they were men's pyjamas.

"Why don't I have a pair of pyjamas on the plane?" she asked.

"Perhaps you never wear them."

He spoke softly, but the words zinged to her heart. She shivered at the thought that she slept naked next to Ishaq Ahmadi. She wondered what past delights were lurking, waiting to be remembered.

"And you do?"

"I often fly alone," he said.

It suddenly occurred to her that he had told her absolutely nothing all night. Every single question had somehow been parried. But when she tried to formulate words to point this out, her brain refused.

Even at its tightest the drawstring was too big for her slim waist, and the bunched fabric rested precariously on the slight swell of her hips. Ishaq turned away and lifted the feathery covers of the bed to invite her to slip into the white, fluffy nest.

She moved obediently, groaning as her muscles protested at even this minimal effort. Once flat on her back, however, she sighed with relief. "Oh, that feels good!"

Ishaq bent to flick out the bedside lamp, but her hand stopped him. "Bring me the baby," she said.

"You are tired and the baby is asleep."

"But she was crying. She may be hungry."

"I am sure the nurse has seen to that."

"But I want to breast-feed her!" Anna said in alarm.

He blinked as if she had surprised him, but before she could be sure of what she saw in his face his eyelids hooded his expression.

"Tomorrow will not be too late for that, Anna. Sleep now. You need sleep more than anything."

On the last word he put out the light, and it was impossible to resist the drag of her eyelids in the semi-darkness. "Kiss her for me," she murmured, as Lethe beckoned.

"Yes," he said, straightening.

She frowned. "Don't we kiss good-night?"

A heartbeat, two, and then she felt the touch of his lips against her own. Her arms reached to embrace him, but he avoided them and was standing upright again. She felt deprived, her heart yearning towards him. She tried once more.

"I wish you'd stay with me."

"Good night, Anna." Then the last light went out, a door opened and closed, and she was alone with the dark and the deep drone of the engines.

Five

"*Hurry, hurry!*"

The voices and laughter of the women mirrored the bubble of excitement in her heart, and she felt the corners of her mouth twitch up in anticipation.

"*I'm coming!*" *she cried.*

But they were impatient. Already they were spilling out onto the balcony, whose arching canopy shaded it from the harsh midday sun. Babble arose from the courtyard below: the slamming of doors, the dance of hooves, the shouts of men. Somewhere indoors, musicians tuned their instruments.

"*He is here! He arrives!*" *the women cried, and she heard the telltale scraping of the locks and bars and the rumble of massive hinges in the distance as the gates opened wide. A cry went up and the faint sound of horses' hooves thudded on the hot, still air.*

"They are here already! Hurry, hurry!" cried the women.

She rose to her feet at last, all in white except for the tinkling, delicate gold at her forehead, wrists, and ankles, a white rose in her hand. Out on the balcony the women were clustered against the carved wooden arabesques of the screen that hid them from the admiring, longing male eyes below.

She approached the screen. Through it the women had a view of the entire courtyard running down to the great gates. These were now open in welcome, with magnificently uniformed sentinels on each side, and the mounted escort approached and cantered between them, flags fluttering, armour sending blinding flashes of intense sunlight into unwary eyes.

They rode in pairs, rank upon rank, leading the long entourage, their horses' caparisons increasing in splendour with the riders' rank. Then at last came riders in the handsomest array, mounted on spirited, prancing horses.

"There he is!" a voice cried, and a cheer began in several throats and swelled.

Her eyes were irresistibly drawn to him. He was sternly handsome, his flowing hair a mass of black curls, his beard neat and pointed, his face grave but his eyes alight with humour. His jacket was rich blue, the sleeves ruched with silver thread; his silver breastplate glowed almost white. Across it, from shoulder to hip, a deep blue sash lay against the polished metal.

The sword at his hip was thickly encrusted with jewels. His fingers also sparkled, but no stone was brighter than his dark eyes as he glanced up towards the balcony as if he knew she was there. His eyes met hers, challenged and conquered in one piercingly sweet moment.

Her heart sprang in one leap from her breast and into his keeping.

As he rode past below, the white rose fell from her helpless hand. A strong dark hand plucked it from the air and drew it to his lips, and she cried softly, as though the rose were her own white throat.

He did not glance up again, but thrust the rose carefully inside the sash, knowing she watched. She clung to the carved wooden arabesques, her strength deserting her.

"So fierce, so handsome!" she murmured. "As strong and powerful as his own black destrier, I dare swear!"

The laughter of the women chimed around her ears. "Ah, truly, and love is blind and sees white as black!" they cried in teasing voices. "Black? But the prince's horse is white! Look again, mistress!"

She looked in the direction of their gesturing, as the entourage still came on. In the centre of the men on black horses rode one more richly garbed than all. His armour glowed with beaten gold, his richly jewelled turban was cloth of gold, ropes of pearls draped his chest, rubies and emeralds adorned his fingers and ears. His eyebrows were strong and black, his jaw square, his beard thick and curling. He lifted a hand in acknowledgement as those riders nearest him tossed gold and silver coins to the cheering crowd.

Her women were right. Her bridegroom was mounted on a prancing stallion as white as the snows of Shir.

"Saba'ul khair, madame."

Anna rolled over drowsily and blinked while intense sunlight poured into the cabin from the little portholes as, *whick whick whick whick,* the air hostess pulled aside the curtains.

Her eyes frowned a protest. "Is it morning already?"

The woman turned from her completed task and smiled. "We here, madame."

Anna leapt out of the bed, wincing with the protest from her bruised muscles, and craned to peer out the porthole. They were flying over water, deep sparkling blue water dotted with one or two little boats, and were headed towards land. She saw a long line of creamy beach, lush green forest, a stretch of mixed golden and grey desert behind, and, in the distance, snow-topped mountains casting a spell at once dangerous and thrilling.

"Where on earth are we?"

"Shower, madame?"

"Oh, yes!"

The hostess smiled with the pleasure of someone who had recently memorized the word but had produced it without any real conviction and was now delighted to see that the sounds did carry meaning, and led her into the adjoining bathroom.

Anna waved away her offer of help, stripped and got into the shower stall, then stood gratefully under the firm spray of water, first hot, then cool. This morning her body was sore all over, but her headache was much less severe.

Her memory wasn't in much better shape, though. It still stopped dead on the night before she had been due to leave for France. Now, however, she could remember a shopping expedition with Lisbet during the afternoon, going home to dress, meeting Cecile and Lisbet at the Riverfront Restaurant. Now she could remember leaving the restaurant, and almost immediately seeing a cab pull up across the street. "You take that one, Anna, it's facing your direction,'' Lisbet had commanded, and she had dashed across the street...

She could remember *that* as if it were yesterday.

Of the two years that had followed that night there was still absolutely nothing in her memory. Not one image had surfaced overnight to flesh out the bare outline Ishaq Ahmadi had given of her life since.

When she tried to make sense of it all, her head pounded unmercifully. The whole thing made her feel eerie, creepy.

Last night's dream surfaced cloudily in her mind. She had the feeling that the man on the black horse was Ishaq Ahmadi.

She wondered if that held some clue about her first meeting with him. Had she seen him from a distance and fallen in love with him?

That she could believe. If ever there was a man you could take one look at and know you'd met your destiny, Ishaq Ahmadi was it. But he was definitely keeping something from her. If once they had loved each other, and she certainly accepted that, there was a problem now. It was in his eyes every time he looked at her. His look said she was a criminal—attractive and desirable, perhaps, but not in the least to be trusted.

Anna winced as she absently scrubbed a sore spot. The accident must have been real enough. Her body seemed to be one massive bruise now, and she ached as if she had been beaten with a bat.

That thought stilled her for a moment. Panic whispered along her nerves. Suppose a man had beaten his pregnant, runaway wife and wanted to avoid the consequences...

Anna reminded herself suddenly that they would be landing soon and turned off the water. In the bedroom mirror she stared at herself. She was still too thin, just as she had been after losing her baby two years ago. There were dark circles under her eyes to match the bruising on her body.

She had a tendency to lose weight with unhappiness. Anna sighed. By the look of her, she had been deeply unhappy recently, as unhappy as when she had lost Jonathan's baby. But the question was—had she lost the weight *before* she left Ishaq, or *after?*

Her clothes were lying on the neatly made bed. The shirt had been mended, the suede pants neatly brushed. Anna's breath hissed between her teeth. *It's terrific, Anna. Stop dithering and buy it!*

She had bought this shirt on that Friday afternoon and worn it that night to dinner in the Riverfront. These were the clothes that she could remember putting on that night. Her jacket was missing, that was all.

Anna stood staring, her heart in her throat. With careful precision she reached down and picked up the shirt. The tag was completely fresh. Either she was confusing two separate memories in her mind…or she and Lisbet had bought this shirt yesterday.

"Ah, I was just coming for you," Ishaq Ahmadi said, as she opened the door. "We are about to land. Come and sit down."

He sank into an armchair as Anna obeyed. Beside him the nurse sat with the baby in her arms. The air hostess was behind the bar. Anna could smell coffee.

"I'll take the baby," she said, holding out her arms.

To her fury, the nurse glanced up at Ishaq Ahmadi.

"Give me the baby," she ordered firmly.

Ishaq Ahmadi nodded all but invisibly, and the nurse passed the baby over. Safiyah was sleeping. Anna stroked her, the hungry memory of the son who had not lived assuaged by the touch of the tiny, helpless body, the feather-soft skin, the curling perfect hand. Her mouth, full, soft and tender, was twitching with her dream, as were her dark, beautifully arched eyebrows.

Anna glanced up at Ishaq Ahmadi and thought that he had probably once had the same mouth. But now its fullness was disciplined, its softness was lost in firmness of purpose, its tenderness had disappeared.

She wanted to believe that he was telling the truth. That he was her husband and that this was the child of their mutual love. She wanted to believe the evidence of the shirt was somehow false. Her heart was deeply touched by the baby, the man. It was possible, after all. She might have packed the shirt away, left everything with friends, perhaps, and then, fleeing to those friends from her husband, had recourse to her old clothes.

Or confusing the memory of two different shopping trips might be a sign that her more recent memory was returning.

"Where are we?" she asked, watching out the window as the wheels touched down in the familiar chirping screech of arrival.

Palm trees, sunlight, low white buildings, the name on the terminal building in scrolling green Arabic script, the red Roman letters underneath moving past too fast for her to read...

"We are in Barakat al Barakat, the capital of the Barakat Emirates," he said.

"Oh!" She had heard of the Emirates, of course. But she knew almost nothing about the country except that it was ruled by three young princes who had inherited jointly from their father. "Is it—is it your...our... home?"

"Of course."

"Are you Barakati?"

"Of course," he said again.

She had some faint idea that amnesia victims didn't forget general knowledge, only personal. So how was it that she couldn't remember anything about the country that was her home? Her skin began to shiver with nervous fear.

A few minutes later the door opened. Bright sunshine and fresh air streamed into the aircraft, bringing with it the smell of hot tarmac and fuel and the sea and...in spite of those mundane odours, some other, secret scent that seemed full of mystery and magic and the East.

An official came deferentially aboard in an immigration check that was clearly token, and her lack of a passport wasn't even remarked on. Anna flicked a glance at Ishaq as the men spoke. Well, it wasn't surprising that he was as important as that. She could have guessed it just by looking at him.

Down below a sparkling white limousine waited, and the chauffeur and a cluster of other people were standing on the tarmac.

"Give the baby to the nurse," Ishaq Ahmadi said when the official departed with a nod and smile. Anna immediately clutched Safiyah tight.

"She's sleeping," she protested, with the sudden, nameless conviction that if she obeyed him she would never see the baby again.

"Give the baby to the nurse," he repeated, approaching her.

Anna evaded him, and stepped to the open doorway of the aircraft. "If you try to take her away from me, I'll scream. How far does your influence go with the people out there?"

Out on the tarmac her appearance in the doorway caused a little stir. People were gazing her way now.

Ishaq's jaw tightened and his eyes flashed at her with deep, suspicious anger. "How cunning you think you are. So be it."

He came up beside her and, with an arm around her waist, stepped with her through the door onto the top step. He stopped there, and to Anna's utter amazement, two of the men below produced cameras and began snapping photos of them.

"What on earth—?" she exclaimed.

She heard him murmur what sounded like a curse. "Smile," he ordered, with a grimness that electrified her. "Smile or I will throttle you in front of them all."

"What is it?" she whispered desperately. "Who are you?" and then, crazily, after a beat, "Who am I?"

"You will not say anything, anything at all, to the journalists."

"*Journalists?*"

She stared at the photographers in stunned, stupid dismay. What was going on? What could explain what was happening to her?

Ishaq went down the narrow stairs one step ahead of her, turning to guide her down. His hand was commanding, and almost cruel, against her wrist. In crazy contradiction to her feelings, the sun was heaven, the breeze delicious. Light bounced from the tarmac, the car, the plane with stupefying brilliance.

A man with a camera jumped right in front of them, and Anna recoiled with a jolt. "Excuse me!" she murmured, outraged, but he only bent closer. "Please, you'll disturb the baby!"

"*Ingilisiya!*" someone cried. "*Man hiya?*"

"Louk these way, pliz!"

The chauffeur had leapt to open the door of the limousine, and Ishaq shepherded her quickly to it. Before Anna's eyes could adjust to the blinding sunlight she was in the dimness of the car, the door shutting her and the baby behind tinted glass.

The voices were still calling questions. She heard Ishaq's deeper voice answer. A moment later he was slipping into the seat beside her. The nurse got into the front seat. The chauffeur slammed the last door and the limousine moved off as a cameraman bent to the window nearest Anna and snapped more pictures.

She turned to Ishaq.

"What's going on?" she said. "Why are there journalists here?"

"They are here because they permanently stake out the airport. The tabloids of the world like to print photographs of the Cup Companions of the princes of Barakat as they come and go in the royal jets. Usually it does not matter. But now—" he turned and looked at her with a cold accusation in his eyes that terrified her "—now they have a photograph of the baby."

Too late, she realized how foolish she had been to defy him when she knew nothing at all.

Six

The limousine turned between big gates into a tree-lined courtyard and swept to a stop in front of a two-storey villa in terra-cotta brick and stone with a tiled roof. The facade was lined with a row of peach-coloured marble pillars surmounted with the kind of curving scalloped arches Anna was more used to painting on clients' walls than seeing in real life.

Anna's heart began beating with hard, nervous jolts.

"Are we here?" she murmured, licking her lips.

It was a stupid question, and he agreed blandly, "We are here."

The door beside her opened. Anna got awkwardly out of the car, the baby in one arm. She stood looking around as Ishaq Ahmadi joined her. The courtyard was shaded with tall trees, shrubs and bushes, and cooled with a running fountain, and she had a sudden feeling of peace and safety.

"Is this your house?"

He bowed.

The baby woke up and started making grumpy noises, and the nurse appeared smilingly at Anna's side. She clucked sympathetically and made an adoring face at the complaining baby, then glanced up at Anna.

Anna resolutely shook her head and, with a defiant glance at Ishaq Ahmadi, shifted the baby up onto her shoulder. The baby wasn't going out of her sight till she understood a lot more than she did right now.

But he merely shrugged. A servant in white appeared through one of the arches, and they all moved into the shade of the portico.

Her eyes not quite accustomed to the cool gloom, she followed Ishaq Ahmadi into the house, through a spacious entrance hall and into the room beyond. There the little party stopped, while Ishaq Ahmadi conversed in low tones with the servant.

Anna opened her mouth with silent, amazed pleasure as she gazed around her. She had never seen a room so beautiful outside of a glossy architectural magazine. An expanse of floor patterned in tiles of different shades and designs, covered here and there with the most beautiful Persian carpets she had ever seen, stretched the length of a room at least forty feet long.

There were low tables, sofas covered in richly coloured, beautifully woven fabric like the most luscious of kilims, a black antique desk, and ornately carved and painted cabinets. Beautiful objets d'art sat in various niches, hung on the walls, stood on the floor.

A wall that was mostly window showed a roofed balcony overlooking a courtyard, in which she could see the leafy tops of trees moving gently in the breeze. The balcony was faced with a long series of marble pillars

supporting sculpted and engraved stone arches and
walled with intricately carved wooden screens. Beyond
the treetops, she saw a delicious expanse of blue sky and
sea.

Anna closed her eyes, looked again. Heaved a breath.
She felt the deepest inner sense of coming home, as if
after interminable exile. She belonged here. She sighed
deeply.

She turned to Ishaq Ahmadi. "Why was I in London?" she asked.

He raised his eyebrows in enquiry.

"I've been doubting you and everything you told
me," she explained. She closed her eyes and inhaled,
letting out her breath on another deep sigh of relief.
"But I *know* this is home. Why did I leave, Ishaq? Why
did you have to bring me home by force?"

He looked at her with an unreadable expression.

"Do you tell me you remember the house?"

She shook her head. "No…not really *remember*. But
I have the feeling of belonging."

"You are a mystery to me," he said flatly. "Give
Safiyah to the nurse, and let us have something to
drink."

The manservant was waiting silently, and Ishaq turned
to him with a quiet order. With a slight bow the man
moved away.

Meanwhile, with a caress, a kiss and a lingering
glance, Anna let the nurse take Safiyah from her arms.
The woman smiled reassuringly and disappeared through
a doorway, leaving Anna alone with Ishaq Ahmadi.

Who was opening a door onto the magnificent balcony. "Come," he said, in a voice that instantly dis-
pelled her more relaxed mood. "We have things to discuss."

He slipped off his suit jacket and tossed it onto a chair. She hesitated.

"My dear Anna, I assure you there is nothing to fear on the terrace," he said. "No one will throw you over the edge, though it is undoubtedly what you deserve."

What she deserved? Well, there was no answer she could make to that until she remembered more.

"Do I—have I left any clothes here?" Anna asked, rather than challenge him, feeling she could hardly bear any more wrangling. She couldn't remember ever having felt so tired. "Because if so, I'd like to change into something cooler."

"I am sure there is something to accommodate you. Shall I show you, or do you remember the way?" Then, correcting himself, "No, of course, you remember nothing."

She followed without challenging that mockery as he closed the door again and led her along half the length of the room and down a flight of stairs. There they walked along a hall and he opened a door.

If she had been hoping that the sight of her bedroom would trigger memories, that hope died as she entered the utterly impersonal room. For all the feeling that the room had been inhabited for centuries, there was not one photograph, one personal item on view. A few bottles of cosmetics on a dressing table were the only evidence that a woman slept here.

Well, she had known from the beginning that her marriage was troubled, so there was no reason to weep over this confirmation. Anna opened the door of a walk-in closet. Inside there were empty hangers, a few items in garment bags, a pair of sandals on the floor, a case neatly placed on a shelf.

So she had left him. She had preferred to run to London to have her baby in the back of a cab rather than stay with her handsome, passionate husband. Anna bit her lip. And he had come and kidnapped her and brought her back.

And she had no idea what that meant. Was she to be a prisoner now? Would he keep the baby and banish her? Or did he mean to try again to make a troubled marriage work?

She heaved a sigh, but there was nothing to be gained in trying to second-guess him. She was desperately disadvantaged by her memory loss, utterly dependent on him for any description of what had gone wrong between them.

Anna stripped, found some clean underwear in a drawer. Bathing her face and wrists in cool water, she paused and stared at her reflection. The face that looked back at her was not the face of a woman who was happy about having left her husband. Her eyes, normally a deep sapphire blue, looked black with fatigue.

Or perhaps it was the marriage itself that had done that to her.

The bra was too large for her. So she had been away some time? She abandoned the bra, slipping into briefs and a pale blue shirt and pant outfit in fine, cool cotton. The shirt was long, Middle Eastern fashion. It was size medium, and she had always bought petite. Anna shook her head. Nothing fit, in any sense of the word. One of the thong sandals was broken and she decided to go barefoot.

Ishaq, having changed his suit for a similar outfit to her own in unbleached white cotton, and wearing thong sandals, was waiting for her outside the door.

He led her up to the main room again.

''What time is it?'' she asked as he opened the balcony door. He obediently consulted the expensive watch on his wrist.

"Eleven."

"It feels more like six in the morning to me," she remarked, yawning and stepping outside. "I feel as if I've hardly slept."

From here she could see that the house was built in a squared C shape, and the broad balcony she was on ran around the three sides. One storey below, the courtyard was deliciously planted with trees and shrubs around a fountain. Beyond that there were other levels of the terrace, connected with arches and stone staircases, but mostly hidden from view by the greenery.

"It is seven in the morning in London. We have travelled east four hours," he replied.

She laughed at her own stupidity. "Oh, of course! Well, it just goes to show how confused I am!"

"No doubt."

The balcony was partitioned with beautiful wooden arches in the most amazing scrollwork. As they walked through one of these archways, Anna paused to touch the warm, glowing wood. "I paint arches like this on the walls of rooms," she observed. "But I've never before seen the real thing at first hand." Then she turned with a self-conscious laugh. "Well, but except—"

"Except for the fact that you live here," he said blandly.

They strolled through another arched partition, past windows leading to magical rooms. The house seemed very old, the brick and tiles well-worn by time and the tread of generations. Flowering plants tumbled in the profusion of centuries over the balcony and down to the terrace below, others climbed upwards past the opening towards the roof.

"Is this your family's house?"

"I inherited it from my father early this year."

"Oh, I'm sorry," she murmured, and then shook her head for how stupid that must sound to him—his wife, who must have attended the funeral with him, formally commiserating with him months after the fact.

"Sorry," she muttered. "It's hard to…"

Past the next archway a group of padded wicker chairs and loungers sat in comfortable array by a low table near a tiny fountain. Anna sighed. Her weary soul seemed to drink in peace so greedily she almost choked. There were flowers and flowering bushes everywhere. The breeze was delicious, full of wonderful scents. The sound of running water was such balm. The whole scene was luxuriously, radiantly, the Golden Age of Islam.

"This is beautiful!"

As he paused, Anna stepped to the scrollwork railing and glanced down. She could hardly believe that any normal process of life had brought her to such a magnificent home.

The villa was not small. That was an illusion at the entrance level. Below her on various levels now she had a clearer view of the stepped terraces full of flowers and greenery, and discovered that the courtyard led to a terrace with an inviting swimming pool unlike any she had ever seen. It was square, set with beautiful tiles both around the edge and under water.

The house was built on a thickly forested escarpment above a white sand beach that went for miles in both directions. Straight ahead of her, across the bay, she saw the smoky blue of distant hills. To the left, several miles away around a curving shoreline, she could just catch sight of the city. Beyond the bay the sea stretched forever, a rich varied turquoise that melted her anxiety and fatigue with each succeeding rush of a wave onto the sand.

The murmur of voices told her that the servant had reappeared, and she turned to see him pushing a trolley laden with a large cut-glass pitcher of juice and a huge bowl of lusciously ripe fruit. All the glass was frosted, as if everything had been chilled in a freezer. In a few deft movements, the man transferred the contents of the trolley to the table, and at a sign from his master, retired.

As she sank onto a lounger Ishaq poured a drink and handed it to her without speaking. She put the ice-cold glass to her lips and drank thirstily of the delicious nectar, then lifted her feet onto the lounger and leaned back into a ray of sun that slanted in. The breeze caressed her bare toes. Behind her head a flowering shrub climbed up a pillar and around an arch, a carpet of pink blossoms. Anna smiled involuntarily as the heavy tension in her lifted. For a moment she could forget her fears, could forget how he had brought her back home, and simply be.

He sank into the neighbouring chair, facing her at an angle, leaned back and watched her over the rim of his glass. His gaze set up another kind of tension in her, that warred with the peace she was just starting to feel.

"So, Anna," he said. She closed her eyes against the intensity she felt coming from him.

"Ishaq, I'm tired. Can't we leave this for another day?"

"Delay would suit you, would it? Why?"

"I really am at a loss to understand you," she sighed. "I'm here, the baby's here, what else do you want?"

He smiled. "You have no idea what it is I want?"

"If I don't even remember being married to you, how can I possibly be expected to guess what you want?"

she exploded. She could feel that she was very near breaking point.

"All right," he said. "Let us deal with what you do remember. As far as you remember, six weeks ago you gave birth and the child died."

She closed her eyes. There was no softness in his tone, and she wondered what kind of fool she had been to tell him, when she remembered nothing about what kind of man she had married. She must have had good reason for not telling him.

"That's how it feels."

"You were distraught over this loss."

"Yes, of course I was." She gave him a steady look, desperately hoping she would be able to hold her own against him. "And I remind you that you were not then part of my life, Ishaq."

"You wondered about the possibility of adopting a baby, but as a single woman you were not eligible through conventional channels."

"What?" She blinked at him. "I never said that! Why are you putting words in my mouth?"

"Anna, time is short. I intend to find the truth."

"The truth of *what?*" she exploded. "You keep telling me different things! How can you expect me to remember anything when you keep changing your story? What is it you want? Why is time short? Why are you playing these games? Why does the past matter now? It's over, isn't it?"

"You wanted a baby very much," he continued, as if she hadn't spoken.

"Ishaq—"

"You wanted a baby very much?"

"No, I did not want 'a baby' very much!" she said through her teeth. "I wanted *my* baby. My baby, Noah, who had every right to be born healthy and strong. I wanted him. I still do. You're going to have to face it, Ishaq. It's not something that gets wiped out by time. He's there in my heart, and he will never leave. Safiyah joins him there, but she won't replace him. Noah will always be in my heart.''

It was the first time she had spoken of the baby in such a way. Her urgency meant she spoke without defending herself against the pain, and her breath trembled in her throat and chest. She felt the lump of stone in her chest shift, and thought, *Six weeks of hiding from the hurt is one thing. But what kind of marriage can it be if I've been keeping this inside for two years?*

He was leaning forward, close to her, but staring down into the glass he held loosely between his spread knees.

''What drew us together?'' she asked.

He lifted his eyes without moving his head.

''Have I never been able to be open about my feelings before? Is our relationship entirely based on sex or something?''

His eyes took on a look of admiration laced with contempt. ''In spite of having no memory of me, you feel sexual attraction between us?''

''Don't you?'' she countered.

His look back at her was darkly compelling, and her skin shivered. There *was* a strong sexual pull. And if that was the centre of their bond, it would be foolish to pretend to exclude it from their negotiations.

He reached out and ran a lean finger along her cheek, and the little answering shiver of her skin made her heart race. ''Have you forgotten this?''

She gulped. Oh, how had she ever, ever managed to attract him? He was so masculine, so attractive, and yet with an air of risk, of danger. Like the powerful muscles under the tiger's deceptively furry coat, under Ishaq Ahmadi's virile masculinity there was a threat that he would make a bad enemy.

"It seems rather wasteful on my part," she agreed with a crazy grin, wanting him to smile without any edge. "But I'm afraid I have."

"Then I will have the pleasure of teaching you all over again," he said lazily. His hand cupped her cheek and he looked searchingly into her face. "Yes?"

She had no argument with that. She bit her lip, smiling into his eyes, nearer now. "It might even be the thing to bring back my memory."

"Yes, of course! That is the most ingenious excuse for making love that I have heard. But you always were imaginative, Anna."

His lips were almost touching hers, and her skin was cold and hot by turns. His hand cupped her neck and his fingers stroked the skin under the cap of hair.

She felt the rightness of it. She wanted to lean against him and feel the protection his strength offered, feel his arms clasp her firmly, feel herself pressed against his chest again. For in his arms, just as in this house, she knew she was home.

He moved his mouth away from hers without kissing her, moved to her eyelid. She closed her eyes in floating expectation, feeling the sun's heat and Ishaq's warmth as if both derived from one source.

He trailed light kisses across her eyelids, brushed her long curling lashes with his full lips, trailed a feathery touch down the bridge of her nose. His thumb urged her chin upwards, and her head fell back in helpless longing.

She felt starved for the touch, as if she had been longing for it for months. Years. Her arms wrapped him, her hand on his neck delighting in the touch of the thick hair.

At last he kissed her lips, and it was right, so right. As if some deep electrical connection had been made. She felt it sing against her mouth and melt her heart, and she felt his hand tighten painfully on her arm and knew that he felt it, too. Whatever had gone wrong between them, it was not this.

He was gnawing on her lower lip with little bites that sent shafts of loving and excitement through her. His other hand came up and encircled her throat, too, and he held her helpless in his two hands while his mouth hungered against hers, stealing and giving pleasure.

Anna pressed her hand against his chest, thrilling to the strength of heart and body she felt there. It was both new and old. She felt as if she had loved him in some long-distant past, some other life, and at the same time that it was all totally new. She seemed never to have been warmed with such delight by a kiss, never yearned so desperately for a man's love.

He wrapped her tight in his arms and drew her upper body off the lounger and across his knees with a passion that made her tremble. Now his mouth came down on hers with uncontrolled longing, and he kissed her deeply and thoroughly until her bones were water and her heart was alive with wild, wild need.

His mouth left hers, trailed kisses across her cheek to her ear, down her neck to the base of her throat, and slowly back up the long line of her throat.

"Ishaq!" She cried his name with passionate wonder before his kiss could smother the sound on her lips. "Ishaq!"

His lips teased the corner of her mouth and moved up towards her ear.

"Tell me the truth, Anna," he whispered. "Tell me, and then let me love you."

"Tell you?" She would tell him anything, if only he would carry on kissing her. But she had nothing to tell. "Tell you what?" He did not answer, only stared compellingly at her, and she slowly turned away her head. "I don't remember," she protested sadly, feeling the passion die within her. "Why won't you believe me? What have I done to forfeit the trust you must once have had in your wife?"

His eyes squeezed shut, and she felt how he struggled for control of himself and bit by bit gained it. Then he lifted her to rest in the lounger again, took his hands away, and sat looking at her. She saw burning suspicion in his eyes.

"What is it?" she pleaded. "What do you want me to tell you? What have I forgotten?"

He shook his head, reaching for his glass, and nervously she picked up her own. He drank a long draft of juice, and set the glass down carefully.

"What have you forgotten, you want to know?" He looked at her levelly. "You have forgotten nothing, Anna. Except perhaps the humanity that is the birthright of us all. Tell me where Nadia is."

Anna closed her eyes, opened them. Swallowed.

"Nadia?" She repeated the name carefully. "Who is Nadia?"

Ishaq smiled. "Nadia, as you very well know, is the mother of the baby you kidnapped and have been pretending is your own."

Seven

The storm of passion he had raised in her body was now a dry emptiness that left her feeling sick. "What?" An icicle trailed along her spine. She blinked at him, mouth open, feeling about as intelligent as a fish. "What are you talking about?"

He watched her in silence. When she moved, it was to set her glass down on the table very carefully.

"I don't know anyone nam…the mother of the baby? Of Safiyah?" Her voice cracked. "She's not my baby?"

He was silent. She stared into his face. Was this the truth, or some kind of mind game?

"You're trying to break me," she accused hoarsely. "Tell me the truth. If you have any humanity at all, if you have one ounce of human feeling in you, tell me the truth. Is Safiyah our baby?"

"You know very well that she is not," he said. "Will

you never come to the end of your play-acting? What can you stand to gain from this delay?''

Anna heard nothing except *she is not.*

''She's not?'' she repeated. ''She's not?''

He sat in silence, watching her, his sensual mouth a firm, straight line.

''If she's not mine, then...I haven't forgotten two years of my life, either,'' Anna worked out slowly. She wrapped her arms around her middle and looked away from his gaze, rocking a little. ''And we aren't married, and this is not my home. It was all lies.''

She looked into his face again, saw the confirmation of what she had said, and turned hopelessly to gaze around her. A quiver of sadness pierced her. It had seemed so right. Being here, the baby, the man—it had felt real to her. She shook her head. ''But how...is one of us crazy?''

He looked like someone sitting through a badly acted play. ''You, if you imagined you could get away with it,'' he offered.

Her mouth was bone-dry. One hand to her throat, she tried to swallow, and couldn't. ''I don't know anyone named Nadia,'' she began, with forced calm. ''I was in an accident and I woke up in hospital and they told me my baby was okay. You said you were my husband and I had amnesia. That's all I know. That is literally all I know.''

Ishaq Ahmadi—if that was his name—leaned back in his chair. ''You knew enough to pretend the baby was your own,'' he pointed out dryly.

She shook her head in urgent denial. ''My memory was a complete jumble. You can't know what it's like unless you've experienced it. First I thought I was back at the time I was in hospital for...when my baby died.

When they said, 'Your baby's fine,' I thought…'' She stopped and swallowed. ''I thought Noah's death had been a bad dream. I thought I'd dreamt the whole six weeks since. I thought I had another chance.''

She forced down the taste of tears at the back of her throat.

''And then you came along,'' she said, in a flat voice. ''You turned everything on its head.''

It was all so crazy, so horrible, she could hardly take it in. She put a hand to her aching forehead. ''Where did the baby come from? Why did you tell me we were married?'' she demanded, fighting to keep sane. He'd be convincing her the world was flat next.

''For the same reason you pretended to believe me.''

''No!'' she cried. ''No! You know perfectly well—'' She broke off that argument, knowing it was futile. ''What is this? Why are you doing this?''

''You can guess why.''

She shook her head angrily. ''I can't guess anything! How dare you do this to me! Messing with my mind when I was concussed, telling me I was suffering from amnesia! What do you want? What can you possibly want from me? Why, *why* did you say she was our baby?''

''Because husbands have rights in such cases that others do not have.''

She blinked at the unexpectedness of it. It was perhaps the first time he had given her a straight answer to any question.

''Are you the baby's father?''

He paused, as if wondering how much to tell her. ''No. Nadia is my sister. ''

''How did I come to be in the hospital with her baby? Did you plant her on me somehow?''

One eyebrow lifted disbelievingly. "Not I. That's what I want you to tell me. I found you there together."

Anna shook her head confusedly. "I don't understand. Then how do you know this is your sister's baby?"

"By the al Hamzeh mark." He rubbed his eye unconsciously.

"By the—*what?*" She jerked back in her chair. "Are you telling me that you abducted a baby and a total stranger from a hospital and brought us across four time zones on the strength of the baby's *birthmark?*" she shrieked incredulously.

He gazed at her for a moment. Anna shifted nervously.

"Nadia was in labour and on her way to the hospital when she disappeared. A few hours later you turned up in another, nearby hospital, pretending to be the mother of a newborn baby with the al Hamzeh mark."

"How did you know I *wasn't* her mother? The nurses told me it was my baby. So how did you know better? Is there really nobody else in the world with that mark except you and Nadia?"

"The nurse who examined you knew very well it was not your baby. She had written notes on your chart to that effect. You may read the notes, if you doubt me. I have them. She made a note for the hospital to check with the police for any reported incidents of baby stealing from maternity wards and to keep you in for observation till the matter was investigated."

Anna blinked and opened her mouth in amazed indignation. "But then why—but they—I *told* them my baby died, and they said, No, here's your baby, she's alive!"

He shrugged.

Anna couldn't fit any one piece of the puzzle with another. She shook her head helplessly, feeling how slowly her mind was working. "Anyway, if you knew I wasn't Safiyah's mother, why bother to abduct me? Why didn't you just take the baby? I wouldn't be likely to complain, would I, if I was faking it?"

"I wanted information from you. And you were in no state to—"

"Information about what?" she interrupted.

"About how you got possession of Safiyah."

This was unbelievable.

"Like for example?" she demanded. "What are you suggesting? That I—jumped Nadia while she was in labour, dragged her off somewhere, and then stole her baby when it was born?"

"That is one possible scenario, of course. Is that what happened?"

"Well, thank you, I'm starting to get a picture here," Anna said furiously. "On no evidence whatsoever, you have decided that I am a baby snatcher. And that gives you the right to treat me like a criminal. You don't owe me an iota of respect, or the decency of truth. Nothing. Because of what you *suspect*. Have I got that now?"

Now she understood the reason for his questions earlier. The ugliest doubt of her own sanity brushed her. Was it possible? Had grief made her crazy enough to want a baby at any cost? Could she have done such a thing and forgotten all about it? Was that even the reason for her amnesia? No. *No.*

"And what do you imagine I did with Nadia?" she went on, when he didn't speak.

"That is one of the things I want you to tell me," he said.

Anna leapt to her feet. "How dare you talk to me like this? I did not do it! You have absolutely no grounds *whatsoever* for making such an appalling accusation!"

"I have not accused you. But you were in that cab with a newborn baby who is not your own. That needs some explaining."

She was not listening. She stormed on. "How dare you take such extreme action on no evidence at all...lying, abducting me, making me believe I'm half crazy! Telling me...my God, and we almost made love!" she raged, her cheeks blazing as she suddenly remembered the scene.

"Was that my doing?" he asked dryly. "Or was that your attempt to get my guard down?" He was speaking as if this were only another such attempt. As if he believed nothing she said.

The flame of rage enveloped her, licking and burning till she felt something almost like ecstasy.

"Don't *you* accuse *me!*" she stormed. "*I've* never said anything but the truth! All the manipulation has come from your corner! You even lied about your name, didn't you? Last night it was the Ahmadi mark. Just now you called it the al Hamzeh mark!"

Ishaq Ahmadi looked bored. "Never lied to me? You lied to me not half an hour ago."

"I have not lied to you!"

He got to his feet, facing her over the lounger, and Anna stepped back, but not fast enough to prevent his grasping her wrist.

"What do you call it? You told me you recognized this place, that you knew you had come home! You have not been within a thousand miles of this place."

Her eyes fell before the searching gaze. "Why did you say it?" he prodded.

She was silent. She had felt a sense of homecoming, probably only because she wanted to feel it. Wanted the baby to be hers, wanted him to be her husband. So desperately wanted all the sorrow and anguish of her terrible loss to be years in the past. There had certainly been enough clues that he was lying, if she had wanted to put them together.

"What did you hope to gain?" he pressed.

"Suppose you tell me!" she blazed, pain fuelling her anger in order to hide from him. She wrenched her wrist from his hold. "What advantage could there possibly be in saying something like that?"

"Perhaps you hoped to lower my guard and make your escape?"

"By sleeping with you, I suppose! Sexually amoral, too. That's quite a charming list you've made up there."

"You lied. You must have had a reason."

"Dear Kettle, yours sincerely, Pot!" she exclaimed mockingly. "I have only your word for what's going on, you know. And your word hasn't exactly proved unassailable. You…"

She stopped. "Why did you think I would believe you in the hospital, if things are as you say? You must have known I had amnesia. You must have been deliberately playing on the fact. Otherwise, why wouldn't I just tell the nurse you were an impostor?"

"I did not imagine that you would believe me. I thought you would prefer to pretend to do so, however, rather than run the risk of being revealed as a kidnapper and arrested by the police." Now she remembered that curious, warning pressure on her hand as she lay so dazed in the casualty ward. "And I was right. You could not afford to make a stand, because that would mean an immediate inquiry. And any inquiry would have shown that the baby could not be yours."

"If I hadn't been totally out of it I would have made a stand soon enough," she said. She suddenly felt too weak to support her own anger. All her energy had been used up; she was empty. She had no more strength for holding pain at bay.

Her baby seemed to reach for her heart, the touch of that tiny soul unlocking the deepest well of grief in her. She shook her head and forced herself to confront Ishaq, to cloak her weakness from this dangerous adversary.

"If you hadn't lied about absolutely *everything*... If a lie is big enough, they'll believe it! Are you proud to be taking your lead from a monster?

Anger flickered in his eyes.

"I do what is necessary to protect those I love," he said coldly. She believed him. She saw suddenly that he was a man who would make a firm friend as well as an implacable enemy and, in some part of her, she could grieve for the fact that she was destined to be his enemy.

"Well, bully for you!" she cried, her voice cracking with fatigue. "I want to get out of here and go home to my life. So suppose you tell me what you want from me?"

Ishaq Ahmadi inclined his head. "Of course. You have only to tell me where Nadia is and how you got her baby. Then you are free to go. I will of course pass the information and your name on to Scotland Yard."

With a grunt of exasperation that almost moved into tears, Anna whirled to stride away from him. Against the wall of the house a railing protected a worn brick staircase running down to the courtyard below, and again she felt that crazy sense of belonging. *I have gone up and down that staircase a hundred times.*

She shook her head to clear it, stopped and turned to face him.

"Why don't you believe me?" she demanded. He lifted an eyebrow, and she fixed her eyes on his. "No,

I really mean it. My explanation of events is as reasonable as anything else in this—'' she lifted her hands ''—in this unbelievable fantasy, so why won't you even give it a moment's consideration? You absolutely dismiss everything I tell you. Why?''

A sudden, delightful breeze whipped across the terrace, stirring her hair and the leaves, whipping the cloth on the table, snatching up a napkin and carrying it a few yards. Her nostrils were suddenly filled with the heady scent of a thousand flowers. The servant appeared as if from nowhere to chase down the napkin.

''Because what you tell me has no logic even of its own. How did you come to be in the hospital with this baby?''

''Funny, that's exactly why I *believed* you,'' she said on a desperate half laugh. ''How did I get there? That's the question, all right.''

''Your story has no foundation. It rests on sand.''

''What about the cab driver?'' she exclaimed. ''What did he say about it?''

''He was quite seriously hurt. He cannot yet be questioned.''

''Where did the accident happen?''

''The taxi pulled into the path of a bus on the King's Road at Oakley Street,'' he replied, as if she already knew. ''You were in the back with the baby. There can be no doubt of that.''

She damned well was not, but she didn't waste time on what he thought he knew. She wanted to sort this out.

''Oakley Street. That's only a couple of minutes from the Riverfront.'' The Riverfront Restaurant was moored near Battersea Bridge. ''What time was the accident?''

"Not long after midnight, according to the police report."

She wondered how he had got access to the police report, but didn't waste time asking. "We asked for our bill around midnight, I'm pretty sure."

She squeezed her eyes shut. That meant her memory loss covered a very short period. If only a few minutes had elapsed from the time she got into the cab till the accident...

"If you're right, the only possible explanation is that the baby was in the cab when I got into it," Anna said, and as she said it, the truth finally pierced her heart. That darling baby whom she already loved was not to be hers to love...any more than her son had been.

Ishaq Ahmadi snorted. "Excellent. If only you had thought of this explanation a few hours ago."

Anna shook her head, swallowing against the feeling that was welling up inside her, a flood of the deepest sadness. She had no right after all to hold and love that beautiful, perfect baby, no matter how empty her arms were, how much she yearned.

"Perhaps a little later you will remember this. At a convenient time you will perhaps remember getting into a cab and discovering a baby cooing and kicking there."

His words hurt her. *Noah,* she thought. *Oh, my baby! You never kicked and cooed....*

Suddenly all her defences were gone. She felt like a newborn herself. She dropped her arms to her sides.

"Maybe I didn't catch that cab. I don't actually remember getting into it. Drivers change shift around midnight, don't they? Maybe he wouldn't take me and we went up to the King's Road to try and get cabs there. Maybe..."

She was babbling. She didn't know if she was making

sense. She blinked hard against the unfamiliar tears that threatened, against the sudden pressure on the wall that had held down her feelings for so long. She wanted to put her head back and howl her loss to the whole mad world that had let it happen, let her perfect baby die.

"Yes?" he prompted.

"I don't know," she said, despair welling up. How could she sort anything out when she could not remember? It was boxing in the dark. Was it possible she had forgotten some horrible conspiracy? Had her grief driven her to the madness of taking someone else's baby to fill her empty heart? Women did such things.

Tears began to slip down her cheeks. She couldn't seem to control them. Her head was pounding; it must be the heat. She staggered a little.

"I'm tired," she realized suddenly. "Really tired." She put out her hand to an arch for support, but it was further away than it seemed. A sob came ripping up from her stomach, bringing with it bile and the juice she had just drunk, and feeling came surging on its heels.

"Oh!" she cried. "Oh, I can't..." Her fingers caught at something, a branch, perhaps, but she couldn't hold on, and at the next sob her knees gave way.

The branch was Ishaq's arm. He caught her around the waist when she buckled, supporting her as grief and bile spilled from her amid howls of anguish.

"My baby!" she cried desperately, as the image of Safiyah blended with that of her own darling son, and seemed to be torn anew from her arms and her heart. Her throat opened, and at last she howled out the uncomprehending, intolerable misery that had been her silent companion for so many days and weeks. "Oh, my baby! My baby! Why? *Why?*"

Eight

"Princess, it is too dangerous!" pleaded the maidservant. She stood wringing her hands as her mistress, gazing into the mirror, tweaked the folds of the serving girl's trousers she wore.

She glanced up, eyes sparkling in the lamplight. "He is a brave man, the Lion. He will admire bravery. If I could, I would challenge him in the field of battle."

"If anyone discovers you—"

"I will flee. And you will be waiting for me, with my own raiment," she said firmly.

She admired herself one last time in the mirror. The short jacket just covering her breasts, the pants caught tight below the knee, the delicate gold chain around her ankles fanning out over her feet to each toe, the circlets of medallions around her waist and forehead, the glittering diaphanous veil that did not hide the long dark curls…the costume of her father's winebearers suited a woman well.

A smile pulled at her dimpled cheek as she turned away and kissed her maid. "Fear not," she said. "I am quick of mind and fleet of foot and I shall elude all save him I would have capture me." A delicious thrill rushed through her and she picked up the white rose that lay waiting and tucked it into her waist.

A few minutes later the two women crept together down the dark, secret passages of the palace towards the sounds of revelry in the great banqueting hall.

Inside the hall, the narrow doorway was hidden by a large carpet hung upright to provide a narrow passage against the wall, but as they glided in behind it, light from the banquet beyond revealed more than one spy hole in the fabric. She pressed her eye to one and gazed hungrily.

The men sat and lay around the laden cloth on cushions and carpets, drinking and eating, laughing, toasting the bridegroom, who sat beside her father. At the far end of the room musicians played. Serving men moved about the room, carrying huge platters massed with food. A whole roast sheep was being set down before the bridegroom.

But she had no thought for her intended. Her eyes searched the faces of the men seated nearest the prince, looking for the one they called al Hamzeh. The Lion. The birthmark made her search easy, even at such a distance, and her heart thudded in pain and delight as her eyes found him.

She took the golden pitcher from her frightened maidservant's hands then and glided stealthily out into the room, her movements measured by the bell-like tinkle of her jewellery. She walked down the room towards the

*Lion, as if in answer to a summons, as she had watched
the cup bearers do.*

*He sat cross-legged on the carpet, leaning against a
mound of silken cushions at his elbow, listening as someone described some feat of the bridegroom's at the hunt.
His dark hair, glowing in lamplight, fell in tousled curls
over the glittering gold embroidery of his jacket. On his
fingers heavy carved gold held rich rubies and emeralds;
high on his arm she noted the seal of his office, a signet
in gold and amber. He seemed to glow independent of
the lamplight. She watched in a fever of desire as he bit
into a sweetmeat and his tongue caught an errant morsel
of powdered sugar from his full lower lip.*

*She approached, and bent over to fill the cup that he
held in one strong careless hand. The scent of him rose
up in her nostrils, spices and musk and camphor from
his clothes, and from his skin the clean perfumed smell
of a man just come from the hammam.*

*As if he sensed something in the winegirl, the Lion
lazily turned his head and let his eyes follow the smooth
arms up to her white breast, her half-hidden cheek. Instead of turning her face demurely away, she met his
gaze with a look of passionate challenge. He started, his
lips parting with questing amaze.*

*She let fall the white rose by the goblet, the little note
fluttering like a lost petal from its stem. His eyes flicked
to the rose, and she saw by his stillness that he understood. He turned and looked up at her, and now his gaze
devoured the sweet face so passionately that her own
eyes fell.*

*His hand moved possessively to gather up the rose
before it could be noticed by anyone else—enclosing it
jealously to keep it from other eyes, crushing it in a*

signal of all-consuming passion. She melted into answering passion as she felt his gesture on her own skin.

A thorn pierced his flesh and he smiled, as if a little pain was no more than to be expected from love.

Anna awoke in a strange bed and gazed around her.

Her headache was gone, and she felt deeply refreshed, as if she had made up for all the lost sleep of weeks past in one go. But the sunlight filtering through the shutters was still bright.

She had wept till she was completely drained and exhausted. She had wept it all out, for the first time, and then had fallen into a deep sleep. And now a burden had lifted from her. The heavy weight was gone.

Now healing could begin.

And of all people it was Ishaq Ahmadi who had sat beside her and witnessed her grieving. He had not said much, but his quiet presence had been exactly right. Someone to listen without feeling driven to reassure. Someone to hear and accept while understanding that nothing could be done to change her world for her.

With more interest in life than she had experienced for weeks past, Anna leaned up on one elbow and gazed around her.

She was in a different bedroom entirely from the one she had changed her clothes in. This was a very spacious room, beautifully decorated in blues and dark wood, with a door leading to the terrace. There were two other doors, and in the hopes that one of them led to a bathroom, Anna sprang out of bed and crossed an expanse of soft silk carpet woven in shades of blue and beige.

She got the bathroom first time, and when she returned to the bedroom, there was a smiling maid waiting for her. The bed was made as neatly as if Anna had never slept in it, and on the bed were laid clothes, as if for her choice.

"Saba'ul khair, madame," the maid murmured, ducking her head.

Anna smiled. *"Salaam aleikum,"* she offered. It was the only phrase she knew in Arabic.

It was a mistake, because the woman immediately burst into delighted chatter, indicating the terrace beyond the windows and the clothes on the bed.

Laughing, Anna shook her head. "I don't speak Arabic!" she said, holding up her hands in surrender, but when she saw that among the offered outfits were several swimsuits, she turned towards the windows. The woman was opening the slatted wooden shutters so she could see more clearly what was out there.

The room was at one of the tips of the C. On the far side of the broad terrace was the swimming pool she had seen from above. Ishaq Ahmadi was sitting at a table in a beach robe, reading a newspaper. A meal was being served to him.

Anna's stomach growled. She turned to the bed and picked up a swimsuit in shades of turquoise. It was beautifully cut and looked very expensive. Underneath that was another one, identical except for the size. With a frown of interest Anna picked up a few other items. Everything had been supplied in two sizes.

It might be conspicuous consumption, but as for refusing to accept his casual largesse, well, Anna was dying for a swim. So she stripped off her clothes and inched into one of the blue suits. It had an excellent fit, and she turned to examine herself briefly in a large mirror. She was thin, but the antique mirror was kind. Her shape was still unmistakably feminine. The suit emphasised her slender curves. The gently rounded neckline produced a very female cleavage, and her back, naked to the waist, had an elegantly smooth line. Her legs were lean but shapely, even if the large purple bruise on one thigh showed cruelly against her too-pale skin.

It was a long time since she had examined her reflection for femininity and attractiveness. Now it was perhaps a sign of her return to feeling that she was anxious to look attractive.

The maid held a cotton kaftan for her, and she slipped her arms into the sleeves with a murmur of thanks. It was plain white with an oriental textured weave and wide sleeves, and she knew without looking at the label that it had cost a small fortune. She chose a purple cotton-covered visor and a pair of sunglasses from a small spread of accessories.

He had thought of everything. He must have phoned a very exclusive boutique—or had one of his servants do so. Well, she would be glad if the utter stupidity of her trip here was relieved by a few hours of sun before she flew back to a wintry Europe. And though the items would be beyond her budget, they wouldn't amount to much for a man who owned a house like this.

The maid drew open the door for her, and Anna stepped out under the arched overhang and into the luscious day and walked across the tiled paving, past shrubs and flowers, past palm trees and small reflective pools, towards the swimming pool.

The air was cooler, and the sun had moved in the opposite direction to what she would have expected. She had thought the courtyard faced south, but in that case the sun was setting in the east.

Before she could reorient herself she had arrived at Ishaq's table beside the pool in a corner where the house met the high perimeter wall, nestled attractively under an arching trellis thick with greenery and yellow blooms.

He closed his paper as the servant pulled out a chair for her. A second place had been set.

"Good afternoon," she said, sinking down into it.

"Afternoon?" Ishaq queried with a smile, and she simultaneously took in the fact that his meal was composed of fruit and rolls.

"Café, madame?" murmured the servant, and she smelled the strong, rich odour and demanded, "What time is it?"

"Just after nine," said Ishaq Ahmadi.

"In the morning!" A breathless little laugh of comprehension escaped her. "Have I slept an entire day?"

"I am sure you needed it. You must be hungry."

"Ravenous!" She flung down her sunglasses, then leaned back out of the shady bower so that the sun caught her face, and felt that she was happy in spite of everything. "Oh, this is heaven! What a wonderful place!"

He smiled. He had lost some of the hard edge of suspicion he had carried since they first met. And she— well, she had shown him things about herself that no one else in the world had seen. So it was only natural that she felt closer to him now.

He offered the basket of rolls. "Perhaps you would like what you call a full English breakfast?"

Taking a roll, Anna smiled up at the servant who was setting cream and sugar just so by her coffee cup. "I could devour a plate of bacon and eggs," she told Ishaq, then checked herself. "Oh, but—"

"I am sure the cook has some lamb sausage."

"That sounds delicious."

Ishaq translated her wishes to the servant. As the man

slipped away, he said, "I do not ask my staff to cook pork for non-Muslim guests. I hope you will not object to doing without it during your stay."

"My *stay?*" She looked at him. "I want to go home. Are you planning on forcing me to stay here beyond today?"

"Force you? No," he replied calmly. "But you might reconsider when you look at this."

His hand was resting on the arm of his chair, holding the newspaper he had been reading. He lifted it to present her with the paper, front page up.

Trahie Par Son Milliardaire De Cheikh! screamed the French headline, which she could vaguely translate as *Betrayed By Her Millionaire Sheikh,* and Anna only shook her head. But then her eye was drawn further down the page, to a large photograph.

"That's me! That's you and me!" she cried in astonishment, snatching the paper without apology and spreading it under her horrified nose.

It was a photo taken at the airport, of herself, holding Safiyah, and Ishaq Ahmadi with one arm around her, guiding her to the limousine. An inset photo showed a sultry, big-lipped blonde whose face Anna vaguely recognized.

Very clearly marked—and too dark, so someone had obviously retouched the photo—was the al Hamzeh mark on the eye of Ishaq and of Safiyah.

"Oh, good grief!" Anna cried weakly. "Is this…" She glanced at the stack of papers on the table beside him, knowing the answer even as she asked. "Is it in the English papers?"

"Very much so," he agreed lazily.

She jumped up and ran to the stack. Of course, today

was Sunday. The English Sunday tabloids were notorious for their love of scandal among the rich and famous.

Sheikh Gazi's Secret Baby!

Sheikh's Mistress In Baby Surprise!

Mystery Beauty Has Playboy Gazi's Baby!

All the tabloids save one had run it on the front page, with a variant of the photograph she had already seen. Every headline insinuated or said outright that the woman in the photo was the sheikh's mistress and the mother of his child. Worst of all, in virtually every photograph Anna's face was clear and unmistakable. She looked exactly like herself. And her arms were around the baby in a firm maternal hold that spoke louder than the headlines.

Still in a state of stunned disbelief, Anna chose one of the papers and returned to her seat, sinking slowly into it as she read the story.

Sheikh Gazi al Hamzeh, the wealthy, jet-setting Cup Companion and trusted confidant of Prince Karim of West Barakat, startled the world yesterday with the revelation that his long-time English mistress has given birth to his child.

The infant is thought to be over a month old. "The birth was kept secret till Gazi could gain the prince's approval to acknowledge the child," said a source close to the sheikh.

Prince Karim, whose own son was born in July, is understood to be urging the sheikh to marry his so far unidentified mistress, seen here with the sheikh on arrival at Barakat al Barakat.

"Sheikh Gazi has gone to extraordinary lengths to protect the privacy of his mystery girlfriend," says our own society columnist, Arnold Jones

Bremner. "Virtually no one outside his circle knows who she is."

Although the couple have been seen in some of London's most exclusive private clubs over the past year, they use a service entrance. This is the first photograph of them together.

Insiders say the couple are unlikely to marry.

Anna lifted her eyes to "Ishaq Ahmadi."

"*'Long-time mistress!'*—where did they get this?" she demanded. Her gaze hardened. "Is this what you told them?"

He laughed. "They did not trouble to ask me. The truth might have got in the way of invention. Suppose you had been the baby's English nanny! Where would their front page be then?"

"They asked you questions at the airport," Anna said stonily. "I heard them. And you answered."

His jaw tightened. "Recollect that it was you yourself who insisted on presenting them with the tantalizing sight of the baby. But for that our arrival would have been unremarkable."

"What does *Paris Dimanche* say?" she asked, to catch him out. If the stories matched, surely that meant there had been one source?

He looked as if he saw right through her suspicious mind, but made no comment, merely lifted the paper and negligently began to translate.

"Sheikh Gazi al Hamzeh, the Hollywood-handsome, polo-playing millionaire considered one of the world's most eligible bachelors, has dashed the hopes and broken the heart of beautiful model/actress Sacha Delavel, his close friend, with the rev-

elation that he is on the point of marrying the
mother of his child. 'It comes as a total shock,'
Mademoiselle Delavel reportedly told friends from
the privacy of a villa in Turkey, where she is said
to have fled as the news broke. 'I never knew of
her existence until today.'''

He tossed the paper aside as Anna's breakfast was
placed before her. He deliberated over the fruit in the
bowl and chose a ripe pomegranate as if he had nothing
else on his mind. Then he neatly began to slice into the
rind.

For some reason this story was much more infuriating
than the other.

"I suppose when you're next seen with Sacha Delavel
I'll be the one billed as having the broken heart," Anna
snapped.

Ignoring her, he delicately, patiently prised open the
pomegranate to reveal the luscious red rubies within.
Anna shivered as if she were watching him make intimate love to another woman.

"Sacha Delavel and I danced together at a charity ball
given for Parvan war relief a few months ago in Paris.
They have searched their picture library and found some
nice photos of the two of us, which are on page seven.
The rest is invention."

She watched as he sank strong white teeth into the
red fruit. Liquid spurted from the seeds over his hands
and mouth, but he was concentrated on his pleasure. A
thrill of pure sensation pierced her, and with a little gasp
Anna dropped her eyes to her own breakfast.

"Did they get your name right? You're Sheikh Gazi
al Hamzeh?"

"In the West I commonly use that name," he admitted wryly.

"Oh!" she remarked with wide-eyed sarcasm. "*It's* not your real name, either?"

"My name is Sayed Hajji Ghazi Ishaq Ahmad ibn Bassam al Hafez al Hamzeh," he said, reeling the name off with the fluency of poetry. "But this is difficult for English speakers, who do not like to take time over other people's names. Nor do they trouble to pronounce consonants that don't appear in English."

She couldn't think of any comeback to that. They ate in silence for a few minutes. With little flicked glances she watched him enjoy the pomegranate, and marvelled that anyone could believe that ordinary Anna Lamb was the mistress of such a powerful, virile, attractive man, or that he had dropped someone as beautiful as Sacha Delavel for her.

But she was pretty sure that people *would* believe it, now. It had been in the papers, after all. Probably even her own friends would wonder. Not Cecile or Lisbet, of course. But others less close to her.

"What do we do about this?" she finally asked, indicating the papers.

"Do?" Sheikh Gazi shrugged and wiped his hands and mouth with a snowy napkin. "Ignore it."

"*Ignore* it? But we have to make them retract. We could sue."

"And sell more papers for them."

"But it's all lies!"

Sheikh Gazi smiled at this indignation. "People will soon forget."

"But—aren't you going to do *anything?*"

"The editors hope that I will. Then they would have something to run with. A story denied is a story. Do you really want to see *Sheikh Gazi Denies Baby* as next Sunday's headline? Or do you prefer *Gazi Is Not The Father, Says Anna*?''

''But people will think—it says that you and I are...''
She licked her lips and faded off, startlingly aware of the day, the heat, the luscious taste of fruit in her mouth, the smell of the sun on his skin. *They think we're lovers.* The thought hovered between them, shimmering like heat.

''And the more you say now, Anna, the more they will go on thinking it,'' he said.

''But I—I have to go back to London immediately. To France,'' she amended. ''What if the papers find out my name?''

''They will certainly do so,'' he warned her softly. ''As soon as the papers are read in London this morning—'' he glanced at his watch ''—it is nearly six o'clock there now—someone who knows you will call a journalist and name you.''

They were reading the story before most people in England were awake. She realized he must have some mechanism for getting the Sunday papers as soon as they rolled off the presses at midnight and flying them out to Barakat.

''Your price per copy must be astronomical,'' she observed dispassionately. ''Do you have a regular Sunday delivery of the European papers?''

''No,'' he said.

The servant came with a new pot of coffee. He whisked their half-drunk cups away and poured fresh coffee into clean cups. Even with her worries, Anna had attention to note the luxury of that.

''Today was special, huh?'' She had always dreamed of being famous one day, but for her work, not for something like this. "Well, so some friend or client will spill the beans. Then what? Will they phone me?"

"Phone you? They will phone you, they will phone your friends, they will come to your front door. At least one paper will offer you money for an exclusive, and if you accept, the editor will do everything to convince you to make the story of your sheikh lover more extreme and exciting."

"What do you mean?"

"Before they are through you will be tricked or persuaded into confessing that we have made passionate, death-defying love in the back of a limousine as it drove through London and Paris, in moonlight on the deck of my yacht, high in the air in the royal jet, on the magical white sand beach down there, and even on the back of my favourite polo pony as it galloped through the forest. Naturally we have been insatiable lovers. And of course they will publish photos of you posed in my favourite piece of sexy underwear."

His words sent electric twitches all across her scalp and down her spine, and Anna sat up abruptly and sugared her coffee. Was he being assailed by the same treacherous thought she was—that since everyone believed it anyway, they might as well make it the truth?

Nine

"**I**'m not going to be selling anyone any story," she said, setting the spoon in the saucer with a little snap. "Your polo pony's reputation is safe from me."

He lifted his hands in a shrug.

"But it really burns me that everyone I know is going to half believe I had your baby. What am I going to tell *them?*"

"That the story is false."

Her anger exploded on a little breath. "Oh, sure! You seem to forget that I actually have been pregnant. Only my close friends know my baby died. I haven't told anyone. I've hardly seen anyone since it happened. Everybody is going to wonder."

He looked at her. "I see."

"And what happens when I don't have the baby with me? People are going to think I walked away and let you keep her."

"Is it so bad? Fathers do get custody," he pointed out, so offhand she gritted her teeth. "And you have a career that takes you—"

She ground out, "I would no more give up my baby to its father for the sake of my career than—" She broke off with an exasperated sigh.

"Blame it on me," he suggested. "Everybody knows Arabs are an uncivilized bunch of barbarians who kidnap their own children."

"Will you stop laughing at me?" she demanded hotly.

"I will stop laughing when you stop being foolishly outraged by something so unimportant. It is not the end of the world, Anna. People will accept that the story was false when you tell them, or they will not. Either way they will cease to care within a week. These things—" he flicked the pile of newspapers with a gesture of such deep and biting contempt she flinched "—they feed the lowest tastes in humans, and like any junk food the purveyors of it make it addictive and completely without nutrition in order to create a constant demand for more. One story runs into another in people's minds. It is a taste for scandal and outrage this feeds, not a desire for factual information."

"I want to make them print a retraction," she said doggedly.

"Anna, by next Sunday, if we give them no more fuel for their fire, no one will remember whether you had a sheikh's baby or bribed a government minister, and no one will care! Do you know how many times my picture has appeared in these rags? Do you think anyone who gobbles such stories along with their Sunday toast remembers my name? I am 'that sheikh' if they think of me at all, and they confuse me with half a dozen other Cup Companions, or even with the princes themselves.

Even with something like the al Hamzeh mark to distinguish me, people say to me, *Oh, you were in the paper, weren't you? What was that about again?* when the story was about the ex-Sultan of Bagestan.''

''You just told me a minute ago that they're going to chase me down like dogs,'' she said irritably.

''*Yes,* if you put yourself in their way.'' He gazed compellingly at her, lifting his closed fist, the first knuckle extended towards her, for emphasis. ''*Yes,* if you give them fodder by complaining. This is a story that has another one or two headlines in it at most—*if* we give it to them! If not, it will die now. This is not, as they say, a story with legs.''

''What does that mean?'' she asked doubtfully, half convinced. He seemed to know so much about it.

''To have legs? It is newspaper jargon. It means a story that is going to run under its own steam.''

She sat in silence, her chin in her hands, absorbing it.

''There is nothing to be gained by issuing a denial, Anna. The best you can do, if you wish it to go no further, is stay out of sight for a while.''

She tried again. ''It's not as though I'm a celebrity, is it? It's you they're really interested in. If I can just get to France, I'll be fine. Alan's house is pretty remote.''

''Let me offer you an alternative to France, Anna.'' His gaze was now utterly compelling. Although he was trying to disguise it, she realized that he wanted something from her, and the butterflies in her stomach leapt into a dance so wild she was almost sick.

She licked her lips. ''And what would that be?''

''You could stay here with me until the heat dies down,'' he said.

* * *

A long moment of stillness was interrupted by the shrill cry of a bird in a nearby tree. Anna dropped her napkin by her plate with a matter-of-fact gesture.

"I—" she began, and then broke off. Her blood pounded in her stomach, making it feel hollow in spite of the meal she had just eaten.

"Do not turn me down without giving it some thought, Anna. There is advantage to you in staying away from the press for the moment. And I assure you I will do everything in my power to make your stay enjoyable."

Anna licked her lips. What was he really offering her here? A mere bolt-hole, or her very own Club Med holiday complete with dark lover? With any ordinary man, she would be in no doubt, but he was a man whose interest would flatter the most famous and beautiful women in the world. Why should he want her?

"For how long—a week?" she asked.

He shrugged and lifted a hand. His hands were graceful and strong, and she wondered if he played a musical instrument. Or perhaps a man got hands like that playing music on women's bodies...she stomped on the little flames that licked up around her at the thought.

"Perhaps a week, a few weeks. It depends."

On what? she wondered. Not on newspaper interest, obviously, when he had already assured her that would scarcely last till next Sunday.

Was he imagining that he would put her through her paces and see how long she kept him interested? She was unlikely to keep a millionaire playboy sheikh who hung out with the likes of Sacha Delavel interested for long. She had never studied sex as an art, and she would bet that he had.

"But people would find out I was here, wouldn't

they? It would just confirm the story. So whenever I went back I'd have to face journalists wanting me to talk about it. Wouldn't I?''

He shrugged and plucked a grape from the bowl. She had the feeling again that he was hiding something.

''Where's the advantage in delaying the inevitable? At least if I go back now I can deny it. If I stay here even for a week no denial is ever going to sound credible.''

It suddenly occurred to her that she sounded like someone wanting to be convinced, and she shut up.

''Can you think of no advantage from such a holiday? Barakat is a very exclusive holiday destination. No package tours come here. We have only a few resorts. That beach is as crowded now as it ever gets.''

She couldn't refrain from a glance in the direction he indicated. The strip of white sand curving around the bay in front of them was virtually deserted. So it actually wouldn't be stretching credibility too far to suggest that they had made love there, she found herself thinking absently...

Some part of her urged her to simply capitulate, and let nature take its course. But a little voice was warning her to be wary. Sheikh Gazi was not disinterested. What purpose would her staying serve for him? Was he really attracted to her, or was he deliberately letting her think so to disguise his real motives? And if he *didn't* want her sexually, what did he want?

Had he in fact been offering *her* sex as a bribe? He wanted her to stay and he knew she was attracted. Plenty of women would jump at the chance for a holiday in this paradise with a man like Gazi—and a sheikh, too!—devoting himself to them. Was he assuming she was one of them?

Anna, examining the grape between her fingers with minute fixity, blushed to the roots of her hair. After a moment she slipped it into her mouth.

"I would of course reimburse you for your time," he said, and that certainly proved the suspicion. He was simply trying whatever was handy by way of a bribe. If sex wasn't enough, he would throw in cash. God, what that said about his opinion of her!

"Really," she observed, her voice distant, almost absent.

"At your professional rate, of course."

She flicked him a look. "Which profession would that be?"

He chose to ignore the irony. "Which profession? I don't—you are an artist, you say. Artist, designer, interior decorator, whatever fees are your usual fees."

"Since you're doing me the big favour by allowing me to hide here, I don't really see why *you* should pay *me*," Anna said sweetly. "Isn't the shoe on the other foot? Or perhaps you have some reason of your own for wanting me to stay?"

He sat for a moment tapping a thumb on his cup, considering.

"Yes," he said at last. "I also have reasons for wishing it."

"Well, well! And what would those reasons be?"

"I cannot discuss it with you," he said. The look in his eyes was an assessment, but a long way from sexual assessment. She realized abruptly that he did not trust her, or fully accept her version of events, even now. But he might be willing to make love with her if that was what it took to keep her here. Rage swept her, with a suddenness that astonished her.

"Suppose I take a stab at guessing?"

He watched her.

"Let's see, now," she began. She tilted her head and looked at him. "You're sure about that judgement, are you—that this story hasn't got legs, as you call it?"

"That a Cup Companion has a child with his mistress may offend the religious in Barakat, but for a Western audience it means nothing. You must be aware of the truth of this. As you pointed out, you are not a celebrity yourself. That gives the story only limited interest."

She nodded thoughtfully. "That's okay as far as our affair and our secret baby go, but that's all lies anyway. But there's something you're leaving out of the calculation, isn't there? I mean, that's not the only story here, not by a long way."

She saw a flicker of feeling in his eyes, instantly veiled. He fixed her with a dark, impenetrable gaze. "And what else is there?"

Anna did not stop to consider how unwise it might be to show such a man how thoroughly she understood his motives.

"You abducted a baby from an English hospital, Sheikh Gazi—and according to the papers, you're one of the trusted Cup Companions of Prince Karim. That's got legs, don't you think? You also abducted an Englishwoman. And you got us out of England and into Barakat without passports. That's got legs, too. In fact, it's got so many legs it's a centipede.

"And forgive me if I suggest that you wouldn't have done any of that just for sheer amusement. So the real reason you took such risks, Sheikh Gazi, whatever it is— that's a story that'll have legs, too."

He was silent when she finished, and her ears were suddenly filled with the thunder of her own agitated

heartbeat. Too late, Anna reflected that perhaps her reasoning processes hadn't fully recovered from her accident. What on earth had made her challenge the man
here on his own ground?

"How well you grasp the facts," Sheikh Gazi said
softly, tossing his napkin down beside his plate. "But I
advise you to consider a little longer before you try to
blackmail me, Anna."

His eyes were absolutely black. His gaze stabbed her,
and her heart pounded hard enough to make her sick.

"I am not trying to blackmail you!" she shouted, re-
jecting her own dimly realized understanding that her
little summation might well have sounded like it. "Why
are you constantly accusing me of the lowest possible
crimes?"

"What, then?" he said, his lips a tight line in a face
that suddenly seemed sculpted from stone. "Just a pleasant little gossip to pass the time of day with me?"

She gritted her teeth. "Tell me, is it your wealth and
position that give you the right to trample over other
people, or is it just that women in general are beneath
contempt?"

"I do not hold women in contempt," he said in flat
repudiation.

"I have a life," she interrupted rudely before he had
finished. "Forgive me if I find it offensive to be offered
a holiday on the casual assumption that my career can
be put on hold in order to save you from the consequences of your own actions." She tilted her head.

"I also resent being taken for such a fool. It's not me
who's going to suffer if I deny this ridiculous story, is
it? It's you. I have nothing at all to fear from the truth.
Now—" She held up her hands. "I have no intention
of telling anyone anything, except that you are not my

lover and I am not the mother of your baby. But I do intend to get out of here and back to my own life. So unless you're considering adding forcible confinement to the list of your crimes—''

"You are annoyed because I have underestimated your intelligence," he interrupted with a sudden return to reasonableness that secretly irritated her. "Fair enough, but if you can see so far, a little more thought will tell you—''

"Please don't spell out anything more for poor little me," Anna snapped, lifting a hand. "I really think I understand enough. The rest I don't want to know. You might decide at some future date that I am a danger to you if I learn any more now."

His face closed, and she saw that he could be deeply ruthless when he chose.

"You are determined to consider only your own convenience."

"Me?" She could hardly speak for outrage. With biting sarcasm, she began, "I quite understand that *you* feel your concerns should come first with everyone you meet, Sheikh Gazi—no doubt it follows from having more servants than is good for you. But forgive me if *I* consider it quite reasonable that I should put myself and my clients first."

He gazed at her for a moment. "My concern is for my sister," he said quietly. "Let me—''

She lifted her hands, pushing the palms towards him. "Well, that's admirable! But I have already told you I know nothing about your sister. She is a total stranger to me. And my life has been quite disrupted enough on her behalf, thank you! Now I'd like to get it back on the rails."

Sheikh Gazi acknowledged this with a hard, business-like little nod. "Let us hope that future generations consider such devotion to your art a worthwhile sacrifice."

"It's no sacrifice on my part, believe me!" Anna exclaimed explosively, if not quite truthfully. "Not that I would *begin* to suggest that you rate your claims too high!"

He went absolutely still with fury. For a moment they stared at each other. Anna's skin twitched wildly all over her back and breasts as emotion flared in him, and she wondered what her reaction would be if he reached for her. If he started to make love to her, it was entirely possible she'd end up agreeing to anything he asked her to do, short of murder.

As if in answer to her thoughts, Sheikh Gazi shoved back his chair and got to his feet. He shrugged out of his bathrobe, letting it fall onto the chair. Then he stood there, naked except for a neat black swimsuit in body-hugging Lycra. She could not avert her fascinated gaze.

Wind seemed to blow up out of nowhere, seducing all the flowers on the trellis overhead to give up their perfume, tousling her hair and robe, caressing her skin, so that all at once her whole body came alive.

He was gorgeous—there was just no other word. Beautifully proportioned legs, powerful thighs, neat-muscled waist curving up to a very male expanse of chest with just the right amount of curling black hair, broad shoulders that were held with the minimum of tension, strong arms.

Probably she would never get another chance at such death-defying sexual excitement as he had just offered. When she was an old woman probably she would look back on this day and call herself seventeen kinds of fool for turning him down.

Her gaze locked with his, her heart jumping, her stom-

ach aquiver. She was acutely aware that the bed she had
spent the night in was only yards away across the terrace.

He could convince her to stay. Even knowing his passion was totally calculated, a payment for services ren-
dered, she would still burn up if he touched her. The
thought of him using his sexual expertise to reduce her
to willing cooperation in his plans, whatever they were,
made her legs weak.

Sheikh Gazi al Hamzeh's lips parted. "Then you will
not wish to avail yourself of my offer," he said, with
bone-chilling politesse. "I will arrange for your return
to London as soon as possible." Then he turned, stepped
to the edge of that delightful pool, and dove in.

Ten

It wasn't as easy as that. Anna would of course not be allowed to re-enter Britain without a passport. Her passport was in London, however, in her flat. The keys to her flat were in her handbag, which was presumably still at the hospital. Before anything else, someone had to be nominated to go to the hospital and pick up her belongings, then go to her flat, find her passport, and send it to her.

Anna wanted to ask Lisbet to do it, but Sheikh Gazi frowned when she suggested it. ''The hospital must be dealt with very diplomatically. And anyone going into your flat may be questioned by journalists,'' he warned.

''Lisbet's an actress. She'll know how to handle that.''

''*Allah!*'' he murmured in horrified tones. ''You surely do not want someone to whom publicity is the breath of life being asked by the press about your private life?''

''Lisbet won't say anything. If anyone is going to be rooting around my flat in my absence, I'd rather it was Lisbet,'' she said doggedly.

''And your other friend—Cecile?''

''If Cecile was challenged by a reporter, she'd collapse and give them my entire life back to when I sucked my thumb, and be under the impression that she had handled them very well. I love her, but really, she just has no idea.''

''There must be another way,'' said Sheikh Gazi. ''I will consider.''

Anna had to insist on being allowed to call her client to explain her delay. ''What is the point? You will be there in a day or two,'' Sheikh Gazi argued.

''The point is I was due there yesterday,'' Anna said, thinking how different the perception of time was in the Barakat Emirates. It was true there was no one at the villa to worry, but what if Alan phoned from London and got no answer? A day or two was plenty of time to get worried.

Sheikh Gazi gave in very gracefully when she explained how Sunday meant Sunday to the English, and a delay till Tuesday or even Wednesday was significant.

''Of course, darling. Whenever,'' Alan Mitching said when she tried to explain. ''You relax and enjoy yourself. The villa's not going to disappear. No one's using the place till Christmas. You can get the keys from Madame Duval anytime.'' She had the feeling that Alan was sitting there with a tabloid leaning against his breakfast teapot, avidly reading about her and Gazi.

''Will you tell Lisbet that I'll be in touch?''

''Of course.''

Having won this argument, Anna found it harder to press the other. So when Sheikh Gazi suggested that it would be best for someone from the Barakati Embassy in London to get her passport, since they could put it in the diplomatic pouch, she felt almost obliged to be as gracious as he had been in giving in.

He insisted on her being examined by a specialist, in spite of the fact that she would be back in London within a day or two and could see her own doctor. Although the man spoke German and French, he knew so little English Gazi had to translate for him.

"He says you are well, there is no lasting damage," Gazi told her, and she suddenly discovered, by the depths of her own relief, how frightened she had been, and was grateful to him for insisting.

Two days later, when she was expecting to hear that her passport had arrived in that day's diplomatic pouch, word came through that the hospital would not give up her handbag without a signed authorization.

It seemed things were going to move at a Middle Eastern speed. It was hard to find the energy to push for a faster conclusion, though, especially as the surroundings were so blissful. Her fatigue seemed to be taking this opportunity to catch up with her. Anna found she had no physical energy for anything but swimming, lying in the sun, or wandering around the beautiful house, and no mental energy at all.

She signed a permission and Sheikh Gazi sent it off by special messenger, and another day drifted past like the others.

The desert sky was black as a cat, with a thousand eyes. The wind blew, hot and maddening, around the turrets, driving her thin robe against her body, biting sand against her cheeks and into her eyes. She crept precariously along the parapet, feeling how the wind clutched at her, trying to fling her down.

He was there before her with a suddenness that made her gasp, his arms around her, dragging her against himself.

"You came," he whispered hoarsely.

The wind whipped at her, but not so harshly as his passion. Her back arched over his arm as her eyes glowed up into his. "How could I not?" she half laughed, half wept. "Am I not lost, and are not you the polestar? Am I not iron, and you the lodestone?"

Holding her with one powerful arm, he bent over her and tenderly drew the scarf from her mouth to gaze at her face in the moonlight. He drank in her beauty with a hunger that melted her, his eyes burning with desire.

"How beautiful thou art," he murmured, and his hand captured one of hers and drew it to his mouth. He pressed the fingers, then the palm, against his burning lips, water in the desert.

He kissed her throat, white in the moonlight, and she trembled with her first taste of such passion. His eyes pierced hers again. "Thou art no slave girl!" he said.

She smiled. "No. No slave girl."

"Tell me thy father's name, and I will send to him for thee. I will make thee my wife."

She shook her head. "Thou art the trusted companion of a prince," she whispered. "And truly, I am no better than a slave. Do not seek to know my father, but only know that I willingly give up all for one taste of thy love. The world holds nothing for me."

He bent his head and his mouth devoured hers with a violence of passion. The wind gusted with a sudden fury, dashing sand cruelly against them. He tore his mouth from hers.

"Your lips are nectar. Tell me thy father's name, for I will not take thee like a slave, but wed thee in all honour."

"Ah, do not ask, Beloved!" she pleaded, but when he insisted, she smiled sadly and said, "Mash'Allah! My father is King Nasr ad Daulah."

He stared at her. "But the king has only one daughter! The Princess Azade, and she—"

"True, oh Lion! Three days hence the Princess Azade is destined to become the wife of the prince to whom you are sworn in allegiance. But for one taste of your love she forsakes all."

The baby was a source of deep delight. Safiyah seemed to have cast off the trauma surrounding her birth completely. She was a happy, deep-thinking spirit who loved to lie with Anna on the terrace under a flowery, shady trellis and watch the blossoms just overhead dance in the constant, cooling breeze.

"There couldn't be a better crib toy," Anna told Sheikh Gazi. Because, whatever their differences, they were united in a deep fondness for the baby. "It's even got musical effects." The birdsong from the trees planted around the terrace and the forest beyond was nearly constant, and it was clear from Safiyah's expression that she loved to listen.

Anna was picking up a little Arabic from the nurse, in the usual women's exchange of delight and approval with a baby. *Walida jamila* was the first expression she learned. She was pretty sure it meant *pretty baby,* and she and the nurse could say it back and forth to each other, and to the baby herself, with endless delight.

And every day she felt a little more of her long-standing fatigue and unhappiness being leached out of her body and self by her surroundings.

The only fly in the ointment was Sheikh Gazi himself. His job had to be very fluid, because he worked from home, and he was almost constantly around. He sat beside the pool in his trunks, tapping away at his laptop or talking into a dictaphone or telephone, while Anna swam and sunned and played with the baby. She was constantly aware of him.

They ate together at nearly every meal. He had a powerful radio, on which he regularly listened to the news from several countries, and in different languages. They often discussed what was happening in the world, and although he was insightful and seemed very informed, he always listened to her opinions with respect.

He talked only a little about himself, though. When she asked, he told her that his job was to coordinate the publicity and public relations side of West Barakat's trade relations with the world, but spoke little more about it. Instead he talked about Barakat's history and culture.

He played music softly as he worked. Anna, who had rarely listened to Middle Eastern music, found it haunting, and in some mysterious way perfect for her surroundings. At intervals, too, could be heard from the city the wail of the muezzin, the Islamic call to prayer, and it all seemed to fit into one marvellous whole.

Sometimes it seemed as if the accident had been a doorway to another reality. A curious little space-time warp had appeared, and she had been shunted through—into some other life stream, where she joined up with a different Anna. An Anna who had made a different choice long ago, and now belonged here. Sometimes it seemed just as if Gazi had been telling the truth—as if they had been married for years.

Except for one thing.

However delicious the weather, however exotic the food his servants brought them, however sexy he looked emerging from the pool, his strong body rippling and his smoky amber skin beaded with water, however electrically she felt his presence—he never again suggested to Anna, by word or by deed, that her holiday out of time might include him as a lover.

He seemed totally immune to her physical presence. Whatever had made him kiss her with such passionate abandon on two occasions, he wasn't interested now.

She had never before met a man who had given up a pursuit of her after one little rejection, but that was what Gazi had apparently done. Or maybe it was simply that, in turning down his request to stay, she had lost her chance at the free lovemaking. In short, since she had refused his actual invitation to stay and was here only from necessity, he didn't feel obliged any longer to pretend he wanted to make love to her.

In every other way, they were practically the ideal family.

The fact that the constant delay getting her passport meant she had ended up staying after all never was mentioned between them. Anna sometimes wondered what his reaction would be if she made the suggestion that since she was, however inadvertently, acceding to his demands, he ought to live up to the original offer.

If you left out of the reckoning a teenage crush on a rock star, it was the first time in her life that she had felt such powerful romantic interest in a man who felt none in return, and it wasn't a sensation she enjoyed. Half the time she was determined not to accept even if he did change his mind, and the other half she had to restrain herself from making a clear pass.

He really was moving heaven and earth in the effort to understand her concept of time, and when she reminded him that another day was passing, he shook his head in frustration with his own stupidity and picked up the phone at once. But unfortunately, he was met with the same lack of focus at the other end. He ended up shouting in outraged impatience down the phone to a Barakati Embassy employee and hung up cursing.

"They understand nothing, these government employees!" he exploded. "To them nothing can be done without the correct documentation and by following established procedure! The person who collected your keys from the hospital put them in the safe last night, and today there is no one in the embassy to give permission for opening this safe." He glanced at her hesitantly. "I can phone Prince Karim, Anna. He is very absorbed with certain affairs of state, but...if I explain, he would call and order them to open the safe. Shall I do this?"

Anna blushed. "No, no, of course not! You can't bother the prince for that!" she exclaimed. And although he hid his relief, she could tell that it was not a request he had wanted to make.

And so another day slipped away.

Though she had told him she wouldn't be here long enough for it to be necessary, Gazi had been adamant about providing her with clothes suitable for the climate. So she had chosen a small but lovely wardrobe of mixed Middle Eastern and Western clothes from a selection sent in for her approval by a couple of city boutiques.

During the day she often wore nothing more than a bathing suit under a cotton kaftan. She never left the house, but for the moment she had no desire to do so, and it was great to be able just to slip off the kaftan any time and dive into the delicious pool.

The water was salt because the pool was, in accordance with Barakati law, Gazi told her, supplied by the ocean and not from the limited fresh-water resources of the country. So there was no smell of chlorine hovering over the garden or on her skin, and it felt like bathing in a natural pool.

She loved the sun, and although in this climate she was careful with exposure, she knew it was a source of deep healing. Her pale skin was a mark of her unhappiness and ill health, and she was delighted when it turned a soft brown.

The healthier she felt, the more physically she responded to Sheikh Gazi's constant presence, reading, tapping into the computer, talking on the phone. Sometimes she would lie on her lounger feeling the sun's hot caress and feel such a surge of desire for him she was convinced he was on the point of coming over to her, but when she glanced over he usually wasn't even looking at her. Or if he was, his face was tight with disapproval.

Every evening Anna dressed for dinner with the casual elegance her new clothes allowed. Made herself as beautiful as she could, without ever fooling herself she was competition for anyone like Sacha Delavel. She was being a fool, she knew, but she couldn't help wanting to see in his eyes, if only once, that she was attractive enough to disturb him.

Sometimes she would remember those moments when he had kissed her. She had felt such passion in his arms and his mouth, seen such burning desire in his eyes, that she had responded by going almost out of her skull with delight.

But now she had to wonder if that had been entirely faked. If he had merely been offering her a sample of the treats on offer. No doubt he could fake the whole thing if necessary. But she never felt that intensity in him now…and she found that was what she really wanted. She wanted to know she could touch his mind, his heart, his feelings. Not simply that he could perform a sexual service like a gigolo, if she insisted. That was how she stopped herself making a move.

They talked and laughed together over the delicious, candlelit meals until she was weak with wanting him. She was almost sure that the dark fire she sometimes surprised in his eyes held admiration.

Sometimes she couldn't believe that things he said could be anything other than a prelude to lovemaking. But if so, his feeling never lasted more than a brief moment. Although she was somehow kept in a constant fever of anticipation and wishing, he never touched her. And if she touched him, even with a spontaneous pat on the arm as she spoke, he would stiffen and look at her with an unreadable look that made her lift her hand.

It didn't help her get a handle on her feelings to discover Gazi was the best listener she had ever met in her life. He drew her out as if he was really interested in her life and her opinions, her experiences and her dreams. He showed particular interest in her art, wanting to know what had drawn her to want to reproduce Middle Eastern art on the walls of England's houses.

The house itself was like the magician's cave, with masterpieces of ancient scrollwork and sculpture in every corner. The patterned tilework was unbelievably artistic, the colours from a palette of magic. Anna spent hours wandering and examining the treasures.

At her request Gazi would explain the significance of

certain symbols, read and translate the beautiful calligraphic designs, so thoroughly she felt she was in a personal tutorial with a professional expert.

"How do you know so much about it?" she asked him in amazement when he had described how certain tiles had been painted and fired, and he threw her a look.

"This is my people's culture and history and art," he said, in a voice like a cat's tongue on her skin. "It is some of the greatest artistic and architectural achievement in the history of the human race. How should I not be familiar with it? Every Barakati is familiar with such things, as familiar as an English person with Shakespeare. But in addition it is my job to know such things."

She was certainly learning more about her area of interest than she had ever learned at art college, and bit by bit she was packing in a wealth of inspiration that could probably carry her for years.

If only she didn't feel that she was also packing in future heartbreak.

"Something has to give," Anna muttered after several days of inaction.

Sheikh Gazi was on the phone trying to get through to the Barakati Embassy in London.

"Yes, today I will insist—why does no one answer?" Gazi said, exasperatedly listening to a recorded message. "It is noon in London, where is everyone? Ah, of course!" He lifted a hand. "Today is Friday, *juma,* they are all at the mosque." He put down the phone. "I will try again later."

"Friday?" she murmured, almost unable to believe that so much time had passed.

"The Friday prayer is the minimum required act of

worship in the week. It is my own fault, I should have remembered.''

He had certainly remembered earlier in the day, Anna thought absently. A bit before noon, he and the entire staff had left the house in a minivan, everyone dressed in their best. She and Safiyah had been left alone for an hour, and when the van returned only Gazi and the nurse were in it.

''Is that where you all went earlier? To the mosque?'' Anna asked.

''Yes, all of my household who wish it have the right to be driven to the mosque for *juma*. It is far to walk. Then they go home to their families. Tonight you and I will eat at the hotel.''

A little later Anna poured a subtle, spicy perfumed oil into her bath and afterwards dressed with care in a flowing, ivory silk *shalwar kamees* embroidered at breast and sleeve with deep blue thread and flat beads of lapis lazuli. Her tiny silver ear studs and silver rings were all the jewellery she had, but they at least suited the outfit. A gauzy navy stole and pair of navy leather thongs on her bare feet completed her outfit.

In the early evening she joined him at the front door, where a sports car was waiting. He drove them up the road to the Hotel Sheikh Daud for dinner in luxurious elegance on a balcony overlooking the sea. From here the view was much more open; she could see the whole stretch of the shoreline around the shallow bay, out into the water of the Gulf of Barakat.

Lights twinkled from the city, on the yachts out in the bay, and in the sprinkling of houses nestled in the forest along the shore. The sea and the sky were one deep, rich black, so that it seemed to her that the sky itself rushed onto the shore and retreated again, with that hypnotic roar and hiss.

A young woman sang haunting Barakati love songs, the food was deliciously cooked, and Gazi's eyes were on her almost constantly. Anna found herself floating away on a dream. A dream that was composed of Gazi's mouth, Gazi's eyes…

He watched her, knowing what she wanted. Her wide mouth stretching in a tremulous smile, her head tilting back to offer her slim throat, as if she knew how that posture in her excited him. His own mouth was tight with control.

"This song is so beautiful," she said dreamily, at the end of the meal, when their coffee cups were drained and the singer sang again. "Tell me what the words mean."

He unlocked his jaw. "They mean that a man is refusing to fall into a trap that a woman has set for him," he replied. "A woman he desires but does not trust. She dresses in beautiful jewels and robes, she perfumes her hair, she smiles, until he is driven mad with passion. But he cannot give in."

In a brief pause in the music, his voice rasped on her ears, and Anna pressed her lips together. "He can't?"

"He knows that she is forbidden to him."

The music resumed on a haunting, wailing note, like a woman in the act of love. She made a little face of disappointment, and he thought that she would not look so if he made love to her.

"Why?" Her eyes, inviting him, were dark as the night sky, her face beautiful as the moon.

"Because she is a cheat," Gazi said harshly.

The singer's voice joined the music again with a keening plaint. Fixed by his narrowed gaze, Anna could not turn away.

"So what happens?"

"He decides to make her admit her betrayal," Gazi said softly. "He will pretend to love her, so that she will confess."

"And he calls *her* a cheat?" she asked.

"The song is about how the man fools himself as to his own motives. He is lying to himself. It is not for the reason he gives himself that he is going to make love to her, but because she has succeeded—before he even began."

The music stopped, amid applause from the restaurant patrons.

"You are beautiful, Anna," he told her in a voice like gravel. "You tempt me, with your soft looks, your willing mouth. I lie awake at night, wishing I were fool enough to believe that I could make love to you without danger. But it is not to be, Anna. You will not succeed."

Eleven

At first, hearing the word *danger,* her heart thrilled, because she believed he meant that he was in danger of falling in love with her. But his voice and the expression in his eyes were so hard...and suddenly she understood.

She drew back into her chair, her brain sharp with suspicion. "My God, you still think—!" Suddenly it all fell into place. "I've been here a *week* now, waiting for someone to perform a simple errand that Lisbet could have done in an hour! You've been delaying deliberately! What is going on?"

"I thought this way would be easier," he said, but she knew it was a lie.

"Easier for you!" she stormed. "Easier for you to keep me here against my will. Did you call back the embassy today, when the staff returned from the mosque?"

Gazi slapped a hand to his head. "Ah! I forgot!" He

lifted his wrist and glanced at his watch. "Too late now. It is past seven o'clock in London."

"You forgot. And today's Friday, and I suppose the Barakati Embassy in London closes over the weekend?"

"All embassies in London, I believe, do so. I am sorry, Anna."

Anxiety choked her. Most of a week had gone by. He had manipulated her into doing exactly what he wanted, and fool that she was, she had spent the time dreaming.

"Is there a British Embassy in Barakat al Barakat?" she demanded.

"But of course!" he assured her blandly. "The British have always been on excellent diplomatic terms with Barakat, even though they never conquered us. The embassy is in Queen Halimah Square."

"If my passport isn't here by Monday, I want to go to the embassy and ask them to issue me a temporary travel document so I can go home," Anna told him sternly.

"Very wise," he said, nodding. "Yes, an excellent solution."

"I want to stay here in the hotel tonight," she said.

He shrugged. "As you wish. Will you go now and check in?"

Anna half got to her feet. "Yes, I—" She stopped, one hand on the back of her chair, and a nearby waiter came to her aid. She stood up because she had to, but stayed looking down at Gazi al Hamzeh. "I don't have a credit card or anything."

"Perhaps if you explain your situation, they will give you credit. Foreigners need passports to register in hotels here, but I am sure you can convince them to wait until you can apply to your embassy on Monday."

Before she could come to any decision he was on his

feet beside her, and the maître d' was hurrying over to bow his distinguished guest out.

Anna had always believed she had her fair share of courage. But she could not summon enough to make a stand now. The thought of trying to make herself understood, in a foreign language, a foreign country, while making a charge of abduction against a leading citizen— a Cup Companion of the ruling prince! And Gazi, as if knowing exactly what she was trying to get the courage for, remained deep in friendly conversation with the man, all the way to the door.

And only she knew, and he knew, that the dark expression in his eyes as he smiled at her was the look of a watchdog guarding a criminal.

They did not speak on the drive back to his house. Anna went straight to her own room, without a word.

She spent a restless night. Only the fact that, thanks to the tabloids, half the world knew where she was kept her from complete panic. She tossed and turned and looked back over the week and realized how easy a mark she had been. Time had slipped by, with sun and food and good talk…. He had her exactly where he wanted her. He had accused her of trying to tempt him. But it was Gazi who had been using constant temptation to keep her brain muddled.

How easily manipulated she had been by his interest in her! He had let her talk and talk. *It's a known brainwashing technique!* she reminded herself disgustedly. *It's what cults do with their marks—give them massive doses of attention. Love-bombing.* And even knowing that, how easily she had fallen for it.

And his Arab incompetence, his lack of appreciation of Western ideas of time—she began to blush for how easily she had fallen for the stereotype. Of course he had been faking all that. She had never met a man with a more incisive, better-informed mind. He spoke at least three languages! What could have possessed her to fall into the trap of believing that he could be so inefficient and ineffectual, could lack a basic understanding of Western culture?

She saw now that he had begun this act only after she refused his invitation. He had deliberately become a caricature Arab. Anna snorted. It must have taken an extremely efficient organization to effect the abduction of her and the baby. That was a plan he had certainly conceived on his feet, and it had been flawlessly executed. From the time he found her in the hospital to the time the plane took off scarcely two hours had elapsed.

Clearly he had a crack team. Yet somehow he had fooled her into believing he couldn't organize getting her *handbag* from the very hospital he had abducted her and the baby from!

And still she had no idea why. What did he want from her? Why did he continue to think she was engaged in some kind of dishonesty? And above all, what was his reason for wanting to keep her here?

"Fly with me!"

"Willingly would I fly with thee, Beloved. But where can we fly, that is not ruled by your father or my prince?"

"India," she breathed.

He smiled at her, knowing she knew nothing save the name. "India is far, very far."

"For you I would suffer any hardship!" she cried.

"Beloved, if they catch us before we reach India, they will not let us live."

She smiled. "Choose fleet steeds, then, my Lion!"

He stood gazing out over the far horizon. "And if I say, stay here and live thy life as thy destiny demands—"

"I will fling myself from this parapet tomorrow night rather than wed him."

He turned and caught her to his chest, and stared into her eyes, his love a torment, because he was destined never to enjoy her beauty. But he could not tell her so. He put his lips on hers and tasted their deaths.

"Why then, we will fly to India," he said.

The dreams were profoundly disturbing, though she never quite remembered them. She would awaken suffocating with love and anguish, her heartbeat pounding through her system, yearning for him so desperately she could almost feel her dream lover beside her, as if his arms had only now let her go.

Her dream lover was Gazi al Hamzeh. And the dream seemed another reality, one that she half watched, half lived...always yearned for.

"I have had a phone call," Gazi said at breakfast. "Your passport has been picked up from your apartment. Today, if you wish, you can fly back to London. I will arrange for someone to meet you at the Immigration desk at Stansted airport with your passport."

She looked at him, one eyebrow raised. "If I wish? Of course I wish."

"You are determined to return?" he said softly. They were at a table on the balcony, looking out over the sun-kissed courtyard in the cool of the morning.

"Has not my home seemed to you like a good place to recuperate from your accident and restore yourself after your sorrows?" he asked, gesturing out to the paradise below them.

"In case you haven't noticed, I've had a week of that," she said. All her hackles were rising as she scented danger. Did he mean to prevent her again?

Gazi took another sip of the perfectly brewed coffee, set the cup in the saucer, and with an almost invisible flicker of his eyes, dismissed the attentive serving man, who nodded and slipped away.

"Anna, I would like to tell you…to explain something to you."

"With a view to changing my mind about leaving?"

He hesitated. "Perhaps. No—not necessarily. But in hopes that what you learn may change your mind about other things that you might plan to say or do."

"Such as talk to the media."

"And other things."

Anna was curious, but she hesitated. "Suppose you tell me what you want to tell me and it turns out you don't change my mind about anything at all?"

Gazi shrugged. "Then of course you will do whatever suits you."

She wondered if that was the truth. He had already kept her here a week against her will. What new ploy might he come up with? But, she reflected, at least she would know more about why. That had to be an advantage.

"Fire away," she said, with a casualness she was far from feeling.

"Nadia, my sister, the mother of Safiyah, is missing. This you know. We are very worried about her."

"Who is 'we'?"

"I and my family. If you permit, I will tell you Nadia's story from the beginning," he said, and waited for her nod before beginning. "Three years ago, my father announced that he had chosen a husband for my sister.

None of us knew until that moment that he was even considering such a step. It was an even greater surprise when we learned that he had chosen a man named Yusuf Abd ad Darogh. This was not a man my sister had any admiration for. She begged my father to go no further in it."

"Oh," she murmured.

"I tried to reason with my father." Anna picked up the echo of frustration and sorrow in his voice and tried to stop her heart softening towards him. "But my father was of the old school. In spite of all that we said, in spite of her deep unhappiness, Nadia was married to Yusuf."

He gazed down at his coffee cup, which his hand absently clasped in a strong, loose embrace. Following the direction of his abstracted gaze, Anna had to close her own eyes. Something in the incipient power of the hold made her want to feel it close around her arm, her body....

"Yusuf's job then took him to the West," he was saying as she surfaced. "He works for a large Barakati company, and he and Nadia moved to London. I am in London frequently, and of course I visited or spoke to Nadia on each visit. One of my brothers also.

"For the first year or so, things were apparently not intolerable. Then time went by, and Nadia did not become pregnant. She was becoming more and more anxious about it. We suspected that Yusuf was blaming her for it."

Anna was listening now with her mouth soft, her eyes fixed on him, her sympathies entirely with Nadia. She heard an anxiety in his tone that proved that he loved his sister, and she couldn't help wanting to help him.

"Then at last Nadia became pregnant. But it made

Yusuf no happier. It became difficult for us to get any reading on how Nadia was. More and more there was some excuse why visits were not convenient just at the moment, or she could not come to the phone. When we did visit we somehow were never allowed time with Nadia alone. And we gradually came to understand that she was only allowed to speak to any member of her family on the phone when Yusuf was in the room with her.''

Anna shivered. ''She must have felt totally helpless,'' she said.

''I am sure you are right, but if so, she was never able to express it.''

He paused and cleared his throat. ''My father died. When they returned to Barakat for the funeral, Nadia was wearing *hejab*. Here in Barakat even a simple headscarf is not worn outside of the mosque except by the religious old women. Nadia was wearing full black robe and scarf, no lock of hair showing, which is extreme by Barakati standards, and nothing she herself would have wished. It is certain that she was made to do it by Yusuf.

''Shortly after this, when they returned to England, Nadia became ill with the pregnancy. Too ill to speak to us when we phoned. Or there were other excuses.''

Gazi paused, and an expression of self-reproach tightened his mouth for a moment. ''There was a great deal to see to about my father's estate. I was here in West Barakat virtually full-time for weeks. One day my brother and I realized that neither of us had been allowed to speak to Nadia for almost two months.''

Anna was listening too hard to be capable of making a sound.

''We knew it was fruitless to try to phone again. Yusuf would only put us off. My brother and I flew in together on Friday last week and arrived unannounced at their apartment. We found—we found Yusuf running around the streets like a wounded animal, screaming for Nadia and saying that she had disappeared.

"He said that she had gone into labour shortly before our arrival, and he had gone out to the garage—it is in a mews behind the house—for the car. When he drew up at the front door, it was open and Nadia was gone. That is what he said."

Anna bit her lip. "Was it—do you think he was lying?" she whispered.

"There is no way to be sure," Gazi replied. "It is possible he had warning that we were on our way and staged a show for our benefit. What reason could Nadia have for running away at such a time? She would want to go to the hospital to have her baby safely."

"You don't think she was desperate and it was maybe—her only chance to escape?" Anna offered quietly.

At this, Gazi bent forward, his hands clasped between his knees. "Perhaps it is so, Anna, perhaps it is so. But now do you see how important your involvement is? You are the only lead we have. The question we must ask is, how did you come to be in a taxi with Nadia's baby? The answer to this may tell us much."

She gazed at him, feeling how strong the pull was. He had half hypnotized her, made her want to declare she was on his side. It was like pulling a tooth to stand up and walk away, out of his potent orbit. But she needed to think clearly, and she couldn't sitting so close to him. She had to do it.

Moving a little distance from the table towards an archway covered with greenery, she turned and said, "Well, thank you for telling me that. But it's *still* not the whole story, is it?"

"Why do you think so?" asked Sheikh Gazi. His gaze was just slightly wary, but she noted the change, and it proved her right.

She lifted her hands. "Because it's got more holes than a sponge! Excuse me, but there you are out combing the streets for your pregnant sister, and you just happen to search the casualty ward of the Royal Embankment Hospital, is that what I hear?"

He was watching her with steady disapproval. "There was an item on the radio that made me think I would find Nadia and her baby there. Instead I found you."

"On the radio?" she demanded disbelievingly.

"Yes, Anna," he said, and she was glad to make him understand how it felt to have his word doubted. "A silly item, meant to be amusing—'mother, baby *and* cab driver all in hospital and doing well.'"

"Ah! Okay, you found me. And you found a baby you were instantly convinced was Nadia's. And what do you do? Do you call the police and tell them your suspicions? Do you claim the baby and take it home to Papa? No, strangely enough, you *kidnap* me and this infant you are convinced is your niece, and you immediately cart us off to Barakat! Now, that needs a little more explaining than the current version of your story offers. Because even a man with your influence and connections, it seems to me, and no doubt they reach to the very top, isn't going to risk breaking the laws of two countries without a very substantial reason.

"Unless, of course, your contempt for women runs so deep you forgot that Safiyah and I had any human rights at all. You're quick to condemn your brother-in-law for keeping your sister a prisoner, but have you noticed that you are at this moment doing exactly the same thing to me?"

She saw that he was angered by that. "I do not keep you prisoner!" he exploded.

"What do you call it?" Anna cried. She suddenly doubted whether the best course after all was challenging him. Her safest alternative probably had been to pretend to go along with whatever he suggested and then, when his guard was down, make good her escape. But she was too late.

"Why don't you tell me the truth, Sheikh Gazi?"

"I have told you the truth, so far as it goes." His eyes were hard. "Recollect that you have still offered no coherent account of how you came to be in possession of my sister's baby."

"Recollect that you have offered no convincing proof that the baby *is* your sister's!"

"There can be no question of it. My brother remains in London, pursuing enquiries. If any woman had reported her child missing, he would have discovered it."

"How do you know that some past girlfriend of your own hasn't given birth and abandoned the baby? Maybe I found her!"

"You are being ridiculous," he said, his face hard. "The baby was in a satchel that had obviously been prepared for a hospital maternity visit. In that satchel, which has now been picked up from the Royal Embankment Hospital, were items recognizably my sister's."

"All right, let's assume Safiyah is your sister's baby, then. What do you suspect *me* of? Your little team has had the keys to my apartment for the best part of a week by now," she told Gazi coldly. "Don't you feel that if there was anything at all to connect me with your sister they'd have found it?"

Gazi took a breath, trying for calm. "Nevertheless, it

is very difficult to imagine any scenario in which you are completely uninvolved. You must see that. What am I to guess? That the hospital mistakenly mixed up two casualties, leaving Nadia with no baby? That Safiyah was abandoned at the precise place where you had your accident?"

"As far as I'm concerned, either of those is more likely than that I went out of my tiny mind and kidnapped a baby, all during the one half hour of my life that I don't happen to have any memory of."

"All right." Gazi's full, usually generous mouth was drawn tight. "I will tell you more. Nadia's husband, Yusuf, may suspect that the baby is not his. In Yusuf's mind his suspicion would be enough. In such a case, it is not easy to guess what he intended to do, but it is almost certain that he would not allow Nadia to keep the child and raise it as his own."

She felt a little chill in the warm breeze, and shuddered.

"It was in the hopes of preventing Yusuf discovering that we had found Safiyah that we rushed her out of the country in the way we did. This would have succeeded, but for your actions. The press has created huge potential risk by running photos of me arriving in Barakat al Barakat with a baby. Yusuf of course now suspects that the child is Nadia's."

His voice was hard with suspicion. Anna frowned and took a step back towards the table where he sat. "You thought I deliberately showed the baby to the cameras to let Yusuf know you had her?"

He was sitting in a casual but not a relaxed posture, one elbow on the chair arm, his hand supporting his cheek. "There seemed very little other excuse for such wanton disregard of the baby's safety."

Anna gasped indignantly. "I did it to protect the baby from *you*!" she informed him hotly, flinging herself back into her chair. "I didn't know the paparazzi were even there. You had convinced me the baby was ours, but you sure hadn't convinced me you had any affection for me! I thought you were going to try to snatch her! You told me nothing but lies! How was I supposed to guess what was going on?"

He raised an eyebrow, but did not comment, merely said, "Fortunately the press blunted the damage by printing that the baby is ours, and even hinted that Safiyah is several weeks old."

She laughed in irritation. How stupid did he think she was? "Fortunately? You told them that, didn't you? You've already admitted that your job is in press relations, so you've got all the necessary contacts."

He waited for her to finish and then went on. "It was of crucial importance in deflecting Yusuf's suspicions. Yusuf will believe what he sees in print if we reinforce it. Or at least, don't contradict it. That is why I hoped that you would agree to remain unavailable for a while. Not to deny the press stories."

"And when I refused, you forced my compliance through trickery."

"There are lives at stake," Sheikh Gazi said.

"Why the hell didn't you tell me there were lives at stake, then, instead of trying to bribe me with sun and fun and money and sex?"

"Sex?" he asked, his eyebrow up. "Do I try to bribe you with sex, or has that been the other way?"

Suddenly danger of a different sort whispered on the breeze. Anna snapped, "What reason could you possibly have for suspecting that I would want to bribe you with sex? What would I hope to achieve?"

"That is something only you know!" he bit out, his own anger flaring suddenly, making Anna jump. "I find you with my sister's baby, you can give no reasonable explanation, you deliberately show her to reporters after I have successfully smuggled her out of England—" He broke off. "Did you give me any reason to trust you? You threatened me with exposure for having abducted Safiyah! What—"

"I *never* threatened you! I told you I had no intention of exposing you! I said I would do nothing more than deny—"

They were by this time almost shouting.

"To go back to England and to deny that Safiyah is our child is to send Yusuf a notarized declaration that she is Nadia's daughter," Gazi said coldly. "Now, if you are involved with Yusuf in any way, I ask you to tell me what your involvement is. And if you are not involved, I ask you to go on with the charade that has been created until we find the truth.

"For the love of God, Anna!" he cried as she hesitated. "My sister may be at this moment her husband's prisoner. Or hiding in some alley, snatching food from rubbish tins. Have you a heart, Anna, to appreciate what she may be suffering, and to help her?"

Twelve

She met him at the stables, in her disguise as a page, while the sounds of revelry still rose on the air from the palace. He dared use no light, nor kiss her, but only turned silently to lead her through dark, tortuous passages to the great city wall.

She climbed the rope ladder ahead of him, bravely, without a murmur of fear, and he thought what a wife she would have made him, if things had been otherwise.

On the other side, still without speech, he led her to the outcrop within which he had tethered two horses. With one quick embrace only, one whispered word of courage, he tossed her into the saddle.

They rode out towards the dawn.

They arrived in London at midmorning, and it was only when she felt the wheels touch down and saw the familiar landmarks that Anna started breathing again.

She had agreed to return to London and make her arrangements as quietly as possible, to head straight to France and hide out at the villa of her clients without speaking to the media.

At Immigration, they were met as promised, by an escort of three bodyguards, one of whom handed over her passport. Sheikh Gazi, she noticed, was travelling on a Barakati diplomatic passport, and they were allowed to enter Great Britain with barely a nod. No one even questioned why or how she had left the country without a passport.

Then they came through the doors into the terminal and were faced with a crowd of excited paparazzi.

Anna stopped as if she had walked into a wall. She could hear the noise of clicking cameras, but the shouted questions might as well have come from the Tower of Babel for all she could understand. She swayed.

"How on *earth* did they find out we were arriving?" she cried, astonished at the sheer numbers.

"Anna, Anna!" "Can you look this way?" "Smile for the folks, Anna!" "Are you happy? How's the baby, Anna?" "Did the baby come with you?" "What's your baby's name, Anna?"

Then a strong arm was around her, and Sheikh Gazi's hand was gripping her arm above the elbow, urging her forward. He leaned into her ear and murmured, "Walk quickly but on no account run. Let me handle them."

This was a command she was only too relieved to obey.

His voice was low and for her ear alone, and in spite of everything it raised yearning in her heart, and heat in her blood. "Look at me."

She looked nervously over her shoulder into his face, and met a glance of such lazy, sexy approval her stomach rolled over. Anna stumbled, and his strong embrace steadied her. She smiled involuntarily, her whole self stretching and basking in his unexpected admiration like a cat in a sunbeam.

The photographers cried out their satisfaction. "Kiss her, Gazi!" someone cried, and Anna's heart thumped. But the sheikh only laughed lightly and shook his head.

They moved quickly after that, his bodyguards doing no more than create a little breathing space as the group of journalists ran beside them through the terminal to the exit, calling questions.

"How do you feel about the baby, Sheikh Gazi?"

"What do you think, Arthur?" he called, as if it should be obvious.

"Did you get Prince Karim's approval?"

"He has never disapproved, to my knowledge."

"When's the wedding? Have you set the date?"

"No," the sheikh's deep voice responded above her ear.

"Are you going to?"

Sheikh Gazi threw the last questioner a smile. "Julia, you'll be the first to know."

Questions and answers were following each other in such a rapid-fire way it was a moment before Anna took it all in. She blinked and turned to him. "What are you—?" she began, but he put a warning grip on her arm.

"Let me handle it, Anna!" he said again.

It terrified her. He was doing it again. Forcing her into compliance through circumstance. She had not agreed to look the press in the eye and pretend it was true, and now she was frightened. Had he ever told her the truth? Was she a pawn in something she didn't know about? Suddenly she doubted the truth of everything he had said. He had a much deeper reason for this constant manipulation of her. He must.

Anna swallowed, coughed and forced herself to turn to the nearest man with a notebook.

"I am not Sheikh Gazi's mistress," she said.

"Great!" he said, scribbling. "Can I say fiancée?"

"No! Don't say I'm his fiancée! And the baby is not—"

"The baby is not with us!" Gazi cried over her, drowning her out. "The doctor thought it better."

His arm went tight around her and he was swooping her through the main exit to where a limousine waited by the curb, the rear door already open.

Anna threw one wild look along the half-deserted road. Wherever she ran now, she would be chased by all these journalists, and they would certainly catch up with her. What would she say then, what could she do? She could not simply deny that she was his mistress and that the baby was hers and then expect to disappear. They would hound her unmercifully for the whole story. And if she told it…Gazi had powerful friends.

Feeling like every kind of coward, Anna got into the limousine. Gazi quickly followed. One of the bodyguards got into the back with them, the other two in front with the driver, and a second later they were pulling away from the happy mob of journalists.

She turned to Sheikh Gazi al Hamzeh. "How did they know we were arriving?" she demanded furiously.

"In a moment," he said, then turned to the other man. "Anything?" he asked.

The man shook his head. He looked younger than the sheikh, and she thought she could detect a facial resemblance between them. "Still not a trace," he said. "She has evaporated into air, Gazi. Yusuf insists he knows nothing, and unless we're willing to show our hand with him, there's no saying if that's the truth or not.''

He had none of the air of a man talking to his employer. As if in confirmation of this judgement, he turned suddenly to Anna. ''Hi, Anna,'' he said, with an engaging smile. ''I'm Jafar. People here call me Jaf.''

''Hello,'' she said slowly. She glanced back and forth between the two men.

''Jafar is my brother,'' Sheikh Gazi said quietly.

''It's great of you to play along, Anna,'' said Jaf. ''We really appreciate it.''

Anna didn't return his smile. ''Thank your brother,'' she said. ''I had nothing to say about it.''

She seemed to herself not to start breathing again until the familiar sights of Chelsea met her eyes and she could believe that Gazi was going to do what he said and take her home.

There were a few journalists on the street in front of the ramshackle Victorian house where she had an apartment, and as the three went up the walk there were more shouted questions.

Anna left it to Gazi to talk to them, already rooting for her keys in the little shoulder bag Jaf had given back to her at the airport. But no key chain met her searching fingers. Anna clicked her tongue and lifted the bag to eye level, just as Gazi produced her keys and unlocked the door.

So Jaf had passed over her keys to Gazi instead of herself.

They all moved inside the small front hall and closed the outer door on the paparazzi. Then she held out her hand and said sharply, ''My keys, please.''

She waited, staring at him, until Gazi put her keys in her hand. A moment later she stepped through her own door, followed by Jaf and Sheikh Gazi, and led the way upstairs.

The phone was ringing. Anna moved into the main room as the answering machine picked up. She stood looking around her for a moment, trying to orient herself in her own life.

The room was long, with windows at each end. The south-facing half, overlooking the street, was her sitting room, with a fireplace, sofa and chairs; the north, whose windows overlooked an overgrown courtyard with a tree, was her studio, with trestle tables, trolleys, rolls of paper, a couple of painted screens that she was working on for a client. Two broad expanses of wall down both sides of the room were covered with sketches, paintings, photos, colour swatches and other bits and pieces of her working life.

Underneath them, painted on the plaster, was a series of arches not unlike those she had seen for real in Gazi's house. Anna blinked and wondered if it was merely her own mural that had given her the idea she was at home there.

It just did not feel like only a week since she had dressed for her meal with Cecile and Lisbet. She felt strange, removed from her old life, as if she hadn't been here for months.

"Hello, Anna. This is Gabriel DaSouza from the *Sun*...."

She mentally shut out the voice coming from the answerphone, and moved towards the sofa. On the table in front of it was spread the week's mail, including a few scribbled notes from the press.

Anna frowned, wondering who had placed them there, and just then heard a step in the kitchen. She whirled, her heart jumping into her throat.

"Hi!" said Lisbet. "I made the coffee while I was waiting. Jaf figured we'd all need it."

Lisbet kicked off her shoes and under Jaf's interested gaze slid her long, black-stockinged legs behind Anna on the sofa as she accepted the cup of coffee Anna had poured for her.

"Frankly, it's a mystery to me, too," she told Anna. "You ask what happened—absolutely nothing. Someone pulled up in a cab and got out, you got in. The cab drove off. It took Ceil and me a couple of minutes to flag another one. Ceil dropped me at home. That was all I knew until someone phoned me at sparrow's peep Sunday morning to say was that Anna Lamb in this morning's *Sun?* I said it couldn't possibly be you. And then Alan said you'd called him...."

Jaf leaned forward, taking his own cup from Anna's hand. "Someone got out of the cab, you say. Did you notice who?"

Lisbet pursed her lips and shook her head. "It was on the other side of the street and I wasn't really paying attention."

"Try to think back. You may have seen something. One person, a couple?"

Lisbet obligingly closed her eyes and tried to visualize the scene. "There was a tree just there—someone came past it, but whether that was whoever got out of the cab or not...one person, I think. Dressed in black, maybe, with street lighting it's—wait! There was someone in black a couple of minutes later, too. I wonder if it was the same person? By the bridge."

Lisbet opened her eyes. "I noticed her because she seemed to be wearing one of those black things that cover a woman from head to foot and I thought it was strange to see a Muslim woman by herself there at night.''

"Battersea Bridge?'' Jaf prompted.

Lisbet nodded. "Yes, the Riverfront isn't far from there, and we were sort of strolling in that direction after Anna left, looking for a cab. This woman crossed the road ahead of us and went onto the bridge. But I don't know that she was the person who got out of the cab Anna caught. There was something about her that drew my eye, I can't really say what it was.''

Anna, meanwhile, put her hands up to her face. A woman in black. She smelled the scent of the river at night, autumn leaves.... She dropped her hands again and found Sheikh Gazi's eyes on her.

"What have you remembered?'' he asked softly.

She shook her head sadly. "Nothing.''

They sat drinking coffee without speaking for several minutes. Lisbet was lost in thought. She surfaced and said, "Unless something completely weird and incredibly unlikely happened after you got into that cab, Anna, the accident must have happened within a couple of minutes. He turned the corner, drove straight along Oakley to the King's Road and smashed into the bus. Five minutes max.''

"That's what I think.''

"So either someone walked up to the accident scene and slipped the baby into the crashed cab knowing that an ambulance would be coming, which, let's face it, is pretty far-fetched, or...or you got into a cab with a baby already in it.''

"Yes.'' Anna nodded.

"Or else some completely off-the-wall thing happened in the hospital.''

As her friend put into words just what she herself had

been trying to say to Sheikh Gazi, Anna felt what a huge relief it was to have her integrity reaffirmed after his suspicions. She glanced at him to see how he was taking this, but his face gave nothing away.

Lisbet went on, "So putting myself in Nadia's place…I'm running away from an abusive husband, but I'm already in labour, right? So I—what? Give birth in the back of a cab? But then the driver would have radioed an emergency call to get an ambulance to the scene, wouldn't he? Was there such a call?"

"No," said Jaf, sitting forward. Lisbet was certainly convincing while she was getting into a part.

"Or he would get her straight to a hospital. What he *wouldn't* do is pull up on the Embankment and drop his passenger, with or without her baby. So, let's assume for the moment that Nadia was the person who got out of the cab that you got into, Anna, and that she left the baby in it. Doesn't it follow that she had already given birth, and *then* flagged the cab to take her somewhere?"

"Yes…" Anna said slowly, the excitement of discovery building in her. This was starting to feel right.

Jaf said, "The baby was absolutely newborn, wrapped in a woman's bathrobe and laid inside a satchel. She had not been washed. The hospital guessed that the driver had stopped to assist in the birth and then had hastily wrapped the baby and resumed the journey to the hospital, when the accident occurred. He is still not able to be questioned."

Anna glanced at Gazi. "She might have given birth in the apartment, and when he went for the car, she just ran out into the streets."

Lisbet pursed her lips.

"You and your brother were both out of town, right?

Who in London could Nadia go to, with her baby? Who could she trust not to call her husband?''

Jaf shook his head. ''She had no childhood friends in London, only those she had met since moving here three years ago. And we think her social life was very restricted.''

''So maybe something like a women's shelter would have been her only option. Was she on her way to one? Have you checked whether there are any shelters in the neighbourhood of Battersea Bridge?''

Jaf smiled. ''We have not before thought about concentrating on this area, of course. I will see what can be done, but women's shelters are very secretive.''

''The big question is, what changed Nadia's mind? Why did she leave the baby in the cab? If she *was* going to a shelter, surely…'' Lisbet faded off thoughtfully.

Sheikh Gazi intervened at last. ''That is the flaw in an otherwise excellent argument. If she went to a women's shelter, why not take the baby with her? And in addition, whether she went to such a place, or to friends we know nothing about, why has she not called us?''

Lisbet hesitated. ''I hate to—uh.'' She glanced at Anna for guidance. Anna, catching her meaning, shrugged.

Lisbet turned to Gazi. ''I have one advantage over you here. I *know* that Anna isn't involved in the way you suspect. I know that she doesn't know any guy named Yusuf, and that she wouldn't be involved in anything like baby-snatching if she did,'' she said firmly, and Anna suddenly felt like crying. ''I also know that if she says she was confused after the accident and has amnesia about a critical moment, that's the exact truth. So.''

She heaved a breath. No one else spoke. ''I don't want

to distress you, and please forgive me if this suggestion is way off beam, but is it possible that…I mean, unhappy people have been known to…do you think Nadia went to the bridge because jumping seemed the only way out?''

Thirteen

"**I**'ve got to go," Lisbet said, looking at her watch a few minutes later. "We've got a night shoot up on Hampstead Heath tonight and I'm due in Makeup in an hour." She turned to Anna. "Do you want to come and hang out for a while?"

The question was put casually, but Anna knew that it was her friend's way of extricating her from a difficult situation. If she went with Lisbet, Sheikh Gazi and his brother would have no option but to leave.

But she found herself shaking her head. "I've got to get to France, Lisbet. I'm only half packed and I have to organize my ticket."

Lisbet lifted an eyebrow as if she understood more than Anna was confessing. "Well, phone me on my mobile later. I'll probably be hanging around doing nothing most of the night."

"All right."

Lisbet slipped into her shoes and a smart little jacket, put sunglasses on her nose.

"Would you allow me to take you where you have to go?" Jaf offered, and Lisbet's mouth was pulled in an involuntary, slow smile.

"Sure," she said easily.

"They will photograph us," Jaf warned, gesturing towards the windows and the photographers still waiting in the street below. "Do you mind?"

Lisbet laughed. "I'm an actress, Jaf. Publicity is everything."

A moment later Gazi and Anna watched from the windows as Lisbet and Jaf braved the journalists and slipped into the back of the limo. As the limo pulled away she turned to look at him, and all at once the silence weighed very heavily in the room.

"Well," Anna said. "Sorry we couldn't be more help."

Sheikh Gazi took her hand, but not in a handshake, and stared into her eyes. "You can be of more help," he said, in a rough, urgent voice. She felt a surge of energy from him travel up her arm to her throat and chest.

"I really—" Anna coughed to clear her throat. "I really can't, you know, unless I remember something. But I do think Lisbet's right. The baby had to be in the cab when I got into it."

"That is not what I mean, Anna."

Her heart began a wild dance in her breast. She stared at him, licked her lip unconsciously and, taking her hand from his, turned away to hide the heat she felt burning up in her cheeks.

He was mesmerizing, he really was. He had the most extraordinary ability to turn himself off and on. A few minutes ago, listening to Lisbet, he had gone to low voltage, Anna thought wildly, effacing himself in some mysterious way to watch and listen. Now he was high-powered again.

"I'm almost afraid to ask," she joked, nervous of her own deep response.

He looked at her with a frown and turned her towards him, his eyes searching her face till she felt exposed and vulnerable, was trembling. She had never felt so emotionally fragile just at a man's look. Almost shaking with nerves, she lifted her hands up and placed them against his chest. She felt his body react to the jolt of the connection, and his eyes darkened suddenly, like a cat's.

And then his arms were around her, and he was staring down into her upturned face. "Anna," he murmured, his lips inches from her own. She felt him tremble and with fainting pleasure recognized in him a mixed desire to cherish her and yet crush her against himself.

Then he closed his eyes, and she felt him tense with a huge effort of will. In the next moment she was released. He dropped his arms and stepped back.

"We must talk," he said.

A little laugh of bitter disappointment escaped her. So she was still the woman who was a cheat, whose temptation he must resist.

"Must we?"

"Anna, what your friend said has changed the picture. You must see this."

"Yes, and how does it affect me?" she asked, blowing air out hard and turning away as she tried to get a grip on the passionate ache her arms felt to hold him.

"It is no longer enough, Anna, that you agree simply to disappear to France and say nothing to the press."

She turned to look over her shoulder at him with deep hostility. "Why not?" she demanded.

"They are out there, Anna. They know you now—they will chase you for the story."

"And whose fault is that? Are you suggesting it was *not* your brother who notified everyone and his dog of our arrival time?"

"No, you are right. It was Jaf who did this. I am sorry. We thought only to take one last advantage of your presence, to get one more story that might convince Yusuf. But now things are more desperate."

"But Lisbet didn't tell you anything you didn't already know—or guess."

"Yes," he contradicted. "May we sit down again?"

It was a command, and her reaction was to turn towards a chair. A sudden draft made her feel how the temperature was dropping outside—or perhaps it was inside her own heart—and Anna stooped and flicked on the gas fire in the fireplace before flinging herself into an armchair on one side of it.

The gas ignited with a whoosh. Sheikh Gazi took the chair opposite her, on the other side of the fireplace. Then for a moment he turned his gaze to blink thoughtfully at the flames leaping up around the fake coal.

She watched him. The bone structure of his face was emphasized by the firelight flickering over it in the gathering dusk, revealing sensitivity at temple and mouth. In this light he looked like an old portrait of a saint, sensuous and ascetic together. She suddenly saw, behind the playboy handsomeness, that he was a man used to the rigours of self-discipline. And he was exerting it now.

Sheikh Gazi stared into the fire. He began speaking slowly. "Ramiz Bahrami has been my close friend most of my life. His family is from one of the ancient tribes in the mountains of Noor, but his father moved to the capital to serve the old king. Ramiz and I went to school in the palace and later to university together. He is a close, personal friend of Prince Karim. Highly trusted.''

Anna blinked, her lips parting in surprise, and he flicked his eyes from the fire to her face. She saw open pain in them, and her heart hurt for him.

''My sister Nadia and Ramiz fell in love. She could not have chosen a better man. It was when Ramiz approached my father to ask for permission to marry Nadia that we were all rocked by the information that my father had already chosen Yusuf for her.

''I told you I argued with my father. I tell you now I never pleaded so strongly with him about anything before or since. But he would not give in. Ramiz was a university-educated, moderate Muslim with political ambitions, and Yusuf was mosque-educated, ignorant of the world, devout. It was one thing for my father to let his sons be educated at university. It was another thing entirely to give his daughter to such a man.''

He was silent for a moment, staring into the flames.

''How did Ramiz react to his refusal?'' she prompted softly.

''They both took it hard. Very hard. Ramiz appealed to the prince to intervene, but although Prince Karim did make a request, he knew very well that a father cannot be ordered even by a prince in such a matter.

''Ramiz wanted to run away with her. I would have assisted them, but Nadia was raised with a strong sense of religious duty. She felt it right to obey my father, even in this. And she knew that such a thing in any case would ruin Ramiz's political career.''

He breathed. ''She said no. I was sorry for it, and yet I knew she was right.''

If he was trying to get her onside with this recital, he was succeeding. Anna's heart was deeply touched.

"Ramiz left the country before the wedding—Prince Karim kindly sent him on some mission abroad. He did not return until Yusuf and Nadia had come here to London."

"Has Ramiz married?" Anna asked softly.

He looked at her, shaking his head once. "No. He devoted himself to work. Karim trusts him absolutely. For the past year he has been engaged on something that took him to various countries. For a while he was in Canada.

"It is only since Nadia's disappearance that I have learned from the prince that Ramiz spent part of the past year here in London."

She gasped. "Do you think they met?"

"Now that the pieces come together a little, I begin to believe that they met. I think that this was the root of Yusuf's jealousy, of his suspicion that Nadia's baby was not his own."

"Did Yusuf know that Ramiz and Nadia were in love?"

"It is possible that my father confided something to Yusuf. I cannot say it is not so. My father might have hoped in this way to prevent trouble by alerting Yusuf to the danger."

She could say nothing. What a wholesale betrayal of a daughter.

Gazi took a breath. "Anna, the story is not over. Ramiz disappeared several months ago, and Prince Karim cannot be certain where he was at the time of his disappearance. But it is very possible that he was in England."

"Are you...are you saying Yusuf killed him?"

Again pain was mirrored on his face. "We can't be certain. Ramiz may even be alive. But it seems more of a possibility now that Ramiz's disappearance, rather than being connected with his secret work for Prince Karim, was because of his personal life."

"Do you think that Yusuf is right? Is Safiyah Ramiz's baby and not his own?"

"How can I be certain unless we have tests done? It will be some time before this can be arranged. And time is something we do not have.

"Anna, if your friend is right, and it was Nadia she saw that night…if Nadia is dead and Ramiz also, then it is possible that Safiyah is the only heir either of them will ever have.

"As things stand, as the legal father under English law, Yusuf has the right to custody of Safiyah. I cannot give up custody of the only child my sister and my friend will ever have to such a man as this, and with such a motive to hate her.

"Anna, I ask you, as a woman who knows the value of one child's life, to go on with the pretence we have started. Let the world think we are lovers. Pretend Safiyah is our child. Stay with me until we have discovered the fate of Nadia and Ramiz."

He wasted no time acting on her capitulation. By the time she had hastily thrown a few things into a bag, completed her half-made arrangements for leaving the flat unoccupied for a few weeks, and written a note for the downstairs tenant, another limousine was waiting to sweep them off to London's most prestigious hotel.

There they went to a huge suite on the top floor, with wonderful views overlooking Hyde Park. "We must give the press as much fodder as we can," he told her.

"The more Yusuf reads about us in the papers, the more he will believe."

Before anything else, Gazi insisted that Anna should be examined by another medical expert on head injury. The surgeon, who seemed to be a personal friend, however, was as cheerful as his counterpart in Barakat had been.

"It's not uncommon for accident victims to experience amnesia such as yours," he reassured Anna. "The period of time immediately surrounding the trauma is lost. In fact, it's unlikely you'll ever regain those minutes. But there is absolutely nothing to worry about."

After that she went to the private Health Suite, where she had a steam bath and a massage, and emerged feeling totally pampered. Then she went downstairs to see a top hairdresser, and then a makeup artist.

She returned to the suite to find that several outfits had been sent up from a boutique downstairs for her choice.

"Choose something for tonight," Gazi ordered her. "We will have dinner in a club. Tomorrow we will go shopping in the stores."

She chose a simply cut, utterly luxurious full-length coat and spaghetti-strap dress in black velvet. She had never worn anything so expensive in her life. The outfit clung to her, emphasizing her fashionable thinness.

She emerged from her bedroom, feeling she had never looked so stylish in her life, to find Gazi at a desk in the sitting room of the suite. He looked up, and for an instant his eyes burned her. Then he dropped his eyes and snapped open one of several cases on the desk.

"Diamonds, perhaps," he said with forced casualness, offering it to her.

Anna gasped when she looked inside. "Oh, goodness, where did these come from?"

He raised an eyebrow. "From the jeweller downstairs." He lifted from its silky bed a fabulous necklace that seemed to burn with cold fire, and when he slipped it around her neck she was almost surprised that it didn't scorch her skin. "Do you like diamonds, Anna?"

She laughed, delighted at the utter madness of her life, and turned to the mirror above the fireplace. "I've never really been on speaking terms with diamonds," she said. "But I'm quite happy to wear a necklace like this tonight, I promise you!"

Later, sitting at the table beside her on an intimately small, semicircular bench seat in a place so famous Anna had to pinch herself to believe it, Gazi observed, "Diamonds are too cold for you. You should wear coloured stones. Sapphires, to match your eyes."

Anna only laughed, shaking her head, and fingered one of the earrings.

"You must wear a variety of jewels over the next day or so," he said. "Then, it will please me if you will choose the set you like best to keep. As a gift of gratitude."

Anna almost choked on the tiny garlic mushroom she was eating as a starter. "Choose a *set* of jewels?" she exclaimed, putting a hand to her throat, and feeling the diamonds glowing there. "You're joking! These must be worth a fortune!"

"What you are doing for Nadia is worth much more to me," Gazi said.

Anna gazed down at the beautiful diamonds encircling her wrist, shaking her head. "Thank you. Not that I have anything against jewellery, Sheikh Gazi, but there's something else that I'd much rather have." She looked up. "It would be a real favour, if you—"

His face darkened with an unreadable expression. His gaze raked her with an intensity that held more fire than the diamonds, leaving her gasping for air. Anna breathed and thought, *God, he thinks I'm going to ask him to make love to me*— But before the thought was completed, the sheikh was in control of himself again.

"Whatever you ask for, if I can," he said levelly.

She could hardly speak, for the thought of what that unguarded moment had told her was choking her. Desire pulled at her, drew her lips into a trembling smile. She could not control that, for what else could his look mean, but that he wanted her, and for some reason known to himself, was exercising rigid control?

In the moment when that control had slipped, she had felt a powerful passion emanating from him. Her whole body seemed to be made of butterflies now, all fluttering, so that nothing but thought held her being together. She was so fragile she would dissolve in the smallest gust of wind.

She knew that he could not remain in control if she challenged him. The thought was like champagne to her system, making her drunk.

She swallowed and tried to speak.

"Tell me," he commanded, and Anna struggled to bring her own thoughts back in line.

"I just—it just occurred to me that you could maybe mention to people that I'm a mural artist, specializing in Middle Eastern themes. It would be such fabulous publicity for me. And if as a result I got even one commission from—" she lifted a hand and gestured around the room, where more than one table had recognizable faces

"—from someone like this, well, I'd be muralist to the stars, wouldn't I?"

He stared at her, his eyes narrowed. "And you would rather have this than precious stones?"

Anna smiled, biting her lip. "It would be a lot more useful over the long term."

"You are a very unusual woman."

Jealousy clawed her, and she didn't think before she spoke. "But then I suppose the favours I'm providing are a little different than what you're used to, too."

His eyes went black as he got it, and his hand found hers on the table between them and crushed it as he stared into her eyes. All the breath left her body in one grunting moan at the suddenness of the change in him. She thought, *I've done it, he's lost control,* and the thought made her blood wild.

"It will not be a favour, Anna, from me or from you, when it happens," he growled between his teeth, and kissed her hand with a mouth drawn tight with passionate control. "It is a necessity between us. You know it."

She felt passion like burning heat in his touch, saw it in his eyes, felt it rush through her body so powerfully she was dimly grateful she was not standing. Gazi was trembling as his hand released hers and came up to stroke her temple, her cheek. She shivered.

"Is it not so? Do you not feel it so?"

She couldn't have said a word to save her life, she was so swamped with feeling. She tried to swallow, but her throat was choked.

"I have seen it in your eyes, Anna! In every move you make!" he insisted. "Do you deny it?"

She opened her mouth and dropped her head back, trying to catch her breath. Electric sensuality roared through her, setting every part of her alight.

"I have wanted you until I was mad," he whispered hoarsely. "Your perfume, your mouth, your body stretched out in the sun...what it cost me, hour after hour, day after day, to see you there, to feel how you wanted to tempt me—*ya Allah!* how I wanted you!"

"Gazi!" she whispered helplessly.

"And do you challenge me now with talk of favours? Favour?" His voice grated over her charged nerves, blinding her with sensation, making her faint. "Shall I ask you for this as a favour, and offer you jewels in return? How much will you ask, I wonder? A diamond for each kiss, Anna? Another for every thrust of my tongue into your sweet mouth, to make us both mad with wanting more? And what, to touch your breasts? A bracelet of sapphires?"

His voice dropped to a tiger's hungry growl. She could feel his breath against her neck. "To open your legs for me, Anna, what for this favour? A necklace, a tiara? I give it to you, yes! If it were necessary I would bury you in jewels, make love to you on a bed of diamonds and rubies and then give them all to you."

His eyes burned her, heat licking through her body, melting everything into wild need.

"But it will not be necessary, Anna—will it? Do you think I do not know that to make you open your legs I need only ask with my tongue for entry? If I press my kiss on you there, Anna, who does whom the favour? Tell me that you too do not want this, if you can. Tell me the thought of my tongue on your body is not part of your dreams as it is of mine."

"Stop," she moaned helplessly. "My God, Gazi, stop, I'm—"

"Think of opening your legs to my kiss, Anna," he commanded, watching how desire burned her and made her tremble, devouring her need. "Think of my tongue, my mouth, think how the heat will stir you, make you need what only I can give you. How you will cry out, and beg for more."

"Gazi," she pleaded. "Gazi, I can't take it."

"Yes," he said, deliberately misunderstanding her. "Yes, you can take more than this. You must. Do you think I can stop there? No, once we start, Anna—"

He lifted her hand to his mouth again, and bit the fleshy part of her palm between strong white teeth. A thousand nerves leapt into wildest reaction, and she could scarcely stifle the moan that rose to her throat.

"What comes next, Anna? Who will beg whom for the favour of my body inside you, hmm? Will we not beg each other for it? Say it!" he commanded.

She wondered dimly how she would survive. She opened her eyes and mouth at him, struggling for control.

"Tell me!" he commanded again.

She licked her dry lips, opened her mouth for air. "Tell you what?"

"Tell me whether you will ask me for the favour, Anna. Tell me that you will want it, too. Or will it be a favour you grant me when I ask?"

Feeling coursed up and down her body, through every cell.

She dropped her head. "You know I want you," she said, scarcely getting the words out.

It was as if she struck him with all her strength. She saw his back straighten with a jolt, his head turn to one side. His eyes never left hers, and she saw blackness like the centre of a storm, and realized that he had, at last, been driven beyond his strength.

Fourteen

It was at that moment that their lobsters arrived. She saw Gazi flick an unbelieving glance at the waiter, and at the plate, saw his hand clench. Then his eyes moved from the deliciously steaming lobster slowly up to her face, and he smiled a smile that sent little rivulets of sensation all over her.

They were silent as the pepper grinder made its ritual pass over both plates and then Gazi picked up a claw of the lobster between his strong fingers. His hands clenched till the knuckles showed white, and she quivered where she sat, knowing it was a sign not of exertion, but control. The shell broke open to reveal the tender white meat.

His hand not quite steady, he dipped the triangular wedge of flesh in butter, lifted it and held it out invitingly to her mouth. Anna tried to speak, failed, licked her lips and then submitted, leaning forward a little to take the meat between her teeth and pull it delicately from the shell.

He watched her chew and lick the butter from her mouth, with a smile that took her breath away. She dropped her eyes to her own plate, picked up the cracker and broke a piece of shell, then did as he had done, dipping the tender juicy flesh into butter, and holding it for him to eat.

When his teeth closed firmly on the meat, biting it, drawing it out, and then eating it with sudden, uncontrolled hunger, a shaft of purely sexual sensation went through her. Anna grunted, and his eyelids flickered.

The meal that followed was torment, the torment of overcharged senses. Anna had never experienced a sensuality to equal it in all her life. They fed themselves and each other without plan, with their bare hands, with forks, biting, chewing, licking, and fainting with delight at each touch of lips and tongue on buttery flesh.

And all the time he talked to her, in a low, intimate voice that was another charge on her drunken senses. "You lay in the sun, Anna, the sweat breaking out on your skin, on your thighs, till I could think of nothing but my tongue licking it off, till I could taste the salt of you actually in my mouth...and you knew it and I knew you knew it."

"No," she whispered.

"How I wanted to punish you for tempting me. I dreamed of how I would do this, how I would make you weep with desire and wanting. How my hands and mouth would touch you, caress you, stroke you...my hands on your damp skin, stroking your feet, your thighs, your stomach, your breasts. Sometimes, when you lay on your back, it was like death, the wanting to walk over to you, to put my hand on the fabric of your suit and draw it aside and kiss you there.

"I told myself my tongue would torment you till you wept for the thrust of my body, and then I would refuse, so that you should know what torment was mine.

"But I knew I was a fool. If once I had touched you, I would have lost all. If I made you beg, at the first pleading I would have to thrust into you. I could not have resisted then."

"Gazi," was all she could whisper.

"Yes, I dreamed of you saying my name in this way," he said roughly, as if the sound of her voice was too much, and held another delicate morsel up to her lips. "And you will say it again for me, in every way that I dreamed."

He looked down at her body, at the bare, soft brown shoulders, the slender curved arms, the soft folds of the fine velvet that covered her breasts. Her nipples pressed against the delicate velvet cloth, announcing her sexual arousal.

She was constantly half fainting. Her blood ran between head and body with a wild rushing that drowned her. She saw him looking down at her body, saw his eyes darken.

He offered her another buttery bite. Looking into his stormy, hungry eyes, she thought of how she would kiss his flesh, too, and gently took what he offered onto her tongue, half smiling at him in sensuous promise.

The breath hissed between his teeth. "You drive me to the edge," he said in a voice like gravel.

When the meal was over, Anna could scarcely stand. She staggered, her knees turned to butter, and was sure she must look drunk, if anyone were watching them, but she didn't want to find out. Gazi took the coat from the attendant and held it for her, and she could feel his arms like iron with the effort it took not to pull her into his embrace as she slipped her arms inside the sleeves.

Neither of them even noticed the photographers' cameras as they went, hand in hand, his grip so possessive it hurt her, out to the waiting car.

His control lasted until the limousine door shut them in. With a steady hand he pressed a switch, and a blind hummed up to cover the glass between the passenger compartment and the driver's. Another switch plunged them into darkness. Music was already softly playing. Outside the black-tinted windows, the city lights began to slide past.

He reached for her, passion tearing at them both, and with a cry she was in his arms. He drew her across his lap, her head in one possessive hand, his other arm wrapping her waist under the velvet coat, and lifted her up to his mouth for the wildest, hungriest kiss either of them had ever experienced. They were pierced with passionate sweetness, and moaned their pent-up need against each other's lips.

Never had a kiss sent so much pleasure through her body, so that she trembled and clung, shivering with desire. Never had his mouth been so hungry for a woman, so that no matter how he drank, he could not get enough of her. Her arms wrapped his head, her fingers threaded the dark curls, while her mouth opened to his wild demands.

The car stopped, a door slammed, and at last, heaving with breath, they broke apart. She lay looking up at him, seeing nothing but the glint of light on his curling hair; he stared blindly down at her. Like two animals, scenting each other in the darkness.

"We are at the hotel," he murmured.

Her hand was clenched in his hair and Anna had to command her fingers to let him go. She felt the hard, uncomfortable pressure from his groin against her side and smiled as he helped her to sit up.

"All right?" he asked, and she heard the click as he unlocked the door. The chauffeur opened it, and a moment later they were inside the hotel and stepping into the luxurious, golden-lighted elevator that carried them upwards.

In the darkened sitting room, two lamps cast soft pools of light, and a fire had been lit in the grate. They moved towards it without speaking. Beside the fireplace a small table held a decanter and glasses.

"Will you have a brandy?" Gazi asked as he helped her out of her velvet coat. The silky lining brushing her skin was almost more than she could bear. She nodded mutely as he tossed the coat onto a sofa, and he turned to the table.

He lifted the stopper out of the decanter and set it down with a small sound that seemed to resonate around them. The slight gurgling of the liquid, even, was another branch laid on the erotic fire.

He handed her the goblet, the brandy a glowing, rich, warm amber in the bottom. Picking up his own, he swirled, drank, and set the glass down again. Then he bent and hungrily kissed her.

The taste of brandy hit all her senses as he kissed it into her mouth, onto her tongue. Anna felt shivers of sensation from her brain to her toes, and with her free hand clutched at his jacket front, her head going back to allow him the fullest access to her mouth.

His hands enclosed her, one arm around her waist, one hard on her naked shoulder. He lifted his mouth from her mouth, and moved hungrily down the line of her throat. The taste of brandy on her tongue smoked through her system, and hot on its trail little flames of sensation licked their way.

His hand found the little velvet buttons at her back, and one by one began to undo them. Her eyes closed dreamily, the better to follow the progress of his determined fingers down her spine, from between her shoulder blades, down and down along her spine to her waist, while her skin became ever more sensitive.

The buttons stopped below her waist, leaving the whole long stretch of her back naked and accessible to his teasing, tasting hands, and he stroked and caressed the bare skin while his mouth sought hers again.

The room was warm. All her shivers arose in his touch, a curious heated chill running crazily all over and through her. She buried her hand in the thick curls on his head and obediently bent backwards as he pressed her body tight against him.

Her glass was slipping from her grasp, and as he straightened he took it from her and set it down. Then he stood close, looking down at her. The straps of her dress had loosened and were slipping off her shoulders, and she instinctively bent her elbows up, placing her hands against her throat.

"Let it fall," Gazi commanded softly, and his voice, too, was all erotic sensation, compelling her obedience. She dropped her arms to her sides, and the velvet whispered slowly, slowly down over her breasts, leaving them naked to the touch of the fireglow.

He closed his eyes, opened them again, and that, too, created sensation in her. The dress rested precariously on her hips for a moment, clung there, and then, as if reluctantly, slithered down the gentle curve and fell with a little swoop to her feet.

She stood revealed in tiny black briefs, smoky lace-top stockings, delicate high-heel mules, and the diamond circlets at throat and wrist.

His hands reached out to slide with possessive heat down her back and encircle her rump, and he drew her against him, gazing into her eyes with a hotter, brighter flame than the fire provided.

"You will drive me out of my mind," he growled, and as her head fell helplessly back he pressed his lips against the pulse at the base of her throat. Her hands wrapped his neck, slid down his back onto the silky fabric of his jacket.

"Take this off," she murmured, as her hands moved to his chest and slipped inside and against his shirt, pushing the jacket down his arms. He shrugged out of it and let it fall, and now she flirtatiously pulled at his neat black bow tie, untied it, and with a hungry, teasing smile, slowly pulled it away.

He smiled, his eyes dark, and let her work on the tiny buttons, one by one, of his shirt. His chest was darkly warm in the firelight, and as she pulled the shirt down his arms, she laid a line of kisses in the neat curling mat of hair, up and across his shoulder to his throat.

"You have not taken off my cuff links," Gazi murmured protestingly, as his mouth smothered hers in a kiss so hungry she moaned.

Anna smiled. "You're at my mercy, then," she whispered, drawing the shirt further down his arms to pinion him.

He smiled a smile, and lifted his arms, the muscles bulging for a moment of exertion, and then she heard the sound of tearing fabric and the distant clink of but-

tons hitting somewhere, and his arms were free, each
wrist carrying a tattered half shirt. He stopped a moment
to tear himself free, tossing the remnants of the shirt
wildly away. Then his arms wrapped her tight, dragging
her against him with a ruthlessness that told her she had
released a demon in him, and swung her up to carry her
to his bedroom.

"A little further, Beloved, before we rest."

"Ah, how weary I am with riding! How far to India
now, my Lion?"

He looked over his shoulder at the cloud in the distance. "Not far, my princess. Courage."

But her eyes followed his, and now she, too, saw the
signs of pursuit. "Riders!" she cried. "Oh, Lion, is it
my father?"

"A caravan," he lied. "On its way, like us, to India.
We shall join them."

She spurred her mount to a gallop again, and bit her
cheek not to cry out against the pain and weariness.
They rode in silence, as those behind grew steadily
closer.

"Will they catch us, Lion?" she asked.

He did not answer.

Anna awoke from the dream just before dawn, still in
his arms. Rain drove against the windows and she lay
listening to the music of it.

Never in her life had she been held with such passion
as she had felt in Gazi's hands, never had she experienced such a wild storm of pleasure and need as had
swept her in his embrace.

When he entered her, it was all fresh, all new, for the
joy she experienced had touched a part of her that no

one had ever touched in her. Everything that had gone
before was like a sepia photograph in comparison. She
had clung to him, accepting the thrust of his body from
the depths of her self, weeping as pleasure suffused her.

She loved him. She looked into his face now, the faint
glow of dawn showing her the mark on his eye, and a
passion of tenderness overwhelmed her. Her heart
melted in its own burning, and was reborn stronger,
surer, understanding things that until yesterday she had
only dimly glimpsed.

Of course he did not love her. He was attracted, but
for a man like him sexual passion was more a part of
his being than her effect on him. She had no illusions
about ordinary Anna Lamb's ability to touch his heart.

It would break her heart when her time with him was
over. Maybe it would have been better for her if she had
resisted the temptation of his lovemaking...but Anna
had the feeling that, however much this affair cost her
in the end, when she was an old woman she would look
back on her moments with Sheikh Gazi as something
she was glad to have experienced.

She felt chilly suddenly, and instinctively slipped
closer to him. Still asleep, he reached for her, and drew
her in against his warm, naked body as if that was where
she belonged.

The Sunday papers were delivered to the suite, and as
they sat over their breakfast at a table set cozily in front
of a bright fire, Gazi and Anna glanced through them.

The story of their arrival in London was not exten-
sively reported, though it had got a few mentions in
gossip columns. Only one paper ran a picture on the
front page. It was a shot of her looking up at him, and

she thought the look between them should set the paper on fire.

Gazi glanced from the paper to her with a look that made her heart jump with sadness, though she couldn't have said why. Perhaps because her pictured face was that of a woman deep in love, and that troubled him.

He shook his head over the favourite story, a rehashed royal scandal. "We must do better than this," he said matter-of-factly, tossing the last tabloid aside and picking up his coffee. "Yusuf cannot be counted on to read gossip columns."

Anna gazed at him. "Do better, how?"

"First things first," Gazi said, with a smile that stopped her heart. "I must take you shopping."

Anna had only ever dreamed of the kind of shopping trip that followed. He seemed to want to buy her everything he saw. She protested several times that he was buying too much, but he simply ignored her.

"Never has so much been purchased by so few in so short a time," she joked, as he signalled his approval to yet another outfit, one only suitable for a yacht cruise. At last he said, in a bored voice, "Anna, you must have clothes if we are going to carry this off."

"But where will I ever wear these?"

"On my yacht," he said with surprise.

"But, Gazi—" she began again, and he made an impatient sound.

"Anna," he told her in a low voice. "I ask you to remember that you are the pampered darling of a rich Arab, and the mother of his only child. Please, Anna! Cannot you find it in you to be capricious, difficult to please, even a little greedy? You should be saying, 'Can't I have both, darling?' not 'Gazi, you are spending too much on me!' You are doing me a great favour, much more than you know, and it is only right that I should reward you according to my means. Do you think a few thousands spent on clothes means anything to me?''

Then she gave herself up to it—total, guilt-free shopping.

''Can I buy one for Lisbet?'' she asked, when he encouraged her to buy several fashionable pashminas in a variety of colours. Gazi shrugged his approval. ''Buy her a dozen, Anna,'' he said.

His cellphone rang several times as they shopped, and he had brief discussions with the callers. When they had finished their shopping at one famous store, Anna was surprised to hear Gazi say that they would take everything with them.

The store produced several uniformed footmen to carry their packages. Gazi chose a medium-sized shopping bag and handed it to Anna. ''Carry this, Anna,'' he said, and took two small boxes under his own arm.

Followed by the footmen, whose arms were full, he led the way to the exit. Outside they were met by two or three photographers, who snapped their cameras as the little procession, the image of conspicuous consumerism or remnant of a vanished era, depending on your point of view, walked along the pavement to the limousine waiting a few yards away.

When they got into the car, she grinned at Gazi. ''You're really good at this!'' she said.

''It is a part of my job to be good at it. In any case, it is not difficult to manipulate something like the media,'' he said. ''Greed is the biggest weakness anyone has, whether an institution or an individual.''

She eyed him. ''Do you think it's right to manipulate people?''

"Anna, if I said to the editors of those papers, 'In the hope of saving my sister's life I need you to run a certain story,' do you think they would agree?"

She thought. "I don't know. Wouldn't they?"

"It is possible. But it is also possible that one of them at least would consider the fact that I am afraid for my sister's life at her own husband's hands a much better story. I do not wish to see a headline tomorrow reading *Save My Sister, Pleads Arab Playboy.*"

She was silenced.

They returned to the hotel, where they had a few hours to prepare for a black-tie function in the evening. Anna had the full treatment again, massage, manicure and pedicure, and professional makeup job.

By the time she was ready for the party she was feeling utterly pampered, and she knew she had never looked better in her life. Her hairstyle wasn't violently different from her old one, but it was a thousand times better cut. Little locks of hair tumbled this way and that over her scalp and down the back of her neck in charming confusion, with half a dozen sapphire-and-diamond trinkets nestling artistically among them, which seemed to reveal a dark sensitivity in her sapphire eyes. Her individual looks and fine bone structure had been dramatized with subtle shading and black eyeliner, and her wide, expressive mouth was coloured dark maroon.

She wore an ankle-length coat dress with a stand-up shirt collar, bodice snugly fitted to the waist, and slightly flaring skirt that was open at the front to well above the knee. It was made of soft-flowing midnight-blue and creamy tan silk brocade that matched both her skin and the deep blue of her eyes. It gave the impression that she was naked under a covering of lace. For warmth she carried one of her new cashmere pashminas, in matching midnight-blue.

She was all blue, black and tan. With clear nail varnish on her short artist's nails, and stockings that matched the navy of the dress, the only flash of real colour was her wine-dark lips. Anna looked dramatic and sensational and, staring at herself in the mirror, she thought that, although she would never be a beauty, perhaps tonight it was just a little less unbelievable that she might be the consort of a man like Sheikh Gazi al Hamzeh.

He was looking extremely rich and handsome himself, in a black dinner jacket with diamond cuff links and diamond button studs nestling among the intricate pleats of an impeccable white silk shirt.

He lifted his head from the contemplation of the fire as she entered the room, and his eyes found her in the huge slanted mirror just above the mantel. His glance darkened in a way that sent blood rushing to her brain, and for a moment neither moved.

Formal wear seemed to emphasize the patch around his eye. He really was a swashbuckler tonight. Anna shivered with a frisson of pure sexual excitement.

"Hi," she said, lifting a hand to shoulder height and waggling her fingers at him, a crazy grin splitting her face.

He turned. "Hi," he returned, smiling with one corner of his mouth, his eyes still intent. "You are very lovely tonight, Anna."

"Amazing what money can do, isn't it?" she quipped, to hide from both of them what admiration in his voice could do to her heart.

"Money can do many things, Anna, but it cannot invent beauty like yours in a woman."

His tone was not consciously caressing, but there was a timbre to his voice that always drew a reaction from her, and coupled with a comment like this, it made her mouth soften tremulously. She couldn't think of anything to say.

"Come and see if you like these," he commanded softly, and opened another jeweller's box to reveal a breathtaking spangle of diamonds and sapphires to match those in her hair. She chose a large square-cut sapphire ring and diamond teardrop earrings, and waved her hands airily.

"I could get used to this!" she joked.

He was watching her with a smile that turned her insides to mush. "Good," he said.

Fifteen

It was a party at a very exclusive private address, with a long line of limos waiting in the sweep drive to disgorge celebrities, and several photographers snapping continually. Anna realized just how exclusive it was, though, only as they moved through the rooms, sparkling with glowing chandeliers, brilliant conversation and an array of jewels on nearly every inch of bare skin. She recognized numerous faces—from film, from television, and even one or two from *Parliamentary Question Time*.

"Gazi, how fabulous of you to come!" a glamorous redhead exclaimed exuberantly. She was covered head to toe with glittering gold and had an accent Anna couldn't quite place. "And this is Anna! Hellooo!" she crooned, grabbing Anna's hands and kissing her on both cheeks.

"Hello," Anna returned, unable to place her.

"Gazi says that you paint wonderful murals of Moor-

ish palaces that he can't tell from the real thing,'' the
woman said, her eyes searching the crowd for a waiter
and summoning him over to offer a tray of champagne.
''I hope you will paint something for me. You must
come to see me, Anna, and I will show you my small
dining room and you will tell me if you can do something Greek with it.''

As Anna expressed her enthusiastic willingness, a
photographer ambled over. ''Can I get one of all three
of you?'' he called, and the redhead struck a pose, smiling a practised smile. Anna tried to do the same, wishing
she had asked Lisbet for a few pointers.

''Of course, we want the publicity,'' the hostess murmured to Anna. ''The editor has given us a two-page
photo spread in the weekend magazine.''

''Thank you, Princess,'' the photographer said, moving away again.

''My God, that was, that was Princess...Princess...''
Anna muttered in a low voice, groping for the name of
one of the uncrowned heads of Europe, as they moved
on a few minutes later. Gazi smiled down at her.

''She is the patroness of the charity,'' he said.

''Charity?'' Anna repeated, and then threw a glance
around the glittering assembly. ''Is this a *charity* function?''

Her sense of humour was sparked, and she flicked a
look up into his face, trying to suppress a smile, an effort
that only added to the charm of her expression. As she
met the appreciative glow in his own eyes she bit her
lip and her head went back, and a crack of delighted
laughter burst from her throat, causing a few heads near
them to turn.

''Sheikh al Hamzeh, my dear chap! What a very great
pleasure!'' a white-haired man cried in the crusty tones

of the Establishment, and a moment later they had been absorbed into the group and Anna was talking to a famous television host.

The evening that followed was one she thought she would always remember. Gazi was blandly informing everyone who asked—and everyone did—that they had met when he bought a painted screen from her to put in his Barakat home.

So Anna was asked for her business card by several people who said they were in the middle of redecorating or about to redecorate and would love to have her do something, and also by the television host, who seemed to have a more personal interest in mind. That boosted her sexual confidence amazingly, because Gazi gave the man a look that would have quick-frozen strawberries in June.

Then she reminded herself that he was here to manipulate people into believing he cared. She must be careful not to fall for the act herself.

But the whole evening was made delicious by his constant attendance, the possessive brush of his hand over her back, the look of sometimes lazy, sometimes urgent desire in his eyes. She knew it was only partly true, but then it was only partly false. And it was headier than the champagne.

They stayed till after midnight. Then, as they left the party, she discovered just how much Sheikh Gazi al Hamzeh was a master of media manipulation.

"The first editions have now gone to bed," he explained quietly as they moved to the door. "They now would like something new for the later editions. Will you play along with me, Anna?"

"All right," she said nervously. "What are we going to do?"

"We are going to have a spat and make up," he murmured.

The temperature had dropped while they were inside, and when they emerged on the pavement the waiting photographers were huddled under the awning, looking miserable and stamping their feet against the cold. Most of them only eyed the couple. They had pictures of them going in, and there was nothing to be gained by another identical shot of them coming out.

Gazi paused to tip the doorman. "Don't be stupid!" he murmured over his shoulder to her in low-voiced masculine irritation, as if continuing an argument begun inside.

The lights showed a driving wet snow coming down at an angle, and although the doorman had clearly been busy with the broom on the red carpet that covered the pavement under the awning, snow was settling again.

"Why is it stupid?" Anna muttered furiously. Her blood was singing with mingled nerves and excitement. He looked so handsome and powerful in his navy cashmere coat, his white silk scarf over the black bow tie, mock anger flashing in his eyes. "It's not stupid!" She turned away from him towards the curb.

"Anna!" he commanded, striding after her, and reaching a hand to clasp her arm. Anna whirled and snatched her arm away.

"I don't appreciate being called stupid!"

The gusting wind suddenly cooperated. It whipped the split skirt of her dress out behind her, revealing all the length of her slim legs, thighs bare above her lace-top stay-ups, and incidentally freezing her where she stood. The photographers, who had slowly been waking up, now snapped to attention.

As she whirled, Anna accidentally put her foot straight

onto a little mound of cold slush. She slipped, half gasped, half screamed, and instinctively clutched at Gazi. A second later she felt her feet go entirely out from under her as electric warmth embraced her. Gazi was scooping her up in his arms.

"Excellent, Anna!" he murmured in her ear, and she felt the heat of him rush through her chilled blood.

He had his arm under her bare knees. As he lifted her, the skirt fell away, revealing her legs right up to the hip. Her shoes dangled from her toes. The photographers were scrambling now, calling encouragement and approval, as Anna, freezing, futilely groped for the panels of her skirt.

"Don't cover your legs! You will soon be warm," Gazi whispered in her ear in a firm command that was suddenly charged with an erotic nuance, and set her heart racing. "Look at me, Anna, and relent!"

Her breath catching in her throat, she lifted one arm to his shoulder and glanced uncertainly into his face. He paused for a few moments, smiling down at her with sexy promise, as if his imagination, too, had suddenly moved into high gear. Cameras clicked and flashed all around them, and then Gazi stepped to the limousine that was just purring up the drive, and after a moment she was inside.

Instantly she was locked in his arms, being ruthlessly kissed. His hand slid up her stockinged thigh with a touch like cold fire, because his flesh was chilled but still heated her blood.

Haunting music played, the windows were all covered, and recessed light glowed softly, enclosing them in their own little world. Anna was half sprawled on the luxurious leather under him, her legs angled, her dress up around her hips, revealing everything as Gazi lifted his mouth, straightened and gazed at her. But as she made a move to sit, he pushed her back with one hand, while the other unerringly found its way to the lace at the top of her stockings, traced its way over the bare skin above, and then, with ruthless precision, to a spot behind the lace of her bikini panties.

Anna gasped. She found she could make no move, no protest, to prevent what he intended. Sensation shot through her, as much from the look in his eyes as from his touch, as he carefully stroked and stroked the potent little cluster of hungry nerves.

They responded obediently to his dictates, as if instantly recognizing their master. A breathless little grunt escaped her, and her hips moved hungrily. She saw the corner of his mouth go up, and one strong arm was on her thigh then, lifting her leg over his head as he sat, and resting it on his other side—spreading her wide for his eyes, his hands…his mouth.

She understood his intent as he bent forward. His hand stopped its delicate stroking and instead his fingers slipped under the lace of her briefs and pulled it to one side, and then, just as he had promised, his mouth was against her, his tongue hot, teasing, hungry.

Her hands clenched in his hair. She could do nothing, say nothing. She was completely at his mercy, melted into submission by the shafts of pure, keening pleasure that his mouth created in her.

"Gazi!" she cried, hitting the peak with a suddenness that made her heart thump crazily. Honeyed sweetness poured through her as her back arched and her muscles clenched.

"Another," he urged her in soft command, and she felt how expertly his fingers toyed with her and his tongue rasped her to pleasure again. She felt completely open, completely helpless, as if the pleasure he gave her put her in his power. "Again," he said, and like an animal going through a hoop, her body had to obey.

After an endless time in a world of pleasure, she found him relenting. He restored her clothing, and drew her body up so that she sat in his embrace, her back against his chest, his face in her hair.

"What's happening?" she begged, hardly knowing where she was.

"We are almost at the airport," he murmured, and she could still shiver as his voice whispered against her ear.

"Oh!" she exclaimed. She had completely forgotten that tonight he had said they would fly back to West Barakat. She lifted a bare foot. "My shoe's gone," she said stupidly.

He felt behind him and eventually found it, and Anna marvelled that she had the muscle coordination necessary to slip it onto her foot. Then the limousine rolled to a stop and it was only moments before they were back on the private jet again, very like the first time, except that this time, Gazi was looking at her with a promise in his eyes that tonight she would not spend the hours in that bed alone.

They weren't long in the air when the hostess approached them with a small tray of Turkish delight and a low-voiced query. Gazi turned to Anna. "Would you like a nightcap or a hot drink, Anna? Or do you prefer to go straight to bed?"

She did not like being offered a choice. She wanted him to want to take her to bed as much as she wanted to go. So perversely, she said, "Oh, let's have some coffee."

She bit into a deliciously soft sugary cube and then stared absently at the shiny green inside of the half still between her fingers.

"Of course," he said, and she couldn't read his expression. "How much sugar?"

"Sweet, please."

He spoke to the hostess, who smiled, nodded, and disappeared into the galley.

Meanwhile Anna unbuckled her seat belt and settled more comfortably in the big plush armchair. With a little whisper of silk, her dress slithered away to reveal all the length of one leg, encased in the dark cobweb of expensive stocking he had bought for her.

Gazi's gaze was instinctively drawn, then moved up to her face, with a look that abruptly reminded her of what had taken place in the limousine. The heat of the memory invaded her body, burned her cheeks.

As the hostess set a little cup of thick sweet liquid in front of her, Gazi reached for a powdery cube of Turkish delight and put it in his mouth with a lazy hand. Anna felt electricity in the air, felt her eyes forced up to his face. He tilted his head and met her gaze, and Anna's heart kicked as if it wanted to kill her.

"I am glad you do not want to sleep," he said.

She yearned towards him, body and soul; she was almost weeping with love and desire. She said, half meaning it, "I don't intend to waste a moment of my allotted time, Gazi."

His eyes darkened with dramatic suddenness, and only then did she realize with what an iron hold he was controlling himself. He reached to imprison her hand, took the little cup from her fingers with his other, and set it down.

"Then let us not waste a moment," he told her

through his teeth, and a moment later he had pulled her to her feet and was leading her to the stateroom.

The bed with its snowy linens was inviting, the room luxuriously intimate, with the ever-present hum of the engines seeming to cut them off from the world.

She melted into passionate hunger as he unbuttoned her dress and drew it off her shoulders, and kissed him with little hungry bites as she in turn unbuttoned his shirt, his trousers, and stripped everything except his underwear off. Then at last, with desperate hungry kissing, they fell onto the bed and their hands began a passionate roaming over each other's body.

He stroked her silken legs, stripped the fine lace from her breasts, while her hungry hand found his sex and pressed it in demand.

Their blood raced up, too needy to wait, and when he stripped off the last of the lace that hid her from him, and tore off the cloth from his own hips, she cried little cries of encouragement and need, and spread her legs, her body ready for the hard, hungry thrust of his.

It was as much pleasure as he could bear, thrusting so suddenly into her, and he drew out and thrust again, to see the grimace of pleasure on her face. Neither of them knew how long they went on, crying out their pleasure, until desire and love and sensation exploded into a fireball of sweetness that burned new pathways all through their being.

They bathed their faces at the little spring, and then turned towards the dust cloud that told them how close their pursuers approached.

"It is not a caravan, Lion," she said sadly. "It is my father."

"It must be so, Beloved."

"They will kill us," she said. *"I am sorry for one thing only,"* and he marvelled at her bravery, for her voice held no quiver, no doubt.

"What, then, Beloved, do you have regrets? I for myself have none," he said.

"Only one, my Lion. That we had nor time nor place to taste each other's love before we die."

"Ah, that," he said.

"Give me your small sword," she commanded. *"For my life will cost them almost as dear as yours."*

He pulled the little blade from his belt. *"Beloved, do you indeed wish it so?"*

"What, shall I die a coward's death at my lover's hands? How would we face each other in the other world, if I asked this of you?"

His heart wept to see her so stalwart.

"One day," she said. *"One day, we shall meet. Somewhere, somehow. Do not you feel it?"*

He was silent.

"It is so!" she swore. *"If we but wish it! Swear to me that it shall be so!"*

The Lion drew his sword and laid his hand upon the blade. *"As God is my witness, though we die here, I will wander a lost soul until your words are fulfilled, Beloved."*

"So be it," she said. *"And when we have found each other, then we will live all the life we lose now. For God rewards true lovers for their constancy. How can He do else?"*

Sixteen

It was early afternoon at the villa, and they were sitting over a late lunch on the terrace by the pool when the call came through.

Nadia was alive. Jaf had already been to see her. Gazi told her that much before embarking on a long conversation with his brother, while Anna sat waiting in anxious impatience for the details.

"She jumped off the bridge," he told her when at last he put the phone down. "The water level in the Thames was high that night. That saved her."

Anna bit her lip and tried to find the right things to say. He took her hand and kissed it.

"Someone in one of the moored houseboats saw her go. They rescued her. She begged them not to go to the police, told them if her husband found her he would kill her. The man was a surgeon. He admitted her to a private hospital. Since then she has been too ill to say anything.

When she recovered a little, she phoned the only number she could remember. Fortunately it was the number of our apartment in London and Jaf was there.''

He sat in silence, contemplating it, until she prompted him. ''What about Ramiz?''

A shadow crossed his face. ''The reason she felt hopeless enough to jump was—when Ramiz discovered she was pregnant, he promised to return here to West Barakat and ask us to begin divorce proceedings on her behalf. She never heard from him again.

''Yusuf must have suspected something, for suddenly she was a prisoner in her own home. She knew nothing of Ramiz's disappearance, but she knew that if Ramiz had spoken to me she would have heard. She thought Ramiz had proved faithless. Yusuf became more and more jealous, till she was frightened for her life and her child's. You were right, Anna. She went into labour and saw it as her only chance. She fled, and gave birth in a garage.

''Only then did she understand she had nowhere to flee to. We were not in town, and our apartment is the first place Yusuf would look for her. After months of bravery, Nadia broke. She caught a cab, left the baby in the cab without letting the driver know, walked onto the bridge and jumped.''

They were silent, trying to understand her despair.

''And I got into the cab,'' Anna murmured at last.

''Yes, Nadia said a woman was there as she got out. She said she looked at you, silently entrusting her baby to you.''

Anna shook her head. ''I still don't have any memory of it. She must be very relieved to know that you have Safiyah safe.''

''Yes, of course. She regrets very deeply what she

tried to do, and we will bring her home here as soon as possible to be with her baby.''

"But you're still worried," Anna said. "Is it something about Ramiz?''

Gazi looked at her, weighing his words, and the look in his eyes made her sad with fear. "Yes, partly about Ramiz. It concerns more than Nadia, or Safiyah, or Ramiz. It is personal, but also much more than personal. It may involve the national security of the Barakat Emirates.''

Her breath came in on a long, audible intake.

"If I tell you, Anna, it will put a burden of secrecy on you. You can never mention it to anyone, not even your friend Lisbet. Can you accept this? Will you hear me?''

"Are you working for Prince Karim?''

"I am his Cup Companion. Of course I work for him. In this matter, for all the princes.''

"Are you a spy?''

"It is not my usual job. But we all do whatever is necessary.''

Anna gazed out over the terrace to the blue sea and wondered how it was possible for a life to change so dramatically in such a short time. How had it happened that she was sitting here in this fabulous villa, whose existence she had known nothing about two weeks ago, being invited to hear the state secrets of the Barakat Emirates?

"If you tell me all this, you're then going to ask me to do something?''

He swallowed, and her heart clenched nervously. "Yes, I will ask you something. But I want to tell you, not to persuade you to anything, but because I am tired of secrecy between us.''

Her heart began to thud. "From the beginning I have been forced always into a position of suspecting you against my natural inclinations, Anna. I could not do or say the things I wished, because so much more than my personal happiness or even my sister's life was at stake. If I was indeed blinded to your true self, the whole country might suffer. Now I ask your permission to tell you the truth."

Anna swallowed against the lump of fear and nerves that choked her. "Yes," she said. "Please tell me."

"You know already that Ramiz was on an undercover assignment for the princes. What I did not tell you was that his mission was to infiltrate, if possible, a secret group trying to overthrow the monarchy here."

Anna silently opened her mouth. She could hardly breathe.

"We think that it was not by his own design that Ramiz met Nadia again. We have suspected that his investigations led him to Yusuf. What Nadia says seems to confirm this."

"Oh, my God! You mean Yusuf is part of the conspiracy?"

"Yusuf must not have known that Nadia was in love before her marriage. My father kept her secret. If he had known, it is impossible to believe that he would have brought Ramiz home to meet his wife, as she says he did. But Ramiz—Ramiz knew who Yusuf was. Pity Ramiz, whose mission required that he accept the invitation!"

"How dreadful!" she breathed, and bit her lip, feeling how totally inadequate that was.

"Do you now understand, Anna, why I was forced to lie to you and abduct you and accuse you? It is not merely the princes' lives that arc at risk from this conspiracy. A move to overthrow their rule would bring certain civil war to Barakat. Tribe against tribe, brother against brother. It would bring to the surface many rivalries now in abeyance. The repercussions would last beyond this generation, whatever the outcome. Our personal lives were less important than this.

"Can you accept that I thought and acted in this way, Anna?"

She nodded, her head bent, not daring to hope for what might be coming next. "To have you here, to be falling more and more under your spell with every moment that passed, to understand how faulty my own judgement might be…to have to suspect that you did this to me deliberately…to be forced to lie—I hope you did not suffer so much at my hands that you cannot also pity me, Anna."

Still she could not lift her head.

"Look at me," he commanded in a firm, quiet, lover's voice, and her heart kicked protestingly and then rushed into a wild rhythm as she looked at him.

"I love you, Anna. When you are here, this house, the house of my ancestors, is complete for me. Wherever I am, when you are there, too, I am home. Stay with me. I don't ask you to give up your art. Anna, I live more than half my time in Europe—we can work it out.

"You already love me a little, I think. You would not look at me with such eyes when I make love with you, if you did not love me a little. Is it not so?"

She bit her lip and gazed at him. "Oh, Gazi!" she whispered.

"Let me finish," he pleaded. "I see you with my sister's child and I know that you are the mother I want for my own children. I know that somehow, you got in that taxi that night because we had to meet, you and I. And we did meet.

"Don't make me let you go. Marry me, and I will make your love grow. If ever a man could make a woman love him, Anna, I know that I can make you love me."

His urgency impelled him to his feet, and he drew her up into his arms. They stood in the nook formed by the ancient arch, against a trellis spread with flowers and thick greenery, his strong arms protectively around her. A delicate perfume drifted down as their bodies made the flowers tremble.

"Gazi," was all she could say, but that word told him everything.

* * * * *

HER DESERT FAMILY

Barbara McMahon

Barbara McMahon was born and raised in the south but settled in California after spending a year flying around the world for an international airline. Settling down to raise a family and work for a computer firm, she began writing when her children started school. Feeling fortunate in being able to realise a long-held dream of quitting her 'day job' and writing full-time, she and her husband recently moved to the Sierra Nevada mountains of California, where she finds her desire to write is stronger than ever. With the beauty of the mountains visible from her windows, and the pace of life slower than the hectic San Francisco Bay Area where they previously resided, she finds more time than ever to think up stories and characters and share them with others through writing. Barbara loves to hear from readers. You can reach her at PO Box 977, Pioneer, CA 95666-0977, USA.

CHAPTER ONE

THE sun shone through the old stained-glass windows casting a rainbow of hues on the polished casket. Bridget Rossi stared at the colors, numb to all feelings. It still hadn't sunk in that her beloved papa was forever gone. At his insistence, she'd brought him home to Italy. This old church was far grander than the one they'd attended in San Francisco. Today it was filled with relatives she hardly knew. And strangers who had known her father as a young man before he'd emigrated to America.

Aunt Donatella sat beside her in the first pew. On the other side of her, Bridget's brother Antonio sat, quiet and solemn. Probably wondering how long before he could return to the States and get back to business.

Behind them, Bridget heard the hushed murmurs as people waited for the start of the service. How slowly the minutes passed.

The sound level rose, changed in pitch. Curious, Bridget turned to look at the back of the church. Francesca always made an entrance, she thought fondly as she saw her older cousin enter the sanctuary with a flourish. One by one everyone in the place turned to stare. Francesca loved it, Bridget knew. Tossing back her dark wavy hair, she sauntered down the center aisle as if she were on a catwalk, modeling

5

the latest in Italian fashion. The chic black dress looked terrific on her. Her style and flare made everyone else look dowdy.

Bridget glanced at her own black suit. It was subdued and somber. With an inward sigh, she scooted closer to Aunt Donatella to make room for her cousin. She would never have the panache Francesca had if she lived to be a hundred.

Francesca and the stranger who accompanied her came straight to the front pew. She waved at family members, blew a kiss at another cousin, turning to murmur something to the tall man standing beside her.

Bridget hadn't met this one yet. Francesca played the field, bringing a new escort to every event she attended. Still, it seemed odd to bring a casual friend to a family funeral.

"Hello, Bridget," Francesca said when she leaned over to hug her, kissing the air near her cheek. The perfume she wore threatened to choke Bridget, but that was Francesca—over the top on most things.

"I'm so glad you could make it," Bridget whispered, clinging for a moment. Francesca was the only relative she felt comfortable with in Italy.

"Of course I made it. He was my uncle. I loved him, too." Francesca greeted her mother and Antonio, then settled in the pew beside Bridget and turned to the man who sat beside her. "Rashid, this is my cousin from America, Bridget Rossi. Bridget, this is His Excellency, Sheikh Rashid al Halzid.

He leaned forward a bit and offered his hand. Bridget took it, surprised by the gesture. Most of

Francesca's men never took notice of anyone else—
they only had eyes for Francesca.

When had her cousin started dating a sheikh? He
was gorgeous, and so far removed from Bridget's
world she was instantly fascinated. Trust her cosmopolitan cousin to captivate such a sexy man.

"My sincere sympathy on the loss of your father,"
he said in English with a charming trace of an accent
which sounded British.

She nodded and withdrew her hand, reminded instantly of where they were and why. He settled back,
looking as out of place in the church as she felt. Who
was this man with his air of authority and what relationship did he have with her beautiful cousin?

Momentarily her grief had been forgotten as a
spark of interest bloomed. She tried to remember if
she'd heard Francesca was seeing anyone special, but
between caring for her father and working, she'd not
had time to keep in close contact with her over the
last few months. No one had mentioned anything in
the two days she'd been in Italy.

The priest entered and the service began.

It seemed like only seconds passed before they
were heading for the cemetery—the final resting place
for her papa, beside his beautiful, and beloved,
Isabella.

When Bridget exited the church walking quietly
beside her older brother, she was surprised to see a
white limousine parked behind the one dark one the
funeral home provided. She glanced around and saw
Francesca clinging to Rashid's arm heading for the
luxury vehicle. She had not had a chance to say more

than a few words to her. She'd hoped they would ride
to the cemetery together, but it looked as if Francesca
had other ideas. Bridget would ride with her aunt and
brother as originally planned.

"Perhaps your cousin would care to join us," Rashid
suggested to Francesca, pausing to look over at
Bridget. "You two have not seen each other for a
while, and I know this is a trying time."

Francesca smiled, trailing one finger along his
cheek. "If she were not already going with her
brother and my mother, that would be fine. But she'll
have to go back with them as we'll be returning directly to the airport. Maybe it would be less confusing
for her to stay with the original plans."

"Perhaps you wish to ride with them. I know you
haven't seen your mother in several months. We have
time enough after the graveside service to return to
the airport. And if not," Rashid said, "we can always
change our departure time. If you wish to visit with
your relatives, please do."

"That would be nice, Rashid," Francesca said.

Rashid believed in the importance of family and
Francesca's young cousin looked pathetically lost at
the moment. Donatella Bianchetti was speaking with
friends who crowded around. The man who had been
introduced as Antonio Rossi was paying no attention
to his sister. She could use some comfort from
Francesca.

He contrasted the two women as Francesca called
to Bridget. Had he not known they were related, he
would never have suspected. Francesca was tall and

model thin. Her glossy dark hair was thick and wavy. Her eyes held mystery and a hint of recklessness that was appealing. They'd been friends for a number of years. He enjoyed her company for as long as she stayed around. But her lifestyle was more flighty than his. After a brief visit, she'd be on her way to another photo shoot, or a modeling venue.

Bridget Rossi, on the other hand, was what the Americans called wholesome. Her dark auburn hair seemed to catch fire in the sun. Her figure could not be described as thin, but it was definitely all woman. Her eyes were red-rimmed and sad from the service. She'd cried several times, as if the wrench of parting with her father was more than she could deal with. But her skin was translucent and delicately tinted, and she carried herself with quiet dignity.

Rashid caught himself. What was he doing, comparing the two women? He was Francesca's friend. There was nothing between them other than friendship. Bridget he'd just met. He knew nothing about her beyond she had just lost her father.

When Francesca asked her to join them on the ride to the cemetery, Bridget jumped at the chance. She loved being with her glamorous cousin. They spent too little time together. Bridget would be returning to America in a couple of days. Who knew how long before Francesca would visit? The ride would give them a chance to catch up.

Bridget understood a haute couture model was in high demand. Francesca had been a much sought after super model in Europe for as long as Bridget could remember. But she still wished her cousin would come back to the States with her for a few weeks. Just until she had gotten used to her papa being gone.

Bridget brushed her fingers beneath her eyes. She'd cried during the service and hoped the mascara she'd put on was as waterproof as claimed. It was bad enough to be the plain woman in the car without looking like a raccoon.

The ride to the old cemetery was short. Bridget sat between Francesca and Rashid listening as her cousin brought her up-to-date on all her activities. Sometimes Bridget knew Francesca elaborated on actual events. Still, her lifestyle was glamorous and exciting, compared to that of a librarian in San Francisco.

Conscious of Rashid beside her, however, she had difficulty concentrating on Francesca's tales. She should be focusing on what Francesca was saying, or on the coming graveside service, not be so consumed with awareness of the stranger beside her.

His aftershave lotion was spicy and reminded her of wide-open spaces. It was not sweet or cloying like some men wore. She looked at his hands resting on his leg-long fingers, neatly manicured nails. What did a sheikh do, she mused. Probably nothing which involved getting calluses on his palms or fingers. From what she'd seen, he was tall and slender, not an ounce of fat anywhere. She sighed softly. She had to watch everything she ate or she'd be as large as a house. Glancing at her cousin, she wished again she could be as slender as Francesca.

The car was far more luxurious than the one the

funeral home had provided. Did Rashid live in
Tuscany? Was that why he had a limousine handy?
Not only did his clothing reflect his wealth, but his
air of command, the arrogance that surrounded him,
told the world he was a man to be reckoned with. He
was used to getting his way instantly, she suspected.
Of course, sheikhs probably had half a country at their
beck and call. How had he and Francesca met?

"Have you and Francesca known each other for
long?" she asked when Francesca made mention of
Rashid accompanying her today to the funeral. Maybe
small talk would help her deal with the rest of the
day. He'd been kind enough to offer her a ride. He
must expect some curiosity.

"We met a couple of years ago," he said.

"Do you live here in Italy?" His English was much
better than her other cousins. And he had not tried to
speak Italian with her, which was a definite plus in
his favor. Her Italian was poor at best, and when surrounded by this branch of her family who spoke a
hundred miles a minute, she felt lost and awkward.
The patience her father had always shown was missing from her aunt and uncles. And her cousins ignored
her, except for Francesca, or laughed at her attempts
to speak Italian.

Not that she would be long in Italy. Once this sad
task was accomplished, she would return home. To
the loneliness that awaited with her papa no longer
there.

Francesca laughed. "No. Contrary to what my family thinks, Tuscany is not the center of the universe.
Rashid lives in Aboul Sari. He's the youngest son of

the ruling sheikh,'' Francesca said. ''He kindly flew me here today to attend the funeral. I received the news at his home, where we were vacationing.''

''Oh, I didn't know. I thought you were at a shoot or something.'' Bridget looked at her. Francesca seemed relaxed, not annoyed to have her vacation interrupted. Of course her papa couldn't help dying while Francesca was on vacation, but would she have come if he had been buried in San Francisco, as Bridget had wanted?

''I'm taking a few weeks off from work. I can use the rest. Rashid has this fabulous home and some friends over from England. We've all been having a fabulous time.'' Did Francesca's tone convey more than a vacation?

Bridget felt like a fifth wheel. She should have ridden with Aunt Donatella and Antonio. She would definitely return with her aunt and let Francesca and her sheikh return to his wonderful home and not be jealous that she herself would be returning to her flat in San Francisco, and taking up her life again without her beloved papa in it.

The simple service at the grave site was brief and moving. As she turned away for the last time, Bridget caught a glimpse of the tombstone for Isabella Rossi, her father's first wife and Antonio's mother. Her papa had his wish; he was buried by his precious Isabella. Not by Bridget's mother where Bridget thought he should have been. He and her mother had been married far longer than he'd been to Isabella. But he'd been so insistent at the end, she'd acquiesced.

Poor Mama, she thought. Even in death, Papa wasn't hers.

Bridget continued along the pathway, conscious of Rashid following closely.

Francesca had stopped to speak with one of their other cousins. She knew them all so well, having been brought up with them in the family enclave.

"What will you do now?" Rashid asked as Bridget stopped near the car that had brought her aunt.

"Return home. There is nothing for me here," she said gazing around at the peaceful cemetery. The old lichen-covered tombstones and monuments were so unlike the neat pristine headstones where her mother was buried. This cemetery was far older, and much farther from home.

"Yet you brought your father here."

"He insisted. He knew he was dying and made us promise to bring him back to the place he'd been born." She was trying to imprint the setting on her mind. She wouldn't be this way again any time soon. Another regret. She could have visited his grave as often as she did her mother's had he been buried in California.

"You would rather have buried him in San Francisco," Rashid stated quietly.

"My mother is buried there. She was his wife, too." Bridget couldn't keep the hurt from her voice.

He looked back at the grave site, read the stone beside the coffin.

"Isabella was his first wife?"

"Yes, she was Antonio's mother. Molly O'Brien was mine. Hired to take care of his baby son when his beautiful Isabella died. Later they married, and had me.'' Bridget had heard the story all her life. On the surface it sounded so romantic. But her papa had never loved her mother, and Mama had known it. How hard had that been? To live with a man who loved a woman long dead?

''Do you work in San Francisco?'' Rashid asked, leaning against the limo, studying Bridget with dark eyes that seemed to see beyond what others saw.

She looked away, disturbed by the emotions he brought out in her. ''I'm a librarian at a branch in the Sunset district. I have a small flat nearby.''

''You did not live with your father, then.''

She shook her head. ''Maybe I should have. I wonder if I would have known he was sick before he admitted it. Maybe I could have done something.''

''Most likely not.''

She looked at him. ''What would you know about it?''

''What do you think you could have done?''

''I don't know, taken him to the doctor sooner or something.'' She looked into his dark eyes again, and felt the world tilt slightly. Rashid's broad shoulders, dark hair and eyes, made a perfect foil for Francesca. Together they made a striking couple, both gorgeous and self-assured.

Had he and Francesca spent hours at the beach or beside a pool *vacationing* together? What else had they been doing that her summons interrupted?

For a moment, a pang of envy hit Bridget. She'd love to have some wonderful, sexy man sweep her away to some hidden hideaway and make wild passionate love day and night. She'd always thought she'd like to see the south seas. But a bower on the Mediterranean could be just as romantic.

"Has it been suggested that earlier care would have saved his life?" Rashid asked.

It took Bridget a moment to reply. The fantasy of sunbathing at the sea vanished. She shook her head. "No, but I still worry I should have done something."

"What does your brother think?"

"That nothing could have been done."

"Your father was older than most of a woman your age," he commented.

"He was over forty when Antonio was born. Even older when I came along. He immigrated to California as a young man, and had to make his way in the world before he could start his family. He built one of the finest restaurants in Little Italy, near Columbus Street. And another one near the Wharf. When he had money enough, he returned home to find a bride. His beautiful Isabella was fifteen years younger, but such a love they had."

Rashid's eyes held a hint of sardonic amusement. "Or so the story goes. You sound as if you've heard that before," he said.

She nodded. "He spoke often of his beautiful Isabella—especially after my mother died. I guess he didn't think I'd mind, but I wish he'd loved my mother as much."

Francesca looked up, spotting her with Rashid. She waved and began heading their way, only to be stopped by another small group of friends.

"I'm sure their marriage was satisfactory for both.

Not everyone marries for love as you westerners think,'' Rashid said.

"You don't believe in marrying for love?" Bridget knew she read too many romance novels, but to her the greatest bond in life was love. She had loved her father and mother. She adored her older brother and her cousin. Close friends also were loved. How much more love would she and her husband share, once she found the right man?

"There are many reasons for marriage. Love is fleeting. Or nonexistent. Strong foundations can be built on other grounds."

"Like what?" She couldn't believe she was debating love and marriage at the edge of a cemetery with this sheikh. She'd just met the man! She would probably never see him again after today—unless he and Francesca were serious about each other. Did Francesca know he held such cynical views of love?

"Arranged marriages have been the norm in my country for generations. Dynastic reasons are strong bonds. Merging families for financial reasons insures the continuation of many bloodlines."

Bridget looked at Francesca. Maybe she'd misread the situation. Maybe this was no different from any other fleeting relationship her cousin had had over the years. She couldn't imagine her settling for less than passionate, brilliant love.

"So you are not looking for marriage anytime soon?" Bridget said, trying to understand the relationship.

"I have been married."

She looked at him in surprise. "You have? What happened?"

"She died."

"Oh." Bridget didn't know what to say. He certainly didn't seem particularly sad about the fact. Yet she didn't know him at all, so how could she gauge his feelings?

"I'm sorry," she said.

"As was I. Fatima was a beautiful woman. Accomplished. And a delight to be with. I still miss her."

She wasn't surprised to hear that. Rashid was extremely handsome and obviously liked to be with beautiful women. How sad he and his wife didn't get to share their lives together for more years than they had had.

"I'll get a ride back with Aunt Donatella. Francesca said you needed to get to the airport," Bridget said after a moment. The sooner she got away from Rashid, the better for her equilibrium. He was like a movie star, someone to dream about, but as far out of her experience as the landing on the moon. That hint of awareness that plagued her was probably due to heightened emotions because of the funeral. Tomorrow she'd laugh at the notion of being attracted to her cousin's friend.

She had to pack and get ready for her own flight home later tonight. She didn't need to know more about Rashid. If his and Francesca's friendship developed into something more, she'd learn about it in due time. And if not—

"You would be welcome to come stay with your

cousin. I know you both grieve for the loss of your father. She spoke fondly of him on the ride here. Maybe a week or two in a new location would help ease the transition. Give you some breathing space before you return to life without your father in it," Rashid said.

She was struck by his insight. She had been dreading the return to San Francisco, to her flat only a few blocks from the home her father had lived in. There was so much to do with packing up his things, deciding whether to live in the family home or sell it. Her father had left it to her, and left the businesses to Antonio.

She had to learn to move on without her papa's comforting presence in the background.

Had Rashid felt the same kind of loss when his beautiful wife had died?

Bridget looked at her cousin. She'd love to spend a couple of weeks with Francesca. She couldn't remember the last time they'd spent more than two or three days together. Francesca rarely came to San Francisco. Her work was in Italy and other European countries; Bridget's was in California. The one time they'd tried to vacation together in Europe, Francesca had been offered a fabulous opportunity and took it to keep her name in the forefront of the fashion industry. Bridget had spent her week's vacation alone.

"I would not wish to impose," she said, yearning to accept.

"There are currently four other guests at the house, not counting my grandmother and my son who lives with me. One more would not be an imposition.

Everyone will be visiting for another couple of weeks, so it may seem hectic. But come and spend time with your cousin.'' There was a hint of imperialistic command.

''You are very generous to a stranger you just met,'' she said, longing with everything in her to accept. But still she hesitated.

''Maybe I do it for Francesca. Don't you think she'd worry about you alone in San Francisco? How can she enjoy her visit if she has to fret about you?''

''I'm not exactly alone. I have my brother, my friends.'' But his explanation gave her a reason to accept. ''Still, it would be wonderful not to return to San Francisco immediately.''

''Come, visit me.''

''Thank you. I would not wish to have my cousin fret.'' She wasn't sure, but she thought she saw sardonic amusement again in his eyes. But he looked away quickly, maybe she'd just imagined it.

A weight seemed to lift from Bridget's shoulders. She could postpone dealing with the reality of her father's death for a little while longer. Maybe it would be easier in a week or two. And she did have the time from her job.

''We will go with you while you pack,'' he said.

''Won't you miss your flight? I can make arrangements to follow later.''

''I'm piloting the plane. We leave when I leave.''

He snapped his fingers and a man standing beside his limousine hurried over. Rashid spoke to him rapidly in his language. When finished, the man bowed and hurried away.

Bridget listened bemused. She'd never known anyone who traveled by his own private plane, or piloted it himself. Or one who could summon anyone by a mere snap of the fingers. How cool. She had a feeling spending time with a sheikh would be unlike anything she'd ever experienced before. She'd have to make sure she took note of every delightful surprise so she could tell her friends when she returned home.

Francesca was enough of a star to give them endless hours of conversation whenever her friends asked Bridget what her cousin was doing. Now this. Who would ever believe plain Bridget Rossi was going to vacation at the palace of a sheikh?

Francesca bade farewell to the crowd surrounding her and sauntered down the path toward Rashid. Bridget watched her, wishing she had the knack to look so at ease in whatever circumstances she found herself. Wishing she could look sexy and sultry and fascinatingly interesting. Instead she was shy and self-conscious in unfamiliar settings and situations, though years of acting as her father's hostess had taught her ways to cover some of her uncertainty at social events. Even if she grew more confident as she aged, she'd never be as pretty as her cousin. Bridget had inherited her mother's Irish looks, dark auburn hair, fair skin with freckles scattered across her nose. Her blue eyes were boring, never as exotic as Francesca's.

"I'm sorry if I kept you waiting, darlings," her cousin said when she joined them. "Family duties, you know. I'm ready to leave now."

"I've invited your cousin to join us," he said smoothly.

"What?" Francesca looked at Bridget, then back to Rashid. "I'm surprised."

"I thought it would offer her time to come to terms with the change in her family. To give her a chance to spend time with her favorite cousin," he said. "Do you have a problem with my invitation?"

"Not at all. Thank you, Rashid. It's wonderful. We'll be able to talk all night and really visit. I'd never presume to invite her to your home, but since you were so thoughtful, I say terrific!" She gave him a quick kiss on the cheek.

"We'll run by your mother's so your cousin can pack and then we'll be off," he said.

Francesca glanced at her watch, "But our flight plan…"

"I've already changed it."

"I can always stay here," Bridget offered, uncertain once again about what she was doing.

"It would be my honor to have you visit my home," Rashid said gravely.

Bridget blinked. Put that way, how could she refuse?

The driver of the white limousine quickly whisked them to Aunt Donatella's home where Bridget made short work of packing. She had brought very little for her brief stay. Her aunt returned before she finished, so there was no wait to exchange farewells. Her aunt seemed to think time with Francesca would be just the thing for Bridget, though she was reluctant to have her leave.

"Come anytime," Donatella urged with one last

hug. But Bridget wasn't sure she'd visit again. It was
so different without her papa.

She'd never been close to the Italian side of her
family except for Francesca. The few trips made over
the years had primarily been to accompany her father
on his visits to his brothers and sisters. Once Bridget
left home for college at eighteen, she'd stopped making the annual trips to Italy.

She should have tried harder to connect. Her
mother had been an orphan, so she had no family on
that side. Aunt Donatella had been kind but she just
didn't relate to her that well. Bridget sighed softly for
what she couldn't change.

Everything moved swiftly until they were airborne.
She had a seat near the back of the small jet, with an
unobstructed view as they soared over the hills of
Tuscany and the Italian coast before turning to head
south.

Once over the deep blue Mediterranean Sea,
Bridget grew restless staring at the endless expanse
of water. She looked at the other occupants in the
small jet. Rashid and Francesca were in the cockpit.
Her cousin was laughing at something the man said,
touching his arm flirtatiously. Bridget envied her
cousin's ease in dealing with everyone, and wished
she wasn't so shy, so uncertain.

The two solemn-faced men sitting across the aisle
from her remained silent. Bodyguards, she suspected.
Or servants of some kind. She hadn't forgotten how
quickly one of them had responded to Rashid's summons.

Her gaze again moved to Rashid. She'd love to

have an opportunity to sit in the front of the plane and watch as he piloted the craft. Anytime he wanted to go anywhere, he just filed a flight plan and took off as easily as she climbed into her car at home and drove away.

Was her cousin serious about this man? Francesca had never talked about getting married and having a family. Had that changed when she turned thirty? The work span of a model was limited. There were always younger women coming up through the ranks. Not that any of them were as beautiful as her cousin, Bridget thought loyally. But she wondered if Francesca worried about the future. Maybe she was planning to marry and leave her career at its peak.

She herself would like to find a man to love and marry. However, she did not plan to jump into anything just because her father had died and she felt more vulnerable than in the past. But she was already twenty-six, and not growing any younger.

Would she feel so vulnerable if she were Francesca? With such a fabulous career, she enjoyed everything—lovely designer clothes, an apartment in Rome and a flat on the Amalfi Coast. Hobnobbing with the jet set in Europe, and even a brief brush with fame in the United States. It would be hard to leave all that.

Bridget closed her eyes. She was tired, sad and feeling lost. Maybe she'd find renewed energy and determination visiting Rashid's country, she thought as she drifted off to sleep. Getting to know her cousin's friend should also prove interesting. And maybe dangerous to her equilibrium if that flare of awareness didn't dissipate by morning.

CHAPTER TWO

BRIDGET woke when the plane touched down. She felt too groggy and disoriented from so little sleep to be refreshed. When she checked her watch, she saw it was half past six. They would be eating dinner before too long. Then maybe she could escape to bed.

In the flurry of deplaning, and accounting for luggage and the carry-all her cousin had brought, Bridget soon found herself in a car with one of the bodyguards. Rashid had driven his two-seater sports car and her cousin rode beside him.

It seemed they roared along the highway at excessive speeds, but maybe she was imagining things. When they turned onto the private driveway, large wrought-iron gates barred the way. Rashid spoke into a small box and the gates swung wide. He zipped up the driveway, Bridget's car following more slowly. Bridget leaned forward to better see his home.

The asphalt wound around fountains, ponds and lovely old trees. She caught a glimpse of a building from time to time, but the landscaping was so lush and thick, she could only see a small segment at a time. Until they rounded the last curve and the villa stood before them.

Colorful blossoms of hibiscus and oleander crowded this part of the long driveway, providing a perfect frame for the wide veranda that encircled the bottom floor of the lovely structure. The white walls reflected the late-afternoon sun so brightly, Bridget fumbled for her dark glasses. The building looked almost too feminine for Rashid's strong masculinity, with the graceful lines and wide windows opened to the early-evening breeze.

She would have pictured him in glass and steel, or a high-rise soaring over the neighborhood.

The man sharing the back seat with Bridget opened the door and assisted her from the car.

Francesca was already heading for the opened front door, but Rashid remained beside the sports car, waiting for Bridget. He watched as she gazed around, her pleasure clearly evident. She studied each bank of flowers, raised her eyes to admire the old trees, and then the gentle sweep of walks that led to the center fountain.

"This is lovely," she said as she joined him.

He looked around absorbing what she saw instead of taking the gardens and grounds for granted. His staff had done an excellent job.

"I'm pleased you like it," he said formally. Looking at her, he gestured toward the house. "I told Francesca I'd see to getting you settled. You look tired. Would you care to skip dinner and go straight to bed?"

"Oh, no, thank you. I had a nice nap in the plane." She couldn't show up and immediately take to her room.

"We'll do a quick introduction to those who are around when we go inside and then I'll show you to your room so you can freshen up for dinner. We do not dress up unless it's a formal occasion.''

There were a couple of people about when they entered. Rashid introduced Bridget to Jack Dalton. Jack was a dedicated sportsman and long time polo player. He immediately tried to engage her in conversation about polo. Rashid could tell Bridget knew next to nothing about the sport as she nodded, trying to look interested. He rescued her from his friend's passion and found Marie Joulais nearby.

Marie greeted Bridget warmly when she was introduced and motioned at Jack, laughing. ''Stay out of his way tonight unless you want more of the same. Tomorrow is time enough for him to bore you to death about polo. He and Rashid are avid players. But he promised me a quick swim before dinner. I think we just have time.''

''Then we will see you at eight,'' Rashid said, grateful for her taking care of Jack. He enjoyed the man's company—they'd been friends from school days—but too much of Jack at any one time could overwhelm anyone.

Rashid slipped his hand beneath Bridget's elbow and guided her toward the wide curving stairs that seemed almost suspended in midair. ''Come, I'll make sure you get to your room.''

An older woman, attired in black, stood near the stairs. She spoke to Rashid, then bowed and turned.

''My housekeeper, Marsella, would have shown you, but I will have the honor today,'' he said as explanation.

Normally he let his housekeeper see to his guests'

needs. She'd been trained in his father's home and was excellent. But for some reason, he wanted to take Bridget up himself. She seemed lost and sad, which unexpectedly brought feelings of protection to the forefront.

Her arm was soft and warm. He didn't want to let go when they reached the stairs. The reluctance caught him by surprise. She was a guest in his house, no more.

He snapped orders to the man carrying Bridget's bag, and then to a maid standing near the top of the stairs. She scurried away down the wide hall. The sooner he had his guest safely ensconced in her room, the better. Perhaps he should have let Marsella take charge.

The room he escorted her to was done in pale yellow, the gauzy curtains at the windows billowing in the breeze. The rich carpet on the floor gave comfort to tired feet. The bed was huge, and high, with three steps on one side. Without them, he doubted she could reach the mattress without a running start.

Fatima had decorated their home. She'd had excellent taste and he had not found a need to change a thing since her death. Would Bridget like it?

"It's beautiful," she said as she surveyed the room.

"We gather in the solarium at eight for drinks. It's cutting it a little short I know, but we'll eat at eight-thirty and I think you could use some nourishment. It was a long and stressful day." He bowed slightly and left her alone in the lavish room.

His own quarters were in the opposite direction. As he headed there to freshen up, he wondered if Bridget would benefit from visiting, or whether it would prove too much on top of the strain of her father's illness and death. He hoped she would find comfort in Francesca's company. Maybe he could find some activities that would enable her to enjoy herself, while not being in the center of the hectic pace his other guests enjoyed.

Once again he found himself comparing the two cousins. Francesca was beautiful, polished. She conversed easily with statesmen and financiers. Bridget seemed shy and almost lost. He'd make it a point to spend some time with Bridget over the next few days to see if he could erase some of the sadness from her eyes.

Once the door closed behind Rashid, Bridget dismissed the maid and went to her suitcase where it had been placed on a rack and began to take the clothing out. She had not planned to stay anywhere but at her aunt's for a few days, so her variety of attire was limited.

She hung up the few dresses and pants she'd brought with her. Nothing she had was suitable for vacationing with a sheikh. Maybe she should return home.

Or ask for the nearest clothing store.

She smiled to herself. A much better suggestion. Would Francesca like to go shopping with her and suggest what she buy? With her cousin's flair for style, Bridget would come out way ahead.

She took a quick shower and donned a simple navy-blue dress. Brushing her hair back, she tied it with a matching bow. It was the best she could do—

her eyes were still a little puffy from crying. She didn't like the sadness that seemed reflected there. Still, she wasn't out to impress anyone, just to recover a bit from her papa's death.

She started down the long hall wondering where the solarium was. If she'd been faster taking her shower, she might have met one of the other guests in the hall and could have gone with them. Or found Francesca. Now it was after eight. She was late, and lost.

She found the stairs easily. Bridget was surprised to see a small boy sitting on the top step, playing with a toy car.

"Hello," she said. Not that he would understand her, she didn't speak any Arabic.

"Hello." The boy responded and looked up at her. He said something rapidly which Bridget didn't understand.

"Sorry, do you speak English?"

"Yes. I speak French, too. *Parlez-vous Francais?*"

He didn't look old enough to speak three languages, she was impressed.

"No, I speak English and a bit of Italian." Bridget sat beside him on the top step. "I'm Bridget Rossi. I've come for a visit. Who are you?"

"I'm Mo. Mohammedan al Halzid. I live here."

"I think it was your father who invited me to visit."

"Is he home?"

The hopeful look in his eyes tugged at her heart. Bridget wanted to hug him tightly and send him off to find his father. But she didn't know where Rashid was at the moment. Most likely with the other guests in the solarium. Would this child know the way?

"He is home. I'm to join him and his other guests in the solarium. Do you know where it is? Maybe you can show me the way." Would Francesca come to look for her, wondering where she was? Or one of Rashid's servants?

He shook his head. "Little boys aren't allowed to bother his guests." He sighed a little and looked at his car.

"Maybe we can sneak down and find him without bothering the other guests," Bridget suggested. Her heart went out to the child. He looked so lonely. She knew how that felt. Surely his father didn't put guests before the well-being of his son?

For a moment Mo's eyes lit up. Then he shook his head. "I don't think I should."

"Well, I can tell your father you are hoping to see him before dinner. Would that work?"

He seemed to consider the situation before nodding gravely.

"How old are you?" she asked, captivated. What a darling child with his dark solemn eyes and long lashes. His black hair was short and shone beneath the light. Rashid was a lucky man.

"I'm five."

"Five and you already speak three languages? That's pretty impressive."

He nodded, looking proud.

"Good for you." Just then Bridget heard voices from the lower level. Rashid and one of his men walked into the foyer and headed toward the salon she'd seen earlier. He paused and looked up, surprised to see the two of them on the stairs. He said something to the other man and then climbed the stairs.

"What have we here?"

Mo launched into a rapid explanation in Arabic and launched himself at his father. For a split second, Bridget wished she could have done the same thing. The thought shocked her. Slowly she rose and smiled politely at the two. Rashid easily lifted the boy and held him in one arm, Mo flinging his arms around his father's neck.

"He wanted to see you before dinner," she said. "I wasn't sure of the way to the solarium, so I thought Mo could show me. But he said he wasn't allowed to bother the guests, so we were discussing the situation."

The two looked at her. Bridget saw the resemblance instantly. Even if she hadn't known Mo was Rashid's son, seeing them together would confirm it.

"You should be with Alaya," Rashid told Mo in English.

"I'm so impressed he speaks English," Bridget said.

"I have many friends who speak English, so better he learns it at an early age. He speaks French, as well. But he knows he's not to bother my guests."

"He wasn't bothering me. He just wanted to see you before he went to bed. It was nice to meet you, Mo. I expect I'll see you tomorrow?" Bridget said.

Rashid narrowed his eyes. "He usually doesn't associate with my visitors."

"Oh, sorry. I didn't realize that was off-limits."

"It's not. Usually the adults who visit don't come to spend time with a small child."

"I love children. I always wished I'd had lots of brothers and sisters. Antonio is several years older, and our interests don't mesh. Sometimes while growing up it felt as if I was an only child."

"I'm a only child," Mo said from his father's arms.

"And do you like that?" Bridget smiled at him.

"No, I want a brother. My dad has two brothers but I don't have any."

"Enough of that. Time for bed." Rashid and Mo started down the hall in the opposite direction from Bridget's room. He hesitated a moment when his son whispered in his ear. Then he turned. "Do you wish to see Mo's room?" he asked.

"I'd love to." She would be happy to see the little boy's room. It also would give her extra minutes before she had to face the room full of Rashid's guests. She hoped they all spoke English. As far as she knew, Francesca only spoke English and Italian. So if she fit in, Bridget would, too. At least in the language department. She wasn't so sure about the rest. She didn't normally number sheikhs among her acquaintances.

Mo's room was large, as were all the rooms in the villa. A nervous young woman quickly scolded Mo and apologized to Rashid. Bridget suspected it wasn't the first time the child had escaped her watch.

Rashid spoke quickly to her in obvious dismissal. She turned and left.

He set Mo on his feet. "Next time you run off

without telling her, Alaya will get into trouble for letting you out of her sight. You don't want that, do you?'' Rashid said.

Mo shook his head. ''But I wanted to see you.''

''Show Miss Rossi your room and then you have to get ready for bed.''

Mo came and reached out his hand for Bridget's. She was charmed and clasped his small hand as he led her around the room pointing out toys, books, and games. Wistfully he looked back at his father. ''Do you play games?'' he asked Bridget.

''I do. Maybe you and I can play one tomorrow. Or I can read you a book. I see you have several in English,'' she said, spotting familiar covers.

He nodded, excitement gleaming. ''I like the English books. Tomorrow, promise?''

''Mo.'' Rashid said in a warning tone. He would not have his son badger a guest.

''If it's all right with your father, I would love to read to you. But I need to fit in with his plans first.'' She faced Rashid. ''It would be a pleasure.''

''You are here to rest after your loss, not baby-sit my son,'' he said stiffly. Truth to tell, not one of his guests even wished to see his son. Rashid was proud of Mo, but knew a child's place was not with adults.

Soon the boy would be old enough to attend boarding school. Rashid remembered leaving home at seven, and all the years in England and France he spent studying. He wanted to hold on to his son a little longer. Mo seemed much too young to be sent away in two years time.

''If I volunteer, it's okay. Shouldn't I be allowed

to do what brings me happiness if I'm to get over Papa's death?'' Bridget broke into his thoughts.

''And reading to a small boy you just met would do that?'' Skepticism rang in his voice. Was she trying to impress him? he wondered cynically.

''I love assisting the children's librarian at work when she needs help at story book hour. Unless you don't wish for me to read to him?''

Rashid studied them both for a moment. ''It would be unusual, but acceptable.'' What game was she playing? For a moment he wondered if she planned some sort of campaign to show him what a doting mother she could be to his small son. Only, she seemed much more interested in Mo than in him at the moment.

His father would say he had a swelled head, thinking women fawned over him. When they did, he knew it was for his position and wealth, more than anything else. He hoped Bridget wasn't one of those.

She smiled at Mo. ''I'll come by in the morning, shall I? We can read some stories and then maybe play a game or two.''

''Yes. Come early.''

''After breakfast,'' she said gently.

He nodded and flung his arms around her. ''Thank you,'' he said.

Rashid was surprised. Mo was not usually demonstrative.

Bridget hugged him back and then walked quickly to the door, ''Until tomorrow then. Good night.''

''Good night,'' Mo said.

Rashid rested his hand on his son's head for a mo-

ment. "Go to sleep when Alaya says it's time. I'll
see you tomorrow as well."

Rashid opened the door for Bridget, and called
Alaya back into the room.

"Allow me to show you to the solarium," he said
after he bade his son good night.

"I would appreciate it. Do you normally give
guests a road map? This place is huge," she asked
lightly.

"My apologies, I had thought Francesca would
show you the way."

"Maybe she stopped by. I took a shower, and took
longer dressing than I planned. That's why I'm late."

He deliberately blocked the image of Bridget Rossi
in the shower, water streaming down her womanly
body, her hair darkened with the spray. The freckles
would stand out against her pale skin. Did she have
them elsewhere, or only that enchanting dusting
across her nose?

"You won't have time for a cocktail," he said,
reining in his thoughts.

"That's not a problem. I hope I haven't held up
the rest of your guests."

"I'm sure they started without us." Since they
were for the most part longtime friends who had the
run of the house when they visited, Rashid wasn't
concerned.

The solarium was at the end of the house, beyond the
grand salon. It seemed full of people when Bridget
and Rashid first stepped in. She looked quickly for
Francesca, spotting her with a tall, gangly man who

looked totally bemused. There seemed to be more than the half a dozen Rashid said were staying with him.

"There you are, darlings," Francesca said, advancing on them, ignoring the young man left standing midsentence.

"I didn't know the way," Bridget said brightly. "Luckily I ran into Rashid on the stairs."

"And why are you so late?" Francesca asked Rashid. "It's almost time for dinner."

"Business."

"What else? Honestly, you are on vacation, let someone else handle things," she said, smiling. "We have to work on your tendency to put duty before everything else."

"What would you have me do, ignore it?" he asked.

"There's a time and a place for everything."

Bridget smiled, remembering the time they'd been on vacation and Francesca had left in a heartbeat when a coveted assignment had appeared.

Just then a chime sounded.

"Charles, would you escort Francesca in?" Rashid called to the young man Francesca had been talking with.

"I wish to introduce Bridget to my grandmother before dinner. We will join you momentarily." He slipped from beneath her grasp and cupped Bridget's elbow. "Come."

The other guests smiled and called greetings as Rashid led Bridget to a chair near the side of the solarium. An elderly woman dressed in black sat in solitary splendor. She was gazing tranquilly over the blossoms now visible beneath artificial lighting in the garden.

"Grandmother, may I present my guest, Bridget Rossi? Bridget, my mother's mother Salina al Besoud."

The woman smiled at her grandson then looked sharply at Bridget. "Rossi? Related to Francesca?"

"She's my cousin."

"Hmm."

Bridget blinked. Usually people told her how lucky she was to have such a beautiful cousin. She wasn't sure how to respond.

"It's nice to meet you," she said politely.

"How long are you here for?" The older woman rose as she said it, and reached for the arm Rashid held for her.

"As long as she likes. Bridget just buried her father. I thought visiting with her cousin would help the transition before she returns home to San Francisco," he replied before Bridget could.

"Ah, you are from America. Tell me about your home. Is it true San Francisco is always bathed in sunshine?" Madame Besoud asked.

Arriving at the dining room, Bridget was seated next to Salina al Besoud with Francesca on her right.

Rashid made the introductions. Bridget greeted Jack and Marie almost as old friends. Charles Porter gave her a brief greeting. Elizabeth Wainswright, sitting opposite Francesca, seemed very unhappy and barely nodded. Everyone spoke English for which Bridget was grateful.

"Jack and Charles and I were in school together in England. We still get together every chance we get," Rashid explained.

As the dinner progressed, however, it became clear that though they all spoke the same language, Bridget had nothing else in common with the other guests. She listened as Francesca held court with her delightful stories about the world of haute couture. Elizabeth spoke briefly about plans to visit Paris after she left Aboul Sari.

Jack broke in with talk about polo matches. At which point he challenged the gentlemen to a match while they visited so the other guests could see Rashid in action.

"You are quiet," Rashid's grandmother said to Bridget as the meal wound down.

She smiled. "I have nothing to contribute."

The older woman studied her for a moment then looked down the length of the table. "Neither does anyone else. I do believe they talk only to hear themselves."

Bridget stifled a giggle. Some of the inanities Jack spouted could be thought that. Charles had said little, gazing like a love-struck gazelle at Francesca.

Bridget smiled when the agreement made to play a polo match before the guests departed was struck. She would love to see a match, and wondered if there were somewhere she could get a book on the intricacies of the game.

"Do you follow polo?" Rashid's grandmother asked.

"No, I've never seen it played but it sounds exciting."

"What do you do with your time?"

"I'm a librarian in San Francisco."

"What happened to your father?"

Bridget spent a few moments quietly telling Madame al Besoud about her father's death and burial. How Rashid had come to the funeral with Francesca and ended up inviting her to his home. When she came to the part about reading to Mo the next day, the woman evidenced surprise. The first emotion Bridget had seen her display.

"Perhaps you could read to me as well," the woman said. "I speak English but reading it is more difficult. A friend sent me a book, I should like to write back to tell her that I enjoyed it."

"I would be happy to. What book?"

"*Four Hole Swamp*. It's a murder mystery. My friend loves them, but I don't always understand why."

"I've heard of that book. It's supposed to be very good. I should like to read it with you."

"Come to my apartment after lunch tomorrow. Unless you need to lie down then."

"No, I don't." Bridget smiled at the idea of taking a nap every day. She was too busy at work and taking care of her father. Suddenly she remembered. She would never have that task again.

Rashid's grandmother reached out and patted her hand. "The grief gets easier with time."

Bridget blinked back tears. "I know. My mother died a few years ago. I still miss her, but it does get easier. But I've always had Papa, and to know I'll never hear his laugh, or feel his arms tight in a hug is almost more than I can bear.''

''I still miss my father and he died thirty years ago,'' Salina al Besoud said softly. ''But now I have happy memories that bring me comfort. Think of the happy times.''

Dinner ended with the house party returning to the solarium. Soft music played. A table had been set up for cards. Bridget paused in the doorway and sought Rashid. She was too tired to stay and hoped he didn't think she was being rude by retiring early.

She saw her cousin and crossed the wide room.

''I'm going to go to bed,'' she said softly. ''Do you think Rashid will think I'm rude to cut out early?''

''Not at all. Sleep well. Tomorrow we'll catch up on all our news.''

Rashid came up to them. ''Thinking of retiring?'' he asked.

She nodded, suddenly feeling awkward. No one else seemed ready to leave. She hoped he would put it down to grief and not a longing to be by herself for a while, though she needed the time alone.

''Sleep well, then, Bridget. And thank you for your kindness to my son.''

''What kindness?'' Francesca asked. ''When did you meet his son?''

''Earlier. It's really nothing. I'm going to read him a book in the morning,'' Bridget said.

''Well we plan to spend most of the day by the

pool. Come out to swim as soon as you can,'' Francesca said with a hug for her cousin. "A little sunshine will put roses in your cheeks.''

Bridget had started up the stairs when Rashid called to her.

She turned. "Yes?'' He'd followed her from the solarium.

"My grandmother told me of your offer to read to her. I didn't invite you here to entertain my family.'' He looked irritated.

"It's no problem. I love children and would like to spend some time with Mo. And your grandmother has a book we both would like to read, so why not together? Besides, it'll keep me from thinking about things. I do have to get on with life.''

"Wouldn't you rather spend the day by the pool with Francesca? And the others?''

"Not all day. Good grief, I'd look like a boiled lobster with my skin. Francesca tans beautifully, I burn and peel. Besides, I didn't bring a swimsuit. I didn't know I'd need one when I left home.''

"We have swimsuits in the changing room by the pool, as well as sunscreen and umbrellas,'' he said.

Standing just below her on the stairs their eyes were level. Bridget found herself mesmerized by her host. Her heart raced, her mind went numb.

"I'll be sure to check it out, then. And use both the sunscreen and umbrella,'' she said softly. What would he do if she leaned across the inches separating them and kissed him?

What would she do if she lost her mind enough to try?

Turning she almost scampered up the stairs before she made an idiot of herself with a man she'd just met that morning.

Rashid watched her hurry up the stairs and head down the corridor to her room. His hand tightened on the banister to keep himself from following her. To make sure she had everything she needed.

To see if he'd just imagined the spark of awareness that threatened to burst into flames when he stood near her.

CHAPTER THREE

RASHID entered Mo's room the next day midmorning, startled to find it empty. He called for Alaya.

"Sir?" She appeared in the door from the adjoining room.

"Where is Mo?"

"Miss took him to the gardens. They were going to read books in English," she said. "Should I have told them not to?" She looked worried.

"Where in the gardens?"

"I don't know. I told them to be back in time for lunch."

He nodded once, curtly, and left. Alaya followed him into the hall. "Shall I go find them?"

"I'll look for them myself."

Rashid had no idea where they'd be, but they couldn't have gone far. Mo was a little boy and Bridget didn't know the grounds. Ten minutes later, he was baffled. He hadn't found them anywhere.

He even swung by the pool area to see if they'd gone there. Marie and Francesca were lying on chaise longues, but there was no sign of his son or Bridget.

He was about to concede defeat and call in help from the gardeners when he heard Mo's laugh. Following the sound, he found them both up a tree!

Fists at his waist, he gazed up into the wide branches of an old cedar. Snuggled together on a wide, sturdy branch near the trunk, Bridget and Mo were laughing at a picture in a book balanced on her lap.

"What are you doing up there?" he asked.

Mo peered down. "Hello, Father. Bridget and I went exploring and found this perfect hide way."

"Hideaway," she corrected. She peeped through the leaves. "He's safe. I wouldn't let him fall. We're not really that high."

"And you couldn't have read the story just as easily sitting on a bench?"

"Where's your sense of adventure? Wouldn't you've rather been in a tree than on a bench when you were five?"

He stared at her. What had he been doing when he was five? Certainly not climbing trees. He'd had a tutor and was cooped up inside learning his letters and numbers.

"Maybe you're right. Can you two get down? It's almost time for lunch."

"We may need some help," she confessed, looking at the stack of books beside her. "How about I drop the books down to you and then help Mo climb down?"

"Fine."

He easily caught the storybooks she tossed down, placing them beside him. Reaching up, he lifted his son down and put him on the ground next to the books. "You pick them up and carry them to the house," he instructed.

Turning back, Rashid reached up to help Bridget descend.

She landed in a flurry, her hands on his arms, his hands on her waist. For a moment they stared at each other, awareness shimmering between them.

Rashid wanted to draw her closer, feel the soft curves of her body against his. Learn the sweet taste of her mouth. See if the desire that erupted was ephemeral or lasting. He'd only met her yesterday, yet he felt a strong pull of attraction he hadn't felt in a long time. Not since Fatima had died.

He slowly pulled her closer.

"Can we read tomorrow, Bridget?" Mo asked, shattering the moment. He looked up trustingly at Bridget.

Rashid stepped back, dropping his hands to his sides. How could he have forgotten Mo?

"Bridget may have other things to do tomorrow," he said to his son, avoiding his guest's eyes. Hopefully she saw nothing amiss in his helping her down.

"Unless your father has plans for his guests, I don't see why not. I'll let you know before bed, okay?" she said, smiling brightly at his son. Rashid flicked her a glance, wishing she'd turn that smile his way.

"Okay," Mo said happily.

Rashid nudged Mo's shoulder. "What do you say to Bridget for reading to you?"

"Thank you!" Mo gave a big whoop. "It was so much fun. I should like to do this every day!"

"I would, too," Bridget said.

Rashid was certain he imagined a wistful note in her tone. Women liked excitement and adventure, not spending time with little boys. What was her game?

"Run along to Alaya, Mo. She will have your lunch ready for you soon."

"Okay! Bye, Bridget." He gave her a brief hug again and headed happily up the path toward the house, carrying the half dozen books they'd read.

"Okay?" Rashid queried.

"It's the new word I taught him. He is eager to learn," she murmured, brushing down her skirt. "If I'm going to be climbing trees again, I need some different clothes." She looked at Rashid. "In fact, I'm going to need some clothes just to complete the visit. Do you suppose I could get a ride into town and get some things at one of the shops?"

"I will put a car at your disposal."

"Thank you. I thought Francesca might like to go with me."

"Perhaps Marie and Elizabeth would round out the party and enjoy some of the shops as well."

When she hesitated, he knew instantly she wanted time alone with her cousin.

"No, just Francesca," he said. "Perhaps tomorrow. I have to go to my offices in the city, so I could drop you both and pick you up later. Or I can arrange to have a car for your own use."

She smiled so brightly Rashid wished he could have offered something more. What would her smile be like presented with a diamond bracelet, he wondered.

"Thank you. That would be perfect. I'll check with Francesca. I'll look forward to seeing some of your capital city, as well. We whisked through it so fast yesterday I hardly had time to glimpse anything."

She looked at her watch. "Did you come to find us because it's almost lunchtime? I should clean up before joining the others."

"You have plenty of time. Mo eats at noon. Our luncheon will be ready at one." Rashid started back toward the house, Bridget beside him.

"You have the most beautiful gardens," she said, pausing to smell one of the many blossoms that weighed down a bush. "Mo and I walked around exploring. Then we tossed a stick in the pond to watch it float. Then we tried to name all the flowers. I recognized the roses and hibiscus, but you have many varieties I don't know. When we studied the shrubbery and trees, we found that one, so we just had to climb it. There's also a special hiding place behind one of the larger shrubs. Maybe we'll crawl in there for our next reading time."

"Were you a tomboy as a child?" Rashid couldn't imagine any of the women of his acquaintance crawling into a special place made by bushes. But she made it sound adventurous and fun. No wonder Mo had been so happy.

"Not especially, mostly trying to keep up with Antonio. Though being sort of plain, I never was as caught up in makeup and fashion as Francesca. So I tried different activities."

"I would hardly describe you as plain." Had her father compared the two cousins and made Bridget feel less somehow? He knew his own father had employed that tactic with his sons, comparing them, urging them to excel in areas their brothers did not, in hopes of fostering strong men. Rashid didn't feel close to either brother as a result. If he had any other children, he would not take that tactic with Mo or his siblings.

"Well, I'm certainly not in Francesca's category. Even though she's two inches taller, I probably outweigh her by twenty pounds."

He stopped and pulled her in front of him, his hands on her shoulders. The softness of her hair caressed the back of his fingers. She was not all skin and bone which he liked. He couldn't understand being worried about eating too much. She was perfect the way she was. Bridget Rossi was a vibrant woman. He suspected there was more to her than he saw on the surface.

His pulse pounded as he studied her. Her hair was fiery in the sun, not quite red, not brown, shot through with golden strands. Her eyes met his frankly, no guile or games there. The dusting of freckles across her nose were enchanting. He'd like to kiss every one.

Focus, he admonished himself. They were on a path in the garden, not some trysting place. People could wander down the path with no notice. Not to mention she was a guest in his home.

And he was not in line for a relationship at this point. Still, he was intrigued by this American.

"Sometimes there's a problem with people being too thin. Do you think a man likes to hold a woman who feels like she's anorexic? You are perfect just the way you are."

She stared at him dumbfounded.

Slowly his fingers caressed her shoulders, feeling the toned muscles and soft skin beneath her cotton top. He wanted to feel her body against his, to test his theory, that she would be a perfect fit against him, that he would know he was holding an armful of femininity.

The urge to kiss her grew as each moment passed. She never blinked. Her eyes were wide and fathomless. Had he been the only one thinking of a kiss?

She was a guest in his home and he would not force himself on anyone but—

She stepped back, breaking contact.

"Thank you. I have never been told I was perfect before." She turned and hurried toward the house, much as she'd run up the stairs last night.

He began to walk after her, lengthening his stride until he caught up with her.

They came out of the bower of flowers just as Francesca and Marie were heading from the pool back to the house. The sarong skirt Francesca wore was gauzy and flowing, leaving her bikini top the only covering above her hips. Marie had covered herself from head to mid calf with a colorful caftan. Women were more circumspect in Aboul Sari than other countries in North Africa. Francesca knew that, so why did she ignore their custom, he wondered, irritated.

"The pool was fabulous," Marie called when she spotted them. She stopped to wait for them to catch up. Francesca also stopped, her expression definitely curious.

"I thought you were reading to Rashid's son this morning," she said as Bridget drew closer.

"I did. We had a delightful time. He's a sweet little boy. Funny, too. We found a tree to climb."

Francesca smiled at that. "Reminds me of when we were younger and you and Uncle Paolo came to visit."

"Was the pool nice?" Bridget asked.

"Lovely, but I don't want to get too tanned. I need to keep an even coloring for photos."

Rashid listened to the interchange, glancing at Francesca. There was no denying she was beautiful to look at, but he couldn't help looking again at Bridget. She had a warmth and openness that called to anyone around her. A joie de vivre that was almost contagious.

"I thought you both might have joined us at the pool," Francesca said to Rashid.

"I had work to do, then I went to find Mo. He enjoyed Bridget's reading," he said.

"Maybe we can swim together this afternoon."

"Sounds delightful." Not that he planned to spend the entire afternoon lounging by the pool, but swimming would be refreshing. And he needed to spend time with his guests—all of his guests, no matter how much he'd rather spend time with just one.

"Bridget wanted to do some shopping. Would you like to accompany her tomorrow?" he asked as they walked toward the double French doors opening off the solarium.

Francesca didn't hesitate a second. "I would love to. At that boutique you showed me last week?"

"If you like." It was a small, exclusive shop near the center of town. The proprietress had been delighted to have such a well-known fashion model patronize her establishment.

"I do." Francesca's mood seemed to swing to happiness instantly. Cynically Rashid knew it wasn't all due to the promise of more time with her cousin, but the idea of shopping for more new dresses. He'd never known anyone so interested in clothes as Francesca.

She looked at Bridget. "You'll love the boutique, the clothes are fantastic. I assume you won't be coming with us tomorrow," Francesca said to Rashid.

He shook his head. "The last time I went with you, I had to spend my entire time fending off giggles and odd looks from the saleswomen. You and Bridget will enjoy yourself more without me."

Francesca laughed. "We would have more fun just the two of us." She linked arms with Bridget and started walking toward the house. "We'll buy the place out!"

Rashid walked with Marie, his gaze drawn to the two in front of them. He had other guests to see to, he couldn't devote his entire time to the cousins. But for a moment, he wished he could see Bridget trying on a variety of dresses at the boutique.

It was midmorning before Francesca was ready to leave the next day. Rashid had left early, sending the car back for the ladies. Bridget had gone out onto the steps at the appointed time and was waiting for her cousin. She almost went back to find Francesca, when she swept out, dressed in a white linen dress that looked stunning with her recent tan and dark hair. Bridget felt a swell of happiness at the thought of spending time just the two of them.

She wished she could find a way to casually find out if there was something more between her host and her cousin than friendship. She'd watched them yesterday when everyone was together and hadn't detected any special bond between them. But what if she were starting to grow interested in a man her cousin was also interested in?

"Have you known Rashid long?" Bridget asked.

"A couple of years or so. He came to one of the charity events I was modeling at and we met. He's fun, isn't he?"

"Yes." Fun, exciting, mysterious and so sexy she was having erotic dreams at night.

"Sad about his wife," Francesca said.

"He said she died."

"It's always sad when someone like that dies so young. Why can't criminals die young?" Francesca said.

"He said she was beautiful."

"I don't know, I never met her, but I can't imagine him not wanting someone as beautiful as he himself is."

Bridget nodded, feeling her heart drop. Or course a man that handsome would like to have an equally beautiful companion. Someone like Francesca?

"So are the two of you...?" Bridget trailed off, hoping Francesca knew what she was asking.

Her cousin laughed. "Not at all. We're friends. I have lots of friends, but no one special—maybe one day. But, Bridget, we need to enjoy today together. The reason I was late is my agent called—there's this fantastic opportunity."

"Not again," Bridget said. "The last time we tried to vacation together you left."

"I know. I'll make it up to you. But this is a special event featuring Versace originals. I can't turn it down."

"So when do you leave?"

"Tomorrow, if I can get a flight out. The next day at the very latest, and then I'd have no time to rest before the fittings and rehearsals."

"I'll have to leave, then," Bridget said slowly. She had just arrived, gotten a taste of the exotic lifestyle so foreign to her own.

"Nonsense, Rashid invited you for a couple of weeks."

"I don't know him. I can't stay. It was one thing with you here, but I can't stay on my own."

"Of course you can," Francesca said. "He'll insist, you watch."

"I doubt it. And if so, only to be polite."

"It seems to me every time I turn around there you are in private conversation with Rashid," Francesca said. "I'm sure an extended invitation won't be for politeness."

Francesca raised her hand, pointing to the index finger of her left hand with the index finger of her right. "First the night you arrived, the two of you were chummy when you walked into the solarium. Second—" she touched the next finger "—you and he were walking around the garden together yesterday. You said you'd been reading to his son, but I saw no little boy. Third—" another finger "—last night you and he were sure cozy with his grandmother until we called him to join us at cards.''

''You are imagining things. We've spent a short time together every time you've seen us.'' They had not had private conversations. Not really. A time or two, maybe, but only because they'd been alone. It wasn't as if it meant anything.

At least, not to Rashid. Bridget looked out the window. She remembered every word Rashid had said. Her excitement for the shopping expedition had waned. She and Francesca had such a limited time to visit they should be sitting somewhere private and catching up. But Francesca was already talking again about the boutique they would visit.

''I'm not here to spend time with Rashid, I came to spend time with you. I'm glad we're shopping just the two of us. I was afraid Marie or Elizabeth would join us. This is your field of expertise, I hope you can help me pick out some dresses that will really suit me,'' Bridget said, resigned to the inevitable.

''Leave everything to me. You'll want to get a special dress for the reception next week,'' Francesca said, reaching out to squeeze Bridget's hand.

''What reception?''

''There's some state affair that Rashid invited us to attend. His father is actually the host. It's in honor of a visiting ambassador. I expect there will be heads of state, officials from several countries as well as the elite of Aboul Sari. Since I won't be here, you'll have to represent the family. It'll knock your socks off.''

Bridget stared at her cousin. For a moment she remembered the last formal reception she'd attended, with Richard Stewart, the man she'd been dating at the time. He'd been up for partnership in the prestigious law firm he worked in, and they'd been invited to a very formal event at the senior partner's home.

Bridget almost shivered in remembrance. Richard had been furious after the accident. She had not tried to ruin his chances, as he'd claimed. Someone had bumped her arm and the glass of red wine had seemed to float out of her hand.

She'd tried to explain to him, but he hadn't listened at all. And her hostess had been less than gracious, making her feel even more clumsy and inept. White dress, white brocade love seat, white carpet, all with a dark red wine stain.

Bridget had vowed never to attend an important, formal affair again. Yet her cousin was thrilled with the idea.

"I think I'd have a heart attack." She'd never be comfortable as long as she could hear Richard's verbal tirade echo in her mind.

"You'll have a fabulous time. Live a little! Too soon you'll have to return to San Francisco and your regular life. When will you vacation here again?"

That was some of the problem. This vacation was like a fantasy. She was swept up in the wonder of it all. Not forgetting her father, but able to put things in perspective and begin to move on.

This morning, she'd looked in on Mo, promising to find him when she returned from shopping to read to him again. She'd have to ask Rashid if the little boy could swim. They could play in the pool together if so. She would enjoy that more than lying in the sun doing nothing. That allowed too much time for sad thoughts.

When they reached the boutique, the chauffeur slid to a stop before the small shop and escorted them to the entrance.

"Welcome." A small woman met them, bowing in greeting and opening the door wide. "I am honored to have you favor my shop," she said, smiling at Francesca.

"I brought my cousin with me today," Francesca said walking through to the elegant love seats in the center of the room. Several gowns were displayed along the wall, but the shop looked nothing like the stores Bridget normally patronized.

Bridget glanced around and followed her cousin. Sitting on the love seat opposite Francesca, she felt awkward. Were there only a half a dozen dresses for sale? None of them looked practical for her.

"We are looking for some clothing for my cousin. She arrived unexpectedly and didn't bring enough dresses for a visit with Sheikh al Halzid," Francesca recounted as another young woman entered, carrying a heavy silver tray loaded with sweets, biscuits, a lavish teapot and paper-thin cups.

"Resort wear?" the woman asked.

"That and a couple of dresses for dinner and something for a formal reception," Francesca said. She looked at Bridget and winked. "Maybe something casual for playing with children."

Bridget smiled at her cousin.

"But nothing too extravagant," Bridget said.

Francesca laughed. "Don't worry about the bill,

it's taken care of. I'm happy to share this time with you.''

Dresses and pants, shorts and swimsuits were paraded before them. Some Bridget loved, others shocked her, she would never wear such clothes. But she was charmed with the genuine desire of the saleswomen to find just the right attire for her.

Francesca picked out most of the dresses for Bridget, commenting on what went with her coloring. She then chose a couple to try on herself. Bridget was overwhelmed with her cousin's generosity. She wanted to keep an eye on costs. Only, there were no tags on anything. Which probably didn't matter, she didn't understand the country's currency so wouldn't really know how much something cost.

An older woman rapped on the front door of the establishment. One of the saleswomen quickly went to speak to the woman standing outside. The exchange was in Arabic, so Bridget hadn't a clue what was said, but the woman left in a huff.

''Was that another customer?'' Bridget asked Francesca quietly.

''Probably. She'll come back. Time to try on these things, to make sure they fit.''

''Why not come in now and look around?'' Bridget persisted.

''Because we are here, of course. Rashid arranged for an exclusive showing. The boutique is closed to others as long as we are here.''

Bridget was astonished. ''They can do that?''

''They are doing it. His business is important to

them. They'll do whatever he asks. Go try on that aqua dress. That color looks great on you.''

Bridget followed the younger salesclerk into the dressing room. It was the size of her bedroom at home. Floor-length mirrors lined one wall, a free-standing full-length mirror stood nearby, to enable a customer to see the back as well as the front of any creation she tried on.

And that's what Bridget felt like. She was trying on creations, not mere dresses. The materials felt soft and sensuous against her skin. The aqua color did wonders for her, making her skin seem even fairer and her eyes a deeper blue. She liked the way the dress fit.

The rose shirtwaist felt luxurious, and the color looked surprisingly good despite her hair. She wouldn't have tried it without Francesca's urging.

It was an hour later by the time she tried on the last dress the woman had brought. It was a confection, no other word for it. A rich cream color, the single shoulder bodice felt as if it were a specially designed body suit, fitting snugly, yet allowing ease of move-ment. The long skirt swirled around her legs. She loved walking in it, feeling like a princess must feel when everything in the world was perfect.

She couldn't imagine anything better for the recep-tion that loomed. If Francesca would be generous enough to extend to this one, she'd be thrilled. If not, she'd splurge and buy it herself, no matter what the cost.

"Francesca, wait until you sec this!" She swept

into the main salon. But Francesca wasn't there. Rashid was.

He sat on one of the love seats, making it seem absurdly frail and feminine. He rose when she entered and let his gaze travel from her head to her toes.

"Exquisite," he said softly.

"Oh." Bridget didn't know what to say. Her heart rate increased. For a split second she was delighted he could see her in the dress. It was the prettiest thing she'd ever worn. Even if she never wore it again, Rashid had seen her and thought her exquisite.

The salesclerk hovered nearby, reaching out to adjust the dress where no adjustment was needed. She spoke rapidly to Rashid in Arabic and he nodded.

"I have told her that dress is definitely a keeper. She will include it with the others you've chosen. Are you almost ready to return to the villa?"

"Yes. I'll change right away."

"No hurry. Francesca is trying something on."

But Bridget had enough. The pile of clothes that had accumulated would give her more than enough for her stay. She was thrilled with the selections and knew she had her cousin to thank for helping her choose colors and styles she would have hesitated to try on her own.

Dressing in one of the new skirts and tops, she rejoined Rashid in the main salon as soon as she was able.

"I wanted to thank you for making this day so wonderful," she said, sitting primly opposite him on the matching love seat. "I never had a store close to others just so I could see the clothes. It's been fabulous! Did you get some tea? They served us tea earlier. The salesclerks seemed to know my size just by looking at me. Not a single thing I tried on didn't fit. Some I didn't like on as well as off, but they all fit perfectly.''

''And you found enough to tide you over until you return home?'' he asked.

''More than enough. I even found a darling swimsuit, with a modest coverup. I wanted to ask you if Mo swims and if so would you trust him with me? We could use the pool when your guests aren't there, so we wouldn't bother them.''

He raised an eyebrow. ''I was under the impression you were also one of my guests, Bridget Rossi. How can you and Mo use the pool when no guests are there?''

''But I am not bothered by your son. He said he has strict orders not to bother any one. I know others don't always want to be around kids like I do, but he's so delightful.''

''If I suggest you spend more time with Francesca?''

''I'm happy to spend all my time with her, but she just told me she has to leave for an assignment.'' Bridget took a breath. She'd almost forgotten. ''I should probably leave as well.''

''No, stay and enjoy yourself a bit. Refresh yourself before returning home. The duties and sad tasks will await,'' he said.

''Unless Antonio has already started with the estate. He is the executor. Maybe he can wind everything up before I return.'' It wasn't fair to leave everything to her brother, but she wasn't up to the tasks just yet.

She looked at her new skirt. "Do you think I'm frivolous shopping so soon after Papa died?"

"Not at all. One of the hard things to deal with after a family member dies is the fact life goes on. Would your father have wanted you to stop everything for a period of time to mourn him?"

"Of course not. He loved life. He was always encouraging me to try new things, learn to skate, try rowing, things like that. I wish you could have known him, he was so special."

"I wish I had, as well. You speak highly of him. As does Francesca," Rashid said.

"He doted on her, but she rarely came to visit. We mostly saw her as a child when we visited Italy. Are you sure you want me to stay?"

"I am most definitely sure."

Bridget looked at him, caught up in the dark gaze that seemed to hold her in thrall. Her skin grew warm as her heart rate increased. She felt that shaft of awareness again, and for a moment the elegant boutique faded. The world only contained Rashid.

She shook her head, as if breaking a spell. Looking away, she took a deep breath. "I don't want to impose. But if you're sure, then let me know about Mo's swimming. Being with him helps cheer me up!"

"Ah, your universal excuse when I suggest my family is imposing on you," Rashid said.

"You kindly invited me to visit to help in the transition over my father's death," she reminded him.

He inclined his head once.

"Certainly spending time with a child is the best way to do that. A young life with so much ahead of him."

"So how does my grandmother fit in?" he asked.

"That's for fun." She thought about it for a moment. "And for wisdom. She is a wise woman, I think. And gracious in her time with me."

"You gave her pleasure explaining the problematic sections of the book yesterday. She looks forward to your reading more with her."

"As do I."

He leaned forward, closing the distance between them. "Is it enough, Bridget, to help you forget? I can make a car available for you to explore, take you to the beach, share some of the treasures of my country, accompany you to parties and receptions. You should not spend your vacation doing what you would do at home."

"Trust me, Rashid, I never do things like this at home. But I wouldn't say no to a tour of historic sites, or even a view of the beach. Does Mo like the beach?"

Rashid narrowed his gaze slightly. "I don't believe I know if he does or doesn't."

Before Bridget could react to that startling statement, Francesca swept into the room, making a definite entrance, wearing a flame-red slip dress that hugged her slim frame like a second skin.

"Rashid, I didn't know you'd arrived. What do you think?" She twirled around, assumed a sultry pose and walked toward him like she was on a catwalk in Milan.

He rose and studied her. "It's beautiful with your coloring and figure," he said.

She continued toward him until she almost touched him, flirting as she trailed a red tipped finger along his jaw. "I want you to think I'm beautiful in it. A model has to be beautiful, or she loses work."

"You are always beautiful, Francesca," he replied.

She smiled, glancing at Bridget. "Did you get everything you wanted?"

"Yes, thank you. I'm set for the rest of my stay and then some."

"If you are ready to return to the villa, I'll wait. If not, I'll send the car back for you," Rashid said.

"We about bought out the place. I'll just change. Won't be a minute. Then we'll ride back with you and after lunch we can go to the pool. Wait until you see the swimsuit I just bought."

Rashid sat back on the love seat, his eyes once again on Bridget. "She has a love of fine things."

Bridget nodded, wishing their time together wasn't going to be so short. She had some more questions for her cousin—all centering on Rashid.

"She always looks good in anything she wears," Bridget said wistfully.

"That's her job. She wouldn't be a very effective model if she didn't."

Bridget had to believe Francesca's saying the two of them were just friends. Rashid certainly didn't sound that besotted with her cousin.

"I have other commitments tomorrow, but the day after I would be happy to show you some of our historic sights. To view all the ones we treasure in our country would take much longer than a day, I'm afraid," Rashid said. "Though we will see all we can while you are here."

"I should love to see whatever we can in the time you can allot. I haven't been to as many places as Francesca, as I'm sure you know, so this is all wonderfully new to me," Bridget said enthusiastically. Many of the buildings she'd seen were old, with lovely designs and carvings. The entire city had a different feel from San Francisco. She'd love to explore more—especially with Rashid.

"You live in one of the world's loveliest cities. Tell me about your life in San Francisco," he invited.

Bridget knew he was only being polite, but he was her host, so she would comply. She gave him a brief background about growing up as the child of a restauranteur, of helping out in the restaurant during high school and college for extra money. How she'd settled in her flat with the narrow view of the Bay if she leaned out the bedroom window. What aspects she liked best about her job as a librarian. How on occasion she'd act as hostess for her father, less and less as the years had gone by and he'd cut back on activities, turning the day to day running of the restaurants over to Antonio.

"You mention friends from time to time," Rashid commented, "But never one special male friend. You do not have one?"

She shook her head, thinking of Richard. She hadn't found anyone since that episode that she wanted to develop a relationship with. Did it look as if she couldn't attract the attention of one special man? Suddenly she wished her cousin would hurry up so they could leave. She didn't like being reminded that next to Francesca, she was a definite also-ran.

"Sorry, I had to try on one more dress," Francesca said as she breezed into the salon. "Ready?"

"We were just waiting for you," Bridget said, jumping up.

"I was about to tell your cousin the men in San Francisco must be blind and crazy to let someone as lovely as she is remain single for so long," Rashid said also rising.

CHAPTER FOUR

DID Bridget really wish to leave since her cousin was departing early, or was she just being polite, Rashid wondered as they drove back to the villa together. They had not done much in the three days she'd been visiting. Maybe he should make an effort to show her more of the delights his country had to offer.

And learn a bit more about the woman while he was at it.

The clothing purchases were being sent and should arrive at the villa before the end of the day. Rashid reviewed what activities he'd planned for his guests for this afternoon. A few hours at the pool, then time with Jack and Charles for a game of billiards while the women fussed and got ready for dinner.

Charles and Jack were counted among his closest friends, but suddenly Rashid felt their visit had gone on long enough. He almost resented the time he had to spend with his friends. He wanted to spend it with Bridget.

Fatima had doted on their son. Had she lived, he was certain they would have had more children. She seemed happiest when with Mo.

Bridget also liked being with his son. Americans viewed the whole love and marriage situation differently. Was there such a thing as enduring love? What would marriage be like to someone who you truly loved?

His parents had a respectful relationship. He knew they cared for him and his brothers.

His grandmother's life had not been that happy, but she had never complained in his hearing.

And he and Fatima had always been compatible. She had taken care of their home, been a suitable hostess and given him Mo. He'd grown to love her as the years passed. And he missed her, but not with a gut-wrenching feeling that wouldn't end. He would always regret she had died so young. Moving on had seemed impossible for a time, but he had done so. Would he risk developing feelings for another? He had a son, and he was content with his life as it was.

Yet, there was something about Bridget Rossi that intrigued him beyond anything he'd ever felt before.

He leaned forward to see Bridget. She was gazing out the car window at the building they were passing. He knew if he sent his other guests packing, she'd leave as well.

Maybe he should give her a further incentive to remain.

"I hope you plan to attend the reception my father is giving for the ambassador of Egypt. That last dress you tried on would be perfect," he said.

"Which dress?" Francesca asked.

"I don't know if you saw it, the sales lady brought it into the dressing room. It's a cream-colored dress. Quite elegant, I think. But I'm not sure about going to the reception. I really don't care for events like that." Especially not after the fiasco with Richard.

"Anyway, I'm not the ambassador type," Bridget said, leaning forward to see him better. "Thank you for asking me."

"Everyone at the villa will be going, so you'll know some people there. Many others who will be there also speak English. Plan to attend," he said.

Bridget suppressed a desire to snap a salute at his imperial tone. "I'll see," she hedged.

Francesca laughed. "That used to mean no, when your mother said it."

Bridget nodded, remembering how they knew exactly what her mother had meant. From there her thoughts turned to the relationship between her parents. Her mother had loved her father so much, and Papa had never loved her in return. It had been expedient for him to marry—for the sake of his young son. But she wondered why he couldn't have at least pretended to love his second wife.

She couldn't decide if that would have been worse. But how could anything be worse than to love someone, make a life and family with him, and know in his eyes, it was only second best?

She shouldn't be thinking about old family dynamics with Rashid sitting there. Nothing would change the past. She had a more current situation to consider—if he was serious about her attending the reception. What in the world would she do at some state reception? She'd be so tongue-tied and shy she'd be miserable. Not to mention worried she'd dump wine or something worse in the ambassador's lap! She'd have to find a way to decline.

Even the thought of wearing her beautiful dress to

the reception wasn't enough. She'd be totally out of her depth. She might dream of fancy balls and romantic nights but truth to tell, she'd be too worried to enjoy it.

Luncheon was more informal than previous meals, with the staff serving it on the patio next to the pool. Marie and Elizabeth had been swimming during the morning and donned their coverups for the meal.

"You are joining us this afternoon, right, Rashid?" Marie asked.

"We all are, I believe," he said, glancing around the group.

"How about a look at the stables, old man," Jack said. "I'd rather go there than swim. Have to see if you have enough horses for the match."

The polo match had been scheduled for Saturday, and Jack wanted a chance to practice beforehand with a couple of Rashid's mounts.

"We can do both. Visit the stables first then join the ladies for a swim. Would anyone else care to join us?"

Francesca shook her head. Marie responded with a quick, "No thank you, I've seen horses before." Elizabeth accepted. Bridget wished she could accept as well, but knew she couldn't keep up with their conversation about polo. Besides, she'd rather spend time with Francesca before she left in the morning.

During lunch, Charles boasted a bit about his prowess on the polo field and before long, he and Jack were trying to outshine each other with tales of their exploits. Bridget found it funny the two men were so adamant about a game. But she knew how men were about football in the States, and figured it was some universal gene they all shared.

Once everyone had finished eating, the men and Elizabeth headed for the stables. Francesca, Marie and Bridget settled in beside the pool. Bridget chose a chaise in the shade of a large umbrella, wishing her swimsuit had arrived so she could swim.

Francesca sat in the chair beside Bridget. "Tell me what your plans are when you return home. Will you help Antonio in the restaurants or what?"

"I'll continue in my job. I was never that enthusiastic about business. And the only thing I was good at in the restaurants was waiting tables. Antonio will probably make the restaurants even bigger than Papa did. He loves them as much."

"Isn't this place grand?" Francesca said looking around. "I love being here. This is my second visit. I think it's become my favorite place to vacation. I really lap up this luxury. It's so different from my real life."

"And that being?" Bridget asked.

"I know you think being a model is glamorous, but it's darn hard work. And I sure wish I could eat like you do. When I finally am ready to give it up, I expect to grow as large as Aunt Louisa," she said, mentioning their largest relative.

Bridget gave her a glance. "I doubt it. Your mother is not heavy, why should you be?"

"I plan to eat my way through everything I've had to deny myself these last years to stay thin. Speaking of which, I need to go up and pack. See you in a bit."

Bridget dozed for a while, relishing the delightful setting. The warm air caressed her skin gently as the breeze moved across. The water shimmered in the sunshine. The colorful hibiscus and gardenias that segregated the pool area added color and fragrance to a perfect setting.

Time drifted by and Bridget began to feel restless.

A shadow crossed her face and she opened her eyes. Rashid stood beside the chaise, blocking the sun.

"Your clothes have arrived," he said softly.

She sat up, noticing Marie was fast asleep beneath another umbrella.

"I thought you might wish to see them again," he said, offering a hand to help her rise.

"Finished at the stable?" she asked.

"Yes. You should have come."

"Maybe sometime when polo afficionados aren't around."

"We wouldn't have talked polo the entire time."

She smiled up at him, then hesitated as his eyes darkened.

"Come, show me what you bought," he said, taking her arm.

When they stepped inside her room a few moments later, Marsella was busy unpacking the bags piled on the bed.

She smiled and said something in Arabic. The wardrobe door stood open with several dresses already hung. Bridget couldn't help contrasting the available space with the few articles she'd brought.

Shyly, Bridget held up each new dress or skirt,

holding them against her as she watched Rashid's reaction. She remembered doing so for her father many
times as a teenager, but Rashid was very different
from her father. And she was no longer a teenager.

Rashid was a very appreciative audience, urging
her to try on one or two dresses and model for him.
She slipped into the bathroom and donned the first
dress—the aqua one she'd liked so much. Stepping
out, she tried to emulate her cousin. It was like playing dress-ups and to her surprise, once her initial shy-
ness faded, Bridget enjoyed every moment. She
wasn't sure she could ever be a model for a crowd of
critical viewers, but for an appreciative audience of
one, it was terrific.

Lastly she changed into her swimsuit and pulled on
her cover-up. This would not be a part of the im-
promptu fashion show. When she stepped out of the
bathroom, she noted his glance, felt her skin heat even
more at the male appreciation she saw in his eyes
when his gaze slid down her legs. Thankfully the
cover-up was as modest as a dress.

"I'm ready for that swim."

"I'll join you in a few moments," Rashid said.
"We'll have the pool to ourselves, I think."

"Then may we also take Mo?" she asked.

Mo was happy to see her a few moments later and
ecstatic when she offered to take him swimming. His
nanny seemed in awe of Bridget, and hastened to help
Mo change into a swimming suit.

The pool was deserted when they reached it.
Rashid had been correct. They would have it to them-

selves. She shed her cover-up and went to the edge of the pool.

"Can you swim?" Bridget asked as she stepped down the stairs at the shallow end.

"Yes!" Mo launched himself off the side in a cannonball and splashed everywhere.

Bridget laughed when he bobbed up and began swimming furiously toward her. He was like a fish in water. She relaxed and plunged into the cool water, relishing the sensuous feel against her skin. She was going to adopt Francesca's attitude and enjoy the luxury while she could.

They played for a half hour before Rashid joined them. Sometimes they played tag. Then they had jumping contests to see who could make the biggest splash.

Mo laughed so hard after one of Bridget's jumps, she had to hold him up afraid he'd go under. Didn't his father play with him like that? She remembered how often she had played with her father. He may not have had a lot of love for her mother, but she had no questions he had loved her. He had made his children more important than anything in his life.

Rashid hunkered down near the side of the pool where Bridget was remembering.

"Are you ready to stop, or do I still have time to join you?"

To her disappointment, he had not already changed. "We have been having a great time. I taught Mo some new water games. Do join us."

"You are slightly pink. Should you be out this long?" Rashid asked, touching her shoulder lightly.

Bridget shivered at the touch. She looked up at him, caught in the dark gaze of his eyes. She had to swallow before she could reply.

"Probably not, but we're having fun."

"Still, I wouldn't want you to burn. Mo, swim to the side and I'll help you out. Next time I'll come immediately."

Mo did as his father asked, then turned to look at Bridget. "Can we go read a book?" Mo asked, dripping on the cement. "I don't want to go inside."

"We need to change." Bridget looked at the strong hand offered to her. Would he pull her out as easily as he had Mo?

She took the hand and in only an instant was streaming water on the cement as well. Rashid was only inches from her, his eyes holding her as if trying to convey some deeper meaning.

"Can you read me a book?" Mo asked again.

"As long as we do it in the shade," she said, heading for the towels and her cover-up. She was ever conscious of the suit which had seemed so appropriate in the boutique and which now clung to her and revealed more than she'd like.

Quickly she wrapped one of the large towels around herself.

"The tree is in the shade," Mo called.

"So it is. How about the secret space behind the shrub?" Rashid asked.

Mo looked at him, eyes wide. "You know about that place?"

"I bet you and Bridget and I could fit in it with no trouble. I should like to hear Bridget read, as well.

Both you and Grandmother have had her take a turn, don't you think it's my turn now?''

Bridget looked at him. Her hair was wet and hung down around her shoulders. She knew she didn't have a speck of makeup on, and the sunscreen was failing if she was turning pink. Rashid wanted to spend time with her and Mo? Her heart kicked into high gear.

"You're on, though I bet it'll be crowded," she warned.

"Meet you both here in fifteen minutes." Rashid tousled his son's hair.

Bridget walked beside Mo feeling like a kid playing hooky or something. Rashid had five other guests, yet he planned to spend some time alone with her. And his son.

Twenty minutes later the three of them were weaving their way through the thick foliage. The space had seemed big enough when Bridget had first found it, but now with Rashid, it was definitely cozy. Mo claimed one spot, leaving Bridget to sit next to Rashid. Shoulders touched. His knee brushed against hers. Leaves filtered the sunlight, and a light breeze kept the air cool enough to enjoy.

Except for the heat generated by her own thoughts with him sitting so near.

Bridget reached for the first book, hoping her voice sounded normal when she read. Rashid sat so close, that when she turned her head, she could see the fine lines radiating from around his eyes. He wore casual attire which made him much more approachable than he'd ever seemed before. His shoulders were wide, his head just brushed the top of the space. His long legs stretched out drew her eye. She had to forcibly return her attention to the book, much as she'd rather stare at him. He was her host, nothing more.

"The Cat in the Hat," she began, reading the familiar rhyming story that brought such delight to so many children. Mo watched her avidly, as if absorbing the words through his eyes as well as ears.

"If you sit in Papa's lap, you can see the words as I read," she suggested after a few pages.

"Papa?" Rashid said.

Mo twisted his head to look at Rashid. "It's English. Bridget called her father that. It's ..." He looked at Bridget with a question in his eyes. "Why do we call him Papa?"

"It's less formal than Father," Bridget said, looking at Rashid. "I hope you don't mind. He picked it up from my use."

"It's fine. Continue."

Mo happily clamored onto his father's lap, snuggling back so he could see the book when she tilted it slightly in his direction.

Rashid's hand came to rest on his son's hip, and he looked at Bridget, his eyes revealing nothing. "Do continue," he said.

The book was quickly read, along with the second one Mo had brought.

"The end," she finished, shutting the book and smiling at the little boy. He was fast asleep.

"Oops, guess swimming so long tired him out," she said softly. "Maybe we should take him inside."

"Crawling out of this bower would waken him,"

Rashid said, shifting a little, and holding his son close.

"I'm all for staying right here, if you are," she said wondering at her audacity. She knew he had other guests to see to, but she loved having his undivided attention for a short time.

"I've never done something like this," Rashid said softly, looking around the shady hideaway.

"You have the perfect grounds for children. Mo can run, climb, hide and make wonderful memories of a happy childhood. You should have a bunch."

"One needs to be married to have a bunch as you say," he replied.

"You can marry again, just ask your family," she said.

"Ask them what?"

"To arrange it."

He looked at her. "I'm capable of choosing my own wife."

"I thought you were a proponent of arranged marriages," she said.

"Not at all. They can work, they can not work. But when a man reaches a certain age, he's entitled to look where he wants for a wife."

"One suitable for his position," she said, as if to remind herself she would never be in the running. Not that she wanted to be. He was dangerous to her own peace of mind. She was on a vacation. She had come to experience a totally different scene before returning home to her life as it would be. She'd always miss her father, but this respite was helping her forget the worst of her sadness, and make new memories to enjoy when the loneliness encroached.

Besides, she had sworn to herself she would never be like her mother, second place to a memory. When and if she ever fell in love, it would be with a man who came to her wholehearted and unencumbered.

How would a woman marrying a widower with children ever know she was loved for herself and not for the help she could bring to run the family?

"Do you not believe a suitable marriage has a better chance to last than one that is unsuitable, or in which lust plays the primary role? What happens when that lust is assuaged and the novelty wears off?" he asked.

"I believe in lasting love. Love that doesn't wear off," she replied.

"Suitability plays no part?"

"Of course, to a degree. I don't think people fall in a forever love with someone who doesn't share the same values they do, or the same goals. But when I start to see some man, I want to envision him in fifteen years, with bratty teenagers around, or in thirty years, with receding hair and maybe a bit of a softness around the middle. Will I still want to be with him, share my life, my hopes? If so, then I'll know he's the right man," she said dreamily.

"No."

"No? No, what? That I won't believe he's Mr. Right?"

"I can't believe you meet a man and immediately start envisioning him in fifteen years," he scoffed.

She laughed softly, reaching out to touch Mo

gently on his arm. "You're right. Only if I think I might be seriously interested in him."

"And so far not, right?"

"Oh, there've been one or two whom I gave my fifteen-thirty-year test to. Neither passed." Bridget looked at Rashid. Could she envision him in fifteen years? In thirty? She suspected he would not have receding hair, nor a softness around the middle. She couldn't envision him any different from the way he was today—totally male, sexy as could be, and so far from her universe as to be almost a foreign species.

"What similar values would you want to share with your Mr. Right?" Rashid asked.

"Family is important. And I hope to marry a man who would want to have lots of kids. I want a bunch. I only had one half brother who was years older than me. I've always yearned to have brothers and sisters around."

"What about parties, fancy clothes, jewelry?"

Bridget laughed. "I hope we have lots of parties—barbecues with friends, others for family celebrations or holidays. I enjoyed lunch today. Everyone seemed to have a great time eating on the patio. That's the kind of party I like."

"Formal receptions?"

"Scare me to death. Oops." She looked at him. "Sorry, I was angsting over the reception next week. It's not my thing, really."

"But you are going?"

She took a deep breath. "If my host insists, I shall."

"I do."

"Will your grandmother be attending?"

"Of course. Her daughter is the hostess. Tell me more about your fantasy husband," he ordered.

Bridget wondered if he were trying to equate her fantasy man with the arranged marriages common in his country.

"I don't know. I don't have a list per se," she said.

"What about sex?"

"Well, yes. I hope there is some strong attraction between us. How do you think I'm going to get my bunch of kids," she asked with some asperity, embarrassed he brought up the topic. Especially when she had trouble not thinking of sex anytime she was around the man. He raised her hormone level every time he walked into the room.

Mo stirred and rolled over, falling off Rashid's lap and onto the ground, waking up.

He looked around. "Did you finish the book?"

"I did, young man. Time we were heading inside," Bridget said, glad for the interruption. The discussion was becoming too intimate for her comfort.

"Run along, Mo. Alaya will be wondering if you left home for good," Rashid said, lifting his son to his feet.

The little boy laughed and crawled from the shelter. Bridget followed and Rashid came behind her carrying the books. Mo scampered down the path. Rashid reached out his hand to stop Bridget from moving.

"Thank you for being kind to my son."

"No thanks necessary. He's a delight. Thank you for inviting me here, Rashid. It is helping. I know I still have to face what awaits me at home, but this

time gives me a breather. I really appreciate it.''
Impulsively she reached up and gave him a brief kiss
on the cheek.

He tossed the books down, and took her shoulders
in his hands, drawing her against him, closing his
mouth over hers.

CHAPTER FIVE

RASHID stood by the window in his grandmother's sitting room and gazed out unseeing. She was finishing her breakfast and had asked to talk to him before the day started. She'd been speaking about the plans for the polo match but all he could focus on was the passionate kiss he'd given Bridget in the garden yesterday afternoon.

She'd been startled, but then, so had he. What possessed him to grab her like that, kiss her like that? Experimentation? To see if she was as sweet as she looked? To wantonly give into need and desire despite her status as guest?

Her kiss had been a polite thank-you. Could he excuse his as a thanks-for-reading-to-my-son? Hardly. A man didn't kiss a woman like he'd kissed Bridget as a thank-you.

It was more like a prelude to full body contact, under the covers, bare skin to bare skin.

He gave a soft groan as he thought about getting bare with Bridget. Her skin felt like velvet. What would it be like to touch every inch? Kiss her long into the night, nibbling on her, tasting the sweetness, feeling the heat they'd generate until he'd think they would burn up the sheets?

Even a man of his age could dream.

"Rashid!"

He turned. "Yes?"

"Have you heard a single word I've said?" His grandmother pushed aside the empty plate and pulled her cup and saucer closer. She took a sip of the hot chocolate as she watched her grandson with a puzzled expression.

"Something about a catered lunch at the grounds. The club house can provide what we need."

"Is something wrong, my dear?" she asked.

He shook his head. "Just thinking about my guests and what entertainment I can provide."

"All your guests or just one?" she asked shrewdly.

Rashid wondered if his grandmother believed he was thinking about Francesca. Or did she suspect where his thoughts really lay—on Francesca's younger cousin? She was the first woman he felt intrigued by since Fatima died.

"Your mother is coming over this afternoon. We plan to gossip about the ambassador."

He raised an eyebrow. "I hardly think that is something I need to hear."

She smiled secretly. "I wanted to know if you were paying attention. I am concerned about your guests. I do not interfere with your life, but I feel I must say something this time. Elizabeth needs to step up and set Charles straight, or you do. His mooning over Francesca verges on being rude."

"He's thirty-four years old, Grandmother. I don't think I can tell him how to behave." Jack had been married once, now divorced. He was widowed. Charles, however, had never seemed to step up to the commitment.

"I believe at dinner the first night he was here, he mentioned running for Parliament at the next election. He needs to get his priorities straight before such a move. If he can be swayed so easily by a pretty face, I don't hold out hope he'll succeed in public office," his grandmother said.

"Francesca is beautiful. Many men feel fortunate to spend time with her. I don't think it will affect how he deals in the British Parliament," Rashid said.

"I don't see Jack or you making a total idiot over the woman," she snapped.

No, but he could understand Charles' actions. He enjoyed looking at Francesca, she was lovely.

But not talking with her.

He frowned at the sudden insight. She didn't have much conversation that didn't revolve around fashion.

For a moment he wondered if he could begin to use Bridget's rule and envision himself with Francesca in fifteen years? Or thirty years. He couldn't even see them attending the reception together.

But with Bridget—

"Rashid!"

"Yes?"

"Honestly what is wrong with you? That's twice I've had to call you to pay attention. You are worse than Mo. I will be tied up with your mother. Bridget won't be reading to me this afternoon, has she made plans with Mo?"

"Actually, with Francesca leaving, I plan to take Bridget sightseeing."

Salina al Besoud was silent for a long moment,

staring nonplussed at her grandson. She cleared her throat.

"Sightseeing?"

"She'd like to see some of our country while she's here. No one else has evidenced any interest, so I thought while everyone had something else to do this afternoon, I'd show her a bit of Aboul Sari. Maybe we'll even drive to the sea."

"To the Med?"

"She would like to go to the beach. Though, I might make that an excursion for another day when we could take Mo with us. Do you know if he likes the beach?"

"I have no idea. Does it matter?" She stared at him with confusion.

"You don't think it odd I don't even know that about my own son's likes and dislikes?" Rashid asked.

"No. He's only five, what does he know?"

"I'm sure he has an opinion on a lot of things," Rashid said.

"Did Bridget ask if he liked the beach?"

Rashid nodded, wondering what else he didn't know about his son. He saw the boy infrequently. His work kept him from home during the day, and Mo went to bed early each evening.

He'd always loved the beach as a child. He bet Mo did, too. Suddenly he realized the last time he'd been to the beach had been several years ago, when he and Fatima had visited friends in Cannes. It had been shortly before she died. One day on the sand had been enough. Lying in the sun doing nothing had never been his idea of fun.

But he wouldn't just be lying around with his son. They'd swim and build sand castles. He bet Bridget had more ideas for a day at the beach.

"She's an interesting young woman," his grandmother said, sipping her chocolate. "Kind enough to spend some time with me reading that book and explaining the Americanisms."

"She enjoys it. So she says."

"She and her cousin are very unlike. I wasn't sure that first night," she said pensively.

"Very different," he agreed. "Don't worry about Saturday, everything will be fine. Just come to watch the match, do not worry about a thing."

"Enjoy your outing with Bridget," she said politely, her gaze thoughtful.

Rashid nodded and left. He was doing a kindness to a guest. She had expressed an interest in seeing some of the treasures of his country. If he visited San Francisco, he was sure she'd offer to show him around.

Anticipation rose. He looked forward to the day as he hadn't looked forward to something in a long time.

Rashid leaned against the car, checked his watch once more. It was still a minute before ten, the time he'd told her they'd leave. He wondered for a brief moment if she'd show up, or send some excuse. After that kiss, she'd fled the garden like she was in a race. Throughout the evening she'd avoided him as much as possible without causing comment. But he'd seen her gaze turn his way when she thought he wasn't watching. When he'd met her eyes, she quickly looked away.

For the second time since his guests had arrived, he wished them all gone. All but Bridget.

He'd caught her alone before she retired and told her he'd take her to see the sights today. She'd been flustered, her indecision clearly evident. She truly wanted to go. Even if she had to put up with him, or that was the message he read.

Had the kiss meant more to her than he intended?

Hell, he wasn't even sure what he had intended. It had been spontaneous, not preplanned. He wanted her. He'd kissed her. End of story.

Or was it? What about the thought of kissing her again that never left? What about the desire to whisk her away from the others, to spend time with her, to see what might develop.

Not the long-term love she so ardently believed in. But men and women could spend time together without a lifelong commitment.

The door opened and Bridget stepped out. She was wearing one of the new outfits she'd chosen, a sleeveless top in some kind of blue, with a sheer white shirt over it. The skirt was a swirl of colors, her feet shod in strappy sandals.

Her eyes lit up when she saw him.

''Oh, we're taking the convertible, how cool.''

It was the car that brought her delight, he thought wryly, feeling firmly put in his place. It was not a comfortable sensation. Was he as spoiled by attention normally given him from women? The thought was unsettling.

"Unless you fear burning by the sun," he said, opening the passenger side door for her.

"I've slathered on a ton of sunscreen. I would love to ride with the top down!" she said coming quickly down the stairs.

Rashid promptly joined her in the car and started the engine. With one last look at the front of the villa, he drove down the driveway, feeling like they were sneaking away, except, of course, for the black sedan which followed. His bodyguards would see they enjoyed their day safely. His other guests were taken care of. Francesca had already left. He was merely extending his duties as host to show a guest around his country. So why did it feel like freedom?

Bridget settled back in her seat and donned her sunglasses. She'd quickly pulled her hair back into a barrette, so it wouldn't become disheveled while they were driving. The wind against her face felt fabulous. She tilted her seat back, enjoying the freedom. She glanced at Rashid, amazed she had found the courage to come today.

She'd thought of nothing but him since his kiss. It had thrilled her to her toes, and worried her beyond end. She'd bid her cousin farewell, wishing she were staying longer so Bridget could discuss this turn of events. But Francesca had been longing to go.

There was no one else in the group she'd confide in. Maybe he had only been flirting, trying to cheer her up and she was reading too much into a single kiss.

Had her thank-you kiss on his cheek given him a false impression? She'd just been so happy she'd wanted to share that.

As recently as a week ago when her father died, she thought she'd never be happy again. But spending time here had shown her differently. She'd always miss her father, as she did her mother. But life did move on and she could find moments of sheer bliss if she looked for them.

Like riding in a convertible with the sexiest man she'd ever known. Could she get a picture to show her friends? Marcie would never believe it. And Sharon would be green with envy—in a happy way for Bridget. She wished they could meet Rashid.

"Where are we going?" She would put the kiss behind her and enjoy the day. It wasn't likely it would be repeated.

"First we will tour the city. Many of our oldest buildings were designed by the French. There are some public gardens that are in bloom now, with landscaping that is constantly changing. Later, if you like, we can visit a monument on the edge of the desert dating from World War II when the Germans occupied our land for a while."

"Rommel?"

"One of his contingencies."

"I've read about the North African campaign. Did he do much damage?"

"No, but our people did sufficient damage to him

and his troops, that he quickly moved to vacate our
territory.''

"Tell me the history of your country. What is its
primary industry, how many people live here? How
is it you and your family speak such perfect English?
Is that a second language here?''

"I attended school in England, from the age of
seven. My father had before me. His father had gone
to school in France,'' Rashid explained.

"Seven? You were sent away from home at age
seven?'' she interrupted. ''I can't believe that. You
would have been only two years older than Mo. You
aren't thinking about sending him away are you?''

He glanced at her. Bridget couldn't imagine a little
boy leaving all he knew to go to boarding school—
not if his parents were around to take care of him.

"It is the custom.''

"Mo's only a little boy. He needs his family
around, especially after losing his mother so young.
I'm sure you have schools here.''

"Of course we do, but it's been the custom in my
family for the sons to be educated abroad. Strengthens
our ties with other countries and gives us a wider
education.''

"But the girls stay home?''

He nodded.

"Sexist,'' she muttered beneath her breath.

He smiled but wisely kept silent.

Bridget took a deep breath. She needn't get caught
up in Mo's future. She was a one time guest. If their
cultural ways were different from hers, she had to

accept that. But her heart ached for little Mo. Maybe Rashid would send him to school in California. She could visit him then and have him visit her at home.

She shook her head. What was she thinking? She'd enjoy her visit and return home. There would be no reason to keep in touch. Rashid was Francesca's friend. He had extended her an invitation to visit only to help out Francesca's cousin.

"This part of the highway covers the old caravan trails. Merchants used to come from Spain to North Africa and then east on the spice trade. Alidan started as an oasis before it grew into our capital city. Fortunately, as it turned out, there is water enough to support millions. It was an important stopping point for the traders in the old days, now our most progressive city," Rashid began.

Bridget looked around, trying to forget about Mo and take in all she could.

The morning flew by as Rashid proved to be an entertaining and informative tour guide. The city was similar to other large cities, cars vying for space on the crowded streets, pedestrians hurrying along the wide sidewalks. Street vendors sold their wares from kiosks along the major boulevards. The old buildings rose gleaming in the sunlight, dwarfing trees that had been planted along the road side. Elegant and fanciful, the buildings caught her imagination.

Some had inlaid tile, others relief work. Still others had a feel of old New Orleans, with iron balconies and railings. She was fascinated.

When they drove out into the desert a short distance, the countryside changed drastically. Quickly gone was any sign of habitation, only the rising sand dunes marched ahead of them to the horizon. It was hard to remember the large city only a few miles behind them.

"Water is so precious here, isn't it," she said, studying the desolate scene.

"Life giving and life sustaining." He drove into a small parking area. Before them stood abandoned ruins of what had once been a military compound. A lone scraggly tree gave scant shade against the noonday sun.

"This is where the final battle was fought between the Germans and our people. Seventy-three Aboul Sarians died. But many more Germans. Rommel felt it wasn't worth staying when he had more pressing needs with Montgomery on his flank."

Bridget felt as if ghosts haunted the lonely outpost. She glanced around and was sad that their last sights had been of such a bleak place. Alidan was truly a lovely lush city. The contrast was amazing.

"Lunch?" Rashid asked.

She blinked and nodded, still studying the lonely abandoned buildings. "It won't be many more decades before it's totally gone," she mused. "Swept away by the sand."

"Storms waste away the walls. I'm surprised it's lasted this long. By the time Mo has children, I expect there to only be the marker."

"Thank you for bringing me. For taking time to show me some of your country," she said. "So far my favorite place was the City Gardens."

"After seeing you at my estate, I figured they

would be. There's a small café on the edge of the city where we can eat. If you like, afterward, we can head for the sea. It's not a long drive.''

''No, thank you. I'd rather go to the beach with Mo. Maybe we could borrow your driver and spend an afternoon there.''

She'd much rather go with Rashid, but she would be embarrassed if everyone knew of her avid interest in her host. She had to work at hiding her feelings. Keep it light.

''Maybe we should head back,'' she said slowly, knowing he had already spent far more time with her than his other guests. Yet she would cherish the memory of their day together. If only she still believed in fairy tales.

''After lunch. I think you will like the café. We can run by the club on the way home to see where we'll play polo on Saturday,'' Rashid said easily.

''I'd like that. How did you get involved in polo? Do you play often?'' She was curious for any information about him. Treasuring each fact, knowing she'd think about him often when she returned home.

Bridget was delighted that Rashid didn't press returning. He seemed to want to spend more time with her. Trying to feel comfortable in his presence, she was relieved he didn't regret his impulse to take her sightseeing. The others had visited before. Undoubtedly seeing all they wanted earlier, she was the only one interested today.

''My uncle plays. I remember going to matches to see him when I was small. When I was at school in England, I picked up the sport, and have been playing ever since. Jack urges me on, as you might have guessed,'' Rashid said.

She couldn't imagine anyone urging Rashid on to anything he didn't wish to do. He was the most self-sufficient, in command man she'd ever met.

''You have your own horse, then.''

''I have a stable full. I usually change horses between each chukker—period of the match. Jack and Charles will borrow some of my mounts to use on Saturday since neither brought horses on this visit. I have a couple of favorites. When we play, I rotate the horses. They are constantly being trained.''

''You have trainers?'' She tried to visualize how big a venture this was.

''Of course. I also ride the horses in practice. Practice makes a good player, as well as keeps the horses in top form.''

''I'd love to see the horses sometime. I always wanted a horse when I was a child, but we lived in San Francisco. Sort of like living in downtown Alidan and wishing for a horse.''

''We'll go to the stables before we head for home. I have a mare ready to deliver soon. Maybe before you leave, you'll be able to see a new foal.''

''Oh, I'd love that! I used to beg my parents for a horse. My mother would never allow me to even entertain thoughts about one day having one. But on one visit to Italy, my grandfather offered to buy me one if I'd stay with them. My mother was horrified, but Papa just laughed and said he couldn't be apart from his little girl.'' Her voice broke on the last as she remembered that happy vacation, and the fact both her parents were now gone.

"Sounds like your grandfather was a trouble-maker."

"No, he was just teasing, only I was too young to understand. I couldn't have left my parents." She looked at Rashid. "I was nine at the time. Imagine how awful it would be for Mo to leave at even a younger age."

"I don't have to imagine, I can remember," he said dryly.

"Oh, of course. I never thought about that. Were you lonely? Did you feel lost? You seem so self-sufficient, I have trouble remembering you were once a little boy."

"It wasn't all bad. I made friends. I learned a new language, and had a lot more freedom than I had had here. I came home for summers, to make sure I didn't lose my heritage," he explained.

"You could have stayed here for school and gone visiting summers," she countered.

He stopped at a roadside café a few moments later. When they walked into the patio behind the restaurant, Bridget was enchanted. High stone walls surrounded the flagstone area, a large fountain splashed in the center. There were few tables, affording a measure of privacy to all. They were seated at one near a corner of the wall. Deep purple bougainvillea flourished as a background.

"For a desert country, there are tons of flowers," she commented gazing around.

"Water makes the difference. When we have it, we use it. Where we don't, you see the sand."

Bridget opened her menu and promptly closed it. "You'll have to order for me, this is in Arabic."

"What would you like?"

"Something with fruit, please."

A few moments later, their order taken, and a pot of hot tea set on the table, Rashid looked at her.

"About that kiss," he said.

Bridget met his gaze, startled he'd brought it up. She'd done her best to ignore her reactions, to keep a distance last night between them.

"It never should have happened. You're Francesca's friend," she said quickly.

"That's all we are, Bridget, friends. You and I are friends as well, aren't we?" he countered.

"Not close friends."

"Maybe I want to change that."

She hesitated, unsure what was going on. What was Rashid playing at? She was visiting for a few days, then would return to her normal life. She and a sheikh had nothing in common.

"Change it how?" she asked warily.

"Get to know each other, spend some time together while you are visiting." He reached out and took her hand in his, holding firmly when she tried to tug free. "You are on vacation, enjoy yourself while you're here. Let's explore where this attraction takes us."

"That's typical of a man," she complained, pulling harder until he released her.

"What is?"

"Enjoy the moment, then move on to the next one."

"Enjoying the moment is not a good thing?"

"Okay, that's not exactly what I meant. Enjoy the person of the moment, I should have said. Have a vacation fling, isn't that what you're suggesting?"

He said nothing and she felt a wave of embarrassment sweep through her. Heat warmed her cheeks and she knew they'd be bright pink.

"I'm sorry, I thought that's what you were saying," she muttered, wishing she could sink beneath the table.

"I was not offering an affair, only friendship," he said formally. Leaning back, he surveyed the courtyard. Several tables were empty, the others occupied by couples or groups intent on themselves. No one was paying any attention to them.

She'd insulted him. "I'm sorry, Rashid. I misunderstood. I would be honored to be counted as a friend of yours."

He met her gaze and nodded once.

Bridget had known she was out of her league. A kiss meant nothing to most people, a momentary expression of fun, or delight, or affection. A sharing of a special moment. Not a lifelong commitment.

Rashid was a worldly sheikh, a man used to jetting to London or Paris or Cairo at a moment's notice, and smoothly fitting in wherever he went. He was used to sophisticated women—like Francesca and Marie and Elizabeth. Not shy librarians who saw things that weren't there.

She hoped she hadn't ruined their day with her wild

thoughts. Was it because she longed so much for another kiss, for another compliment? He had told her
beautiful cousin that she, Bridget Rossi, was lovely.
She would cling to that thought and try to match her
actions to his, not become suspicious and see things
that weren't there, no matter how much she might
wish they were.

By the time the luncheon was served, Bridget had
her emotions under control. Gradually she opened up
again, and tried to maintain a friendly attitude, even
with every cell in her body attuned to Rashid, every
inch of her longing for a closer touch. She should
have let him hold her hand. She should have seen if
he'd kiss her again.

She should have her head examined if she thought
Rashid thought of her in that way!

After lunch, Rashid stopped at a small shop and
bought Bridget a pair of sturdy shoes to wear at the
stable.

"I told you I could wear a pair I already had," she
said, when he tossed her the package.

"And I said they'd get ruined. You need substantial shoes for walking in the muck."

"I'll pay you back when we get home."

"Bridget, I can afford a new pair of shoes, don't
be ridiculous."

"You shouldn't be buying me anything. I'm the
one who wants to see the stable."

"Are you always so argumentative?" he asked as
they sped toward home.

"Only when I know I'm right."

"Take the blasted shoes or I won't let you see my horses."

She laughed. "Gosh, what a threat. If we don't play nicely, you'll take your toys and go home."

He looked at her and the light in his eyes had her heart speeding up. If they hadn't been going down the highway at a hundred kilometers an hour, she knew he would have kissed her to stop the argument. It was all she could do to stay on her side of the car. She longed to lean against him, snuggle up and find out what might result from two *friends* becoming closer. She had never wanted anything as much in her life.

Prudence kept her on her side of the car.

The stables were huge and in pristine condition. Bridget saw Jack riding a horse in one arena to the right. In a corral adjacent to the stable three horses ran along the fence, as if trying to keep pace with Jack and his mount.

Rashid came around the car to let her out, and gestured to the horses running. "They are some of my new stock, trying to keep up. The mare I told you about is inside. We are keeping her segregated as her time approaches."

They walked into the stable, and while it was clean, there were still puddles, wet straw and the distinctive aroma of horse. But no muck in this pristine stable.

Bridget loved it all, including the Arabian mare who put her head over the stall door and nickered softly when Rashid approached.

"Oh, she's so beautiful," she exclaimed.

Rashid took her hand to hold up near the mare. She blew softly against Bridget's palm, then nudged it. He released her to pet the horse. She was charmed.

"She likes me," she said in delight. Her brief riding forays had been long ago. How wonderful it must be to have horses available at any time.

"She's pampered, and ready to deliver, aren't you Asheera," Rashid said, running his hand over her sleek neck.

"That's her name, Asheera?"

"Yes. This is her first foal, so we are watching her closely." He nodded to cameras mounted high above the stall. "Someone monitors her constantly. When it's time, we'll be there to assist if needed."

"Is she one of the polo horses?"

"She has been trained, but usually I prefer a bigger mount. Most of my polo horses are Thoroughbreds. Come, you can meet Halsin, another favorite."

With a last rub on Asheera's velvety nose, Bridget followed.

Rashid whistled sharply when they went to the other side of the barn and a magnificent black horse rushed to the stall door. He was larger than Asheera, glowing with health and vitality. He tossed his head and pawed the ground, then hung his head over the stall door to nuzzle Rashid.

"He's the first one I will ride on Saturday."

"Wow, I bet he's a handful." And she knew Rashid could master him with no difficulty.

Rashid showed her two more horses. As they were leaving the stable, a pony stuck his head over a shallow door.

"Oh, Mo's pony, no doubt," she said, moving to see him. He was a dapple-gray.

"Yes, he learned to ride last year. Sometimes we ride together."

"Not playing polo, I hope," she said, in dismay.

"You are very protective of my son, Bridget. Do you not think I take care of him?"

"Yes, of course you do. I don't know much about children beyond what I see at the library, but he seems so small, and you, um, have other obligations. Wasn't four young to learn to ride?"

"He never rides unattended. You don't believe I spend as much time with him as I should?" Rashid's tone was silky.

"I would never presume to tell you how much time you should spend with your son," she said. "But if it was me, I'd spend lots of time with him. He's such a darling child and children grow up so fast."

"Next week we'll all go to the beach," Rashid said, taking her hand and starting toward the car. "Even Mo."

"I'll look forward to it. Thank you for today. I've had such a good time."

"It was my pleasure."

He stopped by the car but made no move to open the door, turning he looked at Bridget.

"We are friends, and sometimes friends exchange kisses." With that, he leaned over and kissed her.

Bridget couldn't move. She could only feel, savoring the touch of his mouth, the gentle persuasion as his lips moved against hers. When she opened her mouth, he deepened the kiss and wrapped his arms tightly around her.

She leaned into the kiss, reveling in the sensations that spread through every cell.

His embrace was intoxicating. She forgot her sadness, her concerns for the future, everything, swept away to a magical place where Rashid was her only reality. Time seemed to spin out of control as the kiss went on endlessly. She never wanted it to stop.

But end it did, slowly, as if Rashid were as reluctant as she to stop.

She opened her eyes and found his dark ones waiting.

"No regrets," he said.

She shook her head. Never a regret. She wanted more. But conscious of where they were, she summoned a smile and stepped back until she touched the car.

"I will treasure today," she said, turning to get in before she did something else foolish, like insist he kiss her again.

CHAPTER SIX

BRIDGET felt decidedly awkward when she sat down to dinner that evening. She knew better than to talk herself into believing Rashid wanted to be friends. A playboy's idea of friendship differed from hers. He'd been kind to show her around. How many people did she know who could boast having been kissed by a sheikh? She would treasure his kisses as a precious memory.

But once back in San Francisco, she'd get back in the routine of her normal life and the brief vacation in the Mediterranean would be tucked away.

Watching him throughout dinner, she didn't see any evidence that he paid special attention to any of his guests. It reaffirmed her belief he'd merely been kind.

No one had even hinted at more.

And she would not let herself fantasize about a long-term relationship. She wanted to be married one day. To have a husband to adore her. To have children to lavish her love upon.

Rashid had been married, and Bridget knew first-hand how second wives fared. It was not for her.

Salina al Besoud summoned her when they adjourned to the drawing room after dinner.

"How was your tour of the city?" she asked

Bridget once they were seated at a sofa with a huge silver coffeepot on the table before them.

"It was lovely. I learned quite a bit about your country's history while Rashid kindly showed me around. Some of the buildings in the old part of the city are quite fabulous. I would have loved to have gone inside to see if the decor matched the elegance of the facades."

"Another time, perhaps. I'm glad you went with him. He loves our country. No one else seems interested in such pursuits."

"I love history and exploring new places. I would like to go back and spend more time. Or see a different part of the country," Bridget said.

"It can be arranged. Ask Rashid."

Bridget smiled politely and nodded, knowing she would never ask. She'd treasure today's memory for what it was, a host making sure a guest enjoyed herself.

Laughter rang out from the group near the French doors. Bridget looked over at the same moment Rashid's gaze moved to her. For a second she felt her heart catch, then begin to beat rapidly. She couldn't drag her eyes away. His eyes were alight, his smile warm and contagious. What had amused him? She had never heard him laugh before. The richness in the tone brought a smile to her face. Could she ever say anything to make him laugh so?

A moment later he excused himself, glancing around to make sure his guests were occupied. He walked over to Bridget and his grandmother.

"I hope you don't mind, Grandmother, but I am going to steal your companion away."

"To where?" she replied, studying him with some interest.

"Bridget has not yet seen the gardens at night. I thought she would enjoy it. Rain is expected soon, so this may be our last chance for a couple of evenings."

He held out his hand and Bridget automatically placed hers in it. When he tightened his grip to assist her to rise, she felt as if a live current had jolted through her. She came to her feet quickly and tugged to free her hand.

His eyes told her he knew she had been affected by his touch, but he made no comment, merely motioning her toward the French doors. "Shall we?"

"I should like to see the gardens at night, but won't you be missed?" She put her hands behind her lest she give way to temptation to reach out and touch him.

He shrugged, "My other guests seem occupied. It is not as if I'm the sole entertainment available. We won't be gone for long."

Stepping outside, Bridget was buffeted by a strong breeze. "The forerunner of the storm?" she asked, brushing a strand of hair from her eyes. It felt fresh. She felt exhilarated.

"We will have rain before the night is over. A thunderstorm is predicted, with rain to follow all tomorrow. Come, as you can see, our way is lighted."

Small lamps softly illuminated the paths. Placed several feet apart, the dim lighting was enough to enable her to clearly see where they were walking.

Certain bushes and statues had been highlighted with a spotlight, giving a dramatic flare to the garden.

"It's lovely," she murmured, following another spotlight which rested on a rose bush in full bloom. "It's as if certain plants were singled out for special notice while they might blend in with the rest during the day."

"The gardeners change the spots as different bushes come into bloom," he said. "We can have a different walk each evening of the week with the mere changing of the lamps."

"You are fortunate to have such a lovely estate," she said, delighting in the effects of the lighting. It made the entire garden seem like a fairy-tale setting. The breeze caused the bushes and vines to dance beneath its onslaught, but the refreshing air kicked every sense into full awareness. Including her closeness to Rashid.

"I have pots of plants on my balcony, which are a poor substitute. I inherited my father's home, so I can have a garden again if I move back. It would never compare with this, but I like the idea of movable spotlights. I might try that at home," she said as they ambled along.

"Is your home large?"

"Bigger than I'll need alone. But I hope to marry one day, and it will be perfect for a family."

"Ah, the man whom you can envision being with in fifteen and thirty years," he said.

"Exactly."

The wind gusted and blew another strand in her

face. Rashid reached out and brushed it back, tucking it behind her ear. It felt as if his fingers lingered.

"Whomever you marry will be a lucky man," he said softly.

Her heart warmed. "What a lovely thing to say!" Bridget couldn't remember anyone ever saying they'd be lucky to know her, much less be married to her.

As they rounded the bend, there was only the lighting on the path, nothing was highlighted. The wind seemed to grow stronger, the stars were now completely obliterated by storm clouds.

Bridget felt wound up. She knew some of the feeling was due to the weather, but most of it was due to Rashid. She turned to tell him how much she was enjoying her visit. Before she could say a word, however, he reached out to cradle her head in his hands, leaning closer.

"You intrigue me, Bridget Rossi," he said before he kissed her.

Bridget's sense of adventure went into high gear as she stepped into his embrace. Her own arms encircled his neck, tightening as she pressed herself against him, reveling in the sensations that swept through her. The wind blotted out background noise. The darkness was complete with her eyes shut, the pounding of her heart filled every cell, beating faster and faster.

Thunder rumbled in the distance—or was it her blood pounding a drumbeat? Light strobed behind her lids, or was it lightning shattering the darkness?

Wrapped in Rashid's arms, she felt as if she was sheltered from all of life's harms.

A man hurried around the curve in the path, speaking urgently. Rashid raised his head and uttered a harsh comment in Arabic. The man did not retreat, however, but stood his ground, speaking rapidly.

"Damn." Rashid released Bridget. "There are few things that could end this, but my mare is about to deliver. We do not anticipate any problems, but this is her first and it is wise to watch closely." He snapped out orders to the man who then turned and disappeared.

"I'll escort you back to the drawing room," Rashid said, turning back toward the house.

"Can I come? I should love to see a baby horse born," Bridget said, loath to end her time with Rashid.

He looked at her clothes and seemed to be weighing his decision.

"You would have to change. It can get messy. Wear your oldest clothes. I'll stop by your room in a few minutes. We'll take a car to the stables, the rain won't be far off."

"Will we be in time?" she asked as they hurried along the path. The beauty of the garden was forgotten as she tried to decide what she could wear. Nothing she had with her was old, especially not the pants she'd just bought. The navy pair she'd tucked in at the last moment when packing for Italy would have to do. She just hoped they wouldn't be utterly ruined.

"It could be hours before the birth. However, the storm is frightening Asheera. Perhaps I can calm her," he said, lengthening his stride.

* * *

Rashid bypassed the drawing room, leading Bridget directly to the stairs. He did not wish to have Jack and Charles tagging along. He knew they would both be interested, but this time he wanted only Bridget.

He changed into old clothes before heading back to her bedroom. Fatima had never cared much about his horses, though she rode from time to time. He rarely even talked about them with the other women he'd dated over the years since her death. Bridget was the first to show interest beyond admiring them when on the game field.

He knocked on her door.

"Be there in a sec," she called.

He checked his watch just as she opened her door. Amazed, he gazed at her. He knew of no other woman who could have been ready so quickly.

Bridget wore a dark pullover and navy pants. The sturdy shoes he'd bought were the only thing really suitable, but he knew no one had suggested she bring old clothes suitable for foaling. The navy pants and top would have to do.

"I'm ready," she said breathlessly. Her cheeks were flushed, her eyes sparkled. She looked as if she'd been made love to. He wished for a moment Asheera had chosen another night to foal.

"Come, a car should be waiting."

In only moments they were at the stable. The lights had been turned down low, to provide a more soothing atmosphere for the nervous mare. The grooms stood nearby, ready to lend assistance if necessary, but leaving the mare alone for the time being.

Walking to the stall, Rashid mentally ran through

all the problems that could occur. He'd asked one of
the grooms to summon the vet. Nothing else could be
done unless there were complications. It was all up
to Asheera.

The mare was fretful, stomping in the stall, whin-
nying when the thunder rolled. Her nervousness was
obvious.

He spoke to her in his native tongue, softly, cajol-
ingly. He wanted this birth to go smoothly. He knew
she would deliver fine offspring, especially with the
stallion he'd bred with her. It was unfortunate she
chose such a stormy night, but it couldn't be stopped
now.

The sound of his voice calmed her slightly, but
once the thunder rolled again, she grew agitated.

The rain came with a rush, pounding on the roof.
She neighed long and loud. An answering sound came
from another of the stalls. The stormfront moved in,
pouring rain, flashing lightning and rumbling contin-
uously. Rashid calmly soothed the fretful mare,
Bridget leaning over the door, watching them.
Gradually the storm moved through and the thunder
diminished, soon fading completely. The background
sound of the rain at last seemed to calm Asheera and
soon she was standing docily beside Rashid. He ran
his hands along her neck, down her side, feeling the
belly harden as a contraction took hold. The foal
would be born before dawn he estimated.

"You're doing well, my friend," he said soothingly, glad the worst seemed past.

Bridget hadn't said a word since he entered the
stall.

"She'll be all right, I think," he said in English, stepping back and heading to the door. Slipping out into the walkway, he shut it firmly, leaning on the top to watch Asheera.

"So it's like with a human, then, several hours of labor?" she asked.

"Yes. Often the first one takes the longest."

The mare walked to the door and leaned her head over, snuffling against his shoulder. He stroked her neck. "She wants company. I'll have one of the grooms put some bales of hay in her stall. Chairs might prove dangerous to her if she becomes agitated again. Are you comfortable sitting in there with her? I think she'll remain calm now that the worst of the storm has passed."

Bridget nodded, feeling apprehensive, but not willing to ever let Rashid know that. He would not have suggested it if it were dangerous.

Rashid gave the orders. The stable was cozy with its smell of hay and horses, the dim lights and the soft sound of rain on the roof.

A few moments later they sat side by side on a bale of hay watching Asheera drift around in her spacious stall.

"You've probably seen a lot of births," Bridget said once settled.

"Not that many. My first was when I was just a year older than Mo. Then I went away to school and didn't see another until I was in my twenties. It never grows old."

"I expect it's like a miracle each time," she said.

He nodded, pleased she felt the same way he always felt. Maybe next time Mo would be old enough to attend.

Time passed slowly. The grooms lingered nearby, to be ready for any order he might have. The vet arrived, examined Asheera and declared everything in order. He went to the tack room to get some coffee to pass the time until he was needed.

Rashid looked at Bridget. She had leaned back against the stall wall and her eyes were almost closed.

"You should return to the house, get some rest," he said softly. They'd had a long day, and it was approaching dawn. She'd been up far too long.

"No, I want to be here. But waiting's hard. I'm tired. Why don't you talk to me so I stay awake?" she said, rolling her head toward him and opening her eyes slightly.

He felt a tightening in his gut when she looked at him like that. Sleepy, sexy.

He wanted her.

If Asheera wasn't about to foal, he'd take her in a dark stall and kiss her. Or order the car to return them to the villa where they could be alone in one of the bedrooms, for what remained of the night. Conscious of the men who were nearby, he quelled his desire— for the moment.

"And what shall we talk about?" How I would love to kiss that bridge of freckles across your nose? How I would love to tangle my hands in your silky hair and run the strands through my fingers? How I would love to hear you catch your breath as you do just before my lips claim yours?

"Did your wife share your love of horses?" she asked.

He looked away in frustration. He wanted her, she wanted to talk about Fatima. Or was it merely a ploy to change the subject? He glanced at her again, but she was studying the mare.

"Fatima didn't care for horses. The gardens were her delight. She was an indifferent rider, and only went when we had company who wished to ride."

"But Mo likes them."

"Of course." Rashid couldn't imagine having a son who didn't share his love of horses.

"If you marry again, do you plan to seek a woman to share your love of horses?" she asked lazily, her head still resting against the wall.

"Not necessarily. Her functions would be different."

"Her functions?"

"Her role in my life, should I say."

"Sheesh, you sound like you'll be hiring an assistant or something."

"Aren't spouses assistants to each other? I would want a woman who could play hostess to my friends when I invite them to visit, to deal with the social aspects of my business, to be comfortable talking with ambassadors and presidents as she would be dealing with my family."

"Someone your parents arrange for you to marry, of course," she said.

He thought about that. Fatima had impressed him as being the perfect mate, sophisticated, cosmopolitan and beautiful. His parents had chosen her. Their life together had been pleasant.

But now he had doubts. Did he want the same thing if he married again? He slid a glance to Bridget. Her eyes were shut. Her hair had been hastily tied back to keep it out of her face. She looked tired. And so lovely he ached with wanting her.

"They arranged my first marriage. I plan to arrange my next on my own—if I marry again."

"Would you pick someone like Fatima? You had a common background, but did you share any interests in common?"

"Mo."

She opened her eyes and smiled. He felt his heart kick into high gear. She had the most enchanting smile, probably because of the way it lit up her eyes.

"He would be a common enough interest. Do you want lots more kids?" she asked.

"Lots more?" he shook his head. "Maybe one or two."

"Mmm. I want maybe half a dozen. And dogs and cats and bunnies. I want to give my kids the most perfect childhood so they'll have a strong basis in life when they are out on their own."

"Your own life seems to have a strong basis," he said.

Bridget shrugged. "My father didn't love my mother and I knew it. I know he loved me, don't get me wrong. And I think he had some affection for Mum. But nothing like his passion for his beautiful Isabella."

"That's a western view, that marriage must encompass wild passionate love,'' he scoffed gently. He'd heard this before.

Rashid thought about his cousin Yasmin. She had married for love, and seemed deliriously happy. She was the only one in the family he knew who openly displayed her affection for her husband and children wherever they were. His own mother and father were more formal with each other in public. Were they as formal in private?

Remembering how little Fatima and he had to talk about when alone, he suspected they were. Shared interests would have given them more to discuss when alone with each other than the last party they'd attended, or Mo's antics once he'd been born. Still, he had developed love for his wife. He missed her. And he mourned that Mo would not remember the gentle woman who had borne him.

Asheera gave a whinny. Rashid rose and went to the mare, rubbing her neck, speaking soothingly to her. She seemed more agitated. The vet came to the stall door, a cup of coffee in hand. He looked over at the mare.

''Won't be long, I'd say. Maybe your friend should come on this side of the partition.'' His English was heavily accented.

Rashid nodded and looked at Bridget. ''You should go out now. She's getting close and too many strangers will just make her more nervous.''

Bridget stood slowly and went to stand on the outside of the stall door as the vet changed places and entered. He finished his coffee, looked around and then handed her the empty cup. She leaned against the stall door and watched the proceedings, fascinated.

Despite being tired and undoubtably a bit uncomfortable, she was staying. He was glad.

Time seemed to move quickly as the mare prepared for the final stages of delivery. The foal arrived in a textbook perfect birth, feetfirst, the sack breaking before he was fully delivered.

Rashid glanced at Bridget, struck by the sheer delight on her face. Her eyes shimmered with tears, her smile was wide and honest. She truly was moved by the event.

"He's perfect," she whispered.

The vet checked both the mare and the foal, then stepped back to let nature take its course. The mare nuzzled her newborn, licking, caressing. In a short time the little foal struggled to rise onto his feet. Twice he collapsed, to the giggles of Bridget. Rashid smiled at the sight. Newborns were so awkward. Yet in less than a year, this foal would be a colt, running in the fields, growing into the strong Arabian stallion that would bring a hefty price when sold.

"Oh, Rashid, that was the most amazing thing." She laughed when the creature fell again. "Oh, poor thing, can't you help him up?"

"He'll manage, and be stronger for doing it himself," Rashid said, moving to stand near her as they watched. Soon the foal was on his feet, looking around as if to say, what next? His mother nuzzled him again, showing him where to nurse.

Rashid spoke to the vet and then to the grooms in Arabic. Turning to Bridget, Rashid let himself out of the stall. "They will watch to make sure nothing unforeseen happens and let me know if anything unexpected arises, otherwise, the excitement is over for tonight."

"Thank you for letting me be a part of it. Do you have a name picked out for him?" she asked.

"Not yet. We waited to see the sex. But we'll look at his bloodlines and see what name seems suitable. Come, it's almost morning, you must be exhausted."

It was still drizzling when they left the stable, hurrying for the car that waited. In no time they were back at the villa, and climbing the stairs inside the quiet house. The rest of the guests would be rising soon, but Rashid urged Bridget to sleep as late as she liked.

"It'll rain all day. I'll organize some activities for those who need to be entertained, so don't get up until you feel like it," he said when they reached the top of the stairs.

"I'm reading to Mo in the afternoon. I think he'll be ready for that if he can't go outside because of the weather," she said sleepily.

Rashid took her arms in his hands, holding her in front of him. "I've said it before, you are not here to entertain my son."

"It truly is my pleasure. Mo asks for so little. He's a darling little boy, and smart—you must be so proud of him."

Rashid thought about the son he hardly knew. He suspected Bridget had learned more about Mo's likes and dislikes in the short time she'd been here than he knew. Fatima had been in charge of the household and their child.

"Come join us, if you wish," she said shyly.

He'd rather join her in her bedroom now, shut the door behind them and slowly make love to her. He'd open the windows and let the rain-cooled air flow over them to contrast with the heat they'd generate, then to cool them down for sleep. He'd delight in learning what she liked and what brought her pleasure. Share pillow talk that would bind her closer and make her forget for a time her nebulous dream of a loving husband. He wanted her attention entirely, not to share it with some dream.

But she was a guest in his household. She was young, innocent and nothing like the women he usually slept with. She could be hurt, and for some reason, he didn't want to be the person to cause any hurt to her.

"Sleep well—maybe I will join you and Mo this afternoon." He kissed her, holding on to his control lest the kiss get out of hand and he forgot his principles and swept her into bed.

CHAPTER SEVEN

WHEN Bridget reached her room, her heart still pounded. She was warmed through and through and cracked the window open a bit to let in the cool air before changing to slip beneath the covers. She was tired, yet buoyed beyond anything. What a miracle the birth had been. She'd wanted to hug the mare, hug the baby, hug Rashid. She had never seen anything like it. If she lived here, she'd attend every birth on the place!

Of course, that would never happen. Their discussion about marriage once again pointed out the vast differences in their views and beliefs. Rashid had married to please his parents, then fallen in love with his wife. He saw no need to change that process. But what if he married again and didn't fall in love with his wife?

Bridget was a product of a loveless marriage. She was holding out for something vastly different. Not for her the mistakes of her parents. Or some arranged marriage that might or might not work out.

She wanted to be swept away with love. To know the man she gave her heart to would love her to the end of time. She would be special to him, like her papa's beloved Isabella had been.

But just before falling asleep she let her imagination envision Rashid madly in love with her, and she with him. Without thought, she envisioned him in fifteen years, twenty, thirty. She had no trouble imagining a happy life that would suit her forever if he only loved her.

When she woke, it was almost noon. Hurrying to shower and dress, she joined the others in the dining room just as lunch was served at one. Her gaze went immediately to Rashid. He looked as rested and fit as ever. Had he slept at all, or had the duties of host prevented that?

"So I heard you saw the foal born," Jack said when the meal had been served.

"I did. It was fantastic," Bridget said, smiling in remembrance.

"All foals are born in the middle of the night," Salina al Besoud said.

"It seems that way, but I do think some are born in daylight," Rashid said.

Elizabeth and Marie began to talk about going shopping since the rain continued. Bridget didn't need to go, she had more than enough from her earlier shopping expedition.

"Do you wish to join them?" Rashid asked.

Bridget shook her head. "I have plans to read a book to a certain young man. A rainy afternoon is perfect for that."

When lunch was finished, Elizabeth caught up with Bridget as they walked back to their rooms.

"If you think playing up to Rashid's family is going to change anything, forget it. You are not in the running for second wife. He will be guided by his parents in that matter. So no matter how much you

try to ingratiate yourself by reading to his grandmother and baby-sitting his son, you will not win,''
she said.

Bridget blinked, stunned by the woman's assessment. "I'm not trying to play up to anything. I enjoy
spending time with his son. I'm only here on a visit.
I'll be leaving soon."

"Just didn't want you to get any ideas," she said.
"He's been a widower for several years now, and I
don't see that changing, no matter how much women
flirt with him."

Bridget shrugged. "I have it on absolute authority
I'm not his type." Bridget had no intention of mentioning his kisses. But until he was committed to another relationship, he was free to bestow them where
he would. They were hurting no one. As long as she
could keep in mind that once she left, he'd turn his
attentions elsewhere. She had to remember that or risk
heartbreak.

Elizabeth seemed surprised. "What type is his?"

"He wants someone who is comfortable speaking
with ambassadors, being the perfect hostess and looking beautiful. You and Marie sound as if you're accustomed to his kind of life. I'm not. He's merely
being kind to me while I'm here."

"Well, I have to say staying up all night in a smelly
barn isn't my idea of romance," Elizabeth said with
a sniff.

"His wife Fatima never attended a birth," Bridget
offered. She thought it sad that he and his wife had
had so little in common. Maybe he would be happy

with a trophy bride, but she wished more for him, as she did for herself.

"If you aren't trying to score off points, why do you want to tie yourself up with some old woman who hasn't been doing anything exciting for about fifty years?"

"His grandmother had an American mystery which is entertaining for both of us. I'm not sure what your motives are, Elizabeth, but I'm not getting my hopes up or looking for more of a relationship than exists right now. I'm a guest in Rashid's home, that all."

"No motives beyond giving you a word of advice," Elizabeth said. She tossed her head and took off toward her room.

Bridget watched, wondering if that had been the woman's only motive. Could it be she was so dissatisfied with her own relationship with Charles, she was looking to spread the unhappiness? No matter. Bridget didn't need warnings. She could look after herself.

Rashid checked his watch as he walked toward the playroom. It had taken longer than he had expected to bundle two women into a car and send them on a shopping expedition. He had to give directions to the driver for the different shops they wanted to visit.

Then he had to set Jack and Charles up in the billiards room.

Finally his time was his own.

Opening the door, he faced a white missile headed his way. Snatching the paper airplane from the air before it could hit his face, he looked at Mo.

His son was laughing so hard he could scarcely stand. In Arabic he said, "You caught it, Papa. I would have gone farthest if you hadn't. It doesn't count."

"In English, please, Mo. Our guest doesn't understand," Rashid said, stepping into the room.

Bridget scrambled up from her place on the floor and grinned. "I don't understand the language, but I know interference when I see it. Was he calling foul?"

"He said I stopped him from winning."

She put her fists on her hips and shook her head. "Oh, no, you don't Mo. I would have won."

"Do it again. We have to do it again," the little boy said with relish.

Rashid handed Mo the paper airplane and shut the door behind him. "What did I interrupt?"

Mo rushed over to stand beside her, fairly dancing with anticipation.

"We are seeing who can send their airplane the farthest. Bridget wins more than me, but I won a few times," he explained.

"Have won," she corrected gently. "And you sure have. Did you need something?" she asked Rashid.

"Not at all. I came to see what you two were up to on a rainy afternoon."

"Bridget is playing with me before going to see Grandmother. Then they will read a book and I shall color a picture for her to take home. She lives in America, you know. And if she has a picture I drawed, she will always remember me. Can she come back to visit?"

"I would be delighted to have her return for a visit," Rashid said. "We need to make sure she enjoys this one so she will want to come again." He met her eyes over his son's head. He wanted to reach across the distance and draw her close.

"We are having fun," Mo stated firmly. "She will want to come again."

"Yes, I shall wish to. Maybe your father can judge our planes," she suggested, turning her attention on his son. Rashid felt a twinge of jealousy—of his little boy. He wanted her attention on him.

The afternoon passed swiftly. Mo was delighted to have two adults playing with him. After flying paper airplanes lost its appeal, they played two board games, neither familiar to Bridget, so Mo and Rashid had to explain the rules, and constantly offered her strategic suggestions. Mo won both and was pleased as punch.

Then Bridget suggested a game she sometimes used at children's hour at the library. They had moved to the comfortable sofa beneath one set of windows.

"I'll tell you a situation, and you tell me what you would do," she said.

"Okay," Mo said, sitting beside her and snuggling closer. Rashid sat beside his son, stretching his hand out along the back of the sofa. He almost touched Bridget's hair. He knew how soft it felt, would she notice if he rubbed a strand between his fingers?

"Okay, there's a huge dragon coming down the road. Fierce and breathing fire. What would you do?"

"That's easy," Mo said. "I'd give him a peanut butter and honey sandwich. Everybody loves those and he'd be so happy he wouldn't blow fire no more."

Rashid listened to his son's reply. "Peanut butter and honey? When have you ever had that?"

"Bridget says everyone loves peanut butter and honey sandwiches and it always makes her happy to eat one," Mo said.

She smiled wryly. "Comfort food, you know."

"Ah, and what else is comfort food for you?" Rashid asked.

"Pretty much anything chocolate. Now Mo, you have to make up a situation and ask your father what he would do," Bridget replied.

"Okay." He thought for a few moments, his face scrunched up in concentration. Rashid watched him, glancing once at Bridget to share his amusement at his son's determination. Her answering smile warmed him. It was the first time since Fatima died he felt connected with someone who shared his interest in and love of his son.

With a sudden realization, he knew Bridget loved Mo. She had an open, loving manner that couldn't fail to appeal to a small child who had lost his mother. Heck, it appealed to him, and his mother was still very much alive.

"What if we were at the beach and a giant wave came that would cover the beach and all of us. What would you do?" Mo asked seriously.

"I'd snatch you up, and dive through the wave to the other side where the sea would be calm and safe again," Rashid answered promptly.

"I can swim. I can hold my breath a long time," Mo said solemnly.

"Then we would have no problems getting to the other side of the giant wave. Do you want to take my turn to ask Bridget?"

"Okay. What if Papa showed up with lots of guests and you didn't know they were coming. What would you do?"

Bridget glanced at Rashid. "Is that common?"

He shrugged. "I usually give some notice to the staff."

She looked at Mo. "I would make a big pot of spaghetti and then a salad and make garlic bread. That would feed a crowd and when we were done, I'd take your father aside and scold him for not telling me earlier."

Mo giggled. "No one scolds Papa," he said.

"Maybe they should from time to time," she replied, throwing a saucy grin at Rashid.

"Or maybe I'm perfect just the way I am," Rashid teased.

"Or spoiled," she retorted quickly.

You could spoil me, Rashid thought. Her eyes were sparkling, her cheeks flushed with color. Her ready laughter captivated him. For an instant, he wished Mo wasn't with them. He'd draw her into his arms and kiss her until she didn't know her own name, or he didn't know his.

Before that line of fantasy took hold, he dragged his gaze from hers, focusing on Mo.

"Is that answer satisfactory?" he asked.

"Wouldn't she just tell cook?"

"Not if it was at my house. I do the cooking," Bridget said.

"You do?" Mo's eyes grew wide. "All by yourself?"

"Sure. And the cleaning, and laundry and everything. Not everyone has a staff at their beck and call."

Mo looked at his father for confirmation. Rashid felt a wave of love for his young son. He was still so trusting, relying on him for the truth. Would he grow to become cynical and distrusting? Would life be kind or harsh to his son? Rashid had an overwhelming yearning for Mo to stay as happy as he was this afternoon.

The immensity of his responsibility reared its head for the first time. Rashid had never fully realized the magnitude of the task ahead. For the first time in years, he achingly missed Fatima.

"Here's one for you, Mo," Bridget said. "I'm due to read to your grandmother and I'm late. She was expecting me at three."

"I'd run really fast," Mo said.

"Or you will get scolded," Rashid said, rising. "Mo, would you like to come see Asheera's new foal?"

"Yes!" He jumped up and hurried to the door.

"Go tell Alaya where you will be, and get a jacket, it's cool out with the rain," Rashid instructed.

Mo ran into the adjoining room.

"Thank you, Bridget Rossi, for bringing such happiness into the life of my son," Rashid said, taking her hand in his and bringing it to his mouth. He kissed her palm gently, smelling the sweet scent. Holding her gaze with his, he hoped she could see he wanted more. A brief affair until she had to leave. Would she be willing?

They could continue later in San Francisco. He could visit her, have her make him spaghetti and garlic bread and a peanut butter and honey sandwich. He wanted to see where she lived. To see her at work, to watch her captivate children at her reading hour. None could be more captivated than his son.

"I have to go, I really am late. I hope your grandmother won't be upset," she said, slowly pulling her hand from his.

"Tell her where you were, she dotes on Mo, so I think she'll forgive you."

Bridget closed her fingers over her palm, as if she could hold his kiss forever. She headed for the door, hoping he couldn't tell her knees felt as weak as soggy noodles. Hurrying down the corridor a moment later, she tried to remind herself it had been nothing but a thank-you kiss from a grateful father for her spending time with his son.

But it didn't feel like a grateful father's kiss. It felt wonderful. Daring. Romantic.

"Nonsense," she said aloud.

Knocking on the sitting room door a few moments later, she entered when bade to do so.

"I'm sorry for being late, Madame," she said to the woman sitting on a love seat. "I was with Mo and quite let the time slip by."

"Reading to him?"

"No, we were playing games. Rashid joined us, so Mo was in seventh heaven."

"Ah. I thought he had gone into the city with the other guests," Madame Al Besoud said musingly.

"Apparently not. Now he's taking Mo to see the new foal." Bridget reached for the mystery they'd been reading and opened it to where the bookmark was. "Shall I begin?"

"Would you not have preferred to go see the foal?"

"I was there when it was born. I expect I'll see it again before I leave. Don't you think it's good Mo has some private time with his father?"

"I do indeed, but wonder that you'd rather come here than spend time with them both."

"I'm dying to know how this story ends. I'll be leaving before long, so we need to make sure we finish it."

"You are kind to an old woman."

"No, it is you and Rashid who have been kind to me, inviting me here to help me deal with my papa's passing. I shall always be grateful."

By the time Bridget finished, the rain had stopped and sunshine filled the room.

"Do you think they'll still have the polo match? Or would the field be too wet?" she asked. "I've never seen one and would love to do so before I go home."

"The club has a good field, with proper drainage, since the rain has finally ended, I do believe the field will be ready by Saturday afternoon. I haven't seen a match myself in a while. They do play in the rain, but I don't like to attend those, too cold and wet. I, too, look forward to the match. And maybe expending some of that energy will help.''

''Help?'' Bridget asked.

''Tensions are running high, with Charles supposed to be squiring Elizabeth around, and making a bad job of it. Jack still hasn't asked Marie to marry him, which is what she expects. If their parents had been involved, I'm sure the matter would have been settled ages ago.''

''The famous arranged marriages,'' Bridget murmured.

Madame looked at her sharply. ''It might do some good in your country to have a few arranged marriages. The divorce rate is appalling.''

''You have no divorce in this country?''

The older woman was silent for a moment, glaring at Bridget. ''The rate does not even approach what you have.''

''My parents had a marriage that was not based on love. My father married Mum to provide a constant and steady motherly influence on Antonio's life. They had me, too. I always knew there was a lack of love from him to her. She adored him, however. Can you imagine how awful that would be?''

''There are other reasons for marriages than love,'' she stated firmly.

''Yes, but mutual love brings happiness, isn't that important, too? Were you happy in your own marriage?'' Bridget couldn't believe she'd been so rude as to ask such a personal question. Before she could apologize, however, the older woman slowly shook her head.

"No. I was infatuated with another man when I was married and could only bring my husband respect. I never developed warmer feelings for him."

"Yet you allowed your daughter to marry without love."

"Her father arranged her marriage."

"And then Rashid," Bridget murmured, studying the book cover. "Do you think he was happily married?"

"Not in the way his cousin, Yasmin, is. But yes, he and Fatima were happy enough."

"Yasmin?"

"The spoiled daughter of Rashid's uncle. She vowed she would only marry a man she loved. And her father allowed it."

Bridget hid a smile. Obviously Madame had been scandalized by the decision.

"And she's happy," Bridget said.

"It makes one envious to see her and her husband. They have eyes for only each other. And their new son. I expect if they were the only two people left on the face of the earth, they'd still be as happy as could be."

"That's what I want," Bridget said, trying to keep her thoughts away from Rashid. He'd made it clear love didn't figure into his plans for the future.

Bridget looked out the window at the watery sunshine. The visitors from England were leaving in a few days. She'd stay for the reception, and then make plans for returning home at the same time. The initial tearing grief of losing her papa was easing. Being with strangers, in unfamiliar surroundings had helped. She would forever be grateful for the change, no matter what—like falling for Rashid al Halzid.

She looked quickly at Madame Al Besoud. The older woman was studying her.

"Thank you for reading that book to me, and explaining all the different ways to look at the scenes," she said. "Sometimes the meaning of the English words are not as I learned them."

She enjoyed the quiet time with Madame, as she enjoyed being with Mo. She'd miss them both when she returned home. But not as much as she would miss Rashid.

Great, she thought, the deep longing for her father would be replaced by an even deeper longing for Rashid. She had a feeling it would take longer to get over him, knowing he was living somewhere else in the world.

"Is it getting easier?" the older woman asked. "Adjusting to the loss of your father?"

"I really miss him a lot. I can't even imagine how empty my life will seem when I go home. We always had dinner together on Wednesday nights. And I often saw him and Antonio at some point over the weekend. Now, it'll be so hard for the first few weeks. When I'm here, I can almost pretend he's home in San Francisco."

Bridget wished she felt closer to her brother. Not only were the years a chasm, but he was so focused on the restaurants and business, they had only their father to tie them together. Now Papa was gone. How would she and Antonio deal together now?

"I think he was at loose ends once he turned the restaurants over to Antonio," Bridget said slowly. "I don't think retirement is for everyone. Though he did make several trips to Italy over the last few years. I know he had plenty to do with Uncle Rudolfo and Aunt Donatella, his brother and sister," Bridget explained.

Her father had liked being in the heart of things, visiting with customers, handling temperamental chefs, dealing with challenges that invigorated rather than dampened his joy for life. She missed her mother, but her father had filled that void. Now with him gone, who would fill his place?

CHAPTER EIGHT

WHEN Rashid and Mo returned to the house, it was close to dinnertime. His son had been enchanted with the new foal and had not wanted to leave.

Jack was coming down the stairs.

"So how's the new guy?" he asked.

"Already sturdier on his feet. He's going to be a beauty," Rashid said. Of all his friends, Jack was the most horse mad.

"Want to go with us tomorrow?" Rashid asked, placing his hand on Mo's shoulder.

"I'll go on my own. I'm not much into kids. Didn't you tell me he's going off to boarding school soon?"

"That's not been decided." Even as he said the words, he was startled to realize he didn't want Mo to go anywhere anytime soon. He was discovering his child and liking the son he'd not really known before. Seven seemed too young to be sent from home. Maybe he'd see about having him educated in Aboul Sari.

"I thought it had been decided. You certainly will be much more free without a child to worry about," Jack said.

Mo looked back and forth between the men, his face solemn.

"Mo's my son, I will always worry about him," he said resting his hand on his head. He was getting an entirely new perception about parenting. Attributable to Bridget Rossi, no doubt.

"Of course, I never meant you wouldn't. I'll see you in the salon," he said, giving a two-finger salute to Mo.

Mo and Rashid walked to the top of the stairs together and headed for Mo's bedroom. Rashid wondered if he should think about marriage. Wouldn't Mo like a mother? In the meantime, Rashid wanted to concentrate on getting to know his son.

Bridget was in a pensive mood when she returned to her room. Her visit would be coming to an end soon. She'd heard the others were planning to leave shortly after the reception. She should make her travel plans as well.

But first, she would see a polo match.

And a secret part of her yearned to experience one magical night in a party where the rest of the people were powerful, rich and beautiful. It would be several steps up from the event Richard had invited her to. She would never have the opportunity again. Could she turn her back on that?

Time enough to return to the realities of life when she did return to San Francisco. She was selfish enough to wish to see how the other half lived for one evening.

She heard a soft knock at the door. Crossing over, Bridget was delighted to find Mo standing in the hall. Glancing to his side, she spotted Rashid. He was leaning casually against the wall, watching her.

"I came to see if you wanted to have dinner with

me," Mo said. "Papa said I could invite you. He said maybe you wanted someone uncompecated."

"Compecated?" she asked Rashid.

"Complicated. He's only five."

"And English is his second language. I'm still so impressed." She smiled at Mo. "I should love to have dinner with you. Will it just be the two of us?"

Mo nodded.

"Do I need to dress?"

His eyes widened. "Yes, you have to wear clothes." He looked at his father, panic in his eyes.

Bridget laughed. "Then I shall wear clothes."

Rashid explained what she had meant and Mo nodded solemnly. Then he smiled up at Bridget. "No, you don't need to dress. Maybe you can tell me a story."

"Mo, what did I tell you?" Rashid asked.

"You said she was sad and I should cheer her up. I bet she likes to tell stories, don't you, Bridget?"

"I do. It makes me really happy to tell stories." She looked at Rashid.

"Cook made spaghetti and garlic bread, I asked her specially." Mo chattered as they walked to his suite. The table near the window had been set for two, and Rashid stopped at the doorway.

"This is just for the two of you. Will you join us later downstairs?" he asked Bridget.

"Not tonight, if it is all right with you. I shall enjoy the evening much more here than with your other guests. And I need an early night. I still plan to go to the polo match tomorrow, however."

"I want to go," Mo said. "I like polo. Are you going to play, Papa?"

"Yes. You can accompany Grandmother. Would you like to ride with her as well?" he asked Bridget.

"I would love to. She can explain the finer points of the game to me."

"As could Marie, who I believe knows as much about it as Jack does. I'll make the arrangements."

Bridget enjoyed her spaghetti dinner with Mo. She told him stories that amused him. And he told her about visiting the new foal. When Alaya came to say it was time for bed, Bridget was sorry to see the evening end.

The next morning dawned bright and sunny. Bridget was unsure what to wear to the polo match, but decided one couldn't be too dressy, traipsing around a field and sitting on the sideline watching the horses and players. She donned a gray print skirt and sleeveless yellow top. Slathering on plenty of sunscreen, she was ready.

When she entered the dining room, only Charles was present. Had the others been and gone already?

"Good morning," he said, tucking into eggs, sausages and toast.

Bridget responded and sat at the seat next to his. "I'm looking forward to seeing the game."

"It's been many years since Jack, Rashid and I played on the same team. Rashid was telling us last night that he had no difficulty in getting an opposing team. And he found another rider to make the fourth on ours. Jack is quite excited."

"I do believe Jack would do nothing but play polo if he could," Bridget said.

Rashid strode into the dining room and greeted them both. Bridget's heart skipped a beat. He wore classic riding britches and high, polished black boots. His red polo shirt, aptly named, she thought, covered his muscular chest and arms. He looked good enough to eat. She had never seen him look so sexy or approachable. She forgot he was a sheikh of an important country whose oil reserves kept him in more money than she'd ever see. She forgot about his ideas on love and marriage, or his beautiful first wife.

All she could do was stare and hope she didn't give away the myriad of feelings that overwhelmed her.

She loved him.

She wanted him for herself, forever.

And she knew he was never going to be hers.

Rashid looked at her when he sat. "Are you feeling all right?"

She looked away, smiling brightly. "Definitely. And I'm looking forward to the polo match," Bridget said, feeling her face flame. Thank goodness he couldn't read minds. What was she going to do? She couldn't be in love with a sheikh.

Jack entered, wearing attire identical to Rashid's. While he looked fit and trim, he couldn't hold a candle to Rashid in sheer animal magnetism.

In only a few moments the dining room was crowded with guests, all chatting furiously about the upcoming match. Charles obviously enjoyed the game almost as much as Jack and was holding forth on blunders made in the past, some of which he himself had done. It was in good fun, and laughter frequent.

As soon as Bridget finished eating, she rose, hoping to leave unnoticed. But Rashid spoke before she could reach the door.

"Bridget, my grandmother will be ready to leave at nine."

She turned and nodded.

"Bring Mo down to see the horses if you would once we are all on the field. He'll like that," he said.

"Are you sure a polo match is suitable for a young child?" Marie asked. "He will probably be bored and then fretful."

"I think he'll enjoy it. Would you like to come down to see the horses as well?" Rashid asked.

"We'll see." She grinned at Jack. "Maybe I will come to kiss my man for luck."

Bridget slipped through the door and headed for the stairs. She felt a momentary pang for Rashid. Fatima had not cared for his horses. Marie obviously supported Jack and his interests. Would he find a woman one day who would share his interests? Who would love him as much as she did?

The limousine that carried Madame Al Besoud was luxurious. Bridget knew she'd always love this mode of travel and tried to imagine having a limousine and driver at her disposal in San Francisco. Sure would solve parking problems.

Mo was excited, bouncing in his seat, looking out the window, and chatting a mile a minute, sometimes in Arabic, sometimes in English.

"Do you think Papa will let me ride on his horse with him?" he asked as they turned into the grounds of the polo club.

"If he and his friends win, maybe you can ride the victory lap," Bridget said. "We can ask him."

"Victory lap?" Madame asked.

Bridget looked at them both. "It's a rodeo custom, I guess. When a cowboy wins an event, he then takes a ride around the arena, usually waving his hat to all the applause. Maybe they don't do that in polo."

"You know cowboys?" Mo asked, fascinated.

"Not really. I live in the city. But there is a terrific rodeo each year at the Cow Palace near San Francisco, and I usually go. I always wanted a horse when I was little."

"Now do you have one?" he asked.

"No. There's no place for me to keep one where I live. So I go and watch the rodeo and wander around the exhibits."

"I can ride. I have my own pony," Mo said.

"I know, I saw him when I was in the stable."

"He's bigger than the new baby horse, but the baby will grow up bigger."

"I know, but your pony is still a wonderful animal."

The car had stopped and the driver opened the rear door, assisting Madame Al Besoud from the limo. He then offered assistance to Bridget, while Mo scrambled out himself.

Stands were built on both sides of a wide expanse of grassy field. At either end, goal posts delineating the scoring area rose to a height of eight feet. Bridget gazed around in wonder. There were already quite a number of people on both sides of the field, not filling the stands, but certainly making good use of them.

"I didn't expect so many people," she murmured as Madame led the way to the box seats near the center of the stands.

"There are many people who enjoy watching games. Though this is not a regularly scheduled one on the club's calendar, I'm sure everyone heard Rashid and his English friends wanted a match." She nodded to acquaintances as she climbed the short set of stairs leading to a box with comfortable stadium seats. Elizabeth and Marie were already there, avidly watching the players warm up on the playing field.

Bridget walked beside Madame Al Besoud, sitting next to her when she chose a seat in the front row. Mo hung over the railing, waving at his father.

A moment later, Rashid rode his powerful black horse to the edge of the field and gestured for Mo and Bridget to join him.

He dismounted when they drew near, and Bridget was struck by his ease around the horses. For a moment the polo attire faded and she could see him as he might have been a hundred years ago—a warrior riding the deserts to defend his people. Instead of the helmet and red jersey, she envisioned him in flowing robes, riding his black steed across the burning sand. Her heart cartwheeled and began a rapid beat. She wished she could see him striding into some tent, claiming all he saw for himself. She'd love to be one of the spoils of war for this man.

"Papa, Bridget said you can take me on your victory lap," Mo exclaimed running up to his father.

"Victory lap?"

When Bridget explained, he nodded. "You have a lot of faith we will win, promising such a thing."

"I didn't promise, but I do think you'll win. I suspect you win most of your matches."

Jack rode up and dismounted. "Come to wish us luck?" he asked, grinning at Bridget and Mo.

"Of course, but I bet luck has little to do with it. You'll win easily, right?"

"I hope it won't be too easy, I like a challenge. But I do like to win."

Marie waved from the stands and rose. Bridget watched as she spoke with Elizabeth, who then joined her. In only minutes, they joined them at the edge of the field.

"I wanted to give you a good luck kiss," Marie said as she reached Jack. She encircled his neck with her arms and pulled his head down for a kiss. Her hat sheltered them a little from the view of the rest of the world.

Bridget took Mo's hand. "We better return to our seat."

"Why is that lady kissing him?" he asked, refusing to move, fascinated by Marie and Jack's embrace.

"For luck, darling boy," Marie said when she broke the kiss. "He and your father will win the match."

"Then Bridget should kiss Papa for luck."

Bridget looked at Rashid, and met his amused eyes.

"No, Mo. Too much is not good. Your father

doesn't need any kisses. Come, let's return to our seats.'' With that she turned and headed for the stands.

Rashid caught her arm and stopped her. "A team can never have too many kisses for luck, you know."

She looked at his mouth then met his eyes. "I'm not kissing you."

"Then I'll kiss you," he said, and did. His mouth covered hers in an explosive kiss that she felt to her toes. Almost before she could move, he released her and laughed.

"My luck is running high now," he said to Mo.

The match was thrilling. Madame explained the different plays, the scoring, and penalties. But it was the thundering sound of horses' hooves, the thwack of a mallet against the ball, and the cheers of the crowds which kept the game exciting. By the end, she could almost understand some of the plays.

Her eyes never left Rashid. He made it look like child's play, scoring two of the five goals his team made. The opposition scored only three.

When it was over, Rashid motioned for Mo to join him, and he rode his horse around the field in a victory lap.

Madame Al Besoud watched with a small smile.

"You've given them both a memory they will treasure," she said softly to Bridget. "And maybe started a new tradition with the club."

"Me?"

"Rashid didn't see Mo much before you came. I believe he will now spend more time with him. He is an enchanting child, as you know. I'm happy his father now recognizes that. Fatima kept the baby with her, selfishly, I believe. I think Rashid thought child care was only for women.''

''And you think men should be involved?''

''Don't you?''

''Of course, but I'm an American, we always are looking to have the fathers involved. I wasn't sure other cultures would see it the same way,'' Bridget said.

''Yet every parent wants the best for his or her child. You've shown Rashid he can enjoy his son before he is an adult. Come, my car awaits.''

''What about Mo?''

''His father can see to him. You are not his nursemaid.''

CHAPTER NINE

MEMBERS of the opposing polo team and their wives had been invited to dinner. Afterward the entire match was rehashed in the drawing room. Jack was in high spirits after the game, and Marie matched his exuberance. Charles and Elizabeth were a bit more subdued, but everyone in the losing team took the ribbing in good humor.

Bridget enjoyed the evening, though she had little to contribute. It was interesting to see Rashid with members of his own social circle, not just his friends from England.

Tomorrow evening was the state reception, and the day after that Rashid had invited them all to the beach. By Wednesday of next week, the other guests would be leaving. Bridget planned to ride to the airport with them. She needed to book a flight home first thing Monday morning before they left for the beach. She hoped she could get a seat on such short notice.

For a moment the thought of returning to San Francisco saddened her. She still had the task ahead of her of clearing her father's things, donating the clothes that still had life in them, and tossing those with no further value.

She knew Antonio wouldn't want to help, he'd view that as women's work. It would be easier if they did it together, remembering their father's life, sharing special incidences with each other. Maybe she could talk him into helping her.

Sunday evening Bridget was ready to leave before the appointed time. She stood in front of the floor-length mirror in her room gazing at the sight that met her eyes. Marie had insisted on doing her hair. It swept up, with large curls clustered at the top and a few tendrils that curved down around her face, just brushing her shoulders when she turned her head.

The cream-colored dress was a dream, as lovely as the first moment she'd seen it. It brought out the delicate color on her cheeks, blush not needed. She loved the way it fit, the way it felt like a cloud against her skin, and revealed every feminine curve.

She left her room to go down the hall to see Mo, having promised she would tell him good-night before she left. When she knocked on his door, Rashid opened it. He was dressed in formal attire, and looked stunning. She'd once wished he'd dress informally all the time so she could enjoy the view. Now she knew these clothes made the man. He was devastating. She felt her heart rate increase as a wave of sadness swept through her. She was going home soon, probably never to see him again. How would she stand it?

Rashid stared at the vision before him. Bridget looked as beautiful as any woman he'd ever seen. The dress had been made for her. It could never give that glow of beauty to anyone else so well. Her hair was done up, making his fingers itch to let it down until it tumbled over her creamy shoulders. He knew its softness, he wanted to feel it again.

"I came to bid Mo good night," she said softly. Her eyes seemed larger than normal, color flushed her cheeks.

All thoughts of duty and obligations momentarily fled. He wanted to take her some place private and spend the evening alone, with just her. For a moment he said nothing, then at her quizzical look, he spoke.

"I, too, came to say good night." The urge to shut the door, order Mo to his bedroom and kiss her all night long was almost too strong to resist. But he had duties and responsibilities to see to. He didn't have the luxury of doing only what he wanted.

"Bridget, you look beautiful," Mo said, coming up to stand by his father. "Like a fairy princess."

She smiled, and Rashid felt a reaction deep within. She smiled often at his son. The prick of jealousy he felt was irrational. But it was there. He wanted her to smile at him that way.

"I don't know about that, but it is a lovely dress, isn't it? My cousin bought it for me. I love it."

Bridget twirled around, showing off the dress for Mo. Rashid was sorry for the loss of her father, but suddenly he considered the unexpected bonus of Bridget's presence in his home. He never would have met her had her cousin not asked him to take her to the funeral.

"How nice of Francesca, and did she get you the other things from the boutique?" he asked for clarity.

"Yes. I offered to pay, but she said she wouldn't

hear of it. I never would have bought so much on my own.''

''Mo, tell Bridget good night, but no hugs, you don't want to risk getting anything sticky on her beautiful gown.''

''Nonsense, a hug is worth more than a dress any day,'' Bridget said, opening her arms to his son.

Mo's impish grin let Rashid know he delighted in her contradicting his father. Bridget seemed to have that knack.

''I have butterflies in my stomach,'' she said a few moments later as they walked along the hall toward the stairs.

''Because?''

''Because of the reception, of course. What if I make a total idiot of myself? Or spill a drink on an ambassador. That could cause an international incident. Or what if I become tongue-tied or am the only American someone meets. They'll think we're all dumber than dirt,'' she said.

He wanted to laugh at her assessment, but knew she was serious. She didn't seem to know how easily she could charm anyone with her forthright talk, her honesty, and her delight in everything she saw.

''First of all, if you spill something, we'll have it mopped up. Ambassadors are human just as we are. I am sure somewhere in their lives, they've even spilled a drink or two.''

''I don't think you get appointed an ambassador if you're in the habit of spilling drinks,'' she said.

He did laugh at that. ''Not in the habit, but it happens. Secondly, most people attending tonight have met other Americans. You will be a shining representative of your country.''

She stopped and looked at him, her delight clearly visible in her expression. ''Why, Rashid, that's a lovely thing to say. Thank you.''

He took a step forward, unable to resist. One kiss, that's all he'd take. It would have to last the night, but certainly he was entitled to one kiss.

Marie came from her room at that moment, spotting the two of them and calling a greeting. Rashid took a deep breath. That kiss would have to wait. He nodded to Marie.

''You look beautiful,'' he said sincerely.

''Thank you, Rashid, but I do believe your American guest will be the belle of the ball. The dress is fabulous,'' she said appraising Bridget.

''I love it. Thank you again for helping with my hair. I feel up to anything, I think,'' Bridget responded.

''Are we all traveling together?'' Marie asked, as they started down the stairs.

''I will be traveling with my grandmother. We need to arrive before the invited guests. I have arranged for two more cars for the rest of you,'' Rashid said.

Charles and Elizabeth were in the salon standing near one of the windows, deep in discussion. Jack had not yet come down. Rashid hoped his grandmother would join them soon, it was time for them to leave.

''I'm quite looking forward to meeting your parents again,'' Marie said. ''I met them when they came to Paris a couple of years ago,'' she explained to Bridget.

"Indeed. I'm sure they'll be happy to see all my guests, and meet Bridget," Rashid said.

"Will your cousin Yasmin and her husband be there?" Bridget asked.

"Yes, I'll make sure you meet her. You two will have a lot in common, I think."

Rashid checked his watch just as his grandmother entered the room. She looked elegant as always, dressed in black with the jewels she favored at her throat and wrist.

"I did not keep you waiting, I trust," she said.

"Not at all. The car is out front. Are you ready to leave?"

"Yes." She smiled at Bridget. "I shall be happy to introduce you to my daughter and maybe you can find Yasmin and you two will find a meeting of the minds."

"I told her the same thing," Rashid said.

"I shall look forward to it," Bridget replied, smiling at the older woman.

"Until later," he said.

Bridget watched the two leave, trying to still the butterflies in her stomach. She couldn't help thinking about the fiasco with Richard. She'd be careful to take nothing that could spill or drop, and she'd be fine. She hoped. Thanks to dinner the previous evening, she now knew a few more people who would be attending.

She hoped she could make it through the evening without totally disgracing her host.

"I love events like this," Marie said as they pulled silently away from the villa.

"I don't." Bridget would have been just as happy staying in and reading a good book.

"Why ever not? Lots of interesting people to talk to."

"Interesting men to meet," Elizabeth murmured with a sidelong glance at Charles.

"I'm not big on chitchat with strangers, unless it has to do with books or other things with the library." She was not going to tell these sophisticated people of her gaffe at Richard's party. It was bad enough to remember it in vivid detail.

"Did you see the diamonds Madame Al Besoud was wearing?" Elizabeth asked. "I expect all the women in their family have scads of jewels, diamonds, emeralds and rubies. Do you think they have these receptions just so they can wear all that loot?"

Marie laughed softly. "Wouldn't be surprised. Why don't you buy me something nice like Madame's necklace," she asked Jack.

He groaned. "If I wanted to spend a king's ransom I could. But then I couldn't afford to eat for a year."

"Ah, poor baby."

"Not so poor, just not in Rashid's league."

"Few are," Charles commented.

Another reminder of the gulf between them, Bridget reminded herself. Any feelings she was having toward Rashid needed to be nipped in the bud. He had kindly offered her a place to visit while the immediate shock of her papa's death faded. It was a kindness she wouldn't forget. But there was nothing more to it.

Their arrival at their destination saved Bridget further depressing thoughts. There was nothing wrong with her life in San Francisco. The sooner she returned home, the better.

The palace was ablaze with light. Cars and limousines were lined up on the driveway, discharging their passengers and then smoothly moving on. Several couples stood near the entry talking. Others were entering through the ornate double doors held wide by men in uniform.

Bridget took it all in, imprinting it to memory to tell her friends when she returned home. They would demand to hear every detail. And she wanted to forget nothing. For once she could imagine how Cinderella must have felt showing up for the ball.

Head held high, her resolve firmly in place, she followed the others into the State Hall. There was a receiving line comprised of His Excellency, Sheikh Mohammedan Al Halzid, his three sons and the visiting ambassador. Rashid was a familiar face, but the others were unknown. Bridget could see the family resemblance, and noted all the sons favored their father.

Once beyond the receiving line, she took in the splendor of the room, with crystal chandeliers suspended from the high ceiling, ornate gold leaf decorating the trim and the silk-covered walls, shimmering in the light.

Charles and Elizabeth joined her. "I say, this is

fabulous,'' he said, gazing around. ''I've visited Rashid several times over the years, but never been here before.''

Elizabeth looked animated for the first time Bridget remembered. It was not crowded, yet there were many people in the large room. Dresses of all styles and fabrics were worn with aplomb. Jewels sparkled. Voices spoke a myriad of languages. Bridget had never attended an event like it.

''Miss, your presence is requested,'' a man in military uniform stepped beside Bridget.

''Me?'' she asked.

''I will escort you.'' He offered his arm. She took it and they crossed through the crowd. He led her to Madame Al Besoud. She was talking with another two women, one about Bridget's age, one older.

''Delivered as requested,'' he said in English when they reached the threesome. He gave a slight bow.

''Thank you.'' Madame Al Besoud reached out to draw Bridget into the group. ''My daughter, Sadi, and Rashid's cousin, Yasmin. This is the American woman I was telling you about, Bridget Rossi.''

''How do you do?'' Bridget greeted her hostess and the young woman beaming a bright smile her way.

''I have visited San Francisco,'' Sadi al Halzid said. ''It is a lovely city, though I didn't like the cold fog.''

Bridget laughed. ''It can be cool, but we call it nature's air-conditioning. It does keep the temperatures down. Rashid has graciously given me a short tour of Aboul Sari. I like the oases, but not the desert so much.''

"Me, either. Give me air-conditioning," Yasmin said. "Did he take you to the bazaar?"

Bridget shook her head.

"Then let me tell you the best times to go and where to look for the most fabulous materials and rugs. Better yet, shall we arrange a time to visit together? I'll show you the best stalls." Soon Yasmin and Bridget found chairs and sat for conversation. Time flew by. Time and time again waiters would stop offering beverages or hors d'oeuvres. Bridget declined each offering.

At last Yasmin questioned her refusal. "I'm starving, but don't want to take anything if you don't," she said. "Are you on some diet or something?"

"No, I'm afraid I'll spill everything." Despite her reluctance to tell about the last formal reception she attended, she found it easy to relate the event to Yasmin, embellishing it until both of them were laughing by the time she finished. Had she put the trauma behind her at last?

"The next dance is mine," Rashid said appearing suddenly in front of them.

Bridget looked up, surprised to see him. She looked around, not seeing anyone dancing.

"I didn't know there was dancing."

"In the ballroom, adjacent to this room." He greeted his cousin. "Where is Mikeil? I'm surprised to find you two separated."

"It was a hardship, but I've survived. Your father had some shipping people he wanted Mikeil to speak to. He will find me when he's done."

"Undoubtedly. In the meantime, may I take Bridget?"

"That's her decision, but I can't see why she would want to go off with you when she and I were having such a great talk," Yasmin said cheekily.

Rashid offered his hand and Bridget put hers into his. She rose and smiled at Yasmin. "I've enjoyed visiting, do call if we can go shopping on Tuesday. Otherwise, another time." She knew there would be no other time.

Yasmin rose as well, leaning to kiss Rashid on the cheek. "I like your guest. You should have more visiting like her. You two have fun. I'll make sure you meet Mikeil before the night is over."

Rashid tucked her hand into the crook of his elbow as they crossed the reception area. The noise level was louder than earlier. She glanced around, surprised to realize how crowded the room had become.

The next room held almost an equal number of people dancing to the music played at one end of the large ballroom. Rashid swept her into his arms and moved them onto the dance floor moving in perfect time to the slow tempo.

Bridget was in heaven. She rested her forehead against his chin, breathed in his scent. His legs brushed against hers as they swayed in time to the melody. Her hand held in his tightened slightly when he brought her against him with his other arm. They moved as one.

"I take it you have finished your duties in the reception line," she said a moment later.

"Yes, the formal line disbursed. My father is now

introducing the ambassador to close friends, and people who need personal contact. The discussions will last most of the evening, but I'm not needed for that."

"I met your mother, and of course Yasmin. I liked them both. I hope I see them again before I leave."

"Yasmin will surely call. She has a wide circle of friends you might like. And she loves to shop."

"So I gathered." Bridget loved the implicit intimacy of talking softly while they danced. His breath caressed her cheek when he spoke. She felt as if they were in a world of their own.

When the song ended, Rashid introduced her to friends nearby. Bridget danced every dance, sometimes with men who spoke English, other times with men who did not. She enjoyed herself and the specter of Richard and their last night together faded completely.

Rashid claimed her for another dance near midnight. The lights had been dimmed, and the music was unfamiliar to her, but she didn't hesitate a moment. Not a single partner all evening had compared to him.

"My grandmother left for home an hour ago. You must let me know when you wish to return," he said.

"How long will the reception last?" she asked.

"The ambassador has already left. My parents will leave soon, as some attending will not depart until after they have gone. The rest will stay as long as they are enjoying themselves."

"I'm having a wonderful time, but I will probably want to leave soon. My feet are killing me," she confessed ruefully. She had never danced so much in one night, and the lovely shoes weren't designed for hours on her feet.

He stopped. "Shall we leave now?"

"No! I want to finish our dance." In fact, if she was dancing with Rashid, she'd go on all night, hurt feet or not.

He held her closely, tucking their hands in near to their shoulders, his left arm holding her. Bridget thought he kissed her hair, but wasn't sure. She pulled back to look at him, their faces so close she would only have to lean forward an inch or two to kiss him herself.

If protocol didn't dictate discretion, she might have availed herself of the opportunity. But he was the son of the ruling sheikh. They were in too public a place to risk embarrassing him. But she couldn't help wishing he would kiss her. That would make it all right.

As if he read her mind, he closed the gap and covered her mouth with his. Bridget gave a soft sigh of delight and kissed him back. For the moment she refused to think about the other people in the ballroom or the consequences of such a reckless public display.

She savored every second, relished every touching point between them. Tonight was magical, tomorrow would be time enough to return to reality.

"Rashid, can you have a car brought round for me? I'm leaving. I've had enough of Charles humiliating me in front of everyone!" Elizabeth said, popping the fantasy bubble Bridget floated in.

CHAPTER TEN

RASHID released Bridget and turned to Elizabeth. Assessing her anger, he quickly escorted her from the center of the ballroom, Bridget beside him.

"I'm happy to take you home now, if you like. I'll see to the car immediately. What happened?"

Elizabeth was almost in tears, but anger kept her in control. "I am supposed to be Charles's date to this event. Heck, to the house party. I thought this would be the romantic place he'd propose to me. Instead, he took one look at Francesca Bianchetti and had eyes only for her while she was here. Tonight he's flirting with every pretty woman in the place, and virtually ignoring me. I've had enough. I wish to return to the villa and pack to leave. I'm not going to stay another moment!"

"Come, we will leave. Bridget?"

"Yes, I'm ready to go, too," she said, feeling guilty over her cousin's part in Elizabeth's problems. But everybody at the villa had known Francesca was only flirting. Surely it was harmless. Francesca was too wrapped up in her career to become involved with anyone.

In no time Rashid had summoned a car and they were on their way back to the villa. Elizabeth said nothing after they started, but Bridget knew her anger simmered by the way she clenched her fists in her lap.

"If you feel you wish to leave in the morning, I will take you to the airport," Rashid said at last.

"I wish to leave tonight." Anger laced her voice.

"It's after midnight," Bridget said. Did Elizabeth not realize how late it was?

"I don't care. I don't wish to stay another night. Charles has no feelings for me. I'd just as soon leave before he returns. It's too bad your troublesome cousin isn't still here to console him," Elizabeth said.

"What?" Bridget couldn't believe she'd heard right.

"That's enough," Rashid said calmly.

"Either you are as blind as Charles, or you don't care, Rashid. Are you so besotted by a beautiful face that rational thought goes out the window? Francesca uses people. You, Charles. Who knows where she is now. She lets you buy her expensive clothes and take her to exotic places and gives you what in return? She dumps her cousin on you, letting you buy her clothes, entertain her. What next, an Italian grand-mother, an aging aunt?"

"What clothes?" Bridget felt a sinking in her heart. "Elizabeth, what are you talking about?"

"The very ones you're wearing, of course. Don't tell me you didn't know Rashid paid the bill," she scoffed, clearly on a roll.

"Francesca bought them."

"Tell her," Elizabeth said, glaring at Rashid. "Tell her how Francesca delights in spending your money as if it were her own. Or is she just anticipating a happy event the rest of us don't know about?''

Bridget turned to him in horror. "Rashid, you didn't pay for these clothes, did you?''

"It was nothing, Bridget. I was happy to do it,'' he said.

"I thought Francesca bought them. I can't have you buying me clothes.'' Bridget couldn't believe what she was hearing. She was certain Francesca had purchased the clothes. How could she let Rashid pay for them? He hadn't even known her but a day when she'd bought them. It wasn't some casual meaningless gesture to the cousin of a friend. They had cost a lot of money!

"It doesn't matter,'' he said, his voice tightening in irritation.

"It certainly matters to me. I'll pay you back,'' she said, embarrassed.

Elizabeth gave a harsh laugh. "That's easier said than done, my dear. That's a haute couture gown you're wearing...it probably cost more than a librarian makes in a year. And how about that silk blouse you wore the other day, it probably—''

"Enough!'' Rashid said. "Elizabeth, you will kindly mind your own business. Bridget, I do not wish to hear about repaying me for the clothes. Is that clear to both of you?''

Bridget nodded, fuming. She tried to remember exactly why she'd thought Francesca footed the bill. When she'd asked, her cousin had said it was all taken care of. Naturally Bridget assumed she'd meant her cousin was taking care of the bill. She never would have accepted the dresses had she known Rashid was paying. Francesca had put her in an untenable position. Maybe she was used to taking gifts like this from men, but Bridget certainly wasn't.

"I still wish to leave tonight," Elizabeth said stiffly.

"There are no planes for England at this time," Rashid said reasonably.

"Then I'll find a hotel near the airport."

Bridget gazed out the window. For a moment, she wished she could join Elizabeth in leaving. She was totally embarrassed. Did everyone at the villa know she'd bought the clothes on Rashid's money? Was she the only one who hadn't known?

They arrived at the villa in silence. Rashid helped Bridget from the car, turning then to assist Elizabeth. He sent the driver back for the rest of the guests and escorted them inside the house.

Elizabeth went straight for the stairs. "I'm packing."

"Elizabeth, I will have a car for you at eight in the morning. I cannot let you leave now," Rashid said.

She hesitated a moment on the bottom step, then nodded. "Very well, first thing in the morning, then." She ran up the stairs and disappeared around the corner.

Rashid looked at Bridget. "Are you dashing off to bed now, or would you stay with me a while? Would you care for a drink or something to eat?"

She shook her head. While eating sparingly at the reception, lest she spill something, she was too keyed up to be hungry.

"I'm not quite ready to go up," she said. Nor ready to drop the matter of the clothes, no matter what Rashid said. She would come up with a way to repay him!

"About the dresses—" she started.

He placed a finger across her lips. "I do not wish to discuss the dresses. Enjoy them. You look lovely in them and despite what Elizabeth said, they did not cost a fortune. Come, join me for a little while. We will have the salon to ourselves, I'm sure. Grandmother would have retired upon her return and the others won't arrive for a while."

She didn't want to drop the subject, but temporarily gave in. As they walked into the salon, her curiosity peaked. "What do you suppose happened between Charles and Elizabeth?" Bridget asked as they entered the dimly lit room. The French doors were opened to the night breeze, the path to the gardens visible.

"I expect he paid more attention to other women than Elizabeth wanted. I know she came expecting a marriage proposal, and he has not delivered."

"Cynical Rashid, a proposal should be romantic and wonderful, not something delivered," Bridget said, trying to concentrate on the conversation at hand and not dwell on the other matter.

"Should he have swept her off her feet, strewn roses along her path and wined and dined her in style before losing his freedom forever?" he asked whimsically.

She laughed. "I can't imagine Charles being that romantic. And I question your use of the term loss of freedom. Didn't you enjoy freedom when you were married?''

''Yes, but look at Mikeil, he can't take a step without Yasmin.''

''I think it's very romantic. They adore each other and don't mind who knows it.'' Wistfully she gazed off to the garden. ''That's the kind of love I hoped to have one day,'' she said softly.

''Hoped as in past tense?'' Rashid questioned.

She shook off her yearning and corrected herself. ''Hope for. I think I'd rather remain alone than marry where there was no love.'' Or where the love was all on one side as her mother had known.

''Come, let's walk in the garden. The warm weather won't last forever.'' He tucked her hand in the crook of his arm and led her into the night. Night blooming jasmine sweetened the air. The wind rustled the leaves gently, providing a magical melody. Bridget found another moment she wished to capture for all eternity.

''Did you enjoy the reception?'' he asked as they turned a corner away from the house. Without the illumination from the salon, the night became darker, despite the pathway lights.

''I did, unexpectedly. Thank you for inviting me. I will have lots of things to tell my friends when I return home. Once again I must thank you for your invitation to visit. It has helped me get beyond the immediate pain of Papa's death.''

Of course, now she'd have the pain of heartbreak to deal with, but that was something he must never know. She craved his company so much. Surely a walk in the gardens couldn't hurt anything. One night wouldn't matter in the greater scheme of things. And it would add another memory to treasure.

He stopped and turned to look at her, cupping her face in his hands. "It is my pleasure to have you here, Bridget. Remember that." Then he kissed her.

It was unexpected, and most welcomed. Bridget kissed him back, delighting in the embrace when he wrapped his arms around her and held her close. Moments later she felt his fingers in her hair, the pins flung away, the tresses tumbling to her shoulders.

He pulled back and looked at her in the faint light, quiet satisfaction in his eyes. "I've wanted to do that since I first saw you tonight." He threaded his fingers through the soft strands, sending sensuous shivers of delight down her spine.

"I wish I could see it spread on my pillow, see it in the moonlight, in the early dawn. Stay with me, Bridget, after the others leave on Wednesday. Stay a little longer."

She pulled free, staring at him. For a moment hope blossomed. Then what he said penetrated. As well as what he hadn't said. Was he suggesting an affair? She was dismayed. Had her letting him kiss her given him the impression she would condone such a relationship once it was made?

"No, I can't stay. I need to go home." Bridget backed away another step, yearning for him to sweep aside any doubts she had, tell her he loved her beyond measure and wanted her to marry him and have a half dozen children with him.

"Nothing pressing awaits you at your home. Stay just a little while longer," he urged.

So much for dreams. A little while longer was nowhere near a proposal. Not even close to declaring love.

"I think we had…" she began.

He raised his head, listening. Once again Bridget saw him as a warrior, scenting danger, poised to take action. She wished for a moment things were simpler, that she didn't care so much. Didn't wish so strongly she dare take him up on his offer and say to hell with the consequences.

But she couldn't. How much deeper in love would she fall if she stayed? And the outcome was already assured. He didn't love her. She wouldn't give her all like her mother had, only to be met with indifferent affection. It was too hard.

"The others have returned," he said.

Her hands covered her hair, pulling it back. "I can't go in looking like this," she protested.

He frowned, then turned back toward the house. "Very well, wait here. Once I get them all upstairs, you can come in with no one the wiser."

Bridget followed at a distance, stopping when she could see into the lighted salon. Charles and Jack were arguing, Marie was yawning widely. When Rashid stepped in from the terrace, Bridget instinctively stepped back, even though she knew no one could see her in the darkness.

She couldn't hear the conversation, but it was only moments later when they all left the salon.

Had she made the right choice? She licked her lips,

still tasting him, the yearning in her heart growing. She'd never been with a man who touched her so deeply, but it was like a fairy tale. Surely once she was back home, all this would fade and she'd forget the feelings that threatened to overwhelm her tonight.

Waiting a few minutes longer, Bridget brushed back her hair the best she was able and entered the salon. Was someone coming to lock the doors? She pulled them shut behind her.

When she reached the entryway, she paused, listening. The house was silent.

She climbed the stairs quietly, feeling as if she were sneaking in from an illicit date or something. The charm of the evening had faded. She was tired, drained, and longed for bed.

The next morning, Bridget rose early. She had not slept well. A day at the beach was just what she needed. Rashid had said Mo might be included. She'd spend the day with the child, and ruthlessly ignore Rashid.

Tomorrow she'd do her final packing and depart on Wednesday. She did not yet have a reservation. That she must remedy immediately. Leaving her room, she started downstairs when Elizabeth left her room farther along the hallway. She was dressed for travel.

"Elizabeth, how did you get a reservation?" Bridget asked when she drew near.

"Phone." She walked with her head held high, but Bridget could see the swollen eyes from crying.

"The operators speak English?" Bridget hurried to keep up with her.

"Ask for an English speaking attendant when you dial, they'll connect you. You'll have to use the phone in Rashid's study." Elizabeth paused at the top of the stairs and turned to Bridget. "I apologize for last night. I saw after I spoke that you really didn't know your cousin was allowing Rashid to foot the bill for all the clothes. You did nothing wrong and I apologize for lumping you in with your cousin."

"I'm sorry for the trouble she caused," Bridget offered gently.

Elizabeth's eyes filled with tears. "Me, too," she said, and turned to descend.

Bridget watched her leave. She hadn't a clue where Rashid's study was. Sighing softly, she knew she would have to wait to ask him when she saw him.

It was early, but Mo would likely be awake. Maybe she could eat breakfast with him and avoid the discussion that was sure to take place in the dining room when the others learned of Elizabeth's departure. She could imagine the speculation that would result. Would Charles even notice?

Mo was delighted to see her and it did Bridget's heart good to have at least one member of the family open about his feelings.

She chatted with Mo while they ate breakfast, all the while wishing Rashid had joined them.

Wasn't she setting herself up for the same kind of heartache her mother had endured? There was no question her mother had loved Antonio as much as she had loved Bridget. And she had tried so hard to please Papa, hoping he would love her as much as he had loved his beautiful Isabella.

Bridget knew better than to fall in the same trap, but despite all her intentions, there were a lot of similarities. Of course, the primary one was missing—where Rashid asked her to marry him.

He was attracted to her, he made no effort to hide that. But physical attraction was fleeting. She wanted a love so powerful it would endure forever. Was that too much to ask? Only with Rashid. He had loved his first wife. And nothing indicated he was looking for another one.

Any ideas along those lines were purely wishful thinking. Instead she should be making plans to return home. She had her life to live.

"Do you go to the sea a lot?" Mo asked. "Alaya showed me where you live, right on the water."

"San Francisco is on the tip of a peninsula, so we have lots of water around us. But I don't go to the beach often. The water is very cold, not warm like the Med."

"Sometimes my bath gets cold."

"And then you're glad to get out, right?"

He nodded.

"So you see why I don't go to the ocean often. Do you like the beach?"

"I do. I make castles, and dig for water and dive through the waves like Papa said he would do if the big wave came."

"You are a good swimmer. But don't go far from shore."

"Oh, no, or I might be taken for a long ride and it would be hard for Papa to find me."

Bridget smiled at his solemn tone. Obviously someone had taught him well.

When everyone was ready to leave, they gathered
in the foyer. Rashid snapped orders as to who would
ride with whom. He and Bridget would take his sports
car, he informed the group. Marie smiled. Jack offered to drive it back to save Rashid the chore.
Charles looked uncomfortable.

Bridget wondered if she should not have skipped
breakfast. Maybe Marie would tell her later what had
transpired.

The drive was exhilarating. She wondered if she
should consider getting a convertible when she returned home. It felt so free with the wind in her hair,
the sun warming her shoulders and the terrific view
she had of everything.

Of course it might not be the same having a car of
her own with no special person to share it with.

"You look sad, what is the matter?" Rashid asked,
flicking her a glance.

"Just feeling sad this special time is almost over.
I need to make sure I can get reservations for
Wednesday. I have an open ended ticket."

"I wish you would stay."

"I have enjoyed myself," she said politely. "I will
miss all this when I'm gone." *And you!*

"Then, don't go. Stay, Bridget. Stay with me."

"For how long?" *Please say forever. Tell me you
love me,* she willed.

"As long as we both wish it. At least through the
summer. I can show you more of Aboul Sari, take
you on my yacht. When the others leave, my grand-

mother will also be returning to her home. It would just be you and me.''

''And Mo,'' she said. ''Thank you for the offer, but I need to get home.''

''Don't say no without thinking about it,'' he almost ordered.

''Very well, I'll think about it before I say no.'' She tried to keep it light, lest he guess how much she longed to do just what he asked. But no words of love had passed his lips, and she knew she wasn't cut out for a one-sided relationship.

CHAPTER ELEVEN

WHEN they arrived at the beach, there were already several cars parked in a paved area off the road. Before them lay a stretch of pristine white sand beach, and beyond the gorgeous blue of the Mediterranean Sea. Except for several chairs already set up near the water, and the open tent shading tables of food, the place was deserted.

"This is beautiful," she said when he stopped the car near the sand. "Doesn't anyone else think so?"

"I hope all my guests do."

"It's your private beach?" she asked, looking at him.

"My family's, yes."

Oh wow, as far as she could see in either direction was only empty sand and cloudless sky. Imagine having a perfect beach for only one family. It was mind-boggling.

She grabbed her tote bag and joined Rashid. The sand was warm underfoot. They walked to the tent, where several tables and chairs were arranged. Piles of fluffy towels were stacked near the edge. Food was being unwrapped on the long buffet table.

The chaise longues were nearer the water's edge.

"How perfect," she said, taking in everything. She'd never imagined such a magnificent spread in the middle of the beach. Usually she and her friends

171

either roasted hot dogs, or brought sandwiches when they went to the beach. And the only time the beaches near San Francisco were totally empty was when the weather was terrible.

Before long the others joined them. Mo was excited about swimming and despite Rashid's comment that Bridget needn't take him, because Alaya was there to watch his son, she took the little boy's hand and headed for the water. In only moments, Rashid joined them.

It was like heaven. The sun warm overhead and the water a silky sensation against her skin. The temperature enough to cool her off without being too cold to stay in a long time.

The three of them played for a while, until Mo tired. Rashid sent him back to Alaya, and swam next to Bridget.

"It's so buoyant," she commented, lying back to float on the top of the water. It was almost as flat as glass.

"Much nicer than the stretch of Pacific Ocean by San Francisco," she murmured.

"Another enticement to stay," he said.

She dropped her feet and came upright in the water. Rashid was closer than she expected.

"There's much more enticing me to stay than the sea," she said.

"Good." He pulled her against him and kissed her.

Every inch of her skin inflamed. She wound her arms around his neck pressing even closer. He wore brief trunks, she a modest two-piece swimsuit. There was a lot of bare skin touching, and not for the first time Bridget wished Rashid loved her as much as she loved him. She wanted to know every inch of him. Wanted to touch him, to know her life would be complete with this wonderful man a major part of it.

His legs brushed hers as he slowly kicked to keep them upright. The contact was electric. She reveled in the exquisite sensations that pulsed through her as his kiss deepened.

A sound from the beach penetrated the haze that surrounded her and she pushed back slightly. His dark eyes looked into hers. She shivered despite the heat of the day, seeing the desire he made no effort to hide.

"Your other guests must be wondering what we are doing," she said huskily. Her breasts were pressed against his hard chest. Her legs tangled with his as he continued to keep them above the water.

"If they have eyes, they can see."

"Great." She dropped her head against his, forehead to forehead. "I think I should go in."

"You are a great one for running away," he teased.

"When in over my head, retreat is often the best strategy. At least until I can regroup."

Slowly he released her. "Regroup and come again," he said.

She swam back to the beach and came out of the water some distance from the lounge chairs. Heading for the tent, she took one of the towels a servant handed her, and wiped the water from her face before wrapping the towel around her.

Taking a soft drink offered, she stood in the edge of the shade, watching as Rashid swam parallel to the shore. His strong arms cut cleanly through the water. He was a powerful swimmer.

And powerful kisser, she thought, still feeling her heart pound.

She looked around. Mo was playing some distance away, near the water's edge with Alaya. They were constructing a huge sand castle. He was more intent in digging the moat, from what Bridget could see.

She headed for the lounge chairs. Jack and Marie were side by side. There were two empty chairs before the one Charles sat in. He was staring out at the sea, but something in his manner suggested his thoughts were far away.

The sand was warm beneath her feet, she walked slowly, sipping her beverage.

"...admit it makes sense. I always thought he should have more kids," Jack said. "He could do worse. She likes his son. Is pretty enough to have nice-looking kids. And who wouldn't like the lifestyle he enjoys."

Marie was lying on her back, eyes closed as she took in the sun. "A woman wants more than to be a good mother," she murmured.

"Well, the money he has could buy Bridget whatever she wanted."

Bridget stopped walking, stunned to find herself the topic of conversation.

"Maybe money isn't all that important. Her father made money from those restaurants. She probably has all she wants," Marie said lazily.

"Nothing like Rashid could provide," Jack countered. "I bet he proposes before we leave. She fits in.

She's always in his company. They must find something to talk about.''

''You don't think he's in love with her, do you?'' Marie asked.

''Not that I can tell. But he's attracted to her and that would be enough.''

Bridget knew it didn't pay to eavesdrop, but she was struck by the desire to hear more.

''Is that enough for you?'' Marie asked.

''I don't have a kid who needs a mother.''

''Mo's doing fine without one.''

''No, every kid needs a mother. Want to take my bet?'' Jack asked.

''You're on. I say Rashid won't propose before she leaves.''

''And if he does?''

''Then I'll cook dinner for a month.''

Jack was silent for a moment. Bridget was afraid to move for fear they would detect her. Could she back away without their knowing she'd overheard?

''Actually, I want something different for a bet,'' he said.

Marie turned and looked at him. ''Like what?''

''Not dinner. I'm hoping you'll do that anyway— as my wife.''

Marie sat up, her eyes only on Jack. He looked uncertain, but had his gaze on the woman at his side.

Slowly Bridget backed away until she turned and fled to the tent. It would never do to let them know she overheard their conversation.

Shocked at the thought Jack and Marie thought Rashid would propose to acquire a mother for Mo, she wanted to do nothing more than leave. She had vowed never to be second best to a man. She would not repeat the mistake her mother had made.

If she could leave this instant she would do so. Did Rashid think she was angling for marriage? That she was playing hard to get and would capitulate in the end? Was that his goal, to find a suitable mother for his son?

Charles entered the tent and went to one of the stewards. "I need to return to the villa to get my things, then go on to the airport," he said.

"Yes, sir. A car will take you," the man replied.

"Wait," Bridget said on impulse. "I want to go back with you." She was due to leave in two days. Maybe it would be best to make the break now, leave before she further embarrassed herself. Before Rashid had a chance to push for an answer she longed to give, but knew was wrong.

Charles looked at her, as if seeing her for the first time. "I'm leaving," he said. "Elizabeth was right about me, and I need to make things right with her."

"Can I go with you to the airport?" She would take a chance and book her flight when she got there. If there was nothing immediately, she'd stay in a hotel in the city. Her visit was at an end.

"Tell His Excellency I was called away," she told the steward. Snatching up her cover-up, she slipped it on, slid her feet into her shoes and stuffed the rest of her things in her tote. "I'm ready," she told Charles.

When they reached the villa, Charles alighted first and turned to assist Bridget from the car.

"Wait for me, it won't take me fifteen minutes to get ready," Bridget said.

She entered the house and flew up to her room. A quick shower to get rid of the saltwater and she dressed. In less than five minutes she had packed the clothes she came with and was ready. With a last glance at the room, she hurried down the stairs and out the front door.

The driver had already put Charles's bags into the trunk of the limousine. He took Bridget's without comment. She slid in the back seat beside Charles.

"It's rude to leave without saying goodbye," he said.

"Did you?"

He shook his head.

"Guess we'll both be chalked up as rude," she said, wishing the visit had ended differently.

Bridget looked back as they drove away, committing the house to memory. For a moment she felt a pang so sharp she had to rub her chest. She'd write to Mo, and Madame Al Besoud and Rashid. She'd come up with some excuse that she hoped would placate them. But she wouldn't come again.

Bridget settled back when they turned onto the main road. Her life would never be the same for having known Rashid.

"What do you mean, she's gone?" Rashid asked.

The maid cringed. "I checked her room. There are some clothes hanging up, but everything Miss arrived with is gone, and the suitcase, her purse, her toiletries. All gone."

He paced to the far end of the room. It was midafternoon. He hadn't seen Bridget since she had so suddenly left the beach. Once lunch with Jack and Marie had ended, he'd returned home to look for her. When he asked one of the maids to see if she was all right, he learned she'd left. With Charles? It had to be. No other car had departed today, he would have known it.

He dismissed the maid and called to the garage. The driver confirmed he'd taken two guests to the airport that morning.

She'd left. Without a word of explanation. Without a word of goodbye.

He hung up the phone, staring off into space. He clenched a fist. He had wanted her to stay longer, not leave earlier.

He'd handled the situation badly.

He went to her room. Opening the door, he stood there for several minutes, as if expecting her to rise from the chair near the window, or come from the wardrobe. The room was neatly cleaned. He crossed to the old wardrobe and opened it. He recognized some of the clothes, were they all the new ones? She hadn't taken a thing he'd paid for. A slow admiration simmered. She had been horrified when she'd discovered he had provided the clothes. This was obviously her way to mitigate the situation as far as was in her power.

He had other guests to see to. Bridget had chosen her path. He would have had it different, but so be it.

Slowly he left the room, closing the door behind him.

CHAPTER TWELVE

IT HAD been a month since Bridget returned home. Her friends had rallied round to help her go through her father's things and to ease the transition back to normal life. His suits, dress shirts and silk ties had been donated to New Chance, the place that provided quality clothing to people to have on interviews when seeking a new chance in life after circumstances had beaten them down. The rest she donated to a homeless shelter.

Antonio had taken some mementoes he especially wanted from their papa. And offered her a job at the restaurant. She'd turned it down, resuming her duties at the library.

She was at the family home now, trying to decide if she wanted to rent it out, or move back. Nothing felt right.

Upon her return to San Francisco, she'd written to Rashid, enclosing a note also for Madame and Mo. Not having his address, however, she'd merely sent it to the capital city, having no way of knowing if it reached him or not. Surely he was known throughout Aboul Sari.

Despite her firm hope, her love for Rashid hadn't faded once she took off from Alidan. Given time, she was sure it would. At least she hoped it would.

Funny, she'd longed for love for so long, and when

it came, she had to turn her back and leave it behind. Life wasn't always fair, as her mother had probably known.

Time would heal all aches. She wished it would hurry up. She found herself gazing off into space at the most inopportune times—like now when she should finish the vacuuming of the living room. She remembered telling Mo and Rashid she did all the work in her home. She also remembered the special way Rashid would turn his head and look at her, or the passion of his kisses, or the startled laughter when his friends said something funny.

Someday she'd stop thinking every dark-haired man she saw was Rashid. Like the man climbing the stairs to the house, she thought, her daydreams fading as she focused.

Looking beyond him she saw the black limousine, and a familiar bodyguard standing at the foot of the stairs, a suitcase at his feet.

Good grief, it *was* Rashid!

Bridget hurried to the door before he could knock. She flung it open, stunned to see him.

"Hello, Bridget," he said.

"Rashid. What brings you here?"

"I would have called ahead, but felt you might refuse to see me. I must have offended you a great deal for you to leave so abruptly."

"No, you didn't offend me at all. I left for another reason. A bunch of reasons, actually."

He snapped his fingers and the bodyguard lifted the suitcase, climbing up the stairs and depositing it at Bridget's feet.

"You forgot a few things," Rashid said.

She looked at the suitcase. Her clothes, she knew. "I didn't think I should take them."

"They are yours. If I have to accept payment for them so you will take them, I will do so. But they didn't cost much and it would give me pleasure for you to have them."

"Thank you." She bit her lip. What she really wanted to know was what he was doing here. He hadn't come all the way from Aboul Sari to deliver her dresses. He could have sent them for that matter. Or given them away.

"Are you going to invite me inside?" he asked.

"Oh, yes, of course. Come in. Do your men want to come in as well?"

"No, they're fine."

"In the chilly fog?" The gray mist blew in from the ocean, obscuring the sun, giving a damp chill to the air.

"It's a nice contrast from the heat of Aboul Sari."

When he stepped into the living room, Bridget followed, flustered to see the vacuum cleaner in the center of the room.

He didn't notice.

But he did seem to fill the spacious room, taking what air there was out of it. Or was it only her starved senses, taking in every inch of him? She didn't know why he was here, but she was glad he'd come to see her. Oh, how she wished things had been different.

"Did you get my letter?" she asked.

"Yes. As did my grandmother and Mo. They miss

you. It was…unfortunate…you neglected to bid them farewell when you left.''

"Yes, I'm sorry. That was rude. Charles pointed that out. Of course I knew that, but I just had to go. I…just had to.''

"Apparently.''

She looked at him. No, he hadn't a clue. And she'd make darn sure it stayed that way.

"Have a seat. Do you want anything to drink? Coffee?'' she asked.

"No. Come sit beside me.''

She hesitated. "Why are you here, Rashid?''

He sat on the sofa and stretched out his long legs, studying the tips of his polished shoes. "Mo was very disappointed to discover you had left so suddenly.''

She crossed the room to sit gingerly beside him on the sofa, leaving a healthy buffer space.

"I sent him a note in the letter to you.''

"What precipitated your flight? The kiss in the sea? The invitation to stay?''

Bridget went still, felt the heat rise in her throat and cheeks. She dare not tell him the real reason.

He studied her for a moment, his dark eyes giving nothing away. "Jack and Marie suggested there was something between you and me.''

Bridget cleared her throat nervously. "Something between us?''

He reached out his hand. Bridget stared at it for a long moment, then slowly raised hers as if compelled. When he tightened his fingers around hers, she felt her heart skip a beat.

"I know you think I'm the kind of man who would

accept his parents' ideal of a woman, and never choose one for himself. I am not. I married to please them when I was younger. I grew to love Fatima from the moment we became betrothed and loved her until she died. I would not dishonor my future wife by not loving her in the same way.''

She widened her eyes. ''What do you mean?''

For one wild, crazy second Bridget almost thought Rashid was nervous. She stifled a giggle. The man had never had a nervous moment in his life.

Then he surprised her. ''Will you marry me, Bridget Rossi? Become my wife. I pledge total fidelity as long as we both live.''

He wanted to marry her? He saw her as a suitable wife? Then the conversation overheard at the beach echoed.

''I appreciate your offer but—''

''This time I'm not going for my parents' choice, but mine.''

She was getting confused. His holding her hand didn't help, it scrambled her brains because all she could think of was how much she wanted him to pull her into his arms and kiss her. If he really wanted to marry her, wouldn't he want to kiss her?

''Your parents would probably not find me suitable,'' she said, trying to think.

''I think you are perfectly suitable. But that's not the overwhelming criteria for this marriage,'' he said.

''It isn't? What is?'' Her heart drummed so strongly in her chest she wondered if he could see it. Blood rushed through her veins.

''Love.''

She stared at him. Now she knew she wasn't hearing him correctly.

"Love? I thought you loved Fatima," she said stupidly.

"I did. That changed the day you left."

"I left and you stopped loving Fatima?"

"You left and I was lost. I found myself unable to work because I was worried about you. Unable to sleep at night without dreaming of you. Unable to enjoy my new relationship with my son, without thinking of how you brought it about, and how everything we did was that much more fun when you were there."

"Rashid—"

"You left and I realized you'd taken my heart with you. This past month has been hell. I'm astonished to suddenly discover love that is so overpowering I can't function because of it. That I long for a woman that I met only weeks ago, and I don't even know if she likes me, or can ever return my feelings. I've come to wine and dine you, strew roses at your feet and do all I can to make a romantic proposal. I want you for my wife."

"Oh, Rashid!" She flung her arms around his neck. His kiss swept away any trace of doubt as he hugged her tightly to him, his mouth claiming hers forever.

When they came up for air, he rested his forehead on hers. "So is that a yes?"

"Yes, a thousand times, yes! I love you! I don't need to be wined or dined, or have roses strewn at my feet, but it might be nice, if you really want to."

"I love you." He kissed her again. "I'll order five

dozen roses today. How soon will you become my wife?''

''As soon as it can be arranged. I can't believe this.'' She looked at him suspiciously. ''You're sure you love me? Remember I told you my father loved his first wife all his life, even though he was married to my mother and they had more than twenty years together.''

''I am not your father. I loved Fatima. But she is gone these three years. I love you differently, more than I ever thought possible. Tell me again you love me,'' he ordered.

She smiled as she looked into his eyes. ''I'll probably tell you a hundred times a day. I love you. I have loved you since that day you so kindly invited me to visit to help me deal with Papa's death, I think. You were so kind. No one in my family seemed to understand, but you did. Spending time with you in Aboul Sari only strengthened my feeling until I felt as if I were ripping out my heart when I left.''

''And for nought, except to have me come after you. When I apply your thirty-year scenario, I can't imagine being with anyone but you.''

Bridget snuggled closer, relishing every word.

She looked around the living room of her childhood home. ''I guess I'll be selling this place after all.''

''Only if you wish. Or you could save it for one of our children, maybe they'd like to live in San Francisco.''

She looked up at him and smiled. ''One of our children?''

''You said you wanted a half dozen. If they all turn

out as delightful as Mo, we'll fill our lives with happiness.''

''Being with you will fill my life with happiness, but I would like to have a houseful of babies. Your babies,'' she said.

''The villa is large, we can have as many as you like.'' He brought her hand to his mouth, kissing the palm, holding it against his heart. ''And your leaving convinced me my life would be devoid of all that makes it worth living without you there. I love you, Bridget. Come share your life with me.''

One Year Later

Francesca leaned over the crib, studying the little girl who snuggled so serenely in her soft white blanket.

''So you found the love of your life,'' she said to Bridget, meeting her cousin's eyes across the crib.

''Yes. I'm so happy. Do you feel like a fairy godmother, introducing us?''

''A role I never suspected,'' Francesca said, trailing a finger gently down one rounded, rosy baby cheek. ''He made his own choice, once he met you. I know you still miss Uncle Paolo, but look what came out of that sad time.''

Bridget laughed. ''Aboul Sari is much closer to Italy than San Francisco is. Come visit more often.''

''I'll stay until your happiness drives me away. But I will come more often. Love becomes you both. Thank you for extending it to me.''

''You're my dearest cousin. We want to share it with you,'' Bridget said.

Rashid stood in the doorway. Bridget smiled over at him.

"You're right, Francesca, love becomes us both," he said.

The look in his eyes still set her heart racing. Bridget expected it always would.

THE SHEIKH AND THE BRIDE WHO SAID NO

Susan Mallery

Susan Mallery is the bestselling and award-winning author of over fifty novels. She makes her home in the Pacific Northwest with her handsome prince of a husband and her two adorable-but-not-bright cats. Feel free to contact her via her website at www.susanmallery.com.

Chapter One

"I know marrying the crown prince and eventually being queen *sounds* terrific," Daphne Snowden said in what she hoped was a calm I'm-your-aunt-who-loves-you-and-I-know-better voice instead of a shrill, panicked tone. "But the truth of the matter is very different. You've never met Prince Murat. He's a difficult and stubborn man."

Daphne knew this from personal experience. "He's also nearly twice your age."

Brittany looked up from the fashion magazine she'd been scanning. "You worry too much," she said. "Relax, Aunt Daphne. I'll be fine."

Fine? Fine? Daphne sank back into the comfortable

leather seat of the luxury private jet and tried not to scream. This could not be happening. It was a dream. It had to be. She refused to believe that her favorite— and only—niece had agreed to marry a man she'd never met. Prince or no prince, this could be a disaster. Despite the fact that she and Brittany had been having the same series of conversations for nearly three weeks now, she felt compelled to make all her points again.

"I want you to be happy," Daphne said. "I love you."

Brittany, a tall willowy blonde with delicately pretty features in the tradition of the Snowden women, smiled. "I love you, too, and you're worrying about nothing. I know Murat is, like, really old."

Daphne pressed her lips together and tried not to wince. She knew that to an eighteen-year-old, thirty-five was practically geriatric, but it was only five years beyond her own thirty years.

"But he's pretty cute," her niece added. "And rich. I'll get to travel and live in a palace." She put down the magazine and stuck out her feet. "Do you think I should have gone with the other sandals instead of these?"

Daphne held in a shriek. "I don't care about your shoes. I'm talking about your *life* here. Being married to the crown prince means you won't get to spend your day shopping. You'll have responsibilities for the welfare of the people of Bahania. You'll have to entertain visiting dignitaries and support charities. You'll be expected to produce children."

Brittany nodded. "I figured that part out. The parties

will be great. I can invite all my friends, and we'll talk about, like, what the guy who runs France is wearing."

"And the baby part?"

Brittany shrugged. "If he's old, he probably knows what he's doing. My friend Deanna had sex with her college boyfriend and she said it was totally better than with her boyfriend in high school. Experience counts."

Daphne wanted to shake Brittany. She knew from dozens of after-midnight conversations, when her niece had spent the night, that Brittany had never been intimate with any of her boyfriends. Brittany had been very careful not to let things go too far. So what had changed? Daphne couldn't believe that the child she'd loved from birth and had practically raised, could have turned into this shallow, unfeeling young woman.

She glanced at her watch and knew that time was running short. Once they landed and reached the palace, there would be no turning back. One Snowden bride-to-be had already left Murat practically at the altar. She had a feeling that Brittany wouldn't be given the opportunity to bolt.

"What was your mother thinking?" she asked, more to herself than Brittany. "Why did she agree?"

"Mom thought it would be completely cool," Brittany said easily. "I think she's hoping there will be some amazing jewelry for the mother of the bride. Plus me marrying a prince beats out Aunt Grace's piggy Justin getting into Harvard any day, right?"

Daphne nodded without speaking. Some families were competitive about sports while others kept score using social status and money. In her family it was all about power—political or otherwise. One of her sisters had married a senator who planned to run for president, the other married a captain of industry. She had been the only sibling to pick another path.

She scooted to the edge of her seat and took Brittany's perfectly manicured hands into her own.

"You have to listen," she said earnestly. "I love you more than I've ever loved another human being in my life. You're practically my daughter."

Brittany's expression softened. "I love you, too. You know you've been there for me way more than my own mother."

"Then, please, please, think this through. You're young and smart and you can have anything you want in the world. Why would you be willing to tie yourself to a man you've never met in a country you've never visited? What if you hate Bahania?"

Daphne didn't think that was possible—personally she loved the desert country—but at this point she was done playing fair.

"Travel isn't going to be what you think," Daphne continued before Brittany could interrupt. "Any visits will be state events. They'll be planned and photographed. Once you agree to marry the prince you'll never be able to just run over and see a girlfriend or head to the mall or the movies."

Brittany stared at her. "What do you mean I can't go to the mall?"

Daphne blinked. Was this progress at last? "You'll be

the future queen. You won't be able to rush off and buy a last-minute cashmere sweater just because it's on sale."

"Why not?"

Daphne sighed. "I've been trying to explain this to you. You won't get to be your own person anymore. You'll be living a life in a foreign country with unfamiliar rules and expectations. You will have to adhere to them."

None of which sounded all that tough to her, but she wasn't the one signing up for a lifetime of queenhood.

"I never thought about having to stay in the palace a lot," Brittany said slowly. "I just sort of figured I could fly back home whenever I wanted and hang with my friends."

"Bahania will be your home now."

Brittany's eyes darkened. "I wouldn't miss Mom and Dad so much, but Deanna and you." She bit her lower lip. "I guess if I love the prince…"

"Do you?" Daphne asked. "You've never met him. You're risking a whole lot on the off chance you two will get along." She squeezed her niece's fingers. "You've only had a couple of boyfriends, none of them serious. Do you really want to give all that up? Dating? College?"

Brittany frowned. "I can't go to college?"

"Do you think any professor is going to want the future queen in his class? How could he or she give you a real grade? Even if you did get that worked out, you'd just be attending classes part-time. You couldn't live on campus."

"That's right. Because I'd be in the palace."

"Possibly pregnant," Daphne added for good measure.

"No way. I'm not ready to have a baby *now*."

"And if Prince Murat is?"

Her niece glared at her. "You're trying to scare me."

"You bet. I'm willing to do just about anything to keep you from throwing away your life. If you'd met someone and had fallen in love, then I wouldn't care if he was a prince or an alien from planet Xeon. But you didn't. I would have gotten involved with this sooner, but your mother did her best to keep the truth from me."

Brittany sighed. "She's pretty determined to have her way."

"I'm not going to let that happen. Tell me honestly. Tell me you're completely committed to this and I'll back off. But if you have even one hint of a doubt, you need to give yourself time to think."

Brittany swallowed. "I'm not sure," she admitted in a tiny voice. "I want things to go great with the prince, but what if they don't?" Tears filled her eyes. "I've been trying to do what my parents want me to do and I'm scared." She glanced around the luxury plane. "The pilot said we were landing in twenty minutes. That's about up. I can't meet the prince and tell him I'm not sure."

Daphne vowed that when she returned to the States she was going to kill her oldest sister, Laurel. How dare she try to guilt her only daughter into something like this? Outrage mingled with relief. She held open her arms, and Brittany fell into her embrace.

"Is it too late?" the teenager asked.

"Of course not. You're going to be fine." She hugged

her tight. "You had me worried for a while. I thought you were really going through with this."

Brittany sniffed. "Some parts of it sounded pretty fun. Having all that money and crowns and stuff, but I tried not to think about actually being married to someone that old."

"I don't blame you." The age difference was impossible, Daphne thought. What on earth could Murat be thinking, considering an engagement to a teenager?

"I'll take care of everything," she promised. "You'll stay on the plane and go directly home while I handle things at the palace."

Brittany straightened. "Really? I don't even have to meet him?"

"Nope. You go back and pretend this never happened."

"What about Mom?"

Daphne's eyes narrowed. "You can leave her to me, as well."

Just over an hour later Daphne found herself in the back of a limo, heading to the fabled Pink Palace of Bahania. Because of the long plane trip, she expected to find the city in darkness, but with the time difference, it was late afternoon. She sat right by the window so she could take in everything—the ancient buildings that butted up against the new financial district. The amazing blue of the Arabian Sea just south of the city. The views were breathtaking and familiar. She'd grown to love this country when she'd visited ten years ago.

"Don't go there," she told herself. There was no time for a trip down memory lane. Instead she needed to focus and figure out what she was going to say to Murat.

She glanced at her watch. With every second that ticked by, finding the perfect words became less and less important. Once Brittany landed back in the States, she would be safe from Murat's clutches. Still, she couldn't help feeling a little nervous as the long, black car turned left and drove past elegant wrought-iron gates.

The car pulled to a stop in front of the main entrance. Daphne drew in a deep breath to calm herself as she waited for one of the guards to open the door. She stepped out into the warm afternoon and glanced around.

The gardens were as beautiful as she remembered. Sweet, lush scents competed for her attention. To the left was the gate that led to the private English-style garden she'd always loved. To the right was a path that led to the most perfect view of the sea. And in front of her…well, that was the way into the lion's den.

She tried to tell herself she had no reason to be afraid, that she'd done nothing wrong. Murat was the one interested in marrying a teenager nearly half his age. If anyone should be feeling foolish and ashamed, it was he.

But despite being in the right, and determined to stand strong against any and all who might try to get in her way, she couldn't help a tiny shiver of apprehension. After all, ten years ago she'd been a guest in this very palace. She'd been young and in love and engaged to be married.

To Murat.

Then three weeks before the wedding, she'd bolted, leaving him without even a whisper of an explanation.

Chapter Two

"Ms. Snowden?"

Daphne saw a well-dressed young man walking toward her. "Yes?"

"The prince is waiting. If you will follow me?"

As Daphne trailed after the man, she wondered if he had any idea she wasn't Brittany. She doubted Murat had bothered to brief his staff on the arrival of a potential bride. He'd rarely concerned himself with details like that. So she would guess that his staff member had simply been told to escort the woman who arrived to an appropriate meeting area.

"Someone is in for a surprise," she murmured under her breath as she walked down a wide corridor lined with stunning mosaics and elegant antiques.

Just being back in the palace made her feel better. She wanted to ask her guide to wait a few minutes while she stopped to enjoy an especially beautiful view from a window or a spectacular piece of artwork. Instead she trailed along dutifully, concentrating on tapestries and carvings instead of what she was going to say when she saw Murat.

They turned a corner. Up ahead Daphne saw a large tabby cat sitting in a patch of sun and washing her face. She smiled as she recalled the dozens and dozens of cats the king kept in the palace.

"In here, Ms. Snowden," the man said as he paused in front of an open door. "The prince will be with you shortly."

She nodded, then walked past him into a small sitting room. The furniture was Western, complete with a sofa, three chairs, a coffee table and a buffet along the far wall. A carafe of ice water and several glasses sat next to a phone on the buffet. She walked over and helped herself to the refreshment.

As she drank she looked around the room and shook her head. How like Murat to have a stranger bring his prospective bride to a room and then drop her off. If Brittany had been here, the teenager would have been terrified by now. The least he could have done was to have sent a woman and then have her keep Brittany company.

But she wasn't Brittany, Daphne reminded herself. Nor was she afraid. Ten years had given her a lot of experience and perspective. Murat might be expecting a young, malleable bride who would bow to his every wish and quiver with fear at the thought of displeasing him, but what he was getting instead was a very different matter.

Footsteps sounded in the hallway. She set down the glass and squared her shoulders. Seconds later the prince from her past strolled into the room.

He still moved with an easy grace of one "to the manor born," she thought as she took in his powerful body and elegant suit. And he was still a formidable opponent, she reminded herself as he stopped and stared at her.

Not by a flicker of a lash did he indicate he was the least bit surprised.

"Daphne," the crown prince said with a slight smile. "You have returned at last."

"I know you weren't expecting me," she said. "But Brittany couldn't make it."

He raised one dark eyebrow. "Has she been taken ill?"

"No. She simply came to her senses. Even as we speak, she's on a plane back to the United States. There isn't going to be a wedding." She thought maybe she'd been a bit abrupt, so she added a somewhat insincere, "I'm sorry."

"Yes, I can feel your compassion from here," Murat said as he crossed to the buffet and picked up the phone. He dialed four numbers, then spoke. "The airport. Flight control."

He waited a few seconds, then spoke again. "My plane?"

She watched while he listened. It was possible a muscle tightened in his jaw, but she couldn't be sure. He had to be feeling something, she told herself. Or maybe not. Ten years ago he'd let her go without a word. Why should this runaway bride matter?

He hung up the phone and turned back to her. "I assume you had something to do with Brittany's decision."

He wasn't asking a question, but she answered it all the same. "Of course. It was madness. I can't imagine what you were thinking. She's barely eighteen, Murat. Still a child. If you're so desperate for a bride, at least pick someone who is close to being an equal."

For the first time since he walked into the room, he showed emotion, and it wasn't a happy one. Temper drew his eyebrows together.

"You insult me with both your familiarity and your assumption."

She winced silently. Of course. She'd called him by his first name. "I apologize for not using the proper title."

"And the other?"

"I'll do whatever is necessary to keep Brittany safe from you."

"Just because you were not interested in being my wife doesn't mean that others feel the same way."

"I agree completely. There is a world filled with willing young women. Have them all—I don't care. But you're not marrying my niece."

Instead of answering her, he pulled a small device out of his pocket. It was about the size of a key fob. Seconds later a half dozen armed guards burst into the room and surrounded Daphne. Two of them grabbed her by the arms.

She was too stunned to protest.

"What are you doing?" she demanded.

"Myself? Nothing." Murat returned what she assumed was a security device to his jacket pocket, then adjusted his cuffs. "The guards are another story."

Daphne glared at him. "What? You're arresting me because I wouldn't let you marry my niece?"

"I'm holding you in protective custody for interfering with the private business of the Crown Prince of Bahania."

She narrowed her gaze. "This is crazy. You can't do this to me."

"All evidence to the contrary."

"Bastard."

She tried to squirm away from the guards, but they didn't let her go.

"You'd better not try to turn that plane around," she said, her fury growing. "I won't let you touch her. Not for a second."

Murat crossed toward the door, then paused and glanced at her. "Make no mistake, Daphne. One way or another, there will be a wedding in four months, and the bride will be a Snowden. There is nothing you can do to stop me."

"Want to bet?" she asked, knowing the words were as futile as her attempt to twist free of the guards.

"Of course. I have no fear of wagering with you." He smiled again. "What will you give me when I win?"

She lunged for him and only got a sharp pain in her arm for her reward. Murat chuckled as he walked away.

"When I get my hands on him," she said. "I swear I'll..." She pressed her lips together. On second thought, threatening the prince while still in the presence of several burly guards wasn't exactly smart.

"Where are you taking me?" she asked when the guards continued to just stand here, holding her in place.

The one by the door touched an earpiece, then nodded.

"What? Getting instructions from the crown prince himself?" she asked. "Couldn't he have told you while he was still in the room?"

Apparently not, she realized as the guards started moving. The two holding on to her kept their grips firm enough that she didn't want to risk pulling away. She had a feeling she was already going to be plenty bruised by her experience.

The group of guards, with her in the center, walked down the main corridor, then stopped at a bank of elevators. The one in communication with Murat pushed the down button. When the car arrived, it was a tight fit, but they all made it inside. Daphne noticed how none of the men stood too close to her. In fact, except for the hold on her arms, they were pretty much ignoring her.

She tried to remember the layout of the palace so she could figure out where they were going. *Down* wasn't her idea of a happy thought. Were there still dungeons in the palace? She wouldn't put it past Murat to lock her up.

But when they stepped out of the elevator and headed along a more narrow corridor, Daphne suddenly realized their destination. It was much worse than any dungeon.

"You're not taking me there," she said, wiggling and twisting to escape.

The guard on her left tightened his grip on her arm. "Ma'am, we don't want to hurt you."

The implication being they would if necessary.

I'll get him for this, she thought as she stopped fighting. One way or another, Murat would pay.

They turned a corner, and Daphne saw the famous gold double doors. They stood nearly ten feet tall and were heavily embossed with a scene of several young women frolicking at an oasis.

One of the guards stepped forward and opened the door on the left. The rest marched her inside.

When the men released her, she thought briefly about making a dash for freedom but knew she would be caught and returned here. So she accepted her fate with dignity and a vow that she would find her way out as soon as she could.

The guards left. She heard the heavy clang as the doors closed behind them and the thunk of the gold cross bar being locked into place. Low conversation from the hallway told her that someone would be left on duty to watch over her.

"This is just like you, Murat," she said as she placed her hands on her hips. "You might be an imperial, piggish prince, but I can stand it. I can stand anything to keep you from marrying Brittany."

Daphne looked for something to throw, but the thick, cream-colored walls were completely bare. The only decoration was the brightly colored tile floor.

She moved through the arched entryway, into the large open living area. Dozens of chairs and sofas filled the vast space. The doorway to the left led to the baths, the one on the right led to the sleeping rooms. She recognized this part of the palace from her explorations ten years before. Recognized and fumed because of it.

Dammit all, if Murat hadn't locked her in the harem.

Murat stalked toward the business wing of the palace. Fury quickened his steps. After all this time Daphne Snowden had dared to return to Bahania, only to once again disrupt his world.

Had she come modestly, begging his apology for her unforgivable acts? Of course not. He swore silently. The woman had stared him in the eye, speaking as if they were equals. She had *defied* him.

Murat swept past the guards outside his father's business suite and stepped into the inner office.

"She is here," he announced as he came to a stop in front of the large, carved desk.

The king raised his eyebrows. "You do not sound happy. Has your fiancée displeased you already?"

"She is not my fiancée."

His father sighed, then stood and walked around the desk. "Murat, I know you have reservations about this engagement. You complain that the girl is too young and inexperienced, that she can never be happy here, but once again I ask you to give her a chance."

Murat stared at his father. Anger bubbled inside of him, although he was careful to keep it from showing. He'd spent a lifetime not reacting to anything, and that practice served him well now.

"You misunderstand me, Father," he said in a low voice. "Brittany Snowden is not here in the palace. She is flying back to America even as we speak."

The king frowned. "Then who is here?"

"Daphne."

"Your former—"

Murat cut him off with a quick, "Yes."

One of the many advantages of being the crown prince was the ability to assert his will on others. Ten years ago, when his former fiancée had left without so much as a note, he'd forbidden any to speak her name. All had obeyed except his father, who did not need to pay attention to the will of the crown prince.

"She attempts to defy me," Murat said as he walked to the window and leaned against the sill. "She stood there and told me she would not permit me to marry her niece." He laughed harshly. "As if her desires matter at all to me. I am Crown Prince Murat of Bahania. I determine my fate. No one, especially not a mere woman, dares to instruct me."

His father nodded. "I see. So you complain that Daphne wants to prevent you from marrying someone whom you did not want to marry in the first place."

"That is not the point," Murat told him as he folded

his arms across his chest. "There is a principle at stake. The woman did not respect my position ten years ago and nothing has changed."

"I can see how that would be difficult," the king said. "Where is she now?"

Murat glanced down as one of his father's cats stood on the sofa, stretched, then curled back up and closed its eyes.

"I have offered her a place to stay while this is sorted out," he said.

"I'm surprised Daphne would want to remain in the palace. She has delivered her message."

Murat stared at his father. "I did not give her a choice. I had the guards deliver her to the harem."

Very little startled the king, so Murat enjoyed seeing his father's mouth drop open with surprise.

"The harem?" the older man repeated.

Murat shrugged. "I had to detain her. Although she has defied me and spoken with disrespect, I was not willing to lock her in the dungeons. The harem is pleasant enough and will hold her until I decide I wish to let her go."

Although that section of the palace hadn't been used for its intended purpose for more than sixty years, the rooms themselves were maintained in their original splendor. Daphne would be surrounded by every luxury, except that of her freedom.

"It is her own fault," he added. "She had no right to interfere and keep her niece from me. Even though I was never interested in Brittany and only agreed to meet with her to please you, Daphne was wrong to try to foil me."

"I understand completely," his father said. "What do you intend to do with her now?"

Murat hadn't done anything but react. He had no plan where she was concerned.

"I do not know," he admitted.

"Will you order the plane to return Brittany to Bahania?"

"No. I know you wanted me to consider her, but in truth, Father, I could not be less interested." While Murat accepted that he had to marry and produce heirs, he could not imagine spending the rest of his life with a foolish young wife.

"Perhaps I will keep Daphne for a few days," Murat said. "To teach her a lesson."

"In the harem?" his father asked.

"Yes." He smiled. "She will be most displeased."

She would argue and fume and call him names. She would continue to defy him. Despite all that had gone on before—what she had done and what he had yet to forgive—he found himself looking forward to the encounter.

Daphne discovered her luggage in one of the largest bedrooms in the harem. The sleeping quarters consisted of several private rooms, reserved for those in favor with the king, and large dormitory-like rooms with ten or twelve beautiful beds lined up against the thick walls.

She doubted there was any furniture newer than a hundred years old. Handmade rugs covered the tiled floors in the sleeping rooms, while carved and gilded pieces of furniture added to the decor.

She ignored the suitcases and instead walked close to the walls. No one could have come in through the main door to deliver her luggage—she would have seen. Which meant there was a secret passage and door. The getting in didn't interest her as much as the getting out.

When a careful exploration of the rough walls didn't reveal any hidden doorway, she moved to the hall. It had to be somewhere. She felt around furniture and baseboards, paying particular attention to the inner walls. Still she found nothing.

"I'm sure I'll have plenty of time to keeping checking," she said aloud as she paused in front of a French door that led to a massive walled garden.

Daphne stepped out into the late-afternoon sun and breathed in the scent of the lush plant life. There were trees and shrubs, tiny flowers and huge birds of paradise. A narrow path led through the garden, while stone benches offered a place to sit and reflect. Fluttering movement caught her attention, and she glanced up in time to see two parrots fly across the open area.

"Their loud cries cover the sound of women's voices."

Daphne spun toward the speaker and saw Murat standing behind her. He still wore his suit and his imperious expression. She hated that he was the most handsome man she'd ever met and that, instead of being furious, she actually felt a little tingle of pleasure at seeing him.

Betrayed by her hormones, she thought in disgust. While leaving him ten years ago had been completely sensible, it had taken her far too long to stop loving him. Even the pain of knowing he hadn't cared enough to come after her hadn't made the recovery any shorter.

"Many of the parrots here are quite old," he continued. "But there is a single breeding pair that has given us a new generation."

"You no longer have women in the harem. Why do you keep the parrots?"

He shrugged. "Sometimes there is difficulty in letting go of the old ways. But you are not interested in our traditions. You wish to berate me and tell me what I can and cannot do." He nodded. "You may begin now if you wish."

Suspicious of his motives, she studied him. But his dark eyes and chiseled features gave nothing away. Still, that didn't stop her from wanting to know what was going to happen.

"What are you going to do about Brittany?" she asked.

"Nothing."

Like she believed that. "Are you ordering the jet to turn around?"

"No. Despite what you think of me, I will not force my bride to present herself. She will be here in time."

Daphne glared at him. "No, she won't. Brittany isn't going to marry you."

He dismissed her with a flick of his hand. "The gardens have grown since you were last here. Do you remember? You were quite enchanted with the idea of the harem and disappointed that we no longer used it for its original purpose."

"I was not," she protested. "I think it's terrible that women were kept locked up for the sole purpose of offering sexual pleasure for the king."

He smiled. "So you say now. But I distinctly recall how you found the idea exciting. You asked endless questions."

Daphne felt heat on her cheeks. Okay, maybe she *had* been a little interested in the workings of the harem. Ten years ago she'd been all of twenty and a virtual innocent in the ways of the world. Everything about the palace had intrigued her. Especially Murat.

"I'm over it now," she said. "How long do you intend to keep me here?"

"I have not yet decided."

"My family will come to my rescue. You must know they have substantial political power."

He didn't seem the least bit intimidated by the threat.

"What I know," he said, "is that their ambitions have not changed. They still wish for a Snowden female to marry royalty."

She couldn't argue that. First her parents had pushed her at Murat, and now her own sister pushed Brittany.

"I'm not like them," she said.

"How true." He glanced at his watch. "Dinner is at seven. Please dress appropriately."

She laughed. "And if I don't want to have dinner with you?"

He raised one eyebrow. "The choice has never been yours, Daphne. When will you finally learn that? Besides, you *do* want to dine with me. You have many questions. I see them in your eyes."

With that he turned and left.

"Annoying man," she muttered when she was alone again. Worse, he was right. She had questions—lots of them. And a burning desire to deal with the unfinished business between them.

As for the man himself…time had changed him, but it had not erased *her* interest in the only man she had ever loved.

Chapter Three

Daphne stood in front of her open suitcase and stared down at the contents. While a part of her wanted to ignore Murat's demand that she "dress appropriately" for their dinner, another part of her liked the idea of looking so fabulous that she would leave him speechless. It was a battle between principles and beauty and she already knew which would win.

After sorting through the contents of her luggage, she withdrew a simple sleeveless dress and carried it into the bathroom. She would let it hang in the steam while she showered. She plugged in the electric curlers she'd already unpacked, then pinned up her hair and stepped into the shower.

Fifteen minutes later she emerged all cleaned and buffed and smoothed. The bath towels provided were big enough to carpet an entire room. An array of cosmetics and skin-care products filled the cabinets by the huge mirror and vanity.

Everywhere she looked she saw marble, gold, carved wood or beveled glass. How many women had stood in front of this mirror and prepared to meet a member of the royal family? What kind of stories had these walls witnessed? How much laughter? How many tears? Under other circumstances she could enjoy her stay in this historical part of the palace.

"Who am I kidding?" she murmured as she unpinned her hair and brushed it out. "I'm enjoying it now."

She'd always loved Bahania and the palace. Murat had been the problem.

He hadn't been that way in the beginning. He'd been charming and intriguing and exactly the kind of man she'd always wanted to meet. As she reached for the first hot curler, she remembered that party she'd attended in Spain where they had first met.

Traveling through Europe the summer between her sophomore and junior year of college had meant doing her best to avoid all her parents' upper-class and political friends. But in Barcelona, Daphne had finally caved to her mother's insistence that she accept an invitation to a cocktail party for some ambassador or prime minister or something. She'd been bored and ready to leave after ten minutes. But then, on a stone balcony with a perfect view of the sunset, she'd met a man.

He'd been tall, handsome and he'd made her laugh when he'd confessed that he needed her help—that he was hiding from the far-too-amorous youngest daughter of their host.

"When she comes upstairs looking for me, I'll hide under the table and you will send her away," he said. "Will you do that for me?"

He stared at her with eyes as dark as midnight. At that second her stomach had flipped over, her cheeks had flushed and she would have followed him to the ends of the earth.

He'd spent the entire evening with her, escorting her to dinner and then dancing with her under the stars. They'd talked of books and movies, of childhood fantasies and grown-up dreams. And when he'd walked her back to her hotel and kissed her, she'd known that she was in danger of falling for him.

He hadn't told her who he was until their third date. At first she'd been nervous—after all, even she had never met a prince—but then she realized that for once being a Snowden was a good thing. She'd been raised to be the wife of a president, or even a prince.

"Come back with me," he'd pleaded when he had to return to Bahania. "Come see my country, meet my people. Let them discover how delightful you are, as I have."

It wasn't a declaration of love—she saw that now. But at twenty, it had been enough. She'd abandoned the rest of her tour and had flown with him to Bahania, where she'd stayed at the fabled Pink Palace and had fallen deeply in love with both Murat and every part of his world.

Daphne finished applying her makeup, then unwrapped the towel and stepped into her lingerie. Next she took out the curlers and carefully finger-combed her hair before bending over and spraying the underside. She flipped her hair back and applied more hairspray before finally stepping into her dress.

The silk skimmed over her body to fall just above her knees. She stepped into high-heeled sandals, then stared at her reflection.

Daphne knew she looked tired. No doubt her mother could find several items to criticize. But what would Murat think? How was the woman different from the girl? Ten years ago she'd loved him with a devotion that had bordered on mindlessness. The only thing that could have forced her to leave was the one thing that had— the realization that he didn't love her back.

"Don't go there," she told herself as she turned away from the mirror and made her way out of the bathroom.

Maybe if she arrived at the main rooms early, she could see where the secret door was as the staff arrived with dinner. She had a feeling that Murat would not be letting her out of the harem anytime soon—certainly not for meals. Which meant meals would have to come to her.

But as she stepped into the large salon overlooking the gardens, she saw she was too late. A small cart with drinks stood in the center of the room, but even more interesting than that was the man waiting by the French doors.

She'd been thinking about him while getting ready, so seeing him now made her feel as if she'd stepped into an alternative universe—one where she could summon handsome princes at will.

He turned toward her and smiled.

"You are early," he said.

"I'd hoped to catch the staff delivering dinner."

One dark eyebrow rose. "I fail to see the excitement of watching them come in and out of the door."

"You're right. If they're using the door, it's not exciting at all. But if they were to use the secret passage…"

His smile widened. "Ah. You seek to escape. But it will not be so easy. You forget we have a tradition of holding beautiful women captive. If they were able to find their way from the palace, we would be thought of as fools."

"Is that your way of saying you'll make sure I don't find the secret passage?"

He walked toward the drinks cart. "No. It is my way of saying that it is impossible to open the door from this side. Only someone outside the harem can work the latch."

He held up a bottle of champagne and she nodded.

"I suppose that information shouldn't surprise me," she told him. "So there really is no escape?"

"Why would you want there to be?"

He popped the bottle expertly, then poured two glasses.

"I don't take well to being someone's prisoner," she said as she took the glass he offered.

"But this is paradise."

"Want to trade?"

Amusement brightened his eyes. "I see you have not changed. Ten years ago you spoke your mind and you still do today."

"You mean I haven't learned my place?"

"Exactly."

"I like to think my place is wherever I want it to be."

"How like a woman." He held up his glass. "A toast to our mutual past, and what the future will bring."

She thought about Brittany, who would be landing in New York shortly. "How about to our separate lives?"

"Not so very separate. We could be family soon."

"I don't think so. You're not marrying—"

"To the beauty of the Snowden women," he said, cutting her off. "Come, Daphne. Drink with me. We will leave our discussion of less pleasant matters to another day."

"Fine." The longer they talked about other things, the more time her niece had to get safely home. "To Bahania."

"At last something we can agree upon."

They touched glasses, then sipped their champagne. Murat motioned to one of the large sofas and waited until she was seated before joining her on the overstuffed furniture.

"You are comfortable here?" he asked.

"Aside from the whole idea of being kept against my will, pretty much." She set down the glass and sighed. "Okay. Honestly, the harem is beautiful. I plan to do some serious exploring while I'm here."

"My sister, Sabrina, is an expert on antiquities and our history. Would you like me to have her visit?"

Daphne laughed. "My own private lecture circuit? I'm sure your sister has better things to do with her life."

"Than serve me?"

He spoke teasingly, but she knew there was truth behind the humor. Murat had been raised to believe he was the center of the universe. She supposed that came with being the future king.

He sat angled toward her, his hand-tailored suit emphasizing the strength in his powerful body. Ten years ago he'd been the most handsome man she'd ever met. And now... She sighed. Not that much had changed.

"Did you get a chance to see much of the city as you drove in?" he asked.

"Just the view from the highway. I was pretty intent on getting to the palace."

"Ah, yes. So you could defy me at every turn. There are many new buildings in our financial district."

"I noticed those. The city is growing."

He nodded. "We seek success in the future without losing what is precious to us from our past. It is an act of balance."

She picked up her glass of champagne and took a sip. The cool, bubbly liquid tickled her tongue. "There have been other changes since I was last here," she said. "Your brothers have married."

"That is true. All to American women. There have been many editorials in the papers about why that is, although the consensus among the people is new blood will improve the lineage of the royal family."

"That must make the women in question feel really special."

He leaned back against the sofa. "Why would they not be pleased to improve the gene pool of such a noble family?"

"Few women fantasize about being a good brood mare."

He shook his head. "Why do you always want to twist things around to make me look bad? All my sisters-in-law are delightful women who are blissfully happy with their chosen mates. Cleo and Emma have given birth in the past year. Billie is newly pregnant. They are catered to by devoted husbands and do not want for anything."

He painted a picture that made her feel funny inside. Not sad, exactly. Just…envious. She'd always wanted a guy who would love her with his whole heart, but somehow she'd never seemed to find him.

"You're right," she said. "Everyone seems perfectly happy. You remain the last single prince."

He grimaced. "A point pressed home to me on a daily basis."

"Getting a little pressure to marry and produce heirs?"

"You have no idea."

"Then we should talk about Brittany and why that would never work."

His gaze lingered on her face. "You are a difficult and stubborn woman."

"So you keep saying."

"We will discuss your niece when I decide it is time."

"You don't get to choose," she told him.

"Of course I do. And you do not wish to speak of her right now. You wish to tell me all about yourself. What you have been doing since we last met. You want to impress me."

"I do not."

He raised one eyebrow and waited. She shifted in her seat. Okay, yes, maybe she wouldn't mind knocking his socks off with her accomplishments, but she didn't like that he'd guessed.

"Come, Daphne," he said, moving closer and focusing all of his considerable attention on her. "Tell me everything. Did you finish college? What have you been doing?" He picked up her left hand and examined the bare fingers. "I see you have not given your heart to anyone."

She didn't like the assessment, nor did she appreciate the tingles that rippled up from her hand to her arm. He'd always been able to do that—reduce her to pudding with a single touch. Why couldn't that have changed? Why couldn't time away have made her immune?

"I'm not engaged, if that's what you mean," she said. "I'm not willing to discuss the state of my heart with you. It's none of your business."

"As you wish. Tell me about college."

She clutched her champagne in her right hand and thought about swallowing the whole thing in one big gulp. It might provide her with a false sense of courage, which was better than no courage at all.

"I completed my degree as planned, then went on to become a veterinarian."

He looked two parts delighted, one part surprised. "Good for you. You enjoy the work?"

"Very much. Until recently I've been with a large practice in Chicago. My first two years with them I spent summers in Indiana, working on a dairy farm."

She couldn't remember ever really shocking Murat before, so now she allowed herself to enjoy his expression of astonishment. "Delivering calves?"

"Pretty much."

"It is not seemly."

She laughed. "It was my job. I loved it. But lately I've been working with small animals. Dogs, cats, birds. The usual." She took another sip and smiled. "If your father needs any help with the cats he should let me know."

"I will be sure to pass along your offer. Chicago is very different from Bahania."

"I agree. For one thing, there aren't any words to describe how cold that wind can be in the winter."

"We have no such discomfort here."

That was true. The weather in paradise was pretty darned good.

"You're not very close to your family," he said.

Daphne nearly spilled her champagne. Okay, so it didn't take a rocket scientist to figure out that she didn't fit in with the "real" Snowdens, but she was surprised Murat would say something like that so blatantly. After all…

The light went on in her head. "You mean I live far away," she said.

"Yes. They are all on the East Coast. Is that the reason you chose to settle in Chicago?"

"Part of it," she admitted. "I handle the constant disapproval better from a distance."

"Aren't your parents proud of what you have accomplished?"

"Not really. They keep waiting for me to wake up and get engaged to a senator. I'm resisting the impulse."

She spoke with a casualness, as if her family's expectations didn't matter, but Murat saw the truth in her blue eyes.

Pain, he thought. Pain from disappointing them, pain from not being accepted for who and what she was. Daphne had always been stubborn and determined and proud. From what he could see, little had changed about that.

Her appearance had been altered, though. Her face was thinner, her features more defined. Whereas at twenty she had held the promise of great beauty, now she fulfilled it. There was an air of confidence about her he liked.

She leaned forward. "I've spent the past couple of years studying pet psychology."

"I have not heard of that."

She smiled again, her full lips curving upward as if she were about to share a delicious private joke. "You'd appreciate it. The field is growing rapidly. We're interested in why animals act the way they do. What set of circumstances combine with their personality to make them act aggressively or chew furniture or not accept a new baby. That sort of thing."

He couldn't believe such information existed. "This is what you are doing now?"

"I'm getting into it. I've learned some interesting things about dealing with alpha males." She tilted her head. "Maybe I could use the techniques to tame you."

"Neither of us is interested in me being tame."

"Oh, I don't know."

"I do."

"You're certainly sure of yourself."

"The privilege of being the alpha male."

She continued to study him. Awareness crackled between them. He could smell the faint scent of the soap she'd used and some other subtle fragrance he associated only with her.

Wanting coiled low in his gut, surprising him with both its presence and its intensity. After all this time? He'd always wondered what he would feel if he saw her again, but somehow he'd never expected to have a strong need to touch her, explore her, take her.

He wanted to lead her into one of the many harem bedrooms and make her shudder beneath him. Funny how so much time had passed and the desire hadn't gone away.

"You're looking very predatory," she said. "What are you thinking?"

"I was wondering about your art. Do you still make time to do your sculptures?"

She hesitated, as if she didn't quite believe that was what he'd been thinking, then she answered.

"I still love it, but time is always an issue."

"Perhaps I should provide you with clay while you are here. You can indulge your passion."

"How long do you intend to keep me in the harem?"

"I have not yet decided."

"So we really do need to talk about Brittany."

Just then the large golden doors opened and several servants walked in pushing carts.

"Dinner," he said, rising to his feet.

"If I didn't know better, I would say you did that on purpose."

He smiled. "Even I can't command my staff with just a thought."

"Why do I know you're working on it?"

"I have no idea."

Murat had left the menu up to his head chef, and he was not disappointed with the meal. Neither was Daphne, he thought as she ran her fork across the remaining crumbs of chocolate from the torte served for dessert.

"Amazing," she breathed. "I could blow up like a beached whale if I lived here for too long."

"Not every meal is so very formal," he said, enjoying her pleasure in the food.

"Good thing. I'll have to do about fifty laps in the garden tomorrow." She picked up her wine and eyed him over the glass. "Unless you plan on cutting me loose sometime soon."

"Are we back to that?"

"We are. Murat, I'm serious. You can't keep me here forever."

"Perhaps I wish to resume the traditional use of these rooms."

He held in a smile as her eyes widened. "You are *so* kidding," she said, although she didn't sound quite sure of herself. "I'm not going to volunteer."

"Few women did at first, even though it was a great honor. But in time they came to enjoy their lives. Luxury, pleasure. What more could you want?"

"How about freedom and autonomy?"

"There is power in being desired. The smart women learned that and used it to their advantage. They ruled the ruler."

"I've never been good at subterfuge," she told him. "Besides, I'm not interested in working behind the scenes. I want to be up front and in the thick of things. I want to be an equal."

"That will never be. I am to be king of Bahania, with all the advantages and disadvantages that go with the position."

Daphne sipped her dessert wine. Disadvantages? She hadn't thought there could be any. Even if there weren't, it was a much safer topic than what life would be like in the harem.

"What's so bad about being the king?" she asked.

"Nothing bad, as you say. Just restrictions. Rules. Responsibilities."

"Always being in the spotlight," she said. "Always having to do the right thing."

"Exactly."

"Marrying a teenager you've never met can't be right, Murat, can it?"

His gaze narrowed. "You are persistent."

"And determined. I love her. I would do anything for her."

"Even displease me?"

"Apparently," she said with a shrug. "Are you going to behead me for it?"

"Your casual question tells me you are not in the least bit worried. I will have to do something to convince you of my power."

"I'm very clear on your power. I just want you to use it for good." She set down her glass and leaned toward him. "Come on. It's just the two of us, and I promise never to tell. You can't have been serious about her. A young girl you've never met?"

"Perhaps I wanted a brainless young woman to do my bidding."

Daphne stiffened. "She's not brainless. And she wouldn't have done your bidding. You're trying to annoy me on purpose, aren't you?"

"Is it working?"

"Pretty much." She sagged back in her chair. "I don't want you to be like that. I don't want you to be the kind of man who would marry Brittany."

"Do you think I am?"

"I hope not. But even if you are, I won't let you."

"You can't stop me."

"I'll do whatever is necessary to stop you."

His dark eyes twinkled with amusement. "I am Crown Prince Murat of Bahania. Who are you to threaten me?"

Good question. Maybe it was the night and the man, or just the alcohol, but her head was a little fuzzy. There had been a different wine with each course. She'd only taken a sip of each, but those sips added up and muddled her thinking. It was the only explanation for what she said next.

"You're just some alpha-male dog peeing on every tree to mark his territory. That's all Brittany is to you. A tree or a bush."

As soon as the words were out, she wanted to call them back. Murat stunned her by tossing back his head and roaring with laughter.

Still chuckling, he stood. "Come, we will go for a walk to clear your head. You can tell me all your theories about domesticating men such as me."

He walked around the table and pulled back her chair. She rose and faced him.

"It's not a joke. You're acting like a territorial German shepherd. You could use a little obedience training to keep you in line."

"I am not the one who needs to stay in line."

"Are you threatening me?"

As she spoke, she took a step toward him. Unfortunately her feet weren't getting the right signals from her brain, and she stumbled. He caught her and pulled her against him.

"You speak of domestication, but is that what you want?" he asked. "A trained man would not do this."

The "this" turned out to be nothing more than his mouth pressing against hers. A kiss. No biggie.

Except the second his lips brushed against hers, every part of her body seemed to go up in flames. Desperate hot need pulsed through her, forcing her to cling to him or collapse at his feet.

They kissed before, she remembered hazily. A lifetime ago. He'd held her tenderly and delighted her with gentle embraces.

But not this time. Now he claimed her with a passion that left her breathless and hungry for more. He wrapped his arms around her, drawing her up against his hard body.

She melted into him, savoring the heat and the strength. When he tilted his head, she did the same and parted her lips before he even asked. He plunged inside, stroking, circling, teasing, making her breath catch and her body weep with desire.

More, she thought as she kissed him back. There had to be more.

But there wasn't. He straightened, forcing her to consider standing on her own. She pushed back and found her balance, then struggled to catch her breath.

"Brittany will be in New York by now," he said.

The sudden change in topic caught her off guard. Weren't they going to discuss the kiss? Weren't they going to do it again?

Apparently not. She ordered herself to focus on Brittany. Murat. The wedding that could never be.

"I meant what I said," he told her. "There *will* be a Snowden bride."

"You'll need to rethink your plan," she said. "Brittany isn't going to marry you."

He stared at her, his dark eyes unreadable. "Are you sure?"

"Absolutely."

She braced herself for an argument or at least a pronouncement that he was the crown prince, blah, blah, blah. Instead he simply nodded.

"As you wish," he said. And then he left.

Daphne didn't fall asleep until sometime after two in the morning. She'd felt too out of sorts to relax. While she told herself she should be happy that Murat was finally seeing reason about Brittany, she didn't trust the man. Certainly not his last cryptic agreement. As she wished what? Was he really giving up on Brittany so easily? Somehow that didn't seem right.

So when she woke early the next morning, she felt more tired than when she'd gone to bed.

After slipping into her robe, she hurried toward the smell of fresh coffee wafting through the harem. A cart stood by the sofa.

Daphne ignored the fresh fruit and croissants and dove for the coffee. The steaming liquid perked her up with the first sip.

"Better," she said, when she'd swallowed half a cup.

She sat down in front of the cart and picked up the

folded newspapers. The first was a copy of *USA TODAY.* Underneath was the local Bahanian paper. She flipped it open, then screamed.

On the front page was a color picture of her under a headline announcing her engagement to Murat.

Chapter Four

"I'll kill him!" Daphne yelled.

She set down her coffee before she dropped it and shrieked her fury.

"How dare he? Who does he think he is? Crown prince or not, I'll have his head for this!"

She couldn't believe it. Last night he'd been friendly and fun and sexy with his talking and touching, when the whole time he'd been planning an ambush.

She stomped her foot. He'd *kissed* her. He'd taken her in his arms and kissed her. She'd gotten all gooey and nostalgic while he'd known what he was going to do.

"Bastard. No. Wait. He's lower than that. He's a…a camel-dung sweeper. He's slime."

She tossed the paper down, then immediately bent over to pick it up. There, in perfect English, was the announcement for the upcoming wedding along with what looked like a very long story on her previous engagement to Murat.

"Just great," she muttered. "Now we're going to have to rehash that again."

She threw the paper in the air and stalked around the room. "Are you listening, Murat?" she yelled. "Because if you are, know that you've gone too far. You can't do this to me. I won't let you."

There was no answer. Typical, she thought. He's done it and now he was hiding out.

Just then the phone rang.

"Ha! Afraid to face me in person?"

She crossed to the phone on the end table and snatched it up. "Yes?"

"How could you do this?" a familiar female voice demanded.

"Laurel?"

A choke shook her sister's voice. "Who else? Dammit, Daphne, you always have to ruin everything. You did this on purpose, didn't you? You wanted him for yourself."

It took Daphne a second to figure out what her sister was talking about. "You know about the engagement?" she asked.

"Of course. What did you think? That it would happen in secret?"

"Of course not. I mean there's no engagement."

How on earth had her sister found out? There was a major time difference between Bahania and the American East Coast. "Shouldn't you be in bed?"

"Oh, sure. Because I'm going to sleep after this." Her sister drew in a ragged breath. "What I don't understand is how you could do this to Brittany. I thought you really cared about her."

"I do. I love her." Probably more than her sister ever had, Daphne thought grimly. "That's why I didn't want her marrying Murat. She's never even met the man."

"You took care of things, didn't you? Now you have him all for yourself. I can't believe I was stabbed in the back by my own sister."

Daphne clutched the phone. "This is crazy. Laurel, think about it. Why on earth would I want to marry Murat? Didn't I already dump him once?"

"You've probably regretted it ever since. You've just been waiting for the right opportunity to pounce."

"It's been ten years. Couldn't I have pounced before now?"

"You thought you'd find someone else. But you didn't. Who could measure up to the man who's going to be king? I understand that kind of ambition. I can even respect it. But to steal your only niece's fiancé is horrible. Brittany will be crushed."

"I doubt that."

"I never should have trusted you," Laurel said. "Why didn't I see what you had planned?"

"There wasn't a plan." Except making sure Brittany didn't throw her life away, but Laurel didn't have to know about that. "I told you, I'm not engaged to Murat. I don't know what the papers are talking about, but it's a huge mistake."

"Oh, sure. Like I believe that."

"Believe what you want. There's not going to be a wedding."

"Tell that to my heartsick daughter. You've always thought of yourself instead of your family. Just know I'll never forgive you. No matter what."

With that, Laurel hung up.

Daphne listened to the silence for a second, then put down the phone and covered her face with her hands. Nothing made sense. How could this be happening?

She had a lot of questions, but no answers, and she knew only one way to get them.

She stood and crossed to the heavy gold doors.

"Hey," she yelled. "Are you guards still out there?"

"Yes, ma'am. Is there a problem?"

"You bet there is. Tell Murat I want to see him right now."

She heard low conversation but not the individual words as the guards spoke to each other.

"We'll pass your message along to the crown prince," one of the men said at last.

"Not good enough. I want his royal fanny down here this second. And you can tell him I said that."

She pounded on the door a couple of times for good measure, then stalked back into her bedroom. Suddenly the phrase "dressed to kill" took on a whole new meaning.

* * *

Murat finished his second cup of coffee as he read over the financial section of the *London Times*. Then the door to his suite opened, and his father stepped in.

The king was perfectly dressed, even with the Persian cat he carried in his arms. He nodded at the guard on duty, then walked into the dining room.

"Good morning," he said.

Murat rose and motioned to a chair. The king shook his head.

"I won't be staying long. I only came by to discuss the most fascinating item I saw in the paper this morning."

"That the value of the Euro is expected to rise?" Murat asked calmly, knowing it wasn't that.

"No." The king flipped through the pages until he found the local edition—the one with the large picture of Daphne on the front page. "Interesting solution."

Murat shrugged. "I said I would have a Snowden bride, and so I shall."

"I'm surprised she agreed."

Murat thought of the message he'd received from the guards outside the harem. Even though he suspected they'd edited the content, Daphne's demands made him smile.

"She has not," he admitted. "But she will. After all, the choice of fiancées was hers alone."

"Oh?"

"I told her there would be a wedding, and she said Brittany would not be the bride. That left Daphne to fill the position."

"I see." His father didn't react at all. "Do you have a time line in place for this wedding?"

"Four months."

"Not long to prepare for such an important occasion."

"I think we will manage."

"Perhaps I should go to her and offer my congratulations."

Murat raised his eyebrows. "I'm sure Daphne will welcome your visit, but may I suggest you wait a few days. Until she has had time to settle in to the idea of being my wife."

"Perhaps you are right." The king stroked the cat in his arms. "You have chosen wisely."

"Thank you. I'm sure Daphne and I will be very happy together." After she got over wanting him dead.

By ten that morning Daphne was convinced she'd worn a track in the marble tile floors. She'd showered, dressed and paced. So far she'd been unable to make any phone calls because of the stupid time difference. But she would eventually get through to someone and then Murat would taste her fury. She might not be the favorite Snowden, but she was still a member of the family and her name meant something. She would call in every favor possible and make him pay for this.

"Of all the arrogant, insensitive, chauvinistic, ridiculous ideas," she muttered as she walked to the French doors.

"So much energy."

She spun and saw him moving toward her. "I hate

that you do that," she said. "Appear and disappear. I swear, when I find that secret door, I'm putting something in front of it so you can't use it anymore."

He seemed completely unruffled by her anger. "As you wish."

"Oh, sure. You say that now. Where were my wishes last night when you were sending your lies to the newspaper?" She stalked over to the dining room table and picked up the pages in question.

"How could you do this?" she asked as she shook them at him. "How dare you? Who gave you the right?"

"You did."

"What?" She hated that she practically shrieked, but the man was making her insane. "I most certainly did not."

"I told you there would be a Snowden bride and you declared it would not be your niece."

"What?" she repeated. "That's not making a choice. I never agreed with your original premise. Where do you get off saying you'll have a Snowden bride? We're not ice cream flavors to be ordered interchangeably. We're people."

"Yes, I know. Women. I have agreed not to marry Brittany. You should be pleased."

Pleased? "Are you crazy?" She dropped the papers and clutched at the back of the chair. "I'm furious. You've trapped me here and told lies about me to the press. I've already heard from my sister. Do you know how this is going to mess up my life? Both of our lives?"

"I agree that marriage will change things, but I'm hoping for the better."

"We're not getting married!" she yelled.

Instead of answering, he simply stared at her. Calm certainty radiated from him in nearly palpable waves. It made her want to choke him.

She drew in a deep breath and tried to relax. When that didn't work, she attempted to loosen her grip on the chair.

"Okay," she said. "Let's start from the beginning. You're not marrying Brittany, which is a good thing."

He had the gall to smile at her. "Did you really think I would be interested in a teenager for my wife? Bringing Brittany here was entirely my father's idea. I agreed to meet with her only to make him happy."

Spots appeared before her eyes. "You what?" No way. That couldn't be true. "Tell me that again."

"I never intended to marry Brittany."

"But you…" She couldn't breathe. Her chest felt hot and tight and she couldn't think. "But you said…"

"I wanted to annoy you for assuming the worst about me. Then when you offered yourself in Brittany's place, I decided to consider the possibility."

Offer? "I never offered."

"Oh, but you did. And I accepted."

"No. You can't." She pulled out the chair and sank onto the seat. "I know you're used to getting your way, but this time it isn't going to happen. I need to be very clear about that. There isn't going to be a wedding. You can't make me, and if you try, you'll be forced to tie me up and gag me as you drag me down the aisle. Won't that play well in the press."

"I do not care about the press."

She grabbed the paper again. "Then why did you bother telling them this?"

He sat down across from her. "Make no mistake. My mind is made up. We *will* be married. This announcement has forced you to see the truth. Now you will have time to accept it."

"What I accept is that you've slipped into madness. This isn't the fifteenth century. You can't force me to do what you want. This is a free country." She remembered she wasn't in America anymore. "Sort of."

"I am Crown Prince Murat of Bahania. Few would tell me no."

"Count me among them."

He leaned back in his chair. "You never disappoint me," he said. "How I enjoy the explosion. You're like fireworks."

She glared at him. "You haven't seen anything yet. I'll take this all the way to the White House if I have to."

"Good. The president will be invited to the wedding. He and I have been friends for many years now."

At that moment Daphne desperately wished for superpowers so she could overturn the heavy table and toss Murat out the window.

"I'm going to speak slowly," she said. "So you can understand me. I…won't…marry…you. I have a life. Friends. My work."

"Ah, yes. About your work. I made some phone calls last night and found it most interesting to learn that you have left your veterinary practice in Chicago."

"That was about making career choices, not marrying you."

"And you have been very determined to keep me from your niece. Are you sure you do not secretly want me for yourself?"

She rolled her eyes. "How amazing that you and your ego fit inside the room at the same time." Although her sister had made the same accusation.

It wasn't true, Daphne reminded herself. Murat was her past, and she was more than content to keep him there. She hadn't spent the last ten years pining. She'd dated, been happy. He was a non-event.

"I haven't thought about you in ages," she said honestly. "I'm even willing to take an oath. Just bring in the Bible. I wouldn't be here now if you hadn't acted all caveman over my niece. This is your fault."

He nodded. "There is a ring."

She blinked at him. "What? You want to try to buy me off with jewelry? Thank you very much but I'm not that kind of woman."

He smiled again. "I know."

Her rage returned, but before she could decide how to channel it, the phone rang again.

She hesitated before crossing the room to answer it. Was Laurel calling back to yell some more? Daphne had a feeling she was at the end of her rope and not up to taking that particular call. But what if it was Brittany, and her niece really was upset?

"Not possible," she said as she crossed to the phone and picked it up. "This is Daphne."

"Darling, we just heard. We're delighted."

Her mother's voice came over the line as clearly as if she'd been in the same room.

Daphne clutched the receiver. "Laurel called?"

"Yes. Oh, darling, how clever you are to have finally snagged Murat. The man who will be king." Her mother sighed. "I always knew you'd do us proud."

Daphne didn't know what to think. She wanted to tell her mother the truth—that there wasn't going to be a wedding, that this was all a mistake, but she couldn't seem to speak.

"Your father is simply thrilled," her mother said. "We're looking forward to a lovely wedding. Do you have any idea when?"

"I—"

Her mother laughed. "Of course you don't. You've only just become engaged. Well, let me know as soon as the date is finalized. We'll need to rearrange some travel, but it will be worth it. Your father can't wait to walk you down the aisle."

Daphne turned her back so Murat couldn't see her expression. She didn't want him to know how much this conversation hurt.

"Laurel was pretty upset," she said, not knowing what else to say.

"I know. She got it in her head that Brittany would be the one for Murat. Honestly, the girl is lovely and will make a fine marriage in time, but she's just too young. There are responsibilities that come with being queen, and she simply wasn't ready." Her mother laughed.

"Queen. I like the sound of that. My daughter, the queen. My sweet baby girl. All right, I'm going to run, but I'll call soon. You must be so very happy. This is wonderful, Daphne. Truly wonderful."

With that her mother hung up. Daphne replaced the receiver and did her best not to react in any way. Sure, her eyes burned and her body felt tense and sore, but she would get over it. She always did.

"Your parents?" Murat asked from his place at the table behind her.

She nodded. "My mother. My sister called and spoke with her. She's d-delighted."

The crack in her voice made her stiffen. No way was she going to give in to the emotion pulsing through her.

"She wants details about the wedding as soon as possible. So she can rearrange their travel schedule."

"You did not tell her there wouldn't be a wedding."

"No."

Because it had been too hard to speak. Because if she tried, she would give in to the pain and once that dam broke, there was no putting it together.

"Don't think that means I've accepted the engagement," she whispered.

"Not for a second."

She heard footsteps, then Murat's hands clasped her arms and he turned her toward him. Understanding darkened his eyes.

She was so unused to seeing any readable emotion in his gaze that she couldn't seem to react. Which meant she didn't protest when he pulled her close and wrapped his arms around her. Suddenly she was pressing against him, her head on his shoulder and the protective warmth of his body surrounding her.

"You can't do this," she said, her voice muffled against his suit jacket. "I hate you."

"I know you do, but right now there isn't anyone else." He stroked her hair. "Come now. Tell me what troubles you."

She shook her head. To speak of it would hurt too much.

"It's your mother," he murmured. "She said she was happy about the engagement. Your family has always been ambitious. In some ways a king for a son-in-law is even better than a president."

"I know." She wrapped her arms around his waist and hung on as hard as she could. "It's horrible. *She's* horrible. She said she was proud of me. That's the first time she's ever said that. Because I've always been a disappointment."

The hurt of a decade of indifference from her family swept through her. "Nobody came to my college graduation. Did you know that? They were all still angry because I'd refused to marry you. And they hated that I became a vet. No one even acknowledged my finishing school and going to work. My mother didn't say a word in the Christmas newsletter. She didn't mention me at all. It's as if by not marrying well, I'd ceased to exist."

She felt the light brush of his lips on her head. "I am sorry."

She sniffed. "I'm only their child when I do what

they want. I was afraid it would be the same for Brittany. I wanted her to be happy and strong so I tried to let her know that I loved her no matter what. That my love wasn't conditional on her marrying the right man."

"I'm sure she knows how much you care."

"I hope so. Laurel said she would be heartbroken."

Murat chuckled. "Not to marry a man twice her age whom she has never met? I suspect you raised her better than that."

"What?" She lifted her head and stared at him. They were far closer than she'd realized, which was really stupid—what with her being in his arms and all.

"I didn't raise her," she said. "She's not my daughter."

"Isn't she?"

It was what she'd always believed in her heart but never spoken of. Not to anyone. How could Murat grasp that personal truth so easily?

"I know all about expectations," he said, lightly tracing the curve of her cheek. "There was not a single day I was allowed to forget my responsibilities."

Which made sense. "I guess when you're going to grow up and be king, you aren't supposed to make as many mistakes as the rest of us."

"Exactly. So I understand about having to do what others want, even when that means not doing what is in your heart."

"Except I wasn't willing to do that," she reminded him. "I did what I wanted and they punished me. Not just my parents, but my sisters, too. I ceased to exist."

His dark gaze held her captive. She liked being held

by him, which was crazy, because he was the enemy. Only, right this second, he didn't seem so bad.

"You exist to me," he said.

If only that were true. Reluctantly she pushed away and stood on her own.

"I don't," she said. "I have no idea what your engagement game is about, but I know it's not about me."

"How can you say that? You're the one I've chosen."

"Why?" she asked. "I think you're being stubborn and difficult. You don't care about me. You never did."

He frowned. "How can you say that? Ten years ago I asked you to marry me."

"What does that have to do with anything? If you'd really loved me, you wouldn't have let me go. But you didn't care when I left. I walked away and you never once came after me to find out why."

Chapter Five

Murat left Daphne and returned to his office. But despite the meeting he was supposed to attend, he told his assistant not to bother him and closed his door.

The space was large and open, as befitted the crown prince of such a wealthy nation. The conversation area of three sofas sat by several tall windows and the conference table easily seated sixteen.

Murat ignored it all as he crossed to the balcony overlooking a private garden and stepped outside. The spring air hinted at the heat to come. He ignored it and the call of the birds. Instead he stared into the distance as he wrestled with the past.

How like a woman, he thought. She questioned why

he had not gone after her when she had been the one to leave him. Why would he want to follow such a woman? Besides, even if the thought had occurred to him—which it had not—it wasn't his place. If she wished them to be in contact, then she should come crawling back, begging forgiveness for having left in the first place.

She should know all of this. She came from a family familiar with power and how the world worked. He had known that they favored the match, and he was willing to admit he had been surprised she would stand against them.

Murat turned his back on the view but did not enter his office. The past flashed before him—a tableau of what had been. His father had told him she left. The king had come to him full of plans of how they would go after her and bring her back, but Murat had refused. He would not chase her around the world. If Daphne wanted to be gone, then let her. She had been a mere woman. Easy to replace.

Now, with the wisdom of hindsight, he admitted to himself that she had been different from anyone he had ever known. As for replacing her…that had never occurred. He had met other women, bedded them, been interested and intrigued. But he had never been willing to marry any of them.

He knew he should wonder why. What was it about her that had made her stand out? Not her great beauty. She was attractive and sensual, but he had known women who seemed more goddess than human. Not her intelligence. While hers was better than average, he had dated women whose comprehension of technical and scientific matters had left him speechless.

She was funny and charming, but he had known those with more of those qualities. So what combination of traits had made him willing to marry her and not another?

As he walked back into his office, he remembered what it had been like after she had left. He hadn't allowed himself to mourn her. No one had been permitted to speak her name. For him, it was as if she had never been.

And now she had returned and they would marry. In time she would see that was right. She might always argue with him, but she knew who was in charge.

He moved to his desk and took a seat. In a locked drawer sat a red leather box that contained the official seal of his office. He opened that box and removed the seal, then moved aside the silk lining. Tucked in the bottom, in between folds of protective padding, lay a diamond ring.

The stone had been given by a Bahanian king to his favorite mistress in 1685. He had been loyal to her for nearly thirty years and when his queen died, he married his mistress. Many told the story of how the ring had saved the mistress's life more than once, as other jealous women in the harem sought to do her harm. The stone was said to possess magical powers to heal and evoke love.

Of all the diamonds in the royal family's possession, this had been the one Murat had chosen for Daphne and the one she had left behind when she'd gone. He picked it up now and studied the carefully cut stone.

Such a small thing, he thought. Barely three carats. He'd been a fool to think it contained any magic at all.

He returned the ring to its hiding place, replaced the seal, then put the box back in the drawer and locked it. Later that afternoon the royal jeweler would offer a selection of rings for Murat's consideration. He would choose another one for Daphne. A stone without history or meaning. Or magic.

Daphne spent the morning considering her options. Murat had left in a huff without saying much to make her feel any better. He refused to admit there wasn't going to be a wedding, nor had he told her how her sister and the newspaper had found out so quickly. Obviously, he was to blame, but why wouldn't he just say so?

As she walked through the garden she told herself that an unexpected engagement certainly put things in perspective. Twenty-four hours ago her biggest concern had been how long he would keep her trapped in the harem. She'd been sure he would want to make his point—that she'd defied him and had to be punished in some way—but she'd looked at it as an unexpected vacation in a place not of her choosing. Now everything was different.

She wanted to tell herself that he couldn't possibly marry her without her permission, only she didn't know if that was true. Murat was determined and obviously sneaky. Should anyone be able to pull that off—he was the guy. She was going to have to stay on her toes and prevent the wedding from happening. Finding herself married to him would be a disaster of monumental proportions. Getting out of this engagement was going to be difficult enough.

She needed a plan. Which meant she needed more information. But how to get it?

"Hello? Anybody home?"

Daphne turned toward the sound of the female voice. None of the servants would address her that way. Not after they knew about the engagement. To be honest, none of the servants had addressed her at all—it was as if they'd been told to avoid conversation.

She hurried back into the harem.

"Hello," she said as she stepped into the large, cool main room.

Three women stood together. They were beautiful, elegantly dressed and smiling.

Two blondes and a redhead. One of the blondes—a petite woman with short, spiky hair and a curvy body to die for—stepped forward.

"We're your basic princess contingent sneaking in to speak with the prisoner." She grinned. "Not that you're really a prisoner. There were rumors, of course. But now you're engaged to Murat, which makes you family. I'm Cleo. Married to Sadik." She rolled her big, blue eyes. "How totally *Lawrence of Arabia* to introduce myself in terms of who my husband is."

"You're a disgrace to us all, Cleo," the other blonde said fondly. She was a little taller, even more curvy, with big hair and sandals that looked high enough to be a walking hazard, especially considering her obvious pregnancy.

"Daphne Snowden."

"Hi." The redhead waved. "I'm Emma. Reyhan's wife." She motioned to the pregnant woman. "That's Billie."

Billie frowned. "Didn't I give her my name?"

"No," Cleo and Emma said together. Cleo sighed. "Billie thinks she's all that because she can fly jets. Like that's a big deal."

"It *is* a big deal," Emma whispered. "We talked about it."

"I know, but we don't want her to get a big head or anything."

"It'll match my big stomach," Billie said with a grin.

Daphne didn't know what to say. Just then she heard a rapid clicking sound. She glanced around and saw a small Yorkshire terrier exploring the main salon of the harem.

"That's Muffin," Billie said. "My other baby."

"I didn't know there were any dogs at the palace," Daphne said. "Doesn't the king only keep cats?"

"He's taken a liking to Muffin," Billie said. "Which is great because she gets into all kinds of trouble." She rubbed the small of her back. "Mind if I take a load off?"

"What? Oh, sorry. Please." Daphne motioned to the closest grouping of sofas. "Make yourselves comfortable."

The women sat down. Daphne stared from one to the other, not sure what to make of them. The last time she'd been in Bahania, all of Murat's brothers had been happy bachelors.

"I read about your weddings, of course," she said, then glanced at Emma. "Well, not yours."

"I know," she said as she flipped her red hair over her shoulder. "We were a scandal. But I thought the ceremony to renew our vows was very lovely."

"The pictures were great." Daphne turned to Billie. "You're married to Jefri?"

The pregnant woman nodded. "I'm embarrassed to say he swept me off my feet, and in the shoes I wear, that's a trick."

The women laughed. Daphne sensed their closeness and felt a twinge of envy. She'd never had that kind of relationship with her own sisters.

Cleo scooted forward on the sofa. "There are five of us altogether. I know it sounds confusing, but it's really simple. The king has four sons and two daughters. Of the girls, Sabrina is married to Kardal and they live, ah, out of the country. Zara, his other daughter, is married to Rafe. Zara didn't know the king was her father until a few years ago."

"I remember reading about that. Very romantic."

"I thought so," Cleo said.

Billie groaned. "You think everything is romantic."

Emma sighed. "These two argue a lot. I think they're too much alike. The fighting doesn't mean anything, but sometimes it gets a little old."

"I'm ignoring you," Cleo said to Emma.

"Me, too," Billie added.

Daphne couldn't help grinning. "Do you three live in the palace?" They could certainly make her brief stay more fun.

"*They* do," Emma said, pointing to the other two

women. "As I said, I'm married to Reyhan, and we spend much of our time out in the desert. Reyhan inherited a house there from his aunt. Billie and Jefri and Cleo and Sadik make their home in the palace. Billie and Jefri are involved with the new air force. Billie's a flight instructor. She flies jets."

Daphne couldn't imagine the big-haired sex kitten flying anything more complicated than a paper airplane. "You're kidding?"

Billie grinned. "Never underestimate the power of a woman."

"I guess not."

Emma continued. "I'm in town for a few days while Reyhan has some meetings. We brought the baby." Her face softened as she smiled. "We have a daughter."

"That's two for two," Billie said. "I have a daughter, too. Wouldn't it be funny if there weren't any male heirs?"

"Not to the men in the family," Daphne said.

"Good point," Billie said. "So Zara and Sabrina will be out in a few weeks to meet you. They said to say hi for them in the meantime."

Talk about overwhelming, Daphne thought. "You're very sweet to visit me."

"Not a problem," Cleo said. She fluffed her short, blond hair. "Besides, we want all the details. This engagement has come about very quickly."

"That's subtle," Billie said.

"Well, it has," Cleo insisted.

Emma cleared her throat. "I think what she means is

how wonderful that you and Murat have found each other."

Daphne hated to burst their bubble, but she wouldn't pretend to be something she wasn't. "Murat and I haven't found anything. I don't know why he announced we're engaged, because we're not. And there isn't going to be a wedding."

The three women looked at each other, then at her.

"That changes things," Cleo said brightly.

Daphne smoothed the hem of her skirt. "I know it sounds terrible."

"Not at all," Emma said.

"Sort of," Billie said.

Daphne couldn't help smiling. "You guys are great."

"Thanks," Cleo said, preening a little. "I like to think we're pretty special."

Daphne chuckled for a second, then sobered as she thought about her impossible situation. "My family is big into politics and power," she said. "Years ago I was traveling through Europe during a summer break from college and I met Murat. I didn't know who he was and we hit it off. When he invited me back here, I was stunned to find out I'd been dating the crown prince."

"I know that feeling," Emma said. "Reyhan isn't going to be king, but he's still royal. I had no idea."

Billie put her arm around Emma. "She's our innocent."

Daphne sighed. "Then you can imagine my shock. Before I knew what had happened, we were engaged and everything was moving so quickly."

Billie frowned. "*Were* engaged. Obviously you didn't get married."

"I think I remember reading about that," Billie said. "Ten years ago I was a serious tabloid junkie."

"You still read the tabloids," Cleo said.

"Yeah, and then you steal them from me."

"Ladies," Emma said, holding up her hand to stop their bickering. "I believe Daphne was talking."

Cleo smiled at her. "Go on, Daphne."

"There's not much else to say. Things didn't work out and I left. My family was furious and didn't speak to me for ages. Eventually we patched things up." Sort of. Her mother had never really forgiven her for not marrying a future king. "Then a few weeks ago my niece, who is barely eighteen, told me that she was flying over to meet Murat and get engaged."

Billie raised her eyebrows. "What? That doesn't sound right."

"I agree," Cleo said. "Murat can be all formal with his 'I'm the crown prince' but he's never been into silly young women." She winced. "Sorry. Not that your niece is silly or anything."

"I know what you mean," Daphne said. "She's still a kid in so many ways. She's only had a couple of boyfriends and none of them were serious. Murat is nearly twice her age. I was determined to talk her out of it, which I did, just in the nick of time. We were flying here when she suddenly realized she was making a huge mistake. So she went back to the States, and I stayed to tell Murat there wasn't going to be an engagement. The next thing I knew I was locked in the harem and he was announcing *our* engagement in the papers."

Emma sighed. "That's so romantic."

Cleo and Billie looked at her. "That's kidnapping," Cleo said.

"Well, maybe technically, but he must really love her."

Daphne shook her head. "I hate to burst your bubble, but Murat doesn't love me. It's been ten years. He doesn't even *know* me anymore."

"So why the sudden engagement?" Billie asked.

"I have no idea," Daphne told her.

"He has to have a reason," Cleo said. "Men always do things for a reason. Has he been pining for you all these years?"

"Gee, let's count the number of women he's been out with in that time," Daphne said humorously. "I'm going to guess it's around a hundred or so."

"But he wasn't serious about any of them."

Emma scooted forward in her seat. "If it's not too personal, why did you leave last time?"

Good question. "There were a lot of reasons. Things moved so quickly—I didn't get a chance to figure out if this was the life I wanted before I found myself engaged. When reality set in, I panicked."

"But you loved him," Billie said. "Didn't you?"

"As much as I could at the time." Daphne thought back to how brightly her feelings had burned. "I was pretty innocent, and Murat was the first guy I'd been serious about. I'm not sure I knew what love was. We were so different."

Although getting over him had taken what felt like a lifetime. She still had scars.

Cleo smiled at her. "Ah, to be that young again. Wouldn't you like to go back in time and talk to that Daphne?"

"I don't know what I would say to her."

"Would you tell her to stay?" Cleo asked.

"No."

"Why not?" Emma asked. "Are we getting too personal? Does this feel like an interrogation?"

"I'm okay," Daphne told her. "And I wouldn't have told her to stay because I know what happened after. Murat didn't love her…me. He didn't bother to come after me. Not a phone call or a letter. He never cared enough to find out why I'd left."

She expected the three princesses to look shocked. Instead Cleo sighed, Billie shook her head, and Emma's expression turned sad.

"It's pride," Emma said. "They have too much of it. It's a sheik thing. Or maybe a royal thing."

"I'm not sure what pride has to do with it."

Cleo shrugged. "You have to look at it from his point of view. He offered you everything, and you walked away. That had to have tweaked his tail just a little. Tweaked princes don't go running after women."

"Mere women," Billie said in a stern voice. "You are a mere woman."

Emma grinned. "The princes are so cute when they're all imperious."

Daphne felt as if she'd just sat down with the crazy family. "What are you talking about?"

"That you can't judge Murat's feelings for you solely on whether or not he came running after you when you left," Cleo said. "He's the crown prince and has that ego thing going on even more than his brothers. It's possible that in that twisted 'I'm the man' brain of his, he thought it would show too much weakness."

"But if he'd cared…"

"It's not about caring," Emma said. "You're looking at the situation logically, and like a woman. Reyhan loved me and yet he ignored me for years. His pride wouldn't let him talk to someone he thought had rejected him, let alone admit his feelings. Murat could be the same way."

Daphne thought about all the women he'd seen over the past decade. "I don't think he's actually been doing a lot of suffering."

"Maybe not," Cleo said. "But it's something to think about. If he matters at all."

Just then the gold doors opened and several servants entered with carts.

Billie smiled. "Did we mention we'd brought lunch?"

The women gathered around the dining room table and enjoyed the delicious food. Conversation shifted from Daphne and her situation to how each of them had met their husbands, then to shopping and the best place to get really gorgeous, if uncomfortable, shoes. They left a little after three.

Daphne closed the door behind them, then retreated to the sofa in front of the garden window. Despite everything, she'd had a nice day. Had her engagement to Murat been real, she would have been delighted to know that these women would be a part of her life.

But it wasn't real, and their theory that Murat's pride had kept him from holding on to her was nice to think about but was not in any way true.

"Not that it matters now," she whispered. Somehow she'd managed to get over him. At least she didn't have to worry about that now. Her feelings weren't engaged and her heart was firmly out of reach. She was going to make sure things stayed that way.

Daphne planned a quiet remainder of the day. She assumed Murat wouldn't come back to torment her until the morning, and she was partially right. Around four the gold doors opened again, but instead of the crown prince, she saw the king.

"Your Majesty," she said, coming to her feet before dropping into a low curtsy.

"Daphne."

Murat's father walked toward her and held out both his hands. He captured hers and kissed her knuckles. "How lovely to have you back in Bahania." The handsome older man chuckled. "Most young women today don't know the first thing about a good curtsy, but you've always had style."

"I had several years of training in etiquette. Some of it had to rub off," she said with a smile. While she might not be excited about what Murat was up to, she couldn't help being pleased at seeing the king. He had always been very kind to her, especially when she'd been young, in love and terrified.

"Come," King Hassan said as he led her to the cluster of sofas. "Tell me everything. You and your family are well?"

"Everyone is great." Except for Laurel who was furious about Brittany not marrying Murat. "They send their best." Or they would have if they'd known she would be speaking with the king.

"I'm sure they're very excited about what has happened."

Her good mood slipped. "Yes. My parents are delighted."

King Hassan had to be close to sixty, but he looked much younger. There was an air of strength about him. Authority and determination. No doubt that came from a royal lineage that stretched back over a thousand years. He was considered one of the most forward-thinking leaders in the world. A king who earned his people's respect through his actions and loyalty to his country.

Murat would be equally as excellent a leader, Daphne thought. He'd been born to the position and had never once stumbled. Which made him admirable, but not someone she wanted to marry.

"My son sends you a surprise," the king said as the gold doors opened again.

Servants appeared with the carts they seemed to

favor. But this time instead of food they brought clay and sculpting tools.

Her fingers instantly itched for the feel of clay, while the cynical part of her brain wondered if he thought he could bribe her with her hobby.

"You must thank him for me," she said as the servants bowed and left.

"You can thank him yourself. He'll be by later."

Oh, joy, she thought as she smiled politely.

"You are aware of the date," King Hassan said.

Daphne blinked at him. "Today's date?"

"No. That the wedding date has been set. It is in four months. The challenge will be to get everything done in such a short period of time, but I am sure that with the right staff, we will be successful."

She stiffened her spine and drew in a breath. "Your Majesty, I mean no disrespect, but the problem isn't finding the right staff. The problem is I am not going to marry Murat, and there is nothing anyone can say to convince me otherwise."

She'd thought the monarch might be surprised, but he only chuckled. "Ah, two stubborn people. So who will win this battle?"

"I will. It is the old story of the rabbit and the hound. The rabbit gets away because while the hound runs for its supper, the rabbit runs for its life."

"An interesting point." The king took her hand again and lightly squeezed her fingers. "I have often wondered how things would have been different if you had stayed and married Murat. Have you?"

"No." Well, maybe a little, but she wasn't interested in admitting it. "I wasn't ready to be married. I was too young, as was your son. The position of his wife requires much, and I'm not sure I would have been up to the task."

"Perhaps. There are many responsibilities in being queen, although your questions and self-doubts make me think you would have done well in the position. He never married."

Daphne drew her hand from his and laced her fingers together on her lap. "Murat? I'm aware of that. Had he married I would not currently be a prisoner in the harem."

"You know that is not my point," Hassan said humorously. "You never married, either."

"I've been busy with my studies and establishing my career."

"It is not much of an excuse. Perhaps each of you were waiting for the other to make the first move."

Daphne nearly sprang to her feet. At the last second she remembered that action would be a fairly serious breach of protocol. "I assure you that is not even close to true. Murat has enjoyed the company of so many beautiful women, I doubt he remembers them all, let alone a young woman from a decade ago."

"And now?" the king asked.

"We barely know each other."

"An excellent point. Perhaps this is a good time to change that." The king rose. "Murat wants this wedding, Daphne, as do your parents. As do I. Are you willing to take on the world?"

She stood and tried not to give in to the sudden rush of fear. "If I have to."

"Perhaps it would be easier to give in graciously. Would marriage to Murat be so horrible?"

"Yes. I think it would be." She bit her lower lip. "Your Majesty, would you really force me to marry your son against my will?"

His dark eyes never wavered as he spoke. "If I have to."

Murat found Daphne in the garden. The sun had nearly slipped below the horizon, and the first whispers of the cool evening air whispered against his face.

She sat on a stone bench, her shoulders slumped, her chin nearly touching her chest. The only word that came to his mind at that moment was...*broken*.

He hurried forward and pulled her to her feet. She gasped in surprise, but didn't resist until he tried to draw her close.

"What do you think you're doing?" she demanded, twisting free of his embrace.

"Comforting you."

She glared at him. "You're the source of my troubles, not the relief from them."

"I'm all you have."

She took a step back. "What a sorry state of affairs. What on earth does that sentence say about my life?"

"That at least there is one person on your side."

Little light spilled into the garden, but there was enough for him to see her beautiful features. Her wide eyes had darkened with pain and confusion. Her full lips trembled. It was as if the weight of the world pressed down upon her, and he ached for her.

"Come," he said, holding out his arms. "You'll feel better."

"Maybe I don't want to," she said stubbornly, even as she moved forward and leaned against him.

He wrapped his arms around her. She was slight, so delicate and yet so strong. She smelled of flowers and soap and of herself. That arousing fragrance he had never been able to forget.

Wanting filled him, but something else, as well. Something that made this moment feel right.

He felt her hands on his back, and she rested her forehead against his shoulder.

"No one will help me," she said. "I've been making phone calls for nearly two hours. Not my family— which isn't a big surprise—nor any of my friends. I even called my congressman. Everyone thinks us getting married is a fine idea. They refused to believe that I'm being held against my will, and they all hinted for an invitation to the wedding."

"Then you may add them to the list."

She raised her head. Tears glittered in her eyes. "That's not what I wanted to hear."

He knew what she wanted him to say, but he would not speak the words. To set her free…it would not happen.

"You will enjoy being queen," he said. "There is much power in the position."

"I've never been that interested in power."

"You've never had it before."

"Murat, you know this is wrong."

"Why? You are to marry me, Crown Prince Murat. It is not as if you're being asked to wed a used-camel dealer."

She gave a half laugh, half sob and pushed away from him. The tears had trickled down her face. He wiped them away with his fingers.

"Do not cry," he murmured. "I offer you the world."

"I only want my freedom."

"To do what? To give shots to overweight dogs and cats? Here you can make a difference. Here you will be a part of history. Your children and grandchildren will rule this land."

"It's not enough."

He growled low in his throat. Had she always been this stubborn? Was she trying to punish him for what had happened before? All right. Perhaps he could give a little on that point.

"Why did you leave me?" he asked. "Before. Ten years ago. Why did you go?"

Her shoulders slumped again, and the pain returned to her eyes. "It doesn't matter."

"Yes, it does. I wish to know."

"You wouldn't understand."

"Then explain it to me. I am very intelligent."

"Not about me." She swallowed. "Murat, you have to let me go."

Instead of answering her statement, he stepped forward and kissed her. He caught her by surprise—he could tell by the sudden intake of air and the way she hesitated before responding. But instead of retreating, he settled his hand on her hip and the back of her neck and brushed his tongue against her lower lip.

She parted instantly. As he swept inside he felt the heat flaring between them. Wanting poured through him, making it difficult to hold back when he wanted to rip off her clothing and claim her right there on the bench.

Instead he continued to kiss her, moving slowly, retreating, pulling back until she was the one to grab him and deepen the embrace. When he finally straightened, she looked as aroused as he felt.

"You see," he said, "there is much between us. We will take the time to get to know each other better. That will make you comfortable with the thought of our marriage."

"Don't bet on it," she said, but her swollen mouth and passion-filled eyes betrayed her.

Murat brushed her cheek with his fingers, then walked out of the harem. Victory was at hand. He would wear away Daphne's defenses until she understood that their marriage was inevitable. Then she would acquiesce and they would be wed. She would love him and be happy and he…

He stepped through the gold doors and into the hallway. He would return to his regular life, content, but untouched by the experience.

Chapter Six

Daphne rolled the cool clay in her hands until the combination of heat from her skin and the friction of the action caused the thick rope to yield to her will. She tore off a piece of clay and pressed it flat, then added it to the sculpture in progress.

The half-finished project had finally begun to take shape. There was a sense of movement in the way the man leaned too far to the right. His body was still a squarish lump, but she knew how she would slice away the excess clay and mold what was left. The head would follow, with the arms and the tray of dishes to come last. The tray that would be on the verge of tumbling to the ground.

Around her, the garden vibrated with life. She heard the chatter of the parrots and the rustle of small creatures hiding in the thick foliage. Several of the king's cats stretched out in the sun, the slow rise and fall of their chests the only sign of life.

As far as prisons went, this wasn't a bad one, Daphne told herself, as she picked up another clump of clay. Not that she had a whole lot of experience with which to compare. She'd never been held against her will before. Still, if one had to be, the Bahania harem was the place.

She couldn't complain about the service, either. Delicious meals appeared whenever she requested them. Her large bed was plenty comfortable, and the bathroom was so luxurious that it bordered on sinful. Still, none of these pleasures made up for the fact that she had been confined against her will with the threat of marriage to Murat hanging over her head.

He had spoken of getting to know each other, but she wasn't so sure that was a good idea. Men like him didn't make a habit of letting just anyone see the inner person, and she doubted their engagement gave her extra privileges in that area. Which left her with the distinct impression that his request had been a lot more about giving himself time to convince her that this was a good idea than any desire he had to share his feelings.

Even more annoying was the fact that a part of her *was* interested in learning more about the man. Life was never easy when the one who got away was a future king.

She picked up a sharp piece of wood that was part

knife, part chisel and went to work on the torso of the sculpture. When the rough shape was correct, she added features to the head, creating a face that was a fair representation of the man in question. A smile pulled at her mouth. She only had to complete the arms and the tray.

"Men have died for less."

Daphne heard the voice about the same time the sound of footsteps entered her consciousness. She'd been so focused on her work that she hadn't been paying attention. Now she pressed clay into the shape of a tray and did her best not to react to Murat's nearness.

"I thought there was artistic freedom here in Bahania," she said, not looking up from her clay.

"Most artists are too intelligent to mock me."

Daphne spared him a glance. As always he wore a suit, although this time he'd left the jacket behind. The crisp white shirt he wore contrasted with his dark skin. He'd rolled the sleeves up to the elbow, and she found the sight of his bare forearms oddly erotic.

Sheesh. She really had to get out more.

"My intelligence has never been an issue," she said. "Do you doubt it now?"

He glanced at the tray taking shape in her hands. "You sculpt me carrying dishes?"

She grinned. "Actually I sculpt you about to drop the dishes you're carrying. There's a difference."

He made a noise low in his throat, which she knew she should take for displeasure, but there was something about it that made her stomach clench. Perhaps the noise was too close to desire.

Stop that! She grabbed hold of any wayward emotions and reminded herself she needed to keep things firmly in check. Wanting Murat wasn't in the rules. It would only make things difficult and awkward. Hadn't she already had to deal with a broken heart once where he was concerned? Was she really willing to forget that the man held her prisoner and threatened a wedding, regardless of her wishes?

"Why are you here?" she asked as she felt her temper grow and with it her strength to resist him.

"Am I not allowed to come and visit with my bride?"

She rolled her eyes and set down the small tray. Next up she began to form tiny glasses and plates.

"I will take your silence as agreement," he said.

"You may take it any way you'd like, but you'd be wrong."

He sighed. "You are most difficult."

"Tell me about it. Of course you've made 'difficult' an art form. I'm still little more than a student."

He ignored that, saying nothing as he walked around her and the sculpture. "You have an energy I haven't seen before," he said. "Perhaps you needed this time to relax."

Perhaps, but she wasn't about to admit that to him. "Is there a point to your visit or are you simply here to annoy me?"

"You will be visited by someone later."

"The first of three ghosts?"

He frowned slightly, then his expression cleared. "Are you in need of a visit by the ghosts of Christmas past, present and future?"

"No. I've always kept the spirit of Christmas in my heart."

"I am pleased to hear it is so. That will bode well for our children. They will have a festive season to look forward to."

Her jaw clenched. "Is this where I point out, yet again, that I haven't agreed to marry you, nor am I likely to?"

"You may if it makes you happy. However, I will not listen. Instead I will inform you that Mr. Peterson is an old and valued member of our staff here. He specializes in coordinating formal state events."

She got it right away. "Like weddings."

"Exactly. I would appreciate it if you were polite and cooperative."

She formed a tiny clay bowl and set it on the tray. "I would appreciate being set free. It seems we are both destined for disappointment."

Murat moved closer. "Why do you attempt to thwart me?"

"Because I can't seem to get through to you any other way." She wiped her hands on the damp towel on her workbench, then turned to face him. "I don't get it, Murat. What's in this for you?" She held up her hand. "Spare me the party line about marriage and destiny or whatever. Why on earth are you insisting on marrying a woman who doesn't want you?"

Her gaze met Murat's with a familiarity that should have annoyed him, but this was Daphne, and he found himself enjoying most everything she did. Even her challenges.

He smiled as he moved close, crowding her. Daphne, being stubborn and difficult *and* predictable, didn't move back. She made it so easy, he thought with pleasure. He liked that about her.

"You claim not to want me," he murmured as he cupped her head in one hand and bent low to kiss her. "Your body tells me otherwise."

Then, before she could speak whatever nonsense she had in mind, he brushed his mouth against hers.

She squirmed, but he wove his fingers through her hair to hold her in place. When she pressed her lips together to resist his claim on her, he chuckled, then raised his free hand to her breast.

Instantly she gasped. He took advantage of her parted lips and swept inside. At the same time, he brushed his thumb against her hard nipple.

She held out against him for the space of a heartbeat before she wrapped her arms around his neck and surrendered. Her mouth softened against him, her tongue greeted him with an erotic dance, and her entire body melted into his.

Heat exploded between them, and Murat found himself fighting his own desire. He had touched her in an effort to teach her a lesson, but now he was the one being schooled on the power of unfulfilled need.

Her hands clutched at him, pulling him closer. She tilted her head and deepened the kiss, even as she pressed into his hand. He explored her breast and found himself hungering to know the taste of her hot skin.

But that was not for now, he reminded himself as he

gathered the strength to step back. He would know her soon enough—once she understood that their marriage was as inevitable as the tide.

"You see," he said with a calmness he did not feel. "You *do* want me."

She shook her head as if to clear her thoughts. Her eyes were large and unfocused, her face flushed.

"There's a difference between wanting a man in my bed for a couple of weeks and wanting him in my life permanently," she said, her voice low and angry. "If you were trying to prove a point, I'm not impressed."

"Your body says otherwise."

"Fortunately I make my decisions with my brain."

"Your brain wants me, as well," he told her. "You resist only to be stubborn. I am pleased the sexual spark has lasted so long between us. It bodes well for our marriage. You will be a good wife and provide me with many strong, healthy, intelligent children, including an heir to carry on the monarchy."

"And my reward in all this is your pleasure. Gee, how thrilling."

He refused to be provoked by her. "Your reward is in the honor I bestow upon you. I believe you already understand that, and in time you will grow more comfortable showing me your pleasure in your situation."

She opened her mouth, then closed it. He could almost see the steam building up inside of her.

"Of all the arrogant, egotistical, annoying things you've ever said to me," she began.

He cut her off with a wave of his hand. "Say what

you like, but I know the truth. You're already begging to love me. In a matter of weeks you will want nothing but the pleasure of being near me."

"When pigs fly."

Daphne thought Murat was assuming an awful lot, especially that she was interested in him sexually. Whatever warm and yummy feelings he'd generated a couple of minutes ago with his hot kisses and knowing hands, he'd destroyed with a few badly chosen words.

"I wouldn't marry you if you were the last man alive. I said no before, I'm saying no again. No. No!"

The infuriating man simply smiled. "Mr. Peterson will be here shortly. I trust you will act appropriately."

Anger filled her. She reached for something to throw, but there was only her clay statue, and she loved it too much to smash it.

"Get out!" she yelled.

"As you wish, my bride."

She screamed and grabbed the remaining block of clay. When she turned back, Murat had already walked toward the harem itself. Even though she knew she couldn't throw that far, she pitched the clay at him and had the satisfaction of hearing it splat on the stone path.

"I'll get you for this," she vowed. Somehow, some way, she would come up with a plan, and he would be sorry he'd ever tried to mess with her.

Mr. Peterson might be old and valued but he was also the prissiest man Daphne had ever met.

He was small—maybe five-four—so she towered

over him even in low-heeled sandals. He had the deli-
cate bone structure of a bird, with tiny hands and feet.
Next to him she felt like an awkward and ill-mannered
Amazon giant.

"Ms. Snowden," he said as he entered the harem and
bowed. "It is more than a great pleasure to meet you."

She wasn't sure how it could be *more* than a great
pleasure, but she wasn't the fancy-party expert.

"The pleasure is mine," she said as she led the way
to the sitting area and motioned to the collection of
sofas there.

Mr. Peterson looked them over closely, then chose
the one that was lowest to the floor. No doubt he hated
when his feet dangled.

She sat across from him and wondered how badly
this was going to go. Mr. Peterson wanted to plan a wedding and she didn't. That was bound to create some
friction.

"We're working on a very tight schedule," he began
as he set his briefcase on the table in front of him and
opened the locks with a click.

She noticed that the silk hankie in his jacket breast
pocket perfectly matched his tie. He sounded as if he'd
been born in Britain but hadn't lived there in a number
of years. Perhaps he'd moved here with his parents back
in the eighteenth century.

"Prince Murat informed me that the wedding will be
in four months," he said. "I'll be providing you with historical information on previous weddings, along with my
list of suggestions on flower choices and the like. Some

of my ideas may seem silly to a modern young woman such as yourself, but we have a history here in Bahania. A long and honorable history that needs to be respected."

He drew in his breath for what she assumed would be another long speech specifically designed to make her feel like a twelve-year-old who had just spilled fruit punch on a very important houseguest.

She decided it was time to change the direction of the conversation.

"There isn't going to be a wedding," she said, and had the satisfaction of watching Mr. Peterson freeze in place.

It was amazing. The man didn't breathe or move or do anything but sit there, one hand grasping a sheath of papers, another reaching for a pen. At last he blinked.

"Excuse me?"

"No wedding," she said, speaking slowly. "I'm not marrying Murat."

"Prince Murat," he said.

He was correcting her address of the man who wanted to marry her?

"Prince or not, there's no engagement."

"I see."

She doubted that. "So there's no point in us having this conversation. I do appreciate that you were willing to stop by though. It was very kind of you."

She offered a bright smile in the hopes that the little man would simply stand and leave. But of course her luck wasn't that good.

"Prince Murat assures me that—"

"I know what he told you and what he's thinking, but

he's wrong. No wedding. *N-O* on the wedding front. Am I making myself clear?"

Mr. Peterson obviously hadn't been expecting a reluctant bride. He fussed with his papers for a few seconds, then picked up his pen. "About the guest list. I was told you come from a large and distinguished family. Do you have any idea how many of them will be attending?"

Daphne sighed. So Mr. Peterson had decided to simply ignore her claims and move forward.

"Ms. Snowden?" he prodded. "How many family members."

"Not a clue," she told him cheerfully.

"Will you be providing me with a guest list of any kind?"

"Nope."

The little man shook his head. "If necessary I can contact your mother."

"I'm sure you can." And her mother would be delighted by the question and the chance to influence the wedding.

Wasn't it enough that Murat insisted on this charade? How far was he willing to take it?

"Excuse me," she said as she rose to her feet. "I need to put a stop to this right now."

She walked toward the door and once she got there, she simply pushed it open.

The cross bar wasn't in place, no doubt so Mr. Peterson could leave when he was finished. There were only two guards on duty and neither of them looked as if they'd expected her to come strolling out of the harem.

When they saw her, they glanced at each other, as if uncertain about what to do.

Daphne took advantage of their confusion and started running. She made it halfway down the long hall before she heard footsteps racing after her. Up ahead the elevator beckoned like a beacon of freedom.

"Be there, be there," she chanted as she ran. She skidded to a stop in front of the doors and pushed the Up button. Thankfully, the doors immediately slid open.

She stepped inside and pressed the button for the second floor and watched as the doors closed in the faces of the guards.

Ha! She'd escaped. Probably not for long, but the feel of freedom was heady.

She exited on the second floor and hurried toward the business wing of the palace. She had a vague recollection of the way from her detailed explorations ten years ago. At a T-intersection, she hesitated, not sure which way to go, then followed a young man in a tailored suit as he turned left.

Seconds later she entered a large, round foyer. A middle-aged man sat at the desk and raised his eyebrows inquiringly.

"Crown Prince Murat," she said.

"Is he expecting you?"

In the distance she heard running feet. The guards, no doubt. She suspected reinforcements had been called.

"I'm his fiancée," she said briskly.

The man straightened in his seat. "Yes. Of course,

Ms. Snowden. Down that hallway, to your left. There are guards at the door. You can't miss it. If you'll give me a moment, I'll escort you there myself."

"No need," she said, taking off in the direction he'd indicated. She saw massive, carved, dark wood double doors and two guards standing on duty. One of them had his fingers pressed to his ear as if he were listening to something. When he saw her, he spoke quickly.

"I'm going in there," she said as she hurried toward the doors. "And you can't stop me."

The guards stepped forward and actually drew their weapons. A cold blade of fear sliced through her midsection.

"Murat isn't going to be very happy if you shoot me," she said, hoping it was true.

The guards moved toward her.

More footsteps thundered from behind, and she was seconds from being trapped.

"Murat!" she screamed as one of the men reached for her.

The huge door on the right opened and Murat stalked out.

"What is going on here?" he demanded. He glanced at the guards, then settled his stern gaze on her. "Release her at once."

The man did so, and Daphne quickly stepped behind Murat. "I escaped," she murmured in his ear. "That made them cranky."

He looked at her and raised one eyebrow. "I see. And Mr. Peterson?"

"We didn't much get along. All he wanted to talk about was the wedding, and I kept saying there wasn't going to be one. It wasn't very pleasant for either of us."

Murat didn't respond verbally. Instead he took her by the hand and led her into his office.

"Stay here," he said as he placed her in the center of an exceptionally beautiful rug. "I will return shortly."

With that he turned and left. She heard him speaking with the guards.

Daphne glanced around at the large office, noting the beautifully carved desk and the view of the gardens. None of the royal family had offices that faced away from the palace grounds. Years ago Murat had told her it was for security reasons. She'd been afraid for him at the time, but he had smiled and pulled her close and told her not to worry.

She shook off the memory. Murat returned and closed the door behind him.

"You are safe for now," he said. "I'll be having an interesting talk with my security team later. They should not have let you escape."

"Points for me," she said.

"Interesting that in your moment of freedom, you chose to run here. To me."

"Don't read too much into it. I didn't come here for a good reason."

"No? Then why?"

"Because I want to talk about the wedding, or lack thereof. You can't make me do it, Murat."

He moved close and touched her cheek. She hated how her body instantly went up in flames.

"You enjoy challenging me," he said. "However, I think the real problem lies elsewhere. You have been cooped up for too long. Go change your clothes, and we'll take a ride into the desert."

"And if I don't want to go?" she asked.

He looked at her. "Do you?"

She remembered those long-ago desert rides. The scent of the fresh air, the movement of the horse, and the beauty all around her.

"I do, but I hate that you assume you know best."

"I *do* know best. Now return to the harem and change your clothes. I'll meet you downstairs in thirty minutes."

"Does this mean I'm allowed to roam freely about the palace?"

He grinned. "Not even on a bet."

Chapter Seven

Daphne settled into the saddle and breathed in the fresh air. She'd been spending plenty of time outdoors in the harem garden but for some reason, everything seemed better, brighter now that she was sitting on a horse about to ride into the desert on a great adventure. Or to the nearest oasis, whichever came first.

There were a thousand reasons to still be angry with Murat—not the least was the man continued to hold her prisoner and insist they were to be married. Somehow none of that mattered anymore. At least not right now. She wanted to ride fast and feel the wind in her hair. She wanted to spin in circles on the sand, her arms outstretched, until she was too dizzy to stand. She wanted to drink cool, clear water from an underground spring and taste life. Then she would be mad at him again.

"Ready?" he asked.

She nodded as she pulled her hat lower over her forehead. All the sunscreen in the world couldn't completely protect her fair skin. So to keep herself from reaching the crone years too early, she'd worn a loose fitting, long-sleeved white shirt and a hat. Beside her, Murat looked handsome and timeless in his black riding pants and tailored white shirt. His black stallion was so large and difficult to manage as to be a cliché. Her own mount, a gray gelding of particularly fine build, also danced impatiently but with a little more restraint.

"When did you last ride?" Murat asked, as he urged his horse forward. The stallion leaped ahead several feet before agreeing to a more sedate walk.

"A couple of months ago. I usually go regularly, but I've been caught up with work."

"Then we will take things easily. This is unfamiliar country."

She glanced at him from under her lashes. "I don't mind if we go fast."

He grinned. "Of course you don't. But we will wait until you find your seat again."

She wanted to point out that she hadn't lost it in the first place—it was where it had always been. But she knew what he meant. That she had to get comfortable on her horse. So she contented herself with enjoying the scenery.

The royal stable sat on the edge of the desert, about

a forty-minute drive from the Pink Palace. Daphne knew she could happily spend her life there, studying blood-lines and planning future generations of amazing Ara-bian horses. Not that she wanted Murat to know. He had too much power already—he didn't need to discover more of her weaknesses.

She glanced around as the last bits of civilization gave way to the wildness of the desert. When their horses stepped onto sand, she couldn't help laughing out loud.

"Whatever you thought about me," Murat said. "You always loved Bahania."

"I agree."

"You should have returned for a visit."

"Somehow that didn't seem exactly wise."

"Did you think I would make things difficult?"

She wasn't sure how to answer that. If she said yes, it implied that he had cared for her after she left and she didn't think that was true. If she said no, she risked going in the opposite direction and she didn't think Murat would like that. As a rule, she didn't much care about what he liked, but this afternoon was different. For once, she didn't want to fight.

"I thought it might make things awkward," she ad-mitted.

"That is a possibility," he said, surprising her. "But it is sad that you could not see this for so long."

She glanced around at the beauty of the desert and had to agree. She loved the rolling hills that gave way to vast stretches of emptiness. She loved the tiny crea-tures who managed to thrive in such harsh surroundings.

Most of all she loved coming upon an oasis—a gift from God plopped down in the middle of nothing.

"You can taste the history out here," she said, thinking of all the generations who had walked this exact path and seen these same sights.

"We are closer to the past in the desert. I can feel my heritage all around me."

She grinned. "You come from a long line of men compelled to steal or kidnap their brides. Why is that? Are you all genetically unable to woo women in a normal way?"

He made a noise low in his throat. Daphne grinned.

"I'm serious," she said.

"No, you are tweaking the tiger's tail. Take care that he doesn't turn on you and gobble you up."

As Murat wasn't an actual tiger, she didn't have to worry about being eaten. Instead his words painted a picture of a different kind of devouring…one that involved bodies and touching and exquisite feelings of passion and surrender.

A dull ache settled in her stomach, making her shift on the saddle. Probably best not to think about that sort of thing, she told herself. Under the circumstances, sleeping with Murat would be a disaster. He would take her sexual surrender as a resounding "yes" on the marriage front.

But she couldn't help wondering what he would be like in bed. So far his kisses had reduced her to a quivering mass. Ten years ago she'd been too innocent and out of her element to be much more than intimidated by the obvious sexual experience of the man. Now she found herself wanting to sign up for a weekend seminar on the subject.

Next time, she promised herself. When her future and her freedom weren't on the line.

"Those marriages you mentioned may have started in violence, but they all ended happily."

She glanced at him. "You know this how?"

"There are letters and diaries."

"I'd like to read them sometime," she said. "Not that I don't trust you to tell me the truth…" She smiled. "Well, I don't, actually."

"You think I would lie?"

"I think you would stretch the truth if it suited your purpose."

He muttered something she couldn't hear. "How do you explain a relationship that lasts thirty or forty years and produces so many children?"

"Women don't have to be happy to get pregnant."

"I will give you the diaries," he said. "You will see for yourself that you misjudge my ancestors as much as you misjudge me. Are you ready to go faster?"

The quick change in subject caught her unaware, but she immediately nodded her agreement.

"I'm fine," she said. "Lead the way."

He nodded then urged his horse forward. The powerful stallion leaped from walking to a gallop. Her horse followed.

Daphne leaned forward into the powerful gait. The ground seemed to blur as they raced across the open area. She wanted to laugh from the pleasure of the moment.

Pure freedom, she thought, wishing there was more of this in her regular life. But her rides were sedate, on trails in well-known areas. There was little left to discover outside of Chicago.

Unlike here, where the desert kept secrets for thousands of years. While she could trace her family history back to the early 1700s, Murat could trace his for a millennium.

His name would be carved in the walls of the palace. His likeness stored, his life remembered. He had offered all that to her, as well. The privilege of being a part of Bahanian history. Her body could have been the safe haven of future kings yet to be born.

They sped across the desert for several miles. At last Murat slowed his mount and hers followed suit.

"We will walk them now," he said. "Allow them to cool down. We are close to the oasis."

She nodded, still caught up in her thoughts. What would it be like to be a part of something this amazing? Ten years ago she'd never considered all that he offered. Lately it seemed she could think of nothing else.

"The light is gone from your eyes," he said. "What troubles you?"

"I'm not troubled, just thoughtful."

"Tell me what you have on your mind."

She looked at him, at his handsome, chiseled face, at the power in his body and the authority he wore like a second skin.

"You are Crown Prince Murat of Bahania," she said.

"You will one day rule all that we see and miles beyond. You come from a history that stretches back through the ages to a time when my ancestors lived in huts and shivered through the winter. Why on earth would you choose me to share all this? Why me? Why not someone else?"

Murat didn't look at her. Instead he stared straight ahead. There was no way to tell what he was thinking.

"The oasis is just up there," he said, pointing to the right. "Over that dune."

"You're not going to answer my question?"

"No."

She wanted to push him for the truth, but at the same time, felt a reluctance to do so. There were many things she didn't want to discuss, including the fact—which he'd already pointed out—that when she'd burst free of the harem, instead of heading out of the palace, she'd run directly to the man holding her prisoner. Talk about a mixed message.

They rode in silence until they reached the oasis. Daphne stared at the small refuge in the desert, taking in the cluster of palm and date trees, the clear blue water gently lapping against the grass-covered shore and the bushes that seemed to provide a screen of privacy.

"Lovely," she said as she dismounted and pulled off her hat.

"I am glad you are pleased."

"Oh, yeah, because my pleasure makes your day."

She meant the comment as flip and teasing, but Murat didn't smile.

"Perhaps it does," he said. "Perhaps that is what you don't understand."

Before she could absorb what he'd just said, let alone think up a response, he led his horse over to a patch of shade. "We will rest here before heading back."

She followed. When he stopped, she turned to her horse and began stroking the animal's neck.

"Good, strong boy," she murmured as she examined the shoulder muscles, then bent down to run her hands along the well-formed front legs.

"I assure you I have a most capable staff in my stable," Murat said.

She straightened. "Oh. Sorry. Occupational hazard. I can't help checking." She patted the horse's side. "He's in great shape. Just like the cats back at the palace."

"I will be sure to pass along your compliments," Murat said dryly.

She loosely tied the horse to a tree, then joined Murat as he walked toward the water.

"It's quiet," she said.

"Yes. That is why I enjoy coming here."

She glanced around. "No guards?"

"This area is patrolled regularly, but at the moment we are alone." He glanced at her. "If you wish to kill me, now is the time."

"Good to know, but I'm not that annoyed. Yet."

He smiled. "How you continue to challenge me, but we both know who will be victorious in the end."

"Not you."

"Exactly me." He moved close and stared down at her. "Your surrender is at hand. Do you not feel it?"

What she felt was a trickle of something that could very well have been anticipation slipping down her spine. Her skin got all hot and prickly and she had the incredibly irrational urge to throw herself into his arms and beg for a surrender of another kind. Or maybe that was the surrender he meant. In which case she was more than willing to be the one giving in.

"I'm not going to marry you," she said.

He rested his hands on her shoulders. "You say the same thing over and over. It grows most tiresome."

"That's because you're not listening. If you were, I'd stop having to say it."

"How like a woman to make it the man's fault."

"How like a man to be stubborn and unreasonable."

"I am very reasonable. Right now you want me, and I intend to let you have me."

Before she could even gasp in outrage, he claimed her mouth with his. His firm, warm lips caressed her own until she felt compelled to wrap her arms around his neck and never let go. The outrage melted away.

He kissed her gently, teasing her with light brushes that made her nerve endings tingle. He stroked her lower lip with his tongue, but when she parted for him he nipped her instead of entering. He dropped his hands to her hips and drew her against him so that her belly pressed flat against his arousal.

The hardness there made her gasp, but again he chose not to take advantage of her invitation. Instead he kissed along her jaw and nibbled the sensitive skin under her ear. He made her squirm and gasp as need swept through her with the driving force of a sandstorm. He licked her earlobe, then traced a path down the side of her neck to the V of her shirt where he sucked gently on her skin.

She felt hot and uncomfortable, as if she'd been wound too tight. Her breasts ached, her thighs trembled, and she really wanted the man to kiss her.

Unable to control herself any longer, she dropped her hands to his face and drew his head up.

"Now," she said, her voice low and impatient.

"As you wish," he murmured right before he claimed her mouth.

This time he did as she wanted. He swept inside with the purposeful intent of a man set on pleasing a woman. He circled her tongue with his own. He explored and danced and surged until she was breathless with wanting.

His hands moved from her hips to her back. One slipped around to her waist and she caught her breath in anticipation as he moved higher and higher. Closer until he at last cupped her breast in his long, lean fingers.

The pressure was unbearably perfect, she thought through a haze of desire. As his fingers brushed against her tight nipples, she withdrew from the kiss so she could focus completely on his touch. Her breathing increased. She looped her arms around his neck and held on as her knees began to give way.

He brought up his other hand so he could cup both breasts. The delicious torture make her shiver. He raised his head and looked into her eyes.

"You are more beautiful than the dawn," he whispered. "I feel you respond to me. Can you deny what you want?"

She shook her head.

At that moment she had the sense she could disappear into his dark eyes and that it wouldn't be such a bad fate. Not if there were nights filled with this kind of attention. Not if he kept touching her.

She felt her body swelling in anticipation. Her panties dampened as flesh begged and wept for release.

He moved to the buttons on her shirt and quickly unfastened them. But he only went down to the waistband of her jeans and didn't bother pulling the shirt free. Which meant when he tugged the garment down her shoulders, he pinned her arms at her side.

She knew she could free herself with a quick jerk against the fabric, but for the moment, she felt oddly trapped. As if she were at his mercy. As if he could take her against her will.

Crazy, she told herself. Yet…oddly erotic.

He moved to the hook between her breasts and unfastened it. She watched as he slipped the bra away, exposing her skin to sun and air…and to his heated gaze.

He stared at her like a hungry man facing a last meal. Slowly he traced her curves, touching so lightly he almost tickled her. When he touched the tip of his finger against the very tip of her nipple, she felt the jolt clear down to her thighs.

She groaned. His breathing increased, then he bent low and drew her nipple into his mouth.

The combination of damp heat and gentle sucking nearly sent her to her knees. She struggled to free herself from her shirt so she could cling to him. The wanting grew. She didn't remember ever being this aroused before. She wasn't sure it was possible to need so much and stay conscious.

At last she was able to pull her shirt free of her jeans. She shrugged out of it and her bra, then clutched his head, holding him in place against her breasts.

"More," she breathed as he circled with his tongue.

Tension filled her body. She felt herself getting closer and closer to her release. Passion spiraled out of control.

With her free hand, she tugged at his shirt. He straightened and pulled it off in one easy, graceful movement. Then he stood before her, bare-chested, his arousal clearly outlined in his dark slacks.

"Tell me you want me," he demanded.

"How can you doubt it?"

"Say the words."

She stared into his dark eyes and knew that there was no going back. She had to know what it felt like to make love with Murat. She had to have that memory to take with her when she left.

"I want you."

For a heartbeat he did nothing. Then he gathered her up in his arms and lowered her to the ground.

"We must be practical," he said as he sat next to her. "Riding boots are not romantic."

She grinned as he pulled his off, then went to work

on her. When their feet were bare, she stretched out on his shirt and held open her arms.

"Make love with me, Murat."

He claimed her with a soul-touching kiss and a growl. His clever fingers returned to her breasts where he teased her into a frenzy. She squirmed and writhed, wanting more, needing more to find her release.

At last he moved lower, to the button of her jeans. He unfastened it and lowered the zipper. She pushed down with him, helping him remove the heavy fabric, along with her panties.

And then she was naked before him. Rather than feel embarrassed, Daphne let her legs fall open in a brazen invitation for what she really wanted. He did not disappoint. Even as he lowered his head and began to kiss her breasts, he slipped his fingers between her thighs and into her waiting dampness.

He found that one perfect spot on the first try. Just the slight brush of skin against the swollen knot of nerves made her jump. He shifted slightly so that he could rub that spot with his thumb while slipping his fingers deep inside her.

This was too much, she thought as she found herself caught up in a sensual vortex. His mouth on her breasts, his thumb rubbing, his fingers moving around and around. She was slick and more than ready, and it was just a matter of seconds until the tension filled her.

She tried to hold back, to breathe, to do anything to keep herself from falling so quickly. But it felt too good. She clutched at him and gave up the battle.

"Now!" she gasped as her release washed over her. Wave after wave of pleasure surrounded her, filled her, caught her and then let her fall. She pulsed her hips in time with his movements, slowing as she neared the end. He slowed, as well.

When she'd finished, she sank back onto his shirt and draped one forearm across her eyes. It was one thing to impulsively give in to sex with a man. It was another when he was as imperious as Murat. What would happen now?

She braced herself for some comment about his prowess with women or how easily she'd surrendered, and tried to tell herself it didn't matter.

But he said nothing.

The silence grew until Daphne finally dropped her arm and opened her eyes. Murat leaned over her, but he didn't look overly pleased with himself. Instead he seemed…humbled.

No way, she thought, even as he brushed his mouth against hers.

"Thank you," he said quietly.

She blinked. "Excuse me?"

"Thank you for letting me pleasure you. I know that you could have held back and kept me from taking you to paradise, and you did not."

The man was crazy. She could no more have held back than she could have flown to the moon. But he didn't have to know that.

"I liked what you were doing," she said.

"Perhaps you would like something else, as well."

She thought about how hard he'd been, how long and thick. Then she thought about him inside of her.

"I think I would," she told him with a smile.

He didn't have to be asked twice. Seconds later he was naked and kneeling between her knees. He braced himself on his hands and slowly entered her.

He felt exactly right, she thought as she reached up to caress his back. When he filled her, nerve endings cheered and began to do a little dance. Despite her first release, she felt the tension building again and knew it was going to be even better the second time around.

He moved slowly, giving them both time to adjust and anticipate. About the third time he stroked all the way in, she gave up acting like a lady and pulled him down against her. He wrapped his arms around her and kissed her. As their tongues mated, she shifted so she could hug his hips with her legs. That caused him to push in even deeper and she was instantly lost.

Murat felt the first pulsing ripples of Daphne's release. His plans to dazzle her with his stamina quickly faded as each contraction pushed him closer to the edge. She gasped and moaned and clung to him, begging him to continue. He forced himself to hold back until she had stilled and only then did he allow himself to give in to the building explosion of desire.

Daphne knew that it was best to act as casual as possible, but she wasn't sure how to accomplish the task, given what had just happened. She felt as if Murat had somehow touched every cell in her body and made it scream with pleasure. Still, as he rolled onto his back and drew her close so she could rest her head on his shoulder, she was determined not to gush. He hardly needed the increase in his already impressive ego.

"You are amazing," he said as he stroked her bare back.

"Thank you. I could say the same thing about you."

"As you should."

She laughed. "How like a crown prince to insist on defining the compliments."

"You are made for pleasure."

"I don't know about that, but I don't mind giving in to it from time to time." Especially to a man as skilled as he. He sure knew his way around the female anatomy. Did princes get classes in that sort of thing so they didn't embarrass themselves? Were there—

"You are not a virgin."

The unexpected statement nearly didn't register. Daphne pushed herself up on one elbow and stared at him.

"Excuse me?"

"You are not a virgin."

She laughed. "Murat, I'm thirty. What did you think?"

"That you would not give yourself away so easily."

Her warm, fuzzy feelings began to fade. "You're judging me?"

He put his free hand behind his head and regarded her thoughtfully. "Even though we were engaged ten years ago, I never touched you. You left here as innocent as you arrived."

"So?"

"So tell me the name of the man who has defiled you, and I will have him tortured and beheaded."

She started to laugh, then realized he wasn't kidding. There was some definite rage bubbling under the surface.

She sat up and stared at him. "Wait a minute. You're serious."

"Deadly so."

"That's crazy. You can't kill every man I've slept with."

He frowned. "How many have there been?"

"How many women have you slept with in the past ten years?"

"That is not your concern."

"My answer exactly."

"Your situation is completely different. You are a woman. Men took advantage of you. Tell me who they are."

"You belong in the Dark Ages," she said as she scrambled to her feet and grabbed for her panties. She pulled them on, then found her bra and put that on as well.

"You're also making me crazy," she continued as she glared down at him. "I am a modern woman and have lived a relatively quiet life. Yes, there have been a few men, but I was careful about whom I chose, and no one ever took advantage of me." She threw up her hands. "Why am I explaining myself to you?"

"Because you feel bad about what happened."

"I didn't before, but I'm starting to now."

"I don't mean here," he said as he sat up. "Those other men…"

"Are none of your business." She stepped into her jeans. "You're acting like an idiot. Worse, you're acting like a sexist pig and that's even more unforgivable."

"I care about you. I want to look after you."

She picked up her shirt and slipped into it. "I don't need looking after. I've been fine for years. As for the men I slept with, I will never tell you their names. I don't want or need your protection."

Murat stood. She hated how good he looked naked and the way her body responded. Get a grip, she told herself. He was nothing but trouble. Stupid, sexist trouble. To think she'd actually been attracted to him!

While he collected his clothes, she pulled on her socks and boots.

"You're even worse than I thought," she said when she'd finished. "I don't care how good the sex is, I wouldn't marry you if the entire fate of the human race depended on it. There is nothing you can ever say or do to get me to change my mind."

He paused in the act of shrugging into his shirt. "I am Crown Prince Murat of—"

"You know what? I've heard the speech dozens of times and I'm not impressed. Not by it or you." She glared at him. "You want to know why I left you ten years ago? It's because you couldn't see past who you were enough to notice me. You didn't love me. You barely cared about me. I was just one more item on your royal to-do list. 'Get married and produce heirs.' Here's a news flash, Your Highness. A woman needs to matter to the man she marries. She needs to be with someone who needs her. I wasn't interested in marrying a man who thought of me as a mere woman."

She spied her hat and quickly scooped it up. "I left because you're just not good enough for me."

Murat could not believe what Daphne had just said. How dare she say such things to him? But before he could voice his outrage, she walked away toward the horses, collected her mount and quickly swung into the saddle. When he realized she intended to ride off without him, he grabbed his boots.

"Stop. You don't know the way."

She didn't bother answering or even looking back. Instead she gave the animal its head and took off at a canter.

"Damn her stubbornness," he muttered as he quickly pulled on his boots.

Still buttoning his shirt, he hurried to his horse and went after her.

But her head start and her mount's speed meant it would be several minutes before Murat could catch up with her. By then she had already turned toward the east and the rocky part of the desert.

"Do not go there," Murat yelled into the wind. "Stay on the path."

But Daphne either could not hear or chose not to listen. Instead of staying on the marked dirt road cut into the desert, she headed directly toward the stables in what she most likely thought would be a quicker route back.

His heart rate increased, and it had nothing to do with the speed of his horse. Instead he watched and worried until fear turned to horror as Daphne's horse came to a sudden stop and she went flying over its head and landed heavily on the hard, stony ground.

Chapter Eight

Murat lived an eternity in hell, with time crawling as he raced toward Daphne. He fumbled for his security beacon and pressed it in rapid, frantic movements, signaling an emergency. It seemed that days passed, weeks, until he could vault off his horse and crouch down beside her.

Daphne lay on the rocky ground, her legs bent beneath her, her arm thrown over her face.

He lowered it gently, then sucked in a breath as he saw her still, pale face and the pool of blood on the ground.

"No," he said to whomever would listen. "You will be fine. You must be fine."

But she did not respond, and when he touched her cheek, her skin felt cold.

Pain filled him, and fury. That such a simple mistake could cause so much damage. Then he shook off all emotion and quickly went to work examining her.

The only external bleeding came from her head and it had already begun to slow. He could not assess internal injuries but her pulse was steady and strong. If only she would awaken and start yelling at him again. If only...

The distant sound of a helicopter cut through the silence of the desert. Murat rose and waved it in, shielding her with his body when the blades kicked up dust and sand.

"She is injured," he yelled to his men. "I cannot tell how badly. We'll have to be careful of her neck and spine."

He waited until the men brought out the emergency equipment and went to work securing her before calling the stable and telling them about his horse and hers. His stallion was trained not to wander far, but her mount could be halfway to El Bahar by now.

When she had been carried into the helicopter, he joined her and took her hand in his.

"I command you to be healed," he murmured, his face close to hers, his breath stirring her hair. "I am Crown Prince Murat, and I command that you open your eyes and speak to me right now."

Nothing happened. Murat swallowed hard, then pressed his lips to her cheek. "Daphne, *please*."

* * *

Murat paced the length of the main room in the harem. In the bedroom his personal physician reconfirmed what the doctors at the emergency room had told him. Murat tried to find a measure of peace in the knowledge that there were no internal injuries, no broken bones.

"She was very lucky," his father said from his place on the sofa. "I never thought of Daphne as a foolish young woman. To go riding off like that. You must have annoyed her."

Murat continued to watch the bedroom door. "I do so on a regular basis. It is one of my great talents." Only this time it had had too great a price.

Never again, he thought. He would not permit her to act so hastily. Left on her own, she could seriously hurt herself.

"I will stay while the doctor examines her if you wish to shower and change," the king said.

"No," Murat said immediately, then drew in a breath. "Thank you, Father, but I will stay. She is my fiancée, my responsibility."

"I see."

He doubted the king saw much, and nothing of consequence. This was Daphne. She could not be permitted to die.

At last his doctor appeared. The older man smiled.

"Good news," he said as he crossed to Murat. "It is as the other doctors told you. She has a mild concussion and some slight trauma to the brain. She will stay unconscious for a few hours, maybe a day. Then she should awaken and begin the recovery process. Within a week she will be as good as new."

"Is she in pain?" he asked.

"Not now, but when she wakes she will have a bad headache. I've left some medication to help with that. Once she's awake, keep her in bed for a couple of days, then she should take it easy for the rest of the week. I, of course, will be back in the morning and each day until she is fit again."

Murat nodded. "Thank you."

The doctor touched his arm. "Your fiancée will live to give you many healthy children, Your Highness. Fear not."

Murat heard the words, but he could not let the fear go. Not until she opened her eyes and started calling him names again.

He concluded his business with the doctor, wrote down the rest of the instructions, then hurried into the bedroom. Daphne lay in the center of the bed, hooked up to several monitors. A nurse sat in the corner. The king followed.

When Murat nodded at the nurse, she stood and quickly retreated to the living room.

"Daphne will be fine," his father said. "You heard the doctor. A nurse will be here twenty-four hours a day until she wakes up."

"No." Murat moved closer to the bed and reached for Daphne's hand. "I will be here. The nurse can wait in the living room in case there is an emergency. But until she wakes, I will tend to her."

"Murat."

He glared at his father. "No one but me."

The king nodded slowly. "As you wish."

There was only one wish, Murat thought grimly. That Daphne open her eyes.

Now, he willed her. *Look at me now.* But she slept on, unaware of his command. Even in illness she defied him. Pray God she lived to defy him another day.

Daphne felt as if someone was banging on her head with a frying pan. She remembered a frat party she'd gone to years ago while she'd been in college. She generally avoided loud parties with alcohol, but fresh from her broken engagement, she felt the need to participate in something fun and mind numbing.

So she'd gone with a couple of girlfriends and had stayed up way too late and had had too much spiked punch. In the morning she'd found herself with the mother of all hangovers and had basically wanted to die.

This was worse.

She struggled through what felt like miles of thick, sticky water, before finally surfacing. She felt bruised and sore everywhere, but it was her head that got her attention the most. Even her eyebrows hurt.

She was also, she realized, starving and in bed. The thing was, she didn't remember going to bed. She didn't remember much of anything except...

The horses. She'd been riding. She'd been angry at Murat and she'd gone on ahead, determined not to speak to him again, and then she'd been flying through the air and falling and falling and...

She opened her eyes to find herself back in the bedroom she'd been using in the harem. The walls were familiar, as was the furniture. Lamps illuminated the large space.

She glanced around, relaxing as the rest of her memory returned, only to stiffen when she saw a strange man dozing in a chair next to her bed.

He was big—tall and powerful—she could tell that even while he slept. But his hair was mussed and dark stubble darkened his jaw.

A quick glance at the clock told her the time was two. The lamplight made her think it was probably two in the morning, and turning her head increased the pounding to the point of being unbearable.

She sagged back against the pillow and studied the man. In a matter of seconds she recognized the shape of his firm jaw and mouth, the breadth of his shoulders.

"Murat?" she whispered.

Was it possible? In all the time she'd known him, both ten years ago and present day, she had never seen him anything but perfectly groomed. Why did he look so mussed, and why did he sleep in a chair beside her bed?

One of his hands lay on the blanket. She reached out and rested her fingers against his palm.

He woke instantly and glanced at her. His eyes widened.

"Daphne?"

"Hey."

He leaned forward and studied her anxiously. "How do you feel? Your head will hurt—the doctor warned me about that. I have medication for you. And if you're hungry, you can eat, but only lightly for the first day or so. You are not to get up, either. I know you can be stubborn, but I insist you follow the doctor's orders. Rest for two days, then you may begin to resume your normal activities through the end of the week. I will not accept any arguments on this matter."

Despite her aching head, she couldn't help smiling. "Of course you won't. Because this is all about you, right?"

He took her hand in both of his and kissed her fingers. "No. It is about you getting well."

His tenderness made her want to cry, which only went to show that her head injury had affected her brain.

She squeezed his hand. "How long have I been out?"

"Thirty five hours and—" he glanced at the clock "—eight minutes."

"Wow. What happened?"

"You were thrown from your horse."

"I remember that." She reached up with her free hand and gingerly touched the raised bump on her scalp. "I guess I fell headfirst."

"You did. I was concerned you had hurt yourself elsewhere, but you are fine. No broken bones, no internal injuries."

She returned her attention to him, then pulled her hand free and rubbed his cheek. The thick whiskers there grated against her skin.

"You look terrible."

He smiled. "For a good cause."

She studied his shirt and pants. "You were wearing those clothes when we went riding."

"Yes."

"You haven't showered or shaved since?"

"I wanted to be with you."

She blinked. "I don't understand."

"I have been here, with you, since we returned from the hospital."

Her head felt as if it might explode, yet she didn't feel disconnected from the conversation. Which meant she should understand what Murat was saying.

"In that chair?" she asked, trying not to sound incredulous.

"Yes."

"Beside me."

"Yes."

"Because you were…"

"Worried."

He kissed her fingers again.

Something warm and bright blossomed in her chest. Murat didn't have to stay here to watch over her. She was in his palace and completely safe. He could have an entire hospital medical team at his disposal and yet he'd stayed with her himself.

"I don't know what to say," she admitted.

"Then do not speak. There is a nurse in the other room. Let me call her to bring you the medication for your headache."

Her stomach growled.

He smiled again. "And perhaps some soup."

He rose and crossed to the doorway. As she watched him go, Daphne had to admit that she might have been a little hasty in her judgment of Murat. Sure he acted all in charge and "my way or the highway" but his actions told her something far different and far more important.

He *cared* about her. When he thought she might be in danger, he stayed by her side. What about his meetings? His princely duties? Had he neglected them all while she'd been out of it?

She relaxed back against the pillow and sighed. She'd been so busy resisting his demands that she'd never taken the time to get to know the man inside. Maybe it was time to change that. Maybe—

The nurse appeared in the doorway. She listened while Murat spoke, nodded and left. Seconds later she reappeared with a small plastic container in her hands.

"Take two," she said. "I will order the soup."

Murat carried the medicine over to the bed, then helped Daphne into a sitting position. She felt her head swim, but forced herself to stay upright long enough to swallow the pills. He eased her back onto the bed.

"You will feel better soon," he told her.

"Thank you."

He resumed his seat and took her hand again. "My father was here for a time. He, too, was worried."

"That was very nice of him."

The nurse walked back into the room. "I have ordered a light meal," she said. "It will be here in about ten minutes."

Daphne winced. "I just realized the time. You had to wake someone, didn't you?"

The nurse, an attractive woman in her late forties, only smiled. "The staff was delighted to hear you are awake, Your Highness. No one minded the late hour."

"You're very kind, but—" Daphne froze as her mind replayed the woman's words. "I'm sorry. What did you call me?"

The nurse frowned slightly. "Your Highness." She glanced at Murat. "I was sure that was the right address. Am I incorrect, sir?"

He shook his head. "You did well. Now if you would please go wait for the meal?"

"Of course."

The woman left.

Daphne stared after her. A thousand thoughts bombarded her bruised brain and made it impossible for her to think clearly.

Something was wrong. Very wrong.

"Murat," she began.

"Do not trouble yourself," he told her. "All will be well."

She wasn't about to be put off. Not now. "She called me Your Highness, and you said that was correct."

"It is."

Panic flooded her. She struggled to sit up, but he pressed down on her shoulders.

"You must rest," he said.

"I must know the truth." She glared at him, willing herself to be wrong. Completely and totally wrong. "Why did she call me that?"

He picked up her left hand and fingered the diamond band on her ring finger. A diamond ring she'd never seen before in her life.

"Because you are now my wife."

Chapter Nine

Daphne wanted to shriek loudly enough to cause the ancient stone walls to crack. She wanted oceans to rise up, and thunder to shake the heavens. But she knew if she opened her mouth and really let loose, all she would have to show for it was a worsening of her already pounding headache.

Murat was speaking a foreign language, she told herself in an effort to stay calm, or he was the one with the head injury. Except, she knew neither was true and that this was all real, yet how was it possible?

"You married me while I was unconscious?" she demanded in a voice that was perilously close to shrieky.

"You need to stay calm."

"I need to have you killed," she said, narrowing her eyes, then wishing she hadn't when the pain increased. "What is wrong with you? You can't do that sort of thing. It's horrible and it's illegal."

"Not technically."

Murat continued to rub her fingers. When she realized that, she pulled them free.

"In a Bahanian royal marriage, the bride does not have to agree," he continued. "She merely has to not disagree."

"Silence as consent?" she asked, unable to believe this.

"Yes."

"Did anyone notice that I wasn't in a position to agree *or* disagree? I was *unconscious* with a head injury?"

He shrugged. "It was a matter of discussion."

"That's it? No one protested?"

"No."

Of course not. Because who would? Certainly not Murat and— "Who else was there?"

"The man who officiated and the king."

"That's it? No other witnesses?"

He smiled. "The king is enough of a witness."

She couldn't believe Murat's father had been in on this. Her head continued to throb, and now she felt tears burning in her eyes.

Don't cry, she told herself. Crying would only make her weak, and she had to stay strong, but it was hard. All she wanted to do was curl up in a ball and sob her heart out.

"You can't do this," she said.

"It is already done."

"Then I'll undo it. I'll get an annulment or a divorce. I don't care about the scandal."

"The king must give his permission for the union of a crown prince to be dissolved."

Which meant when pigs fly, what with the monarch being in on the sleazy ceremony.

"You're a lying weasel bastard with the morals of a pack of wild dogs," she said angrily. "I'll never forgive you for this. Mark my words. I *will* find a way out of this."

He had the nerve to brush her hair off her face. "Rest now, Daphne. You can deal with our marriage in a few days."

She smacked his hand away. "Don't touch me. Not ever again. I hate you."

That got his attention. Murat straightened, then stood and walked to the foot of the bed where he loomed over her.

"You forget yourself."

"Not even for a second. If I'm your *wife*—" the word tasted bitter on her tongue "—then I can do as I please."

"You will still remember your place."

"Oh, right. That would be as your slave here in the harem. Gee, how exciting. I'm delighted to be the unimportant plaything of a dictatorial, arrogant, selfish prince."

He glowered at her.

She didn't care about anything he might be thinking.

And the pill must be kicking in because the pain started to fade.

She pushed herself into a sitting position and glared back at him with all her considerable fury.

"You are a most frustrating woman," he said.

"Let me tell you how much I don't care about your opinion."

He drew his eyebrows together. "You complain now, but I did this for you."

"Oh, right. Because I've been begging for us to be married."

"No, because of what happened. You hurt yourself. Someone has to watch over you."

"You married me to protect me from myself?" She didn't dare shake her head in disbelief, although she wanted to. "I guess you're reduced to telling yourself lies so you can sleep at night."

To think that she'd gotten all soft and gooey inside thinking he actually cared about her, that he'd worried while she'd been out of it. Instead he'd simply been protecting his new toy.

"There is also the fact that we made love," he said, as if explaining things to a small and slow child. "You were not a virgin."

What on earth did that have to do with anything? "So?"

"You should have been."

"You married me to punish me?"

"Of course not." The glower returned. "You are being most difficult."

"Gee, I wonder why. So you're saying you married

me because I wasn't a virgin, but if I had been we would have been flirting with defiling territory, so that wouldn't have been much better."

"You are correct. I would have married you if you had been a virgin."

Talk about being between a rock and a hard place.

The sensation of being trapped sucked the last of her energy. Daphne slid down onto the mattress and closed her eyes.

"You are feeling unwell?" he asked.

"Go away."

She heard him walk closer, then he touched her forehead. "I wish to help."

She forced herself to open her eyes and stare at him. "Do you think I will ever care about what you want? Get out now. I never want to see you again. Get out. Get out!"

She screamed as loudly as she could. When Murat still hesitated, she reached for the empty glass on her nightstand and picked it up to use as a weapon.

"Get out!"

"I will check on you in the morning."

"Get out!"

He turned and left.

She put down the glass, then curled up in the big bed and closed her eyes. The pain was still with her, but this one had nothing to do with her head injury and everything to do with the loss of her freedom.

She didn't doubt that Murat had married her and that she was well and truly caught in circumstances that would be difficult to undo. The sense of betrayal hurt more than anything. Her eyes began to burn again, but this time she didn't fight the tears. She gave in to them, even though she knew they wouldn't help in the least.

With the aid of the painkillers, Daphne managed to sleep through the night. She saw the doctor the next morning, who told her to stay in bed at least twenty-four more hours and not to return to her normal routine for a few days.

For reasons she didn't understand but was grateful for, Murat didn't return to visit her, which meant she was left in solitude, except for the quiet presence of the nurse who brought her meals and stayed out of her way.

On day three, Daphne sent the poor woman away. "I'm fine," she said after she'd showered and dressed and found that walking wasn't all that difficult. "You should return to someone who actually needs your help."

"You're very kind, Your Highness," the woman said. "I wish you and the crown prince a long and happy marriage."

Daphne didn't know what to say, so she smiled and thanked her again. Obviously, she'd been out of the room when Daphne'd had her screaming fit. No one witnessing that could ever imagine a successful relationship as the outcome.

She still had bouts of weariness and despair, but when they hit, she used her anger to fuel herself. Murat wasn't going to get away with this. She wasn't sure what she was going to have to do to get away, but she would find out and make it happen.

After finishing her breakfast, she walked to the gold doors and pulled them open. No guards. No doubt Murat had released them from their duties after the wedding. He no longer had to worry about her escaping. As the queen, she couldn't go out unaccompanied. No driver would take her. No pilot would leave the country without express permission. She might have the freedom of the palace now, but that simply meant she'd graduated to a larger prison.

She walked through the quiet halls of the palace. As always the beauty of the structure pleased her. She paused to admire a particularly lovely and detailed tapestry of several children in a garden. She recognized the stone wall and the placement of several trees. The scene might be from four hundred years ago, but the garden itself still existed just outside.

The history of Bahania called to her, but she ignored the whispers. There was nothing anyone could say or do to convince her she had to make her peace with what had happened.

She saw several people hurrying from place to place. When she recognized one of the senior staff, she stopped the man and asked after the king. The man led her outside, and Daphne stepped into bright sunshine.

For a second the light hurt her eyes and made her head throb, but she adjusted, then made her way along the stone path. She heard voices before she saw the people, and when she turned the corner, she recognized Cleo, Sadik's wife, with the king.

They sat across from each other. A pretty baby stood between them.

"You are so very clever," the king said with obvious delight. "Come to Grandpa. You can do it."

The baby, dressed in pink from the bows in her fine hair down to the hearts on her tiny laces, laughed and toddled toward the king. He caught her and swept her up in the air.

"Ah, Calah, I had not thought to find love at this stage in my life, but you have truly stolen my heart." He kissed her cheek.

Cleo grinned. "I'll bet you say that to all the grandkids."

"Of course. Because it is true."

Daphne didn't know what to do. While she had business with the king, she didn't want to interrupt such a private family moment. She felt a twinge of longing for the connection the king had with his daughter-in-law. Cleo might have come from ordinary circumstances, but no one held that against her. Funny how a girl who grew up in foster care and worked in a copy shop could go on to marry a prince and be accepted by all involved, while Daphne had never been as welcome in her own family.

King Hassan looked up and saw her. "Daphne. You are looking well. Come." He patted the bench. "Join us."

She moved forward and greeted Cleo and her daughter. "She's walking," she said, touching Calah's plump cheek and smiling.

The baby gurgled back.

"Barely," Cleo said. "Which is okay with me. She's a complete terror when she crawls. I can only imagine what will happen when she starts running everywhere.

I'm going to have to get one of those herding dogs to keep her out of trouble."

The king shook his head. "You will dote on her as you always do. As will Sadik."

"Probably." Cleo bent down and collected Calah. "But right now we have to deal with a dirty diaper. See you later."

Her exit was so quick and graceful, Daphne wondered if it had been planned in advance. Not that anyone would tell her. She seemed to be the last to know about almost everything.

"How are you?" the king asked as he turned toward Daphne and took one of her hands in his.

The right one, she noticed. Not the left one, now bare of the ring Murat had given her. She'd left that in her rooms.

"I'm feeling better physically," she said. "Emotionally I'm still in a turmoil." She stared directly at the king. "Is he telling the truth? Did Murat really marry me while I was unconscious?"

"Yes, he did."

It was as if all the air rushed out of her lungs. For a second she thought she might pass out.

"Are you all right?" King Hassan asked.

"Yes. I just…" Her last hope died. "I don't understand why you allowed this to happen. What Murat did was wrong."

"The crown prince cannot *be* wrong."

Ah, so they were going to close ranks around her. "I don't believe that, and I don't think you believe it, either. He had no right to trap me into a marriage I don't want. Neither of us will ever be happy. Surely you want more for your son."

"I am confident you can work things out."

She stared in the king's handsome face. He was so much like his son—stubborn, determined to get his own way, and he held all the cards.

"I want an annulment," she said quietly.

He patted the back of her hand. "Let us not speak of that. Instead, we will talk of the beauty of Bahania. If I remember correctly you enjoyed your time here. Now you will be able to explore the wonders of our country. You can meet the people. I understand you have become a veterinarian. Practicing your chosen profession outside of the palace could present a problem, but we can work on that. Perhaps you could do some teaching. Also, I have enough cats to keep you busy."

She felt as if she were sitting next to a wall. Nothing was getting through.

"Your Majesty, please. You have to help me."

He smiled. "Daphne, I believe there is a reason you never married. It has been ten years since you left Bahania. Why, in all that time, did no other man claim your heart?"

"I never met the right man. I've been busy with my career and—" She stared at him. "It's not because I've been pining for Murat."

"So you say. He tells me much the same. But he never found anyone, either. Now you are together, as it was always meant to be."

This wasn't happening. "He trapped me. Tricked me. How can you approve of that?"

"Give it time. Get to know him. I think you'll be happy with what you find."

The hopelessness of the situation propelled her to her feet. "If you'll excuse me," she mumbled before turning and hurrying back toward the side door into the palace.

She felt broken from the inside out. No one would listen; no one would help. The tangled web of her circumstances would tug at her until she gave in and surrendered.

"Never," she breathed. "I'll be strong."

She turned a corner and nearly ran into a young woman in a maid's uniform.

"Oh, Your Highness. I was sent to look for you." The woman smiled. "Your parents have called and wish to speak with you. If you will please follow me."

No doubt her parents had learned about the marriage. They wouldn't care about the circumstances, she thought glumly.

Sure enough, when she picked up the phone, her mother couldn't stop gushing.

"It's wonderful," she said. "We're thrilled."

Her father had picked up the extension. "You did good, baby girl."

Tears burned in Daphne's eyes. Funny how until this moment, she'd never heard those words from her father before. Apparently she'd never "done good" until she'd been trapped in marriage to a man she didn't love.

Her mother sniffed. "We would have liked a big wedding, but this is fine, too. I read that there will be a huge reception in a few months, so as soon as you have the dates, let us know. We'll need to make arrangements to fly over. Oh, darling, I'm so happy for you. Are you happy? Isn't this fabulous? And just think—in a year or so, we'll hear the pitter patter of a little prince or princess. Oh, Daphne. You've made us so proud."

Her mother kept on talking while her father added his few comments, but Daphne wasn't listening anymore. Instead she stared blankly out a window as a horrible, stomach-dropping thought occurred to her.

She and Murat had made love without protection. Right there in the oasis, she'd let him take her to paradise and back never once considering the consequences. She could be pregnant.

"I have to go," she said, and listened as they told her of course they understood. A woman in her position had responsibilities and they would talk soon.

She hung up and tried to shake off her daze.

Pregnant. Oh, God. If that was true… She knew enough about Bahanian law to know that no royal child was ever allowed to leave the country in the case of a divorce. Which meant if she had a baby, she would be forced to stay here forever. Abandoning her child wasn't an option.

"It was just one time," she told herself as she hurried back to the harem. She couldn't get pregnant that easily, could she?

As she stepped off the elevator, she saw another

young woman in a maid's uniform sitting in a straight-back chair by the gold harem doors. When the woman saw her, she rose.

"Your Highness, I was asked to wait until you returned. It is my honor to show you to your new quarters."

Daphne's headache had returned. "New quarters?" Oh. "With the crown prince."

The young woman beamed. "Yes. If you will follow me."

She didn't want to. She wanted to sit down right there and never move again.

"My things?" she asked.

"Have been sent ahead."

Of course. Murat would want the details taken care of so she couldn't put up a fuss.

"Very well," she said, wanting only to find a quiet place and close her eyes until the pain went away. Not just the pain from her head, either, but the aching in her heart.

She allowed the woman to lead her to the elevator, then through a maze of hallways, with them finally stopping in front of a large, carved wooden door. The maid opened it and Daphne stepped inside.

Her first impression was of openness and light. Massive windows and French doors led onto a private balcony with what seemed to be a view of the world. It was only after she'd stared at the vastness of the city and the water did she realize they were at the very top of the palace, on the corner.

To the left was the Arabian Sea, twinkling blue and teal and green in the sunlight. To the right was the skyline of the city. And beyond it all, the desert stretched for miles, compelling in its starkness.

When she returned her attention from the view to the room, she saw comfortable furniture, an impressive collection of artwork and a space big enough to roller blade in. Doors led to other rooms. Most likely a dining area, a bedroom and an office, in case the crown prince wanted to work from "home." Because she had no doubt she had been brought to Murat's suite of rooms. Where else would his wife live?

Her heart ached, her legs felt as if they would give way at any moment and her head throbbed. She thanked the maid and made her way to what she hoped was the bedroom. Unfortunately, when she stepped inside, she found she was not alone.

Murat sat in a chair in the corner. Waiting? She wasn't sure. She ignored him as she made her way to the huge bed and crawled onto the mattress.

"You are ill," he said as he jumped to his feet. "I will call the doctor."

"I'm fine," she told him. "Just tired. Please, leave me alone."

"I cannot."

She turned away, curling up on the embroidered bedspread and doing her best not to give in to the tears. Not again. There had been too many over the past few days.

But the strain was too much and the first tear leaked out of the corner of her eye. She did her best to hide it, but somehow Murat knew. He sat on the bed and gathered her in his arms.

"It is all right," he said quietly.

"No. It's not and you're the reason."

He stroked her hair and her back and rocked her. She wanted to protest that she wasn't a child, that he couldn't make things better with a kiss and a hug, but speaking was too difficult. Right now it was all she could do to breathe.

She wasn't sure how long he held her, but eventually the pain eased. The tears dried up, and when he offered her his handkerchief, she took it and blew her nose.

"I talked to your father," she said. "He won't help me."

"Are you surprised?"

"More like disappointed." She shifted away from him and stared in his face. "You know I will never forgive you for this."

Murat did know. Marrying Daphne that way had been a calculated risk. But once he had made up his mind, there was no going back. He would face her wrath in the short term to gain her acceptance in the long term.

"Time is a great healer," he said.

"Not in this case. My anger will only grow."

He tucked her hair behind her ear and smiled. "I have seen the new sculpture you have started. I believe it is going to be me falling down the stairs. You have found a way to release your anger."

"It's not enough." Her blue eyes flashed fury. "You had no right to—"

He pressed his fingers against her mouth. "Let us not have that conversation again."

"Then which one do you want to have? The one

where I call you a lying bastard? The one where I say that taking away my freedom is an unforgivable act and that you'll never get away with it?"

"They are variations on a theme."

"It's what I want to talk about."

She was so beautiful, he thought. Not just in her fury, but always. There was an intensity about her, and he longed for that energy to be focused on him.

He captured her left hand and held it in his. "You do not wear your ring."

"Why would I?"

"Because it is a symbol of our marriage and your position in my world." He pulled the ring from his pocket and tried to slide it on her finger. She pulled back.

"You are not usually one to act like a child," he said.

"I'm making an exception."

"Very well. I will leave it here until you change your mind." He set the ring on the nightstand.

She drew in a breath. "I'm leaving, Murat. Eventually I'll find a way to escape you and this palace."

"You are not my prisoner."

"Of course I am. I have been from the beginning. I don't suppose you would care to tell me why."

"You have made all the choices, save one."

"Yeah, that last really big one when there was a wedding." She pressed her lips together. "I *will* leave just as soon as I'm sure I'm not pregnant."

Her words crashed into him. He stood and stared at her. "Pregnant?"

She rolled her eyes. "Don't you give me that happy

expectant-father face. It's unlikely. We only did it the one time, and let me tell you how much I'm regretting that incident."

Pregnant. Of course. He had been so caught up in making love with Daphne that he had not taken precautions, which was very unlike him. He had always been careful not to be trapped by that particular game.

A child. A son. An heir.

"Stop grinning," she demanded.

"Am I?" He felt as if he could fly.

"There's no baby."

"You don't know that."

"I'm reasonably confident. It was just one time."

"It only takes one time." He cupped her cheek. "You understand the law, Daphne. You know what happens if there is a child."

Despair entered her eyes. "You win. I couldn't leave my baby, and I would never be allowed to take him or her from the country." She shook off his touch. "But know this. I'm not sleeping with you ever again, and as soon as I know I'm not pregnant, I'm leaving."

Strong words, but he doubted she meant them. Not completely. "Would you leave the people of Bahania so soon? You are their future queen."

"They've lived without me this long. I'm sure they can survive into the future."

"You will change your mind."

"I won't." She stood and faced him. "Murat, you think this is a game, but it's very serious. I don't want to be here. I don't want to be married to you."

"I will convince you."

"You can't."

But he could. He knew that. He was Crown Prince Murat of Bahania, and she was a mere woman. Her will could not withstand the pressure of his.

He knew now he should never have let her go all those years ago. It was a mistake he would not repeat again.

"I want to love the man I marry," she told him earnestly. "I don't love you."

"You will."

"How do you figure? You're going to force me to love you?"

"Yes."

"It's not possible."

"Watch me."

Chapter Ten

Cleo sat in the middle of several boxes of shoes and grinned. "So I guess when you're the once and future queen, you don't go to the accessories, the accessories come to you."

Daphne wove her way between nearly a dozen racks of clothes sent over to the palace by boutique owners and fashion designers.

"The clothes, too," she said as she took a cashmere jacket off a rack and studied the light-blue color. "This is overwhelming."

Cleo held up a pair of strappy sandals. "I hate you for not having the same size feet as me. Just so we're all clear. I don't think I've ever seen a shoe this narrow."

"Or as long," Daphne said. "I have big feet."

"But skinny. I, of course, wear a 6 wide." She wiggled her hot-pink painted toes. "Billie's going to have a heart attack when I tell her what she's missed."

Daphne put the jacket back on the rack and returned to the sofa. "Then please don't tell her while she's flying. She only has a couple more weeks until the doctors ground her for the rest of her pregnancy. Besides, as far as I can tell, the clothesfest is going to go on for several more weeks, so she's welcome anytime."

"Cool." Cleo dropped the shoes back in the box and picked up a leather handbag. "At least I can borrow this. If you're getting it. Are you?"

"I have no idea."

The clothes had started arriving three days ago. At first Daphne had kept the racks in the spare bedroom in their suite, but that space had filled rapidly. She'd finally asked for a large unused conference area and had all the clothes brought down, along with some sofas and several large mirrors. Dressing as the wife of the crown prince was serious business.

"You should be happier," Cleo said. "These are all beautiful."

"I know." Daphne did her best to smile. She wasn't sure she'd been convincing.

The problem was without Calah around to distract her—the baby was currently down for her nap—Cleo was far too observant. Daphne didn't know what to say to her new sister-in-law. That it had been a week and she still felt angry and trapped.

True to her word, she avoided Murat as much as possible and slept in the suite's guest room. He acted as if there was nothing out of the ordinary and insisted on discussing their future in terms of decades.

"Want to talk about it?" Cleo asked.

"I don't know what there is to say." Or how much she was willing to confess.

"I know the marriage happened pretty fast," Cleo said as she stood and walked over to the same sofa and sat at the opposite end. She fingered her short, spiky blond hair. "There was some talk."

"I'll bet. It's just…" She sighed. "I didn't ask for this. I know, I know." She held up both hands. "Boo-hoo for the poor woman who married a prince and will one day be queen. How sad."

Cleo shook her head. "If you're not happy, you're not happy."

"I wish it were that simple." She didn't want to talk about what Murat had done. Somehow she guessed that Cleo wouldn't want the information, nor would she act on it.

"Have you thought about giving the relationship a chance?" Cleo asked. "I know these guys act all imperious, but underneath, they're amazing husbands. You just have to get past the barrier down to their hearts."

"I don't think Murat has a heart."

"Do you really mean that?"

"No." He must have. Somewhere. "I'm finding the situation overwhelming. I'm doing interviews later for my chief of staff. I need someone to help me stay organized. Invitations are pouring in. I don't want to accept any of them, but Murat has to go, which means..."

She still hadn't decided what it meant. Did she go with him? Put on a front and pretend to be the happy bride? Did she refuse? While she wouldn't mind rubbing his face in what he'd done, he wasn't the only one involved. In some ways she felt responsible for the citizens of Bahania. She didn't want them embarrassed by her behavior.

"I don't want to make life easier for him," she admitted, "but my own sense of what is right is on his side. I really hate that."

Cleo leaned close. "You're thinking too much. Just relax and take each day as it comes. These royal things get easier with time. At least you have the advantage of breeding. You should have seen my first few lesson with the etiquette guy. I think I completely scared him."

Daphne stared into Cleo's big blue eyes and easy smile. "I doubt that. I'm sure he was charmed."

"Not when I accidentally poured the hot tea into his lap instead of his fine china cup."

Daphne laughed. "I'll bet that got his attention."

"In more ways than one." She shrugged. "The princes are worth it. That's the best advice I can give you. Know that they're worth every annoyance, every pain. I'm so thankful I met Sadik and fell in love with him. It wasn't easy, but now..." She grinned. "I know this sounds lame, but my life is perfect."

"I'm happy for you," Daphne said, and meant it. Cleo

had grown up in difficult circumstances. She'd more than earned her happy ending.

But not everyone's story was the same. Should Daphne ignore her responsibilities because she was still intent on leaving? Should she play the part while she was here? And if she played it too much, would she become complaisant? She would never forgive herself if she gave in to Murat. Worse, she would have taught him not only was it acceptable to treat her badly, but that there were no consequences. Ignoring everything else, did she want to be married to a man who thought so little of her?

Cleo stood. "Sorry to gush over your clothing and run, but Calah will be waking up soon and I want to be there." She smiled. "Sadik tells me that our nanny has the cushiest job around. Great pay and I never let her do any work."

"Your daughter is lucky."

"I like to think I'm the lucky one." She wiggled her fingers at Daphne and crossed to the door. When she reached it, she turned back. "If you need to talk more, you know where I live."

"Absolutely."

"Good. I'll—" Cleo gave a laugh and turned around "—look who just appeared," she said and dragged Murat into the room. "Your wife needs help," she said. "Too many good clothing choices. Maybe you could talk her into modeling a few things for you."

Murat glanced between the women. "An intriguing proposition. I will consider it."

Cleo left.

Daphne stayed where she was on the sofa while Murat walked through the maze of racks and the boxes of shoes, purses and scarves.

"Have you made sense out of any of this?" he asked.

"Not really. I need a schedule first to figure out what sort of clothing I'll need."

"I see. And you do not want to agree to a schedule because that is too much like giving in."

She shrugged, even though he'd guessed correctly.

"You have time," he said. "No one will expect you to have a full schedule right away."

"And if I don't want one ever?"

He sat down across from her. "There are advantages and disadvantages to any position in life."

"I know your advantages," she said. "You pretty much get whatever you want."

"True, but there is a price to pay."

"Which is?"

"I have much to offer. Favors, knowledge, an interesting circle of acquaintances. Who comes to see me because of who I am and who comes because of what I can do for him?" He loosened his tie. "Now I am aware of the possibilities at the first meeting, but when I was younger, it was not so easy to see those who expected something in return."

Daphne understood exactly what he meant. "I had the same thing, on a much smaller scale. Not so much with friends, but sometimes my teachers were too impressed by my parents to actually pay attention to me."

"Exactly." He shrugged. "Reyhan, Sadik and Jefri were free to roam the city, making trouble, having fun. I was not. While they played, I learned about governments and rulers and history. All in preparation. Each day I was reminded of my responsibility to my people. I did not know who they all were, but sometimes I hated them."

The man sat across from her but she could easily picture the boy. Tired, restless, but forced to stay inside for one more lesson when all he wanted was to go play with his brothers.

Compassion made it difficult for her to want to keep her distance, which meant he was making good on his word to convince her to care about him. Talk about smooth.

"While we are on the subject," he said, "your father called me. He wishes to discuss expanding the family business into Bahania, and from there El Bahar and the Middle East."

Daphne couldn't believe it. Her own father? Heat flared on her cheeks and she had a bad feeling she was blushing.

"I'm sorry," she said. "I'll phone him right away."

Murat leaned back in the sofa and shook his head. "There is no need. As my father-in-law, he is due some consideration. I will put my people on it and he can work through them."

"It's only been a week," she said, angry that after years of ignoring her, her father was now willing to use her situation to his advantage. "He could have waited a little longer."

"Perhaps, but if you allow yourself to get upset over every person who comes looking for something, then you will spend your life in a state of great anxiety. It means nothing, Daphne. Let it go."

Maybe it meant nothing to him, but it meant something to her. Unfortunately, no matter how much she wanted to hate Murat, he was the only person who could understand what she was going through.

She didn't want to live in a world where people used her to get what they wanted, yet that had been his whole life.

"Have you ever been sure about anyone?" she asked. "How do you know if he or she is interested in you or what you can offer?"

"Sometimes the situation is very clear. Those are the people I prefer. When I know what they are after I can decide to give it or not. But when they play the game too well…" He sighed. "I was more easily fooled when I was younger. After college, a few women managed to convince me that their love for me was greater than the universe itself when what they really wanted was the title and money."

She winced. "That couldn't have been fun."

"No. But for every half-dozen of them there was someone sincere. A young woman who didn't know or didn't care. You, for example."

She smiled at the memory. "I didn't have a clue."

"I know, and when you found out, I thought you would run so far in the opposite direction that I would never catch you."

Her smile faded. "And when I did run, you didn't come after me."

He stared at her, then dropped his gaze to her left hand. "You still refuse to wear your ring."

"Are you surprised?"

"No. Disappointed."

"Want to talk about what I'm feeling?"

"If you would like."

She narrowed her gaze. "That's new. Since when do you care about my feelings regarding anything?"

"I want you to be happy."

She couldn't believe it. "You kept me prisoner, then married me against my will. Not exactly a recipe for happiness."

"We are husband and wife now. I would like you to make the best of the situation. You may find yourself pleasantly surprised."

She leaned toward him. "Murat, when will you see what you did was wrong? Why won't you at least admit it? I meant what I said. I want out."

"There will be no divorce. The king will not allow it."

Daphne stood, with the thought of escaping, only there wasn't anywhere to go. She glanced around at all the clothes she had to try on, the reminder about her interviews, the stack of books on history and protocol.

"Did it ever occur to you that whatever chance we might have had for happiness is now dead because of what you did?" she asked quietly.

Murat stood and moved close. He touched her cheek. "In time you will let go of the past and look toward the future. I can be patient. I will wait. In the meantime I have a meeting." He glanced at his watch. "For which I am now late."

"Somehow I don't think you'll get a reprimand."

He flashed her a smile. "Probably not." He nodded at the clothes. "Are you truly overwhelmed?"

"Of course. How could I not be?"

"Would you like to leave this all behind for a few days?"

"Is that possible?"

"Yes. Although it requires you getting back on a horse."

"I can do that."

"Good." He tightened his tie. "Be ready, tomorrow at dawn. You'll need to dress traditionally. I will have someone leave the appropriate clothing in our room."

"Where are we going?"

"It's a surprise."

Daphne spent a restless night in the small guest-room bed. She couldn't stop thinking about Murat, which wasn't all that uncommon, only this time she wasn't nearly so angry.

Maybe it was because they'd discussed a little of his past. She wouldn't have enjoyed being hampered by so many restrictions. While it might be good to be the king, growing up as the prince sounded less fun.

She appreciated his understanding of what her father had done, but hated that such things were common-place to him. Who had ever cared about Murat simply for himself? Who had ever loved him?

She didn't mean family, but someone else. A woman. Had there been even one to care about the man more than the position he held?

She opened her eyes and stared into the darkness. Would she have? Ten years ago, if she hadn't run, would she have loved him more than anyone?

Of course, she thought. She already had. She'd wanted to get lost in him and have him get lost in her. She hadn't run because of her feelings, but because of a lack of his. At twenty, she'd needed to be important, an emotional equal. She'd wanted to matter.

Funny how ten years later her goal hadn't changed.

That's what he didn't understand. Of course she was furious about how he'd forced her into marriage. He was wrong and egotistical and he deserved some kind of punishment. But if he'd come to her and even hinted that she mattered, she might have been willing to accept his apology and give things a try. Not that Murat would ever admit he'd done anything wrong, let alone apologize.

While it was her nature to make the best of a bad situation, she believed down to her bones that he had to understand he'd acted selfishly.

She rose and turned off the alarm, then moved into the small bathroom to shower. Every night Murat invited her to share the large, luxurious bedroom and every night she refused. Now, as she stood under the spray of hot water, she found her body remembering what it had been like to make love with him. She wanted to feel his touch again.

"Which only goes to show you're in need of some

serious therapy," she muttered as she turned away from the spray.

After drying herself and her hair and applying plenty of lotion to combat the dryness of the desert, she slipped on her bra and panties, then a lightweight T-shirt and jeans. Next came her riding boots, followed by the traditional robes that covered her from shoulder to toes. Last, she slipped on her head covering.

As she stared at herself in the mirror, the only part of her she recognized was her blue eyes. Otherwise, she could have been any other Bahanian woman of the desert. Most women who lived in the city had long abandoned the traditional dress, but she and Murat would be heading into the desert where the old ways were still favored.

She left the bedroom and found Murat waiting for her in the living room.

He wore a loose-fitting white shirt and riding pants. She could see her reflection in his boots.

"I can arrange a Jeep if you would prefer," he said by way of greeting.

"I'd rather ride. I won't go off by myself again. I've learned my lesson."

He nodded, then held out his hand. The diamond wedding band rested on it. "We are married. I will not have my people asking questions."

She stared at the ring, then at him. The internal battle was a short one because she agreed that she did not want others brought into their private battle of wills. She took the ring and slipped it on.

His expression didn't change at all. She'd half expected him to gloat and was pleased when he didn't.

"Shall we go?" he asked.

Murat stepped out of the car into the milling crowd by the stable. Nearly fifty people collected supplies, checked horses, loaded trucks or called out names on the master list. His head of security gave him a thumbs-up, before returning to the conversation he'd been having with his team.

Murat helped Daphne out of the car, then waited while she glanced around.

"Did you say something about roughing it?" she asked in amusement. "I was picturing us on a couple of horses, with a camel carrying a few supplies."

"This is not much more than that."

She laughed. "Of course not. You do know how to travel in style."

"Will you feel better knowing we are to sleep in a tent?"

"Gee, how big will it be?"

"Not large. A few thousand square feet."

"However will we survive?"

"Everyone else is housed elsewhere. There is a kitchen tent, a communication tent and so on."

She shaded her eyes as she stared into the distance. "I'm glad we're going."

As was he. Even shrouded in yards of fabric, she was still beautiful. He had not enjoyed the past week—her anger and silence. He hated that she slept in another bed, although he would not force her into his.

Why did she not understand that what was done was done and now they should get on with their lives? Did she really think that being married to him was such a hardship? She insulted him with her reluctance and sad eyes.

"Daphne," he said, drawing her attention back to him. "About our time in the desert. I would like us to call a truce."

"I'm not sure that's possible when only one of us is fighting," she said. "But I understand what you're saying."

She looked at the horses, then the camels and trucks. "Will we be joined by some of the nomadic tribes?"

"Yes. Word has spread that I will be among my people. They will join us as they can."

She looked back at him. "I agree to the truce, but for your people, not for you."

"As you wish."

For now it was enough. If she spent time with him and forgot to be angry, he knew he could win her over. Then when they returned to the palace, all would be well.

"Come," he said, holding out his hand.

She took it and allowed him to lead her to a snow-white gelding.

"Try not to fall off this one," he said as he helped her mount.

She settled into the saddle and grinned down at him. "Try not to make me angry."

"That is never my goal."

"But you're so good at it."

"I am a man of many talents."

Something flashed in her eyes. Something dark and

sensuous that heated his blood and increased his ever-present wanting.

"We're not going there," she said. "Don't think for a moment there's going to be any funny business."

"But you enjoy laughing."

"That's not what I mean and you know it."

"So many rules."

"I mean this one."

"As you wish."

She might mean it but that did not prevent him from changing her mind. The desert was often a place of romance and he intended to use the situation to his advantage. Their tent might be large and well furnished, but there was only one bedroom…and one bed.

"Tell me where we're going," Daphne said after they'd been traveling for about an hour. "Is it a specific route? We're on a road." Sort of. More of a dirt track that cut through the desert.

"Yes. This leads north to the ancient Silk Road. We will not go that far—just into the heart of the desert."

The Silk Road. She'd heard of it, studied it. To think they were so close. There was so much history in Bahania. So many treasures for her to discover.

She shifted slightly in her saddle. After a few minutes of trepidation after finding herself back on a horse, she'd quickly settled into the rhythmic striding and lost her fear. Murat riding close beside her helped.

She supposed it wasn't a good sign that the very man

who made her insane also made her feel safe. "Will we be camping by an oasis?" she asked.

"Each night. Eventually we will make our way to—" He hesitated.

"What?" she asked.

"We are going to a place of great mystery. It is not far out of our way, and I thought you would enjoy reacquainting yourself with my sister Sabrina."

Daphne remembered the pretty, intelligent teenager from her previous visit to Bahania. "She lives out here?"

"Yes, with her husband. My sister Zara resides there, as well."

"Zara. Okay, she's the daughter of the dancer. The American who found out she was the king's daughter a few years ago?"

"Exactly. She is married to an American sheik named Rafe. He is the chief of security."

"Of what?"

Murat looked at her. "That is the secret. You must take a solemn vow to never reveal it to anyone." He seemed to be perfectly serious.

"You know I'm still planning to leave," she said.

"We agreed not to speak of such things."

"Not speaking doesn't take away the truth. But I would never betray the people of Bahania. Or you."

He nodded, as if he'd expected no less. "You have heard of the City of Thieves?"

She thought for a second. "It's a myth. Like Atlantis. A beautiful city in the middle of the desert where those who steal find sanctuary. Supposedly some of the most amazing missing treasures are said to reside there. Jewels, paintings, statues, tapestries. If a country has lost something of great value in the last thousand years, it can probably be found in the City of Thieves."

"It is true."

She blinked. "Excuse me?"

"All of it. The city exists."

"You mean like a real city. Buildings. People. Cool stolen stuff?"

"There is a castle built in the twelfth century and a small city surrounding it. An underground spring provides water. The buildings all blend so perfectly with their surroundings that they cannot be seen from any distance or from the sky." He motioned to the large crowd behind them. "We will leave nearly everyone long before we near the city. Prince Kardal will send out his own security forces to escort us in."

"I can't believe it," she breathed. "It's like finding out the Easter bunny is real."

"Sabrina is an expert on the antiquities there. Due to her influence, several pieces have already been returned to some countries. She will take you on a tour if you would like."

"I'd love it. When do we get there?"

He laughed. "Not so fast. First we must ride deep into the desert and find our way to the edge of the world."

"I've never been there," she admitted, more than a little intrigued.

"It is a place worth visiting."

Chapter Eleven

Daphne might hate the way Murat had arranged their marriage and not enjoy being kept in Bahania against her will, but she had to admit that the man knew how to travel and travel well.

Small trucks with large tires kept pace with the group on horse- and camelback. Several vehicles were designated as moving cafeterias, offering everything from cold water to sandwiches and fresh fruit.

Lunch had been a hit-and-miss affair, eaten while her horse drank and rested, but Murat promised a dinner feast when they reached their camp for the first night.

He had also promised more people would join them, and he was true to his word.

By midafternoon, the number of travelers had tripled. Every hour or so another group appeared on the horizon and moved toward them. There were families with small herds of camels or goats, several young men with carts, and what looked like entire tribes.

Murat's security spoke with them first, inspected a few bags and boxes, then let them join the growing throng. A few of the men rode to the front of the queue and spoke briefly with Murat. She noticed that those brave enough to do so seemed to focus most of their attention on her.

"Why do they do that?" she asked as a man bowed low in his saddle and returned to his family somewhere behind them. "If they want to meet me, why don't they just ask?"

"It is not our way. First they must speak with me and remind me of their great service to me or my father. Perhaps their connection is through a bloodline or marriage. Once I have acknowledged their place, they retreat. Later, at camp, they will bring their wives and children and introductions will be made."

He glanced at her and smiled. "I do not flatter myself that so many people are interested in traveling with me. I have gone into the desert dozens of times. It is their future queen who sparks their imagination."

Daphne felt both flattered and guilty. She was happy to meet anyone interested in meeting her, but she hated the thought of letting them think her position as Murat's wife was permanent.

"Your eyes betray you," he said. "How tender your feelings for those you have not yet met. Perhaps if you opened your heart to your husband, you would be less troubled."

"Perhaps if my husband had bothered to win my affection instead of forcing something I never wanted, I could open my heart to him."

Instead of looking subdued or chagrined or even slightly guilty, Murat appeared pleased. "You have not called me that before."

"What?"

"Your husband."

How like him to only hear that part of the sentence. "Don't get too excited. I didn't mean it in a good way."

"Nevertheless it is true. We are bound." His gaze dropped to her midsection. "Perhaps by a child growing even now."

"Don't count on it."

She knew that if he had his way, he would will her to be pregnant. And if she had hers…she would be gone by morning.

Daphne breathed in the sweet air of the desert. The sounds delighted her—the laughter of the children, the jingling of the harnesses on the horses and camels, the call of the birds following them overhead.

As always the vastness of the wilderness left her feeling both small and yet very much a part of the world. All right—if truth be told, she would not wish herself away just yet. Perhaps it would be better if she left Murat *after* this trip.

"It has been many years since my people have had a queen to call their own," he said.

"Then you should encourage your father to remarry."

"He has had four wives and several great loves. I think he prefers his various mistresses."

"What man wouldn't?"

Murat's expression hardened. "Is that what you think? Do you resist me because you assume I will not keep my vows? I assure you, I have no interest in being with another woman. You are my wife and I seek solace in your bed alone."

Had things been different, the information would have thrilled her. As it was, she felt a slight flicker in her chest, but she quickly doused it.

"For now," she said.

"For always."

He drew his horse so close, her leg brushed against his.

"I am Crown Prince Murat of Bahania. My word is law. I will honor our vows to my death."

The declaration had the desired effect. She felt bad for doubting him and for the briefest moment wondered if she was being incredibly dumb to resist him. Yes, he'd married her against her will, but it wasn't as if he planned to mistreat her.

Wait! Was that her standard for a happy marriage? Lack of mistreatment? What about love and respect? What about treating each other with dignity? What about the fact that for the rest of their lives together, he would think it was all right to ignore her opinion and desires and simply do what he wanted?

"I plan to release you well before you breathe your last," she said.

His gaze narrowed. "You mock my sincerity."

"You ignore my deepest and most sincere wishes."

"I have not tried to bribe you."

She couldn't help laughing. "And that's a good thing?"

"I knew you would not approve. Nor would jewels and money influence your decision."

"You're right about that." How could he know her so well on the one hand and be such a jerk on the other? "You're very complicated."

He smiled. "Thank you."

"I'm not sure it's a compliment."

"Of course it is. You will not be bored with me."

That was true. "We'd fight a lot."

"Passion is healthy."

"Too much anger can chip away at the foundation of a relationship."

"I would not allow that to happen."

"You don't always get to choose."

"Of course I do. I am—"

She cut him off with a wave of her hand. "Yeah, yeah. Crown prince. Blah, blah, blah. You need some new material."

He stared at her with the shocked expression of a man hearing words from the mouth of a beetle. Both dark eyebrows raised, his mouth parted and she half expected him to stick his finger in his ear and jiggle it around.

"You dare to speak to me that way?"

"What's the problem. I am, for the moment at least, your wife. If I don't, who will?"

"No one. It is not permitted."

"Murat, you seem to be a pretty decent ruler, but you really have to get over yourself."

She half expected him to call down thunder onto her. Instead he stared at her for a long moment, then tossed his head back and began to laugh.

The sound delighted her, even as she realized she'd never heard it before. Oh, he'd laughed, but not like this—unrestrained, uncontrolled. He was not a man who allowed himself to be taken off guard very often.

In that moment she knew she could make a difference for him. She could be the person he trusted above all others, the person he depended upon. She could ease his burden, give him a safe place to rest.

Need filled her. All her life she had longed to be a part of something. She'd always felt out of step with her family, and since leaving home, she'd never found anyone to love that completely. With Murat…

He was a man who took what he wanted. She thought of all the dates she'd had with guys who didn't bother to call when they said they would or who were too intimidated by her family to want a relationship with her. Men who hadn't been strong.

Murat was too strong. They had been too weak. Was there any comfortable place in the middle? And if she had to choose one or the other, which was best?

Strength, she decided. Perhaps there was something to be said for a prince of the desert.

"What do you think?" Murat asked as he passed her a bowl filled with a spicy grain dish.

Daphne smiled. "It's amazing. I feel as if I'm in the middle of a giant movie."

A sea of tents surrounded them. Twilight approached, and in the growing dark, campfires stretched out toward the horizon. The last rays of the sun danced off the dozens of banners flying from tall poles.

Scents of a thousand meals prepared on open flames blended with perfumes and oils and the clean smell of fresh straw.

She and Murat dined alone. The guards were always there, ever-present shadows who watched for danger. Yet she felt comfortable and at peace. Should the unlikely occur and someone try to attack Murat, the intruder would be laid low long before he reached the center of the camp. The desert tribes were both fierce and loyal.

"While silence is often welcome in a woman," he said, "in your case it troubles me. What are you plotting?"

"I'm thinking about your people. They have a long and proud history."

"It is true. Many have sought to invade our land and none have succeeded. Now we have an air force to protect us from the skies." He picked up his glass of wine. "Why do I know you care more for the fate of my people than you care for me?"

"Because it's true," she said cheerfully before biting into a piece of chicken.

"You think you can say anything to me."

"Pretty much." She reached for her napkin. "What are you going to do to me? I'm the future queen. You can't really lock me up."

"There are other forms of punishment."

He spoke the words in a low voice that grated against her skin like burned velvet.

"Cheap threats," she told him. "I am the future queen. You must honor me."

"I already do."

"Not enough to admit you were sincerely wrong to hold me prisoner and marry me against my will."

"Perhaps we could put that behind us and move forward."

She glanced up toward the stars. "Oh, look. There's a flying camel."

He growled. "You mock me."

"I'm telling you what it will take for me to forgive and forget. It won't happen without you accepting your part in what you did."

"We will speak of something else."

"I had a feeling you'd say that." She reached for another piece of chicken.

The night was cool but pleasant. Murat sat across from her, looking completely at home in the primitive surroundings.

"Did you come out here much when you were younger?" she asked.

"When I could. There were many things for me to do back at the palace. Studies, lessons. I was presented to visiting dignitaries and expected to sit through many meetings. But when time permitted I escaped to the desert."

Where he could just be a boy. She could imagine him

riding hard and fast as he played with the other children. For an hour or two he wouldn't be the prince, and how he must have treasured that time.

Daphne shifted on her cushion. She wasn't used to sitting so low on the ground. As she got more comfortable, she noticed a group of people walking toward them. There were maybe seven or eight, both men and women. They took a few steps, stopped, seemed to argue among themselves, then moved forward again.

One of the guards rose and spoke with them. After a few minutes, they were waved forward. The walking, stopping, arguing continued as they got closer.

"I wonder what that's about?" she asked, nodding at them.

Murat followed her gaze. "They are not sure if they should interrupt us," he said. "The men resist, but the women insist. Some men should control their wives better."

"Some men are sensible enough to listen to a more intelligent opinion. What should we do?"

"Greet them."

Murat wiped his hands, then rose and helped her to her feet. They stood by the fire and waited as the small group approached.

Everyone bowed. One of the women elbowed one of the men but he didn't speak. Finally the woman took a step forward and bowed again.

"Greetings, Your Highness," she said, speaking to Daphne. "May the new day find you strong and healthy and blessed with good fortune always."

"May the new day find you equally blessed," Daphne replied.

"I fear it will not."

"We should not be here," one of the men said. He looked at Murat. "We are sorry to have troubled you and your bride."

"No!" The woman glared at him. "We are in need."

"How can we help?" Daphne asked.

The woman sighed. "A family who travels with us has a camel in labor. There is trouble of some kind. The man who usually helps with such things did not come with us. We have heard that you are trained with animals. Is it true?"

Daphne took in their robes. While the cloth was clean, it had been mended and patched in several places. She doubted these people could afford to lose a healthy, breeding camel.

The man with her grabbed her arm. "In all this crowd, there must be one other who can assist us. You should not bother the wife of the crown prince."

"There is no time," the woman said. "The mother grows weak." She looked at Daphne. "Please help us."

Daphne wasn't sure of the protocol of the situation. Nor did she know if she could help. "I've never delivered a camel before," she admitted. "I've had a lot of experience with cows and horses. If that is good enough."

The woman sagged with relief. "Yes. Please. A thousand thanks. This way." Then she hurried off.

Daphne started to follow her and wasn't all that surprised when Murat and his guards fell into step.

"You have delivered cows and horses?" he asked. "In Chicago?"

"No. In the country. It's not all that far to the farmlands in the south. I would spend a few months there every summer. Nothing against your father and his hundred or so cats, but it was always a nice change to work on big animals instead of small house pets."

As she walked, she shrugged out of her robes, handing them to Murat who passed them on to a guard. By the time they reached the straw-lined enclosure, she was down to her jeans and a T-shirt. Both of which were going to be pretty yucky by the time this was done. Birth was never tidy.

Three hours later a baby camel teetered on spindly legs. His mother moved close and nudged him until he began to nurse. Daphne leaned against the makeshift fence and smiled. This was the part she liked best—after, when things had gone well.

"Impressive," Murat said, stepping out of the shadows and moving close. "You were very confident."

"All that medical training paid off." She stretched. "I didn't think you'd stick around. It's late."

"I wanted to see what happened." He put an arm around her and led her away from the pen. "While you were working, I spoke with some of the elders of the tribe. The mother has died and the father is ill. There are three boys who tend the family's small herd. They desperately needed this birth."

"I'm glad I didn't know that," she admitted. "I wouldn't have liked the pressure."

"Had the camel died, I would have compensated them, but you were able to give them back their livelihood."

There was pride in his voice, which surprised her. Her parents had never thought much of what she did for a living, why should Murat?

He pulled her close, but she resisted. "I'm pretty stinky," she said. "I don't suppose we have a shower in our tent."

"No, but I can provide you with a bath."

"Really?"

"Of course."

Their massive private tent had still been under construction at dinner so she hadn't had a chance to see the interior. Now she followed Murat inside to a foyerlike opening. They removed their shoes. He held open a flap, and she stepped into an amazing world she hadn't known existed.

The fabric ceiling stretched up at least ten feet. Carpets were piled on top of each other underfoot. Her toes curled into the exquisite patterns and softness.

Low benches and plush chairs provided seating around carved tables. Old-fashioned lamps hung from hooks, providing illumination. The faint but steady rumble of a generator explained the flow of fresh, cool air she felt on her face.

"This way," he said and led her deeper into the tent.

There was a dining area, a huge bed on a dais, and a tub filled with steaming water that nearly made her moan with delight.

She had to resist the urge to dive in headfirst. Instead she tugged off her socks, then glanced down at her filthy T-shirt.

"Good thing I didn't pack light," she said. "I think this one is past recovering."

Murat shrugged out of his robes and left them draped over a low chair. Then, wearing only loose trousers and a white shirt, he moved close and held out his hand.

"What?" she asked.

"Your clothing."

She took a step back. "I'm not getting undressed in front of you."

"You forget. I have seen you bare before."

"That's not the point."

Actually, it was exactly the point. Getting naked with Murat around would only lead to trouble. Even talking about it made her body start to react. Tiny pinpricks of desire nipped at her skin. Her belly felt hollow and hot and an ache took up residence between her thighs.

"I'm perfectly capable of bathing myself," she said.

"I am offering to help." His dark gaze caught her and wouldn't let her go.

"Not necessary."

"Are you afraid?"

"Murat, I'm not playing that game. Now shoo so I can get cleaned up."

Instead of leaving, he moved closer. "I am here to help you with your bath, my most stubborn princess. I give you my word that I will make no attempt to seduce you in your bath. I will not make suggestive remarks or touch you in any inappropriate way. Now, take off your clothes."

Was this how the cobra felt in the face of the snake charmer, she wondered. She didn't want to listen or do as he said, yet she found herself reaching for the hem of her T-shirt and pulling the whole thing off, over her head. She handed it to Murat.

Her jeans were next, leaving her in a bra and panties. Turning her back on him, she unfastened the former and pushed down the latter. They tumbled to the carpeted ground. Then she stepped into the steaming tub and sank down into the water.

The heat soothed aching muscles. She reached up to keep her hair out of the water, but Murat had moved behind the tub and brushed her hands away.

"I will do it," he said as he gently coiled her hair, then took pins from a nearby tray and secured her hair on top of her head.

"Here."

He handed her a bar of scented soap and a washcloth. She breathed in the smell of flowers and sandalwood.

The water was clear, which made her feel awkward about being naked. Murat stayed behind her, and there weren't any mirrors, so she tried to tell herself he wasn't really there…watching. Still, as she smoothed the soapy washcloth across her suddenly sensitive breasts, she felt his gaze on her.

She turned only to find him with his back to the tub.

He stood by the wooden dresser, opening a drawer and drawing out a nightgown. Okay, so her imagination was putting in some overtime. Obviously he'd meant what he said. This was just a bath.

Being female and completely comfortable supporting two opposite ideas at exactly the same time, her next thought was one of annoyance. Didn't he *notice* that she was naked? Didn't he find her sexually appealing? Wasn't he aroused by the situation? They were married, and a man was supposed to want his wife.

She quickly finished washing and wrung out the cloth. Annoyance made her slosh the water as she stood.

"Could you hand me a towel?" she asked.

Murat reached for one and handed it to her. From what she could tell, he barely looked at her naked, wet body. How perfect. Now that he had her, he didn't want her anymore. Just like a man, she thought as she rubbed herself dry. Fine. She could "not want" him, too.

She wrapped the towel around herself and stepped out of the tub. He passed her a nightgown. The soft, pale silk was unfamiliar, but at this point she was too much in a temper to care. She let the towel drop to the floor and slid the nightgown over her head.

The see-through fabric left nothing to the imagination. The front dipped down nearly to her stomach, and the back consisted of a few lacy straps and nothing else. Ha! As if Murat would care.

She wanted to kick him. She walked to stalk out into the night and scream her frustration to the heavens. What was wrong with him not to react? And more important, why did she care? She didn't love Murat. Lately she didn't even like him very much. So why did it bother her that he hadn't pounced on her like a cat on catnip?

"I'm going to bed," she said curtly. "Good night."

"You enjoyed your bath?" he asked from his place just behind her.

"It was fine."

"You would consider it finished now?"

She turned until she could look at him. "As I'm out of it, dry and dressed, I would go with yes."

"Good."

A rush of movement followed the word and she found herself caught up against him as he hauled her into his arms and pressed his mouth to hers.

She had no time to think or react or even feel. His hands were everywhere. Her back, her sides, her breasts. He kissed her hotly, ravishing her. Somehow she managed to part her lips, and he swept inside with the purposefulness of a man set on claiming his woman.

Even as he cupped her breast and stroked her hard nipple through the thin fabric of her nightgown, he squeezed her rear and pulled her into him. She felt the pulsing hardness of his arousal.

"You want me," she murmured, her mouth still against his.

He raised his head and stared at her. "Of course. Why would you think otherwise?"

"Because I was naked and you just ignored me."

"I gave you my word I would not bother you while you were in your bath."

Of all the times for him to keep it, this would not have been her first choice.

"You're the most annoying man," she told him.

He bent down and swept her into his arms. "Let me annoy you some more," he said as he carried her to the bed on the other side of the tent.

There were candles hanging everywhere and fresh-cut flowers in vases all over the room. The white linens had been folded back invitingly. Murat knelt on the mattress, then lowered her onto the smooth surface.

She kept her arms around his neck and pulled him close so she could kiss him.

Once again he claimed her with a kiss that marked her as his. She supposed she should protest, or at least not like it so much, but she couldn't help squirming in delight as he nipped on her lower lip, then drew the sensitive curve into his mouth. He nibbled her jaw and down her throat. Lower and lower until he settled over her tight, aching nipples.

The silk was so thin, he didn't bother pushing it away. Instead he licked and sucked her through the fabric. She ran her fingers through his hair, to touch him as much as to hold him in place. He moved to her other breast, repeating the glorious touching and teasing, until she felt hot and strung far too tightly.

Wanting poured through her. She couldn't seem to keep her legs still, and between her thighs a pulsing hunger began.

"Murat," she breathed as she began to tug at his shirt. "I need you."

"No more than I need you." He took the hint and shrugged out of the garment.

She took advantage of his distraction to pull up her nightgown in a shameless invitation. She knew this wasn't her smartest act of the day, but she couldn't seem to stem the tide of need rushing through her. She might have had other lovers, but she'd never wanted one the way she wanted Murat. Desperation made her reach for his trousers. He had to be in her. Now!

"Impatient?" he asked with a smile as he shed the rest of his clothing, then slipped between her legs. "Let me take the edge off, my sweet."

Instead of filling her with his hardness, he bent low and gently parted her swollen flesh with his fingers. Then he pressed his mouth against her hot, damp center.

She had only a second to brace herself before the impact of the pleasure nearly had her screaming down the tent. Vaguely mindful of their neighbors, she held in her cries of delight as he licked all of her before settling on that one single point of pleasure.

He traced quick circles, making her breathe more quickly. Tension made her dig in her heels and grab on to the covers. She tossed her head from side to side as he gently sucked that one perfect spot.

She rocked her hips in time with his movements, moving closer and closer to her ultimate release. Every brush of his tongue, every whisper of breath pushed her onward. When she finally clung to the edge, so ready to surrender all to him, he slipped two fingers inside of her.

The combination was too much. She tried to hold

back, to enjoy the moment longer, but it wasn't possible. Passion claimed her and she called out Murat's name as she sank into the waves of pleasure.

Fast, at first, then slowing, but not really ever ending. Not even when he raised his head and stared at her with wild, hungry eyes. He continued to move his fingers. Back and forth, back and forth. Mini-waves rippled through her. Climax after climax. As long as he touched her, she came.

She stared at him, unable to control her body's response to his touch.

"Murat," she breathed.

He shifted closer, at last replacing his fingers with his arousal. He thrust into her, filling her until she thought she might shatter.

It was too good. There was too much. She came again and again. Every time he moved into her, she gave herself over to the release. Faster and faster until they were both breathing hard, and then she lost herself again in a violent shuddering that left her both shattered and satisfied down to her bones.

Chapter Twelve

Daphne awoke the next morning with the sense of being one with the world. She could hear the birds outside and the low voices of people in the encampment. The smell of cooking made her mouth water, and the sounds of laughter made her smile. She had a feeling that when she climbed out of bed, there was a very good chance she would float several inches above the carpeted tent floor.

What a night, she thought as she pushed her hair out of her face and sat up. Murat was long gone. She vaguely recalled him kissing her before he'd left their bed sometime after dawn.

They'd continued to make love, each time more passionately than the time before until she'd been afraid she would never be able to recover. Her body ached, but in the best way possible. Her skin seemed to be glowing, and she knew she would be hard-pressed not to spend the entire day grinning like a fool.

Everything had been perfect. Except… She pressed her hands to her flat stomach and wondered if they'd made a baby last night. She and Murat had made love several times without any kind of protection. The thought had never crossed her mind. She knew the price of having his child—she would never be able to leave.

Now, in the soft light of the morning in the beautiful tent, she wondered if perhaps she should make her peace with all that had happened. Was his behavior really that horrible? He'd only—

"Earth to Daphne," she said aloud. "Let's think about this."

Rational thought returned, pushing away the lingering effects of the night of pleasure. Of course she couldn't give in. Even if she wanted to stay married to Murat, she would still need to make him understand that he couldn't have his way in everything. That for their marriage to be a happy and successful union, they both had to make decisions, and he couldn't simply bully his way into what he wanted.

Which meant getting pregnant was a really dumb idea. She was going to have to avoid his bed.

She stood and faced the rumpled sheets. It was a very nice bed and the man who slept in it was nothing short of magical when it came to making love. Still, she had to be strong. At least until she knew if she were pregnant.

She washed using the basin of water on the dresser, then pulled on the garments that had been left out for her. Murat had mentioned something about a tribal council today. He would assemble the leaders from the various tribes and then hear judgments and petitions from the people. She'd agreed to attend.

Intricate embroidery covered her robes. In place of a headdress, a small diamond-and-gold crown sat on a pillow.

Daphne stared at it. While she knew that Murat was the crown prince and that he would one day be king, she never really thought about it all that seriously. But now, staring at the crown, she felt the weight of a thousand years of history pressing on her.

She carefully brushed her long, blond hair until it gleamed, then she set the crown on her head and secured it with two pins. She checked that it was straight, all the while trying not to notice she actually had it on her head, then left for the main part of the tent.

One of Murat's security agents sat waiting for her. When she approached, he stood and bowed.

"Good morning, Princess Daphne," he said. "The judgments are about to begin. If you will follow me."

He led her outside into a beautiful, clear morning. The camp was nearly deserted, but up ahead she saw a huge covering that would easily hold a thousand people. They walked toward it, avoiding the main entrance and instead circling around to the back.

She ducked under a low hanging and found herself behind a dais that held several ornate chairs. Murat approached and took her hand in his.

"We are about to begin," he said with a smile.

He spoke easily, but his eyes sent her another message. One that reminded her of their night together and all that had happened between them.

She wanted to tell him they couldn't do that again. Not until things were straightened out between them, but this was not the time or place.

She followed him up onto the dais and sat in a chair just to the left and slightly behind his. On his right sat the tribal council. In front of them were hundreds of people sitting in rows. A few stood on either side of the room, and an older man with a parchment scroll stood in the center.

He read from the ancient document in a language she didn't recognize. She remembered enough from her previous time in Bahania to know he called all those seeking justice to this place and time. That the prince's word would be final. Judgments against those charged with crimes were covered in the morning, while petitions came in the afternoon.

Several criminals were brought forward. Two charges were dismissed as being brought about by a desire for revenge rather than an actual crime. One man accused of stealing goats was sentenced to six months in a prison and a branding.

Daphne winced at the latter and Murat caught the movement.

"It is an old way," he said, turning toward her. "A man is given three chances. The brand allows the council to know how many times he has been before them."

"But branding?"

"He stole," Murat said. "These are desert people. They exist hundreds and thousands of miles from the world as you know it. If you steal a man's car in the city, he can walk or take a bus. You steal a man's goats or camels in the desert and you sentence him and his family to possible death. They may starve before they can walk out of the desert or to another encampment. They would not be able to carry all their possessions themselves, so they would be discarded. The youngest children might die on the long walk to safety. Stealing is not something we take lightly."

His words made sense. Daphne understood that where life was harsh, punishment must be equally so, but the whole concept made her uncomfortable.

Several more minor cases were brought forward. Then a man in his late twenties was walked in front of the dais.

The guards took his left arm and held it out for all to see. Three brands scarred his skin. Daphne sucked in a breath.

"He is charged with stealing camels," a member of the council told Murat.

"Witnesses?"

Five people stepped behind the men. Two were his accomplices, while the other three—a father and two sons—had owned the camels. The father spoke about the night his camels were taken. He had a herd of twenty, and this man and his friends took all of them. He and his sons went after the thieves only to find that one of the camels had gone lame and the thieves had slit its throat.

The crowd gasped. Daphne knew that to kill such a useful creature because it had gone lame was considered an abomination.

The cohorts spoke of the crime. They had already been charged and had confessed. Each had a fresh brand—their only brand. But the leader had three.

Murat listened to all the evidence, then turned to the council.

"Death," each of them said.

When it was his turn to speak, he said, "You decided not to end your thieving yourself. We will do it for you."

The criminal dropped his head to his chest. "I have two children and no wife."

Murat nodded for the children to be brought out.

A boy of maybe fourteen stepped forward, holding on to the hand of a much younger girl. The boy fought tears, but the little girl seemed more confused, as if she didn't understand what was happening.

"What of this?" Murat asked the boy. "Do you have a brand on your arm?"

The teenager squared his shoulders. "I do not steal, Prince Murat. I protect my sister and honor the memory of my mother."

"Very well." Murat turned his attention to the crowd. "Two children of the thief."

There was a moment of silence, then a tall man in his early forties stepped toward the dais.

"I will take them," he said.

Murat was silent.

The man nodded. "I give my word that they will be treated well and raised as my own. The boy will be given the opportunity to attend college if he likes."

Daphne glared at the man and raised her eyebrows.

He caught her gaze and took a step back. "Ah, the girl, too."

"Better," she murmured.

"She-wolf," Murat whispered back. But he sounded pleased.

Still Murat did not speak to the man making the offer. At last the man sighed. He called out to the crowd. Several people turned to watch as a young girl of eleven or so stepped out and walked to the man.

"My youngest," he said heavily. "The daughter of my heart. I give her into your keeping, to ensure the safety of those I take in."

The girl stared up at him. "Papa?"

He patted her head. "All will be well, child."

Murat rose. "I agree," he said. "The children of the thief will enter a new family. Their pasts will be washed clean and they will not carry their father's burden."

He walked to Daphne and held out his hand. She stood and took it, then followed him off the dais, toward the rear of the tent.

"What was all that?" she asked. "Why did that man bring out his daughter?"

"Because she is insurance. We will check on the condition of the two children he is taking in, but here, desert traditions run deep. Should he not treat them well, they will be removed from his care, along with his daughter. She gives him incentive to keep his word."

She'd never heard of such a thing. "An interesting form of foster care."

"It is more than that. He will take those children into his home and treat them as his own. I meant what I said—they will not bear the stigma of their father's crimes." He urged her toward their tent. "It is often this way with the children of criminals. They are taken in and given a good home. I have never heard of one of them being ill treated. I know the man who claimed them. He will be good to them."

She ducked into the tent and found lunch waiting for them. "I guess it really does take a village."

"For us it does."

He held out her chair, then took the seat across from hers. A young woman carried a tray of food toward them.

"What happens this afternoon?" Daphne asked as she served herself some salad. "More criminals?"

"No. The petitions. Anyone may approach me directly and ask me to settle a dispute."

"That must keep you busy."

He smiled. "Not as busy as you would think. My word is law, and I have a reputation of being stern and difficult. Only the truly brave seek my form of justice."

"Are you fair?" she asked.

He shrugged. "The fate of my people rests in my

hands. I do not take that responsibility lightly. I do my best to see both sides of the situation and find the best solution for all concerned."

He wasn't what she thought. At first she'd described Murat as being just like her family—friendly and supportive as long as he got his way. But now she questioned that. He wanted to be a good leader. A good man.

How did she reconcile that with what he'd done to her? What was the solution to her dilemma? How did she show him that they had to be honest with each other before they had any hope of a relationship together?

After lunch Murat met with his tribal council, and Daphne went for a walk. She strolled by the makeshift stables and stopped to watch several children play soccer. A young woman approached and bowed.

"Greetings, Princess," she said. "I am Aisha. It is a great honor to meet you."

"The honor is mine," Daphne said with a smile.

The girl was maybe sixteen or seventeen and incredibly beautiful. In the safety of the camp, she left her head uncovered. Her large brown eyes crinkled slightly at the corners as if she found life amusing. Her full mouth curved up at the corners. Jewelry glinted from her ears and caught the sunlight.

"I must confess I sought you out on purpose," Aisha said. "I have a petition for the prince, but I dare not deliver it myself."

"Why?"

The girl ducked her head. "My father has forbidden me."

Daphne didn't like the sound of that. "He forbids you to seek justice?"

She shrugged. "He has offered me in marriage to a man in our tribe. The man is very honorable and wealthy. Instead of my father having to provide me with a dowry, the man will pay *him* the price of five camels."

This would be the part of the old-fashioned desert world Daphne didn't like so much. "Is your potential fiancé much older?"

Aisha nodded. "He is nearly fifty and has many children older than me. He swears he loves me and I am to be his last wife, but…"

"You don't love him."

"I…" The girl swallowed. "I have given my heart to another," she said in a whisper. "I know it's wrong," she added in a rush. "I have defied my father and dishonored my family. I know I should be punished. But marriage to someone so old seems harsh. Please, Princess Daphne, as the wife of the crown prince you are entitled to plead on my behalf. The prince will listen to you."

Daphne thought about her own recent marriage and the circumstances involved. "I'm not the right person to take this to the prince. You have to believe me."

"You are my only hope." Tears filled Aisha's eyes. "I beg you."

The girl reached for the gold bangles on her wrists. "Take my jewelry. Take everything I have."

"No." Daphne shook her head. "You don't need to pay for my support. I..."

Now what? She felt bad for the girl, but would Murat give his new wife a fair hearing in these circumstances? He had said he took his responsibility very seriously. She would have to trust that...and him.

"I'll do it," she said. "Tell me what you want from the prince."

Murat listened as the woman explained why she was entitled to have her dowry returned to her. Her case was strong and in the end, he agreed. The husband, who had only married her for her dowry, sputtered and complained, but Murat stared him down and he retreated. Murat spoke with the leaders of the woman's tribe to make sure there would be no retribution and gave her permission to contact his office directly if his wishes weren't followed out.

Next two men argued over the use of a small spring deep in the desert. Murat gave his ruling, then watched as a veiled woman approached. By the time she'd taken a second step, he knew it was Daphne.

Why did she seek him so publicly? To petition for her own freedom?

For a moment he considered the possibility. That she would seek to hold him to the fairness he claimed to offer all. A protest rose within him. There were no words, just the sense that she couldn't leave. Then he remembered their night of lovemaking and the one that had occurred nearly three weeks before. She could not go until they were sure she was not with child. More than anyone, she understood the law of the land.

Relief quickly followed, allowing him to relax as she walked toward him. As she reached the dais, she bowed low, then flipped back her head covering to reveal her features. Many in the waiting crowd gasped.

"I seek justice at the hand of Crown Prince Murat," she said, then frowned slightly. "You're not surprised it's me."

"I recognized your walk."

"I was covered."

"A husband knows such things."

Several of the women watching smiled.

He leaned forward. "Why do you seek my justice? For yourself?"

"No. For another. I call forward Aisha."

A young woman no more than sixteen or seventeen moved next to Daphne. Murat held in a groan. He had a bad feeling he knew what had happened. The girl had approached Daphne and had told a sad story about being forced to marry someone she didn't love. Daphne had agreed to petition on her behalf.

Murat looked at the teenager. "Why do you not petition for yourself?" he asked.

The girl, a beauty, with honey-colored skin and hair that hung to her waist, dropped her chin and stared at the ground. "My father forbade me to do so."

Murat shifted back in his chair and waited. Sure enough, someone started pushing through the waiting throng. A man stepped forward and bowed low.

"Prince Murat, a thousand blessings on you and your family."

Murat didn't speak.

The man twisted his hands together, bowed again, then cleared his throat. "She is but a child. A foolish young girl who dreams of the stars."

Murat didn't doubt that, but the law was the law. "Everyone is entitled to petition the prince. Even a foolish young girl."

"Yes. Of course you are correct. I never dreamed she would seek out your most perfect and radiant wife. May you have a hundred sons. May they be long-lived and fruitful. May—"

Murat raised his hand to cut off the frantic praise. No doubt the thought of a hundred sons had sent Daphne into a panic. He looked at her and raised his eyebrows.

"You see what you have started?"

"I seek only what is right."

Murat sighed and turned his attention to the girl. "All right. Aisha. You have the attention of the prince, and your father is not going to stop you from stating your case. What do you want from me?"

It was as he expected. Her father wished her to marry an old man with many children.

"I am the wife he expects to care for him in his waning years," she said in outrage.

"And the man in question?" Murat asked.

There was more movement in the crowd, and a tall, bearded man stepped forward. He had to be in his late fifties. He bore himself well and had the appearance of prosperity about him.

The man bowed. "I am Farid," he said in a low voice.

"You wish to marry this girl?" Murat asked.

Farid nodded. "She is a good girl and will serve me well."

"Instead of asking for a dowry, he offers me five camels," the father said eagerly. "He has been married before and has lost each wife to illness. Very sad. But all in the village agree the women were well treated."

Murat felt the beginnings of a headache coming on. He looked at the girl.

"There is one more player missing, is there not?"

Aisha nodded slowly. "Barak. The man I love."

Her father gasped in outrage, the fiancé looked patiently indulgent and a steady rumble rose from the crowd.

At last Barak appeared. He was all of twenty-two or twenty-three. Defiant and terrified at the same time. He bowed low before Murat.

"You love Aisha, as well?" Murat asked.

The young man glanced at her, then nodded. "With all my heart. I have been saving money, buying camels. With her dowry, we can buy three more and have a good-size herd. I can provide for her."

"I will not give her a dowry," her father said. "Not for you. Farid is a good man. A better match."

"Especially for you," Murat said. "To be given camels for your daughter instead of having to pay them makes it a fine match."

The father did not speak.

Murat studied Farid. There was something about the color of the skin around his eyes. A grayness.

"You have sons?" Murat asked the older man.

"Six, Your Highness."

"All married?"

"Two are not."

Murat saw the picture more clearly now. "How long do you have?" he asked Farid.

The man looked surprised by the question, but he recovered quickly. "At most a year."

"What?" the girl's father asked. "What are you talking about?"

Murat shook his head. "It is of no matter." He rose and nodded at his wife. "If you will come with me."

He led her to the rear of the tent.

"What's going on?" Daphne wanted to know. "Can you do this? Stop the hearing or whatever it is in midsentence? What about Aisha? Are you going to force her to marry that horrible old man?"

Murat touched her long, blond hair. "That horrible old man is dying. He has less than a year to live."

"Oh. Well, I'm sorry to hear that, but the information means Aisha was right. He's buying her to take care of him in his old age. If he's so rich, why doesn't he just hire a nurse?"

"Because this isn't about his health. It's about his wealth. Farid has six sons. Two are not married. Per our laws, he must leave everything to them equally, which divides his fortune into small pieces. But that is not the best way to maintain wealth in the family. What if the sons do not get along? What if their wives want them to take the inheritance to their own families? If Farid dies married, he can leave forty percent of what he has to his wife. The rest is split among his children. I believe his plan is for one of his unmarried sons to then marry Aisha and together they will run the family business."

Daphne looked outraged. "Great. So she's to be sold, not once but twice? That's pleasant."

"You are missing the point. Farid doesn't want her for himself."

"I get the point exactly. Either way she's been given in marriage to someone she doesn't know or care about. And she's in love with someone else. What about that?"

Why did Daphne refuse to see the sense of the union? "She could be a wealthy widow in her own right in just a few months," he said. "She wouldn't have to marry one of the sons if she didn't want to."

"Are you saying she should agree to this? That in a few months, she could bring in what's his name—"

"Barak."

"Right. She could bring in Barak? That's terrible, too."

Murat shook his head. "Marriage isn't just about love, Daphne. It is about political and financial gain."

"I see that now. What are you going to do?"

"What do you want me to do?"

She raised her eyebrows. "It's my choice?"

"Yes. Consider it a wedding gift."

"I want Aisha to have the choice to follow her heart. I want her to be free to marry Barak."

"Despite what I have told you?"

She stared at him. "Not despite it, but *because* of it."

"And years from now, when she and Barak are struggling to feed their many children, do you not think she will look back on what she could have had and feel regret?"

"Not if she loves him."

"Love does not put food on the table." Love was not practical. Why did women consider it so very important?

"I want her to be with Barak," Daphne insisted.

"As you wish."

He led her back to the dais and took his seat. Aisha had been crying, and her father looked furious. Farid seemed resigned, while the young lover, Barak, attempted to appear confident even as his shaking knees gave him away.

Murat looked at Aisha. "You chose your petitioner well. Daphne is my bride and, as such, I can refuse her nothing. I grant your request, but listen to me well. You are angry that your father would sell you to a man so many years older. You see only today and tomorrow. There is all of your future to consider. Farid is a man of great honor. Will you not consider him?"

Aisha shook her head. "I love Barak," she said stubbornly.

Murat glanced at the boy and hoped he would be worthy of her devotion. "Very well. Aisha is free to marry Barak."

Her father started to sputter, but Murat quelled him with a quick glare.

"I give them three camels in celebration of their marriage. May their union be long and healthy."

Aisha began to cry. Barak bowed low several times, then gathered his fiancée in his arms and whispered to her.

Murat turned to the angry father. "I give you three camels, as well, in compensation for what you have lost in your deal with Farid."

Murat knew that Farid had offered five camels, but he wasn't about to give the father more than he gave the couple.

Finally he looked at Farid. "When it is your time, your family may bring you to the mountain of the kings."

The crowd gasped. The honor of being buried in such a place was unheard of.

Farid bowed low. "I give thanks to the good and wise prince. I wish that I would live to see you rule as king."

"I wish that, as well. Go in peace, my friend." Murat then waited as they all left.

"Who is next?" he asked.

Daphne stayed quiet during dinner. Murat seemed tense and restless. He had been that way since returning to their tent.

When the last plate had been cleared away, she put down her napkin and smiled. "I want to thank you again for what you did today."

"I do not wish to speak of it."

"Why not? You made Aisha very happy."

"I granted the wish of a spoiled girl. She is too young to know her heart. Do you really believe she will love that boy for very long? And then what? She will be poor and hate her husband. At least her father sought to secure her future."

Daphne couldn't believe Murat actually thought the marriage of a sixteen-year-old to a man four times her age was a good thing.

"Her father wanted to sell her," she said in outrage. "That's pretty horrible."

"I agree, the father's motives were suspect, but Farid was a good man, and she would have had financial security."

"Right. To be sold again into marriage with one of his sons."

"She might have fallen in love with one as well."

"Or she might not."

Murat stared at her as if she were a complete idiot. "As a widow, she would be free to marry whomever she liked. No one could force her into the marriage."

"Gee, so it's only the one time. That makes it all right."

He turned away. "You do not understand our ways and our customs."

"I don't think it's that, at all. I think you're angry because I petitioned for the girl."

He stood and glared at her. "I am angry because my wife took the side of a foolish young woman and I did as she requested. I am angry because I believe Aisha chose poorly."

He stopped talking, but she sensed there was more. Something much larger than Aisha and her problems. But what?

Murat walked away from the table into the sitting area of the tent. She followed him.

"You gave a woman her freedom, Murat. What is so terrible about that?"

"What is so terrible about our marriage?" he asked. "Why do you seek to escape?"

Was that it? Did he see her in Aisha?

"I'm not in love with anyone else," she told him. "I would have told you if I was."

"I never considered the matter," he said, but she wasn't sure she believed him.

"Being married to you isn't terrible," she said slowly, still not sure what they were arguing about. "My objection is to the way it happened. You never asked."

"I did and you refused."

"Right. And you went ahead and married me, anyway. You can't do that."

"I can and I did."

She couldn't believe it. "You say that like it's a good thing."

"Achieving my goal is always a good thing." He moved toward her. "We are married now. You will accept that."

"I won't."

"And if you carry my child?"

Daphne pressed both hands to her stomach. They should know fairly quickly. "I'm not."

"You are not yet sure." He loomed over her. "Make no mistake. Any child will stay here. You may leave if you like."

"I would never leave my baby behind."

"Then the decision is made for you."

She wanted to scream. She wanted to demand that he understand. Why was he being so stubborn and hateful?

"I won't sleep with you again," she said.

"So you told me before, yet look what happened."

She felt as if he'd slapped her. "Is that all that night meant to you? Was it just a chance to prove me wrong?"

"Your word means very little."

She turned away, both because it hurt to look at him and to keep him from seeing the tears in her eyes.

"I'm sorry I came on this trip with you," she said. "I wish I'd never left the palace."

"If you prefer to be back there, it can be arranged."

"Then go ahead and do it."

Chapter Thirteen

Murat left the tent without looking back. Daphne wasn't sure what to do, so she stayed where she was. Less than forty minutes later she heard the sound of a helicopter approaching. One of the security agents came and got her, and before she could figure out what had happened, she found herself being whisked up into the night sky.

The glow of all the campfires seemed to stretch out for miles. She pressed her fingers against the cool glass window and wished for a second chance to take back the angry words she and Murat had exchanged.

He'd hurt her. She refused to believe he'd spent last night making love with her only to prove a point. Their time together had to have meant something to him, too. But why wouldn't he admit it? And why had he let her go so easily?

Just like before, she thought sadly, when she'd broken their engagement. He'd let her go without trying to stop her then, too.

The trip back to the palace took less than thirty minutes. She made her way to the suite she shared with Murat and let herself inside.

Everything was as she'd left it, except that the man she'd married was gone. She had no idea when he would return or what they would say to each other when he did.

She wandered through the room, touching pictures and small personal things, his pen or a pair of cuff links. She missed him. How crazy was that?

Something brushed against her leg. She looked down and saw one of the king's cats rubbing against her. She picked up the animal and held it close. The warm body and soft purr comforted her. Still holding the cat, she sank down on the sofa and began to cry.

"So, how was it?" Billie asked the next morning as she threw herself on one of the sofas. "I can't imagine riding through the desert. Flying would get you there much faster."

Cleo sat next to her sister-in-law and swatted her with a pillow. "The journey is the point. When you fly you never get to see anything."

"Yeah, but you get there fast." Billie grinned. "I'm into the whole speed thing."

"And we didn't know that." Cleo fluffed her short, blond hair. "Did you have a good time? I thought you would have been gone longer."

"It was great," Daphne said, hoping the cold compresses she'd used earlier had taken down some of the swelling around her eyes. Crying herself to sleep never made for a pretty morning after. "I enjoyed the riding, and the tent was incredible. Like something out of *Arabian Nights*. There were dozens of rugs underfoot, hanging lights and a really huge bathtub."

Billie smoothed the front of her skirt over her very pregnant belly. "Tubs can be fun. Anything you want to talk about?"

"Not really," Daphne said, trying to keep things light. "The cultural differences were interesting. I enjoyed watching Murat work with the council."

"You weren't gone long enough to get to the City of Thieves, were you?" Cleo asked, then covered her mouth. She winced and dropped her hand. "Tell me Murat told you about it. I *so* don't want to be shot at dawn."

"Not to worry. He did. And, no, I didn't make it there."

She'd been looking forward to it, too. She hadn't really wanted to leave the caravan. She'd acted impulsively in the moment. Why had she reacted so strongly last night? Why had he been so willing to fight with her and let her go?

"I wanted to see Sabrina and meet Zara," she said.

"They're both very cool," Cleo said. "You'll have time later. Or we could plan a lunch. The show-off here can fly us out there in a helicopter."

"Cleo's just jealous because I'm talented," Billie said with a grin.

"It's disgusting," Cleo admitted. "And she brags about it all the time."

"Do not."

"Do, too."

Daphne felt a wave of longing. These women weren't sisters, yet they were closer than Daphne had ever been to anyone in her family. If she stayed, she could be a part of this, as well.

If.

Cleo shifted to the edge of the sofa and laced her hands together. "I'm not sure how to say this delicately, so I'm just going to blurt it out. Something's up. You're obviously unhappy. You're back early and Murat isn't with you. Given how you two came to be married and all, Billie and I were wondering if you wanted to talk. You don't have to, but we're here to listen."

Daphne bit her lower lip. She did want to confide in someone, but… "You're both in very different places."

"Okay." Billie looked confused. "I know you mean more than us sitting on the sofa and you sitting on a chair."

Daphne couldn't help laughing. Cleo stared at Billie and rolled her eyes.

"She means we're in love with our husbands and she's not sure she is." She glanced at Daphne. "Is that right?"

"Yes."

"I knew that," Billie said. "I guess you have a point. But Murat isn't so bad, is he?"

"I don't know."

Daphne realized it was the truth. That while she hated what he'd done to her—how he'd used circumstances and manipulated her to get what he wanted—she wasn't sure how she felt about the man himself.

"There's the whole 'going to be queen thing,'" Cleo said. "Does that count for anything?"

"Of course it doesn't," Billie said. "Daphne has more depth than that."

Cleo sighed. "I actually wasn't asking you."

"Do you two ever stop arguing?"

"Sure," Cleo said. "When we're not together." She linked arms with her sister-in-law. "Billie and I have fabulous chemistry. I love sniping at her more than almost anything. It's like a sporting event."

Billie nodded. "Jefri and Sadik have gotten used to never getting a word in edgewise when the four of us have dinner."

"Shopping is a complete nightmare for the guys," Cleo said. "We have credit cards and we know how to use them." She disentangled her arm. "How can you not want to be a part of this?"

"You're tempting me."

"More than being queen?"

Daphne curled up in the chair and leaned her head against the back. "I remember when I was here before. I was so young, just twenty, and engaged to Murat. The thought of being queen really terrified me. I was sort of a serious kid, and I knew there would be huge responsibilities. I didn't think I could ever manage."

"And now?" Billie asked.

"I don't know. There's a part of me that thinks I could really help Murat. He doesn't have anyone he can confide in. Not to say anything against his brothers."

Cleo and Billie looked at each other, then at her. "I know what you mean," Cleo said. "Sadik is in meetings with Murat and that kind of thing, but he only has to worry about his own area of expertise. Murat has all the responsibility. King Hassan is handing over more and more of the day-to-day ruling. So a wife he trusted could help lighten the load."

"Maybe. I think I could make a difference. As much as I don't get along with my family, I have to admit I've been raised to be married to a powerful man."

"How nice not to have to learn what fork goes where," Billie grumbled.

Daphne grinned. "It's a skill that has served me well."

"So you're okay with the office of queen, which means the problem lies with Murat himself," Cleo said. "I think you're going to have to solve that one on your own."

Daphne knew she was right. "I appreciate the support."

Billie slipped to the edge of the sofa and leaned close. "I'm about to say something I shouldn't, but I have to because I feel bad about what happened. Cleo, you can't tell anyone. Not Zara or Sadik or anyone."

"I won't. I promise."

Billie nodded and stared at Daphne. "If you want to leave, just tell me. I can get you on a plane and back to the States in five hours."

Daphne thought of the long flight over. "How is that possible?"

Billie grinned. "We'd take a jet. No luggage room, but plenty of speed. I need an hour's notice. That's all. If it gets bad and you need to run, I'll take you."

Daphne felt her eyes start to burn. These women didn't even know her and yet they were willing to offer so much support.

"I appreciate the offer. I doubt things will come to that, but if they do, I know where to find you."

The women left after lunch. Daphne walked into the gardens and admired the bronze artwork there. Her favorite piece stood in the center of a large, shallow pool. A life-size statue of a desert warrior on the back of a stallion. As she studied the power in the horse's flanks and the fierce expression on the warrior's face, her fingers itched to be back in clay. She wanted to make something as wonderful as this.

"If only I had that much talent," she said ruefully. But she still enjoyed the process. She had time for that here. Time for many things she enjoyed.

She sat on a bench and raised her face to the sun. Now that she was alone, she could admit the truth. She missed Murat.

Despite his imperious ways and how he made her crazy, she missed him. She wanted to hear his voice and laughter. She wanted to watch him work and know that his strength would one day be their children's. She wanted his touch on her body and her hands on his.

So when exactly had she stopped hating enough to

start caring about him? Or had she ever hated him? What did she do now? Accept what had happened and move on?

Her heart told her no. That giving in would mean a lifetime of never being more than an object in his life. She wanted more than his rules and wishes. She wanted him to care. To woo her. To love her.

She dropped her chin to her chest as the truth washed over her. She wanted him to love her enough to come after her, instead of always letting her go so easily. She wanted to know it was safe to fall in love with him.

But how? How did she convince a man who believed he was invincible that it was all right to be vulnerable once in a while? How did she get him to open up to her? How did she get him to give her his heart?

She touched her stomach. If she was pregnant, she had her lifetime to figure it out. If she wasn't, then time might be very, very short.

Which did she want? If she had to choose right now, which would it be?

Murat couldn't remember the last time he'd been drunk. He usually didn't allow himself to indulge. As crown prince it was his responsibility to be alert at all times. But tonight he couldn't bring himself to care.

He'd waited all day for Daphne to return, but she had not. Even as he and his people rode deeper into the desert, he watched the sky for a helicopter that did not come.

He should never have ordered the helicopter. He knew that now. If he'd ignored her outburst, she would still be with him. But her reluctance to accept their marriage as something that could not be changed made him furious. How dare she question his authority? He had honored her by marrying her. It was done, and they needed to simply move forward.

But did Daphne see it that way? Was she logical and grateful? No. She constantly fought him, making life difficult, looking at him with accusations in her eyes.

He reached for the bottle of cognac and poured more into his glass. The smooth liquid burned its way down his throat.

Time, he told himself. He had time. Unless she wasn't pregnant. Then she would leave as she had before.

Do not think about that, he told himself. She would not leave again. He wouldn't permit it. Nor would the king.

The sound of muted footsteps forced his gaze from the fire. He watched as several of the tribal elders approached, bowed, then joined him by the fire.

"Will you be attending the camel races tomorrow, Your Highness?" one of the men asked.

Murat shrugged. He had wanted Daphne to see them, but now… "Perhaps. After the morning petitions."

"The council sessions went well today," another said. "Your justice, as always, provides a safe haven for your people."

Murat knew the compliments were just a way to ease into the conversation the old men *really* wanted to have with him. He thought of how Daphne would listen attentively, all the while secretly urging them to get to the point.

She played the games of his office well. She understood the importance of ritual and tradition, even when she didn't agree with it. Unlike many women he had met, she would have patience for tribal councils and diplomatic sessions and negotiations.

"You made an interesting choice with Aisha," the first man said. "To give her to Barak."

He decided to help them cut to the chase. "The decision was a gift to my bride. It was her request that the young lovers be allowed to start a new life."

"Ah." The elders nodded to each other.

"Of course," one of them said, "a woman sees with her heart. It has always been the way. Their tender emotions make them stewards of our households and our children. But when it comes to matters of importance, they know to defer to the man."

Not all of them, Murat thought as he took another drink. He wondered what Daphne would make of being called the steward of his household. The title implied employment and a distance between the parties far greater than in a marriage.

One of the elders cleared his throat. "We could not help but notice the princess has left us. We hope she was not taken ill."

"No. Her health continues to be excellent."

"Good. That is good."

Silence descended. Murat stared into the flames and wished the old men would get to the point, then leave him alone.

"She is American."

"I had noticed that," Murat said dryly.

"Of course, Your Highness. It is just that American women can be strong-willed and stubborn. They do not always understand the subtleties of our ways." The man speaking held up both hands in a gesture of surrender. "Princess Daphne is an angel among women."

"An angel," the others echoed.

"Not the word I would have chosen," Murat muttered. She was more like the devil—always prodding at him. If he wasn't careful, she would soon be leading him around by the nose.

"Have you tried beating her?" one of the men asked.

Murat straightened and glared. The old man shrank back.

"A thousand pardons, Your Highness."

Murat rose and pointed into the darkness. "Go," he commanded. "Go and never darken my path again."

The man gasped. To be an elder and told to never show his face to the prince was unheard of. The old man stood, trembling, then crept away into the night.

Murat sank down by the fire and looked at each of the six remaining men. "Does anyone else wish to suggest I beat my wife?"

No one spoke.

"I know you are here to offer aid and advice," he said. "In the absence of the king, you are my surrogate family. But make no mistake—Princess Daphne is my wife. She is the one I have chosen to be the mother of my children. Her blood will join with mine and our heirs will rule Bahania for a thousand more years. Remember that when you speak of her."

The men nodded.

Murat turned his attention to the fire. As much as Daphne frustrated him, he had never thought to hit her. What would that accomplish? He already knew he was physically stronger. Old fools.

"Do you know why the princess left us?" one of the men asked in a soft, timid voice.

Interesting question. Murat realized he did not know. One minute they had been fighting and the next she was gone.

"She angered me. I spoke in haste," he admitted.

"You could demand her return," a man said.

Murat knew that he could. But to what end? To have her staring at him with anger in her eyes? That was not how he wished to spend his days. Yet to spend them without her was equally unpleasant.

"The prince wishes her to return on her own," another man said.

Murat squinted at him through the flames. He was small and very old. Wizened.

"The elder speaks wisely," he said. "I wish her to return to me of her own accord."

The tiny man nodded. "But she will not. Women are like the night jasmine. They offer sweetness in the shadows, when most of the world slumbers. Other flowers give their scent in the day, when all can enjoy them. A very stubborn flower."

"So now what?" Murat asked.

"Ignore her," one man said. "Give her time to get lonely. She will be so grateful to see you when you do return that she will bend to your will."

An interesting possibility, Murat thought. Although Daphne wasn't the bending type.

"You could take a mistress," another suggested. "One of the young beauties who travel with us. A man does not miss the main course when there are many sweets at the table."

He shook his head. Not only was he not interested in any other woman, he had given his word. He would honor his vows until his death.

"A flower needs tending," the little old man said. "Left alone it grows wild, or withers and dies."

The other elders stared at him. "You wish Prince Murat to go to her? To go after a woman?"

Murat was equally surprised by the advice. "I am Crown Prince Murat of Bahania."

The old man smiled in the darkness. "I do not believe her ignorance about your title and position are at the heart of the problem."

Daphne had said much the same thing.

"The gardener yields to the flower," he continued. "He kneels on the ground and plunges his hands deep in the soil. His reward is a beauty and strength that lasts through the harshest of storms."

The cognac had muddled Murat's brain to the point that the flower analogy wasn't making any sense. "You want me to what?"

"Go to her," the old man said. "Provide her with fertile soil and she will bloom for you."

If Daphne grew anything it would be thorns, and she would use them to stab him.

Go to her? Give in?

Never. He was a prince. A sheik. She was a mere woman.

He reached for the bottle, then stood abruptly and stalked into his tent without saying a word. When he reached the bedroom, he stood in the silence and inhaled the scent of Daphne's perfume.

How he ached for her.

"Go to her," the old man had said.

And then what?

Daphne stood her ground with the servants and basically bullied them into helping her set up her art table and supplies in the garden of the harem.

"But the crown prince said you were not to return here," one of the men said, practically wringing his hands.

"I'm not moving in," she said, trying to be as patient as possible. "I just want to work here. It's quiet, and the light is perfect."

With a combination of prodding, carrying most of the stuff herself and threatening to call the king, she got her supplies in place and finally went to work.

The clay felt good against her bare hands. She had a vision for what she wanted the piece to be, but wasn't sure if her talent could keep pace with her imagination. Sleeplessness made her a little clumsy—she'd spent the past three nights tossing and turning—but she reworked what she had to and kept moving forward with the piece.

The sun had nearly set when she realized she'd had nothing to eat or drink all day. Dizziness made her sink onto the bench in the garden. But the swimming head and gnawing stomach were more than worth it, she thought as she stared at the work she'd accomplished so far. She could—

"I forbade you to come to this place."

The unexpected voice made her jump. She stood and turned, only to see Murat stalking toward her.

"I left specific instructions," he said. "Who allowed you to return to the harem?"

He wore a long cloak over his riding clothes. The fabric billowed out behind him, making him seem even taller and more powerful than she remembered.

She'd missed him. The past seventy-two hours had passed so slowly. Only getting back to her art had kept her sane. She longed to hear him, see him, touch him, but now as he stalked toward her, she wanted to ball up the unused part of her clay and throw it at him.

"I'm not giving you any names," she told him. "And for your information, I'm simply using the garden as my art studio. I can't get the right light in our suite, and the main gardens are too busy. All those people distract me. The harem isn't used, so I'm not in anyone's way."

He glared at her. "You are still living upstairs with me?"

"I was, but I have to tell you, I'm seriously rethinking that decision."

She wiped her hands on a towel and walked away.

Murat watched her go. On the helicopter flight back to the palace, he had thought about all the things he would say to Daphne when he saw her. They had been soft, conciliatory words designed to make her melt into his arms. When she wasn't in their suite, he had gone looking for her, only to be told she was in the harem.

He had thought that meant she had moved back, but he had been wrong. Now what?

He walked out of the garden only to find his father entering the harem. King Hassan shook his head.

"I just passed your wife. She seemed to be very annoyed about something."

"I am aware of that."

His father sighed. "Murat, you are my firstborn. I could not wish for a better heir. You have been born to power and you will lead our people with strength and greatness. But when it comes to Daphne, you seem to stumble at every turn. You must do better. I worked too hard to get her back here and into your life to have you destroy things now."

Chapter Fourteen

Daphne reached the suite she shared with Murat in record time, but once there she didn't know what to do with herself. She wanted to burn off some of the excess energy flowing through her. She wanted to throw something, but everything breakable was far too valuable and beautiful.

After pacing the length of the living room twice, she stopped by the sofa where one of the king's cats slept. Petting a cat or dog was supposed to be calming, she reminded herself. She stroked the animal and scratched under its chin, but still her blood bubbled within her.

"Of all the arrogant, terrible, hard-hearted men on the planet. To think I *missed* him." Talk about stupid.

"Never again," she vowed. "Never ever again will I think one pleasant or kind thought about—"

The door to the suite opened and Murat walked in. She stood and glared at him. "Don't even try to talk to me. I'm furious."

Murat closed the door and walked toward her. "I just spoke with my father."

"Unless you're going to tell me he's agreed to us getting a divorce, I'm not interested."

He unfastened his cloak and draped it across a chair. "He took me to task for annoying you."

"Really? Well, he's a very smart man."

Murat ignored her comment. "He was most disappointed we were not getting along better, especially in light of all his effort to bring us back together."

"I…" She blinked. "What?"

He motioned to the sofa. She sank down next to the cat she'd been petting and waited while Murat sat across from her.

"He told me that he has been waiting a long time for me to pick a bride. When I seemed reluctant, despite the various women in my life, he decided there must be some reason from my past. He made a study of my previous relationships and kept coming back to you and our broken engagement."

"That's right," she said. "Broken and not fixed."

"When he discovered you were unmarried, as well, he decided to bring us back together to see what happened."

"That's not possible." She refused to believe it. "I

wasn't brought here for you. I came because of Brittany…"

She felt her mouth drop open and quickly pressed her lips together. Sensible Brittany who, out of the blue, suddenly decided to marry a man she'd never met and move half a world away.

"She was in on it," she breathed.

"Apparently. No one else in your family knew. My father found out that the two of you were close and contacted her. Together they hatched this plan."

"No." Daphne shook her head. "She would never do that to me. She's not that good a liar."

"Apparently she is." He motioned to the phone. "Feel free to check with her."

"I will." She picked up the receiver and punched in the number for her sister's house. When the maid answered, Daphne asked for Brittany.

"Hey, Aunt Daphne, how's it going? College starts in ten days and I'm *so* excited. Mom's still annoyed with you, but she's getting over it. She thinks I should start dating the governor's son. He's okay, I guess, but not really my type. What's up with you?"

Despite Murat's revelation and the possibility that Brittany had been a part of some plan, Daphne couldn't help smiling as she listened to her niece's monologue.

"I'm good," she said. "I've missed you."

"I've missed you, too. Think I could come over there for winter break? We could go shopping and ride a camel. It would be fun. Plus I'd love to finally meet Murat."

"I'll bet you would. Sure. You can come here. But first I need to ask you something. Did the King of Bahania get in touch with you a couple of months ago?"

Brittany sucked in a breath. "What?"

"Did he want you to pretend to be willing to marry Murat to lure me back to Bahania? Brittany, I want the truth. This is very important."

The teenager sighed. "Maybe. Okay, sort of. Yes. He called and talked. He was really nice. Not at all like I imagined a king would be. He said that the reason you hadn't fallen in love with any other guy was that you still loved Murat but you wouldn't admit it to anyone. Not even to yourself. At first I told him he was crazy, but then I thought about it for a while and I decided he might be right."

"Oh, God."

"So I said I would marry Murat so that you'd get all worried and stuff. Which you did. I felt bad on the plane. I was acting so shallow, but it was important. And then you went to see Murat and I came home."

"Did anyone else know?"

"Are you kidding? Mom would never have agreed. I sort of felt bad about how excited she got over me marrying a prince and all. But, sheesh, how could she take it seriously? He's so old."

"Practically in his dotage."

"But it worked out great. Right?" Brittany sounded slightly unsure of herself. "I mean you married him and everything. You're happy, Aunt Daphne, aren't you? I'd never hurt you for anything. You know that, right?"

"Of course I know that. I love you, Brittany. You'll always be my favorite niece."

Brittany laughed. "I'm still your only niece, but I know what you mean. How did you find out?"

"The king told Murat."

"Was he furious?"

"He was unamused."

"But you're okay."

Daphne thought about the young woman she'd loved for eighteen years. Whatever Brittany had done, she'd acted out of love and concern.

"I'm completely fine. I love you."

"I love you, too. Let's talk soon."

"Absolutely. Bye."

Daphne hung up the phone and looked at her husband. "It's true. Brittany was a part of it from the beginning. She pretended to be interested in marrying you to get me on the plane."

He leaned back in the chair and closed his eyes. "And I played right into my father's hands by losing my temper and locking you in the harem."

Not to mention marrying her against her will, but she didn't say that.

"I'm pretty mad," Daphne admitted. "But I also feel kind of stupid. I can't believe those two were able to trick us like that."

Murat looked sheepish. "It does not say much about our powers of reasoning. I kept telling my father I was not interested in a teenage bride, but he insisted she be brought over for my inspection."

"I got all maternal and demanding," she said. "I was terrified Brittany was throwing away her life." She glanced at him. "Not that life as your wife is so terrible, but it wasn't right for her."

"Believe me, I did not want her, either."

Daphne felt as if she'd shown up for a big party only to find out the celebration had been the previous night. She felt both awkward and let down.

"So, um, now what?" she asked.

He straightened. "I should not have yelled at you before," he said, "when I found you in the garden. As I told you, I thought you had moved out of our rooms."

Had Crown Prince Murat of Bahania just apologized? "I know. I'm sorry. I didn't mean to give that impression. I just wanted to work with my clay."

"As you should. I enjoy the things you create." He smiled. "Even when they mock me."

Something tightened her heart. She felt happy and nervous at the same time. She cleared her throat.

"I didn't really want to leave. Before. Our trip into the desert. All this is so confusing and I reacted to that and what happened with Aisha. I don't always know what I'm feeling. Then we were fighting, and you said I could go and I said I wanted to and then I was here."

He stood and crossed to the sofa, where he sat next to her. He took both her hands in his.

"I missed you, Daphne. So much so that the tribal elders came to offer me advice."

She liked him touching her, but even more than that, she liked the sincerity in his gaze and that he'd missed her.

"What did they say?"

"One suggested I beat you. I sent him away."

"Thank you. I wouldn't respond well to a beating."

"I am many things, but I am not a bully."

"I know." He would never use his position of strength to take advantage of someone physically.

"One thought I should take a mistress."

Her stomach clenched. The sharp pain made her gasp. "What did you decide?"

He pulled one hand free and touched her cheek. "I want no other woman. Even if I chose not to be bound by my vows, I would still be true."

The pain eased.

"Finally, the oldest of the elders told me you were like a flower and that I should tend you in your garden."

She frowned. "What does that mean?"

"I was hoping you could tell me."

"I haven't a clue."

He stared deeply into her eyes as he slid his hand from her cheek to her mouth. He brushed his fingers against her lips. "Stay with me."

She didn't know if he meant that night or for always. Her heart told her to give in, that in time Murat would learn to yield, while her head reminded her that to stay based on an expected change in behavior was foolish.

Could she accept Murat as he was? Could she be with him knowing he would overrule her at will and never let her be an equal in their relationship? It wouldn't take much for her to fall in love with him again, but would he return those feelings? Could a man who thought of her as a mere woman ever give his heart?

"Stay," he repeated, then saved her from answering by kissing her.

She surrendered to his touch, still not sure how far to hold her heart out of reach.

"You can't be serious," Daphne said over dinner, several days later.

"It will never happen. The Americans are not ready to elect a woman president."

"But if they did…"

Murat shrugged. "You expect me to meet with a woman as an equal?"

"Of course. Didn't your father meet with Prime Minister Margaret Thatcher?"

"Perhaps. I am too young to recall." He cut into his meat. "You seem agitated."

"I'm trying to figure out what I should throw at you."

He raised his eyebrows. "Such threats of violence over a simple discussion. You see why women are not good in politics. There is too much emotion."

She narrowed her gaze, just as she caught the twitch at the corner of his mouth.

"You're toying with me," she said, both relieved and determined to get him back.

"Perhaps."

"I should have known. You *would* meet with a woman president."

"Of course, but I doubt it will happen during my lifetime. Perhaps our son will have to deal with the situation."

She was about to say that any son of hers would respect women and their rights, only to stop herself at the last minute. Perhaps that wasn't the best conversational tack to take. Not when the truce between them was so fragile.

It had been three days since Murat had returned from the desert. Three days in which she'd slept in his bed, made love with him and toyed with the idea of simply accepting her marriage as permanent.

Her feelings grew, and she knew that the point of no return was at hand. If she fell in love with him, she wouldn't want to go, regardless of their past.

"You grow quiet," he said, setting down his knife and fork. "Are you troubled about some matter?"

"No."

Troubled didn't begin to describe her emotions.

"At the risk of starting another battle between us," he said. "It has been nearly three weeks since the first time we made love. You have not started your period."

"I know. I'm late."

She watched him carefully, but his expression didn't change. She wondered if he was crowing on the inside.

"Do you think you are pregnant?"

She wasn't sure. "I don't feel any different, but I don't know if I should. I could get a pregnancy test and take it if you would like."

"What would you prefer to do?"

"Wait a few more days. Sometimes stress upsets my cycle."

She'd certainly had her share of that in the past month or so.

She expected him to insist that she find out that very evening. Instead he nodded. "As you wish."

She couldn't help smiling. "Are you unwell?"

"No. Why do you ask?"

"You never give in on anything."

He sighed. "I am doing my best to nurture the flower in my garden. Do you feel nurtured?"

She held in a laugh. He *was* trying hard. "Nearly every minute of every day."

"Ah. Now you mock me again." He carefully put his napkin on the table and rose. "I think my flower needs a good pruning."

He had an evil gleam in his eye. Daphne stood and started to back away.

"Murat, no."

"You do not know what I have in mind."

"I can tell it's going to be bad. Now stop this. Think of your delicate flower. You have to be nice."

He made a noise low in his throat and started toward her. She shrieked and ducked away. In a matter of seconds he caught her.

In truth, she didn't mind being dragged against him. Even as he pressed his mouth to hers, he caught her up in his arms and carried her into their bedroom.

"What about dinner?" she asked when he set her on her feet next to their bed and reached for the zipper at the back of her dress.

"I am hungry for other things."

* * *

Murat worked through the messages left for him by his assistant. On the one hand he appreciated his new and warm relationship with Daphne. On the other, he found his workdays long and dull when compared with the nights he spent in her company. While his ministers spoke of the oil reserves and the state of the currency-exchange market, he thought of her body pressing against his and the way she cried out his name when he pleasured her.

Things were as they should be, he thought contentedly. She had made her peace with her situation. Now they would grow together as husband and wife. There would be many children and a long and happy life together.

His assistant knocked on the door.

"Come in," Murat called.

Fouad entered with several folders. "The king wishes to change your lunch meeting to this afternoon. It seems he is to dine with Princess Calah."

Murat smiled at the thought of his father having lunch with the charming toddler. "That is excellent. Have the kitchen send up a second meal to my suite. I will dine with my wife."

"Very good, sir." Fouad set the folders on the desk. "I have had a call from our media office. Princess Daphne turned down an interview request from an American women's magazine. They were surprised, as the publication is known for honest reporting. They were interested in making a connection with her, sir, not doing an exposé."

"Perhaps she is not aware that such interviews are welcome. I will mention it to her."

"Yes, sir."

Fouad completed his business and left. Forty minutes later Murat walked into his suite to find the table set for two.

"This is a surprise," Daphne said as she walked into the living room, then crossed the tile floor to kiss him. "A very pleasant one."

"My father and I were to have lunch, but he chose instead to dine with a very attractive young woman. So I took the opportunity to spend some time with you."

Daphne led him to the table. "Calah?" she asked.

"Of course."

"He loves that little girl."

Murat's gaze dropped to Daphne's flat stomach. Did *his* child grow there? So far she had not gotten her period, nor had she offered to take a pregnancy test. He had decided to let her make the decision. If she was with child, he would soon know.

They sat across from each other and spoke about their morning. As she served them each salad, he mentioned the interview with the American magazine.

"You are welcome to speak with them," he said. "I will not forbid it."

"My flower heart trembles at your generosity," she said in a teasing voice.

He pretended to scowl. "I can see I have been too lenient with you."

"Not to worry, Murat. If I had wanted to give the interview I would have. But I wasn't interested."

"Why not?"

Instead of answering, she mentioned that Billie and Cleo were planning a day trip to the City of Thieves and that she wanted to join them.

"Of course Billie wants to fly us there herself, and the king has said that would not be allowed. She's too far along in her pregnancy."

He watched her as she spoke, noting a slight shadow in her eyes.

"Daphne, why did you refuse the interview?"

"It's not important."

Which meant that it was. "I will not rest until you tell me."

She set down her fork. "If you must know, I didn't know what to say. This was for a big bridal issue they're doing in a few months. They're collecting romantic stories from different couples and they wanted to talk about how we met and fell in love. I didn't think it was a good idea to tell them the truth. That you locked me in the harem then married me against my will while I was unconscious. Rather than having to make up something, I declined the interview."

She continued speaking, changing the subject to the upcoming trip to the City of Thieves, but he could not hear her. The impact of what she had said—a bald statement of a truth he knew well—seemed to render him immobile.

For the first time he understood what she had been

trying to tell him all along. That he had held her captive, like a common criminal. Of course the quarters were luxurious and she had not been mistreated in the least, but he had locked her away. Then, knowing she wanted nothing to do with him, he had taken advantage of a medical condition to force her into marriage.

Had he given her the choice, she would have refused him. She would have left. She was not with him because she wanted to be.

The truth sliced through him like a knife. He had always known that she complained about his treatment, but he had told himself it was all simply the meaningless chatter of a woman with too much time on her hands. He had not considered she had cause for her complaints. Had she been a stranger and appeared with her petition while he had been in the desert, he would have freed her from her marriage and locked away the man in question.

The phone rang in the suite. Daphne excused herself to answer it. Murat took advantage of her distraction to leave the table. He indicated he was going back to his office and she nodded. On his way out, he noticed a new clay sculpture on a table.

Two lovers, he thought. Bodies entwined, arms reaching. The sheer passion of the piece took his breath away. It gave him hope. But as he moved closer, he saw the lovers were faceless.

Did she not see him in the role, or did she wish for another man? He knew he pleased her in bed—her body told the tale all too well for him to think otherwise. But was that enough? Did claiming a woman's body mean anything when a man could not lay claim to her mind or her heart?

Chapter Fifteen

Daphne sat alone in the suite and stared out at the perfect view. The light wind had cleared the air enough for her to see all the way to Lucia-Serrat. Two cats dozed next to her on the sofa, their small, warm bodies providing a comforting presence. But it wasn't enough to heal the ache in her heart.

She wasn't pregnant. Proof had arrived an hour before.

She'd suspected, of course. That was why she'd resisted taking a pregnancy test. She hadn't wanted to *know*. She hadn't wanted to have to choose.

Funny how a month ago she would have been delighted with the chance to escape. She would have already had it out with Murat and been busy packing her bags. But now everything was different.

Instead of relief, she felt a bone-crushing disappointment, which told her a truth she'd tried to deny for a long time—she didn't want to go.

Murat wasn't perfect—he would never understand that what he'd done to her was wrong. He would never see her as a partner, but that didn't stop her from loving him. She wanted to be with him, regardless of his faults. She wanted their children to have his strength and stubbornness. She wanted to be a part of his world and his history. She loved Bahania nearly as much as she loved its heir and she didn't want to go.

Since he'd returned from the desert they hadn't discussed their future. No doubt he assumed her silence meant agreement, but that wasn't her way. She wanted to tell him what she'd decided, even if that meant listening to him say how he'd known what was best all along. She wanted to feel his arms around her as he pulled her close and kissed her. She wanted to take him to bed and get started on making their firstborn.

She stood and walked out of the suite with the intent of finding him in his office. But he wasn't there. His assistant said that he had gone for a walk.

Daphne went to the main garden and saw him sitting on one of the stone benches. His shoulders were slumped as he stared at the ground. An air of profound sadness surrounded him.

"Murat?"

He looked toward her and smiled. His expression brightened and the sadness disappeared as if it had never been. In response, her heart fluttered and she wondered how she had ever fooled herself into thinking she didn't love this man with every fiber of her being.

"I've been looking for you," she said as she walked closer.

"You have found me." He shifted to make room for her, then studied her as she sat next to him. He tucked her long hair behind her ear. "As always, your beauty astounds me."

"I'm not all that."

"Yes, you are."

He sounded so serious, she thought, wondering what was going on.

"Unlike many who shine only for a short time," he continued, "you will be beautiful for decades. Even as time steals the luster of your youth, you will gleam like a diamond in the desert."

"That's very poetic and very unlike you." She frowned. "What's going on?"

"I have been sitting here thinking about us. Our marriage."

Her pulse rate increased. "Me, too. I have to tell you something." She paused, not sure how to say it all—that she loved him, that she wanted to stay and make their marriage work. But the words that came out were, "I'm not pregnant."

He didn't react. His gaze never wavered, his hand on her remained still.

"You are sure?" he asked quietly.

"Very." She waited for him to say something else, and when he didn't, she leaned closer. "What's wrong?

Shouldn't you tell me you're disappointed? That we'll be trying again soon?"

He drew in a breath. "I would have. Before. Now I know that this is for the best."

She jerked back as if he'd slapped her. "What?"

"It is for the best," he repeated. "A child would complicate things between us."

"How can they be complicated? We're married."

"In law, but not in spirit. I am sorry, Daphne. I did so much without thinking of you, and there is only one way to make that right. I will set you free."

She couldn't think, couldn't breathe. Confused and sure she must be hearing things, she pushed to her feet and walked across the path.

"I don't understand," she whispered.

He stood. "I was wrong to keep you here against your will, and I was wrong to marry you without your consent. I thought you did not mean your protests, but you did. We cannot have a marriage where you are little more than a prisoner in a gilded cage. I cannot take back what I have done in the past, but I can set it right." He nodded at the ring on her left hand. "You need not wear that reminder any longer. I will speak to the king and arrange for our divorce. You are free to leave whenever you like."

He turned and walked a few feet, then paused. With his back still to her he said, "Take what you like. Clothing, jewels. Any artwork. Consider it compensation for the wrong done to you. There will be a settlement, of course. I will be generous."

Then he was gone.

She made her way back to the bench where she collapsed. Tears poured down her cheeks. She wanted to scream out her pain to the world, but she couldn't seem to catch her breath.

This wasn't happening, she told herself. It couldn't be that Murat had finally figured it all out, only to let her go.

"I love you," she said to the quiet garden. "I want to stay and be with you."

But he'd never offered that. Was it because he didn't think she would be interested, or was it because he didn't care enough about her? Had she been little more than a convenient bride, one easily forgotten?

She wasn't sure how long she sat there grieving for what could have been. An hour. Perhaps two. Then she straightened and brushed away her tears. All along she'd allowed circumstances to choose her path for her. It was time for her to act. She would find Murat and talk to him. If after she explained her feelings for him and her thoughts about staying in the marriage he still wasn't interested, then she would leave. But she wasn't going to give up without a fight.

Once again she went to his office, but he was not there. Fouad, his assistant, shook his head when she asked what time he would return.

"Prince Murat has left the country," he said. "On an extended trip. He is not expected to return for several weeks."

She couldn't believe it. "He's gone? Where?"

"I have his itinerary here, if you would like it."

She took the offered sheet of paper and tried to read the various entries, but the print blurred.

"Wh-when was this planned?" she asked.

Fouad looked sympathetic. "He has been working on it for a few days now, Your Highness. I'm terribly sorry to be the one to tell you about it."

The paper fluttered from her fingers, but she didn't try to pick it up.

He couldn't have left. Not so quickly. She'd just spoken to him a few minutes ago.

"I don't understand. When did he pack? He can't have just left."

"I'm sorry," Fouad repeated.

Daphne forced herself to smile. "You've been very kind. Thank you."

She left and made her way to the elevator, then to the suite she was supposed to share with Murat. Only, he was gone and she was no longer his wife.

She stepped inside to find the king waiting for her.

"My child," he said as he walked toward her. "I have spoken with Murat."

"He's gone," she said, still unable to believe the words. "He left. For several weeks. I had a list of where he was going, but I…" She glanced around for the paper, only to remember she'd dropped it in his office. "He said I could leave. Did he tell you that?"

King Hassan nodded. "The divorce will be finalized as quickly as possible. You are free to return to your life in America."

"Right." Her life. The practice she no longer had, the family who would never forgive her, the friends who couldn't possibly understand what she'd been through.

"He is very sorry for what he has done," the king said. "He sees now that he should never have held you against your will."

She drew in a breath. "Perhaps you shouldn't have meddled, either."

"I agree." Murat's father suddenly looked much older than his years. "I thought the two of you were right for each other. That you only needed time together to realize how right you were. I was an old fool and I hurt you both. I am deeply sorry."

She swallowed, then shook her head. "You weren't wrong. Not completely. I know that Murat isn't interested in me or our marriage, but I..." Her throat tightened. "I love him. I would have stayed." She touched her stomach. "When I told him I wasn't pregnant, he told me to leave."

The king held out his arms, and Daphne rushed into them. She gave in to the tears.

"I could call him back," King Hassan said. "He still has to listen to me."

Temptation called, but she pushed it away.

"Please don't," she said as she straightened and wiped her face. "There has been too much manipulation already. I wouldn't want Murat to be forced into our relationship. I would only want him there because it was what he desired."

"What will you do now?"

"Go back to the States."

The king bent down and kissed her cheek. "Stay as long as you would like. Despite what has happened, you are welcome here."

"I doubt Murat would be thrilled to come home and find me here."

"You never know."

She was pretty sure. He'd let her go without a fight—as he always had.

It took her most of the next day to gather the courage to pack her things and prepare to leave. She only took a few items of the new clothing she'd received since marrying Murat—the things she'd worn in the desert and the nightgowns she'd worn in their bed. She left all the jewelry, including the diamond band that had been her wedding ring.

"Can we do anything?" Billie asked as she hugged Daphne goodbye. "Are you sure you don't want me to fly you home?"

"I think I'll be more comfortable on the king's plane, but thanks."

Cleo moved in for her hug. "I'm sorry Murat is being such a jerk about all this. Men are so stupid." Tears filled her blue eyes. "What I don't get is I would have sworn he was really crazy about you."

Daphne had thought so, too, but she'd been wrong. About so much.

"Keep in touch," Cleo said.

Daphne nodded even though she knew it would never happen. They might send a card back and forth, but in the end they had nothing in common.

"You've both been terrific," she said. "Please tell Emma goodbye for me. And tell Zara and Sabrina I'm sorry I never had the chance to meet them."

The three women hugged again, then Daphne walked out of the suite with them and carefully closed the door behind her.

She rode alone to the airport. Cleo and Billie had offered to come with her, but she wanted to be by herself. She was done with tears and hopes and shattered dreams. She didn't want to feel anything, ever again.

But the burning ache inside of her felt as if it could go on forever. How was she supposed to get over loving Murat? Only now that she had lost him forever did she realize that he had been her heart's desire from the very beginning.

Murat stepped out of the limo and hurried inside the palace. Urgency quickened his steps as he raced up the stairs to the suite he shared with Daphne. He jerked open the door and stepped inside.

"Daphne?"

The large space echoed with silence.

"Daphne? Are you here?"

He walked into their bedroom. She wasn't there. Nor was the book she kept on her nightstand. He moved to the bathroom next and saw her makeup tray was empty. She was gone.

Defeat crashed through him. He had gone away to forget her only to realize that she was with him always. Even knowing that he owed her the choice, he wanted the chance to convince her to stay. But she hadn't even waited two days.

He walked down the hall and into his office. Two things caught his attention at once—a diamond band placed exactly in the center of his desk and the sculpture of the lovers he'd seen before.

He moved forward and picked up the ring. Funny how it still felt warm, as if she had only just removed it. He squeezed it in his hand, then dropped it into his jacket pocket. Then he turned his attention to the clay.

The intense embrace mesmerized him. He followed the graceful line of arms and torso up to the—

His heart froze. No longer were the lovers faceless. She had pressed in features. Just a hint of a nose, a slash for a mouth, but he recognized both of the faces.

Swearing, he picked up the phone and demanded a connection to the airport.

The luxurious jet raced down the runway. Daphne leaned back in the leather seat and closed her eyes. While she doubted she would sleep, she didn't want to watch as Bahania disappeared behind her.

Faster and faster until that moment just before the wheels lifted off. Then the jet suddenly slowed and sharply turned.

"Everything's fine, Your Highness," the pilot said over the intercom. "A signal light came on to tell us the cargo door isn't closed tight. We need to return to the hangar. It will only take a couple of minutes to fix."

She nodded her agreement, then realized the man couldn't see her. "Thanks for letting me know," she said as she pushed the intercom button on the console beside her seat.

She flipped through the stack of magazines left for her and picked out one on interior design. When she returned to Chicago, she either had to join another practice or go out on her own. That had been her plan when she'd left.

Maybe a change in cities would be nice. She'd never lived in the South or the West. She could go to Florida, or perhaps Texas.

She glanced out the window and saw several uniformed crewmen rushing around the plane. Then the main door opened. Daphne looked up in time to see a tall, handsome, imperious man striding on board.

Her heart took a nosedive for her toes. Rational thought left her as hope—foolish hope—bubbled in her stomach.

Murat took the seat opposite hers and leaned toward her.

"How could you leave without telling me you love me?" he demanded.

"I…I didn't think you'd want to know."

He scowled. "Of course I want to know that my wife loves me. It changes everything."

She couldn't think, couldn't breathe, couldn't do anything but drink in the sight of him.

"You told me to leave," she reminded him.

"I thought you were anxious to be gone." He glared at her. "This is your fault for not confessing your feelings." His expression softened. "I am happy to know my love is returned."

She couldn't have been more surprised if he'd told her he was a space alien.

"You l-love me?" she asked breathlessly.

"With all my heart and every part of my being." He took her hands in his. "Ah, my sweet wife. When I realized how badly I had treated you, I did not know how to atone for what I had done. Setting you free seemed only right, even though it was more painful than cutting off my arm. When you accepted my decision without saying anything, I thought you did not care about me."

"I was too shocked to speak," she admitted. "Oh, Murat, I do love you. I have for a long time. Maybe for the past ten years. I'm not sure."

He stood and pulled her to her feet. "You are a part of me. You are the one I wish to be with for always. I want you to share in my country, my history. I love you, Daphne."

She wasn't sure if he pulled her close or she made the first move. Suddenly she was in his arms and he was kissing her as if his life depended on her embrace.

She clung to him, needing him more than she'd ever needed anyone ever.

He pulled back. "But if you must leave, I will let you," he said.

She couldn't believe it. "But you said—"

He smiled. "You may go, but I am coming with you. I will be next to you always."

She laughed. "I don't want to go anywhere. I love Bahania and I love you."

Right there, in the walkway of a jet, Crown Prince Murat of Bahania dropped to one knee.

"Then stay with me. Be my wife, the mother of my children. Love me, grow old with me and allow me to spend the rest of my life proving how important you are to me."

"Yes," she whispered. "For always."

He stood and reached into his jacket pocket. When he withdrew a ring, she started to shake. Then she realized he wasn't holding the diamond band he'd given her after their marriage. Instead he held a familiar and treasured engagement ring—the one she'd left behind ten years ago.

"My ring," she said breathlessly. "You kept it all this time."

"Yes. In a safe place. I was never sure why, until now. I know I was keeping it for you to wear again." He slid on the ring, then kissed her.

Lost in the passion of his body pressing against hers, she barely heard the crackle of the intercom.

"Prince Murat?" It was the pilot. "Sir, are we still going to America?"

"No," Murat said into the intercom. He sank onto a chair and pulled Daphne onto his lap. "We are not."

"Are we going anywhere?"

Murat leaned close and whispered in her ear. "Do

you have any pressing engagements for the rest of the afternoon?"

She shifted so she could straddle him. "What did you have in mind?"

He chuckled, then pressed the intercom button again. "Once around the country."

"Yes, sir."

"Which gives us how long?" she asked.

He reached for the buttons on her blouse.

"A lifetime, my love. A lifetime."

* * * * *

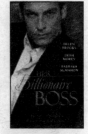

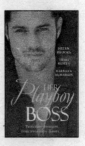
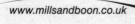